U0928588

认知语言学

第十辑　熊沐清/主编

西南交通大学出版社
·成 都·

图书在版编目（CIP）数据

认知诗学. 第十辑 / 熊沐清主编. —成都：西南交通大学出版社，2021.12
ISBN 978-7-5643-8524-8

Ⅰ. ①认… Ⅱ. ①熊… Ⅲ. ①诗学－中国－文集
Ⅳ. ①I207.2-53

中国版本图书馆 CIP 数据核字（2021）第 275201 号

Renzhi Shixue（Di-shi Ji）
认知诗学（第十辑）

熊沐清 **主编**

责任编辑	居碧娟
封面设计	曹天擎
出版发行	西南交通大学出版社 （四川省成都市金牛区二环路北一段 111 号 西南交通大学创新大厦 21 楼）
发行部电话	028-87600564　028-87600533
邮政编码	610031
网址	http://www.xnjdcbs.com
印刷	成都勤德印务有限公司
成品尺寸	170 mm × 230 mm
印张	15.75
字数	232 千
版次	2021 年 12 月第 1 版
印次	2021 年 12 月第 1 次
书号	ISBN 978-7-5643-8524-8
定价	68.00 元

目 录

名家特稿

认知诗学本土化

认知文体批评

情感研究

认知诗学“关键词”

研究新论

名家特稿

Embodied Social Cognition and Comparative Literature: An Introduction

Lisa Zunshine
(University of Kentucky, USA)

【Abstract】There is a growing sense among scholars working in cognitive literary studies that their assumptions and methodologies increasingly align them with another paradigmatically interdisciplinary field: comparative literature. This introduction to the special issue on cognitive approaches to comparative literature explores points of alignment between the two fields, outlining possible cognitivist interventions into debates that have been animating comparative literature, such as those concerning "universals," politics of translatability (especially in the context of world literature), and practices of thinking across the oundaries of media. It discusses both fields' indebtedness to cultural studies, as well as cognitive literary theorists' commitment to historicizing and their sustained focus on the embodied social mind.

【Key word】cognitive historicism, universals, embodied social mind, world literature, translatability

There is a growing sense among scholars working in cognitive literary studies that their assumptions and methodologies align them with another paradigmatically interdisciplinary field: comparative literature. For instance, as Karin Kukkonen points out in her contribution to this issue, comparative literature and cognitive literary studies "share a global perspective on literature. In the last decades, comparative literature has ventured beyond the European canon and into the system of world literature, where transnational streams of literary texts are investigated" (244); similarly, cognitive literary studies "sees in principle all of literature as its domain, since thoughts and emotions are features involved in texts from any language or country" (244). This special issue thus seeks to articulate points of alignment between the two fields and to propose a range of interpretive models that are self-consciously comparativist in their cognitivist explorations.

If we look for immediate disciplinary contexts of the current comparativist trend in cognitive literary studies, three factors are apparent. The first is the move away from the focus on anglophone literature. Today it is hard to believe that only a decade ago a charge of parochialism leveled against the field of cognitive approaches to literature—that "studies which link cognitive theory and literature often focus on Shakespeare and Austen" (Simerka 2012: 263) —was perceived by its practitioners as both legitimate and worrisome. As the field kept growing, it changed so much that today its center of gravity sometimes seems to be in Spanish and Latino studies (see Aldama 2009; Simerka 2013; and Jaén and Simon 2017), [①] with East Asian studies a close second and Slavic studies gaining. This becomes especially clear if we do not limit ourselves to criticism published in North America and/or sponsored by North American professional organizations and take into account critical and professional trends in other countries. [②]

① Consider, for instance, the rapidly growing Chinese Association of Cognitive Poetics and Cognitive Literary Studies, which has been sponsoring national and international conferences since 2008. The first international conference took place in Chongqing in 2013 and was followed by the ones in Guangzhou in 2015, Beijing in 2017, and Harbin in 2020. For more information, see the inaugural issue of *Cognitive Poetics*, particularly an article by the association's president, Xiong Muqing (2014), as well as www. cognitivepoetics. com/cn.

② This means that graduate students trained in several languages are at a particular advantage when they choose to explore issues in cognition and literature, and they should be aware of their advantage. The unabating cultural interest in the mind/brain and the rapid expansion of academic research networks dedicated to studying those issues thus militate against the current trend of defunding university comparative literature programs and eliminating foreign language requirements.

The second factor is the awareness, on the part of scholars working with cognitive approaches to literature, that they need to put pressure on their explicit and implied claims about the universality of certain features of literary production, by going beyond the confines of a single literature. We know that, in anthropology and psychology, a claim about a particular cognitive pattern receives only so much traction until it is followed up by research conducted with different subject populations, often those from other countries. The practice of literary analysis is different: traditionally, cognitive literary studies have not depended on this kind of cross-cultural scrutiny. Yet it makes sense that a given cognitive-literary hypothesis benefits from being tested across disparate cultures (see Crane 2001; Richardson 2001; Spolsky 2001; Hogan 2003). One can go as far as to argue that responsible cognitivist theorizing would make a point of drawing on case studies from several literary traditions that are, "at most, only sparsely and weakly interrelated" (see Patrick Colm Hogan's contribution in this issue, 194).

The third factor shaping the cognitive-comparative synergy is the continuous repositioning of what started out as a straightforward cognitive-literary inquiry in relation to various sister arts. Again, to get some sense of this development, we may want to look beyond the boundaries of the North American academy and follow, for instance, the disciplinary trajectory of the annual conference associated with the network "Cognitive Futures in the Humanities." As the conference moved from Bangor (2013), Durham (2014), Oxford (2015), and Helsinki (2016), to Stony Brook (2017), Kent (2018), Mainz (2019), and Osnabrück (2020), it has revised both its title (it is known now as "Cognitive Futures in the Arts and the Humanities") and its original focus on literature. What this means, in practical terms, is that students of literature who find themselves at one of the Cognitive Futures conferences encounter panels on the moving image, performance, theater and dance studies, the visual arts, and musicology. While panels on literary studies are present, they are not in the majority, which prompts aspiring cognitive-literary theorists to see connections and possible areas of collaboration among a wider range of media than they may have been used to. In doing so, they effectively expand the conceptual repertoire of comparativism, for "comparative literature has always been a home for scholars interested in thinking across representational modalities" (see Elaine Auyoung's contribution in this issue, 302).

The move beyond Shakespeare and Austen, the commitment to testing a given hypothesis against disparate literary traditions, and the rethinking of the role of sister arts in formulating such hypotheses—these are, then, some of the recent trends that lend cognitivism its strong comparativist outlook. This perspective takes as its starting point the immediate professional contexts of the cognitive literary studies, but yet another way to approach the affinities between the two fields is to look at how they describe themselves.

In *Comparative Literature in an Age of Globalization* (Saussy 2006a), a collaborative report by the American Comparative Literature Association, Caroline D. Eckhardt (2006: 141) emphasizes the importance of moving beyond thinking about comparative literature in terms of what it is; commenting on academic disciplines as "behavioral and performative phenomena," she suggests that "comparative literature can be defined, at least in part, by what we *do*." Similarly, as the editor of the *Oxford Handbook of Cognitive Literary Studies* (Zunshine 2015b: 3), I observed that to define the field of cognitive approaches by what its different strains have in common—and then to present it as its "essential" feature—"would be reductive." Instead, one focuses on processes that hold this community of scholars together, such as the continuous dialogue between "literary critics and theorists vitally interested in cognitive science," who therefore have "a good deal to say to one another, whatever their differences" (Richardson 2004: 2). The emphasis on *doing* as opposed to *being* thus seems particularly congenial to the respective self-perceptions of the two fields.

Here is one issue that comes to the fore when we begin to consciously build on all these points of intersection between cognitive literary studies and comparative literature. On the one hand, comparative literature has always been hospitable, in Haun Saussy's (2006b: 34) words, "to margins and angles of all comers," serving as "the test bed for reconceiving the ordering of knowledge both inside and outside the humanities." This may mean that new, cognitively inflected interpretations could be integrated within the already extensive theoretical repertoire of comparativists, enriching the existing models. In the long run, this is what we hope for. On the other hand, it remains an open question if cognitive literary critics must deliberately engage with controversies that have been animating comparative literature, or if their cognitive approach may allow them to, if not quite sidestep the existing debates, then perhaps reframe some of them. In the rest of this introduction, I focus on some of those debates, those concerning universals, politics of translatability, and practices of thinking across different arts, outlining possible cognitivist responses to them, as represented by the articles in this issue.

1 Universals and Cognitive Historicism

In "Narrative Universals, Emotion, and Ethics", Patrick Colm Hogan demonstrates that comparative literature is uniquely positioned to make valuable contributions to the cognitive science of ethics if it integrates "cognitive and affective science with a study of narrative universals" (188). Using examples from Chinese, European, and Indian works, as well as from the current cultural and political discourse (e. g., Leeann Tweeden's accusation that Al Franken had groped her, without her consent, while she was asleep, in the context of the #MeToo movement), Hogan suggests that our ethical responses to fictional narratives as well as to real-life dilemmas hinge on (although are not defined by) particular emplotments of recurring story prototypes and on corresponding emotional values.

To see what is at stake in Hogan's treatment of universals, we may want to remember that both comparative literature and cognitive literary studies have a long history of grappling with this issue and that they are simul-taneously drawn to its interpretive potential and acutely sensitive to problems inherent in facile evocations of universality. For instance, comparativist Dario Villanueva (2015: 16) has argued that

> A solidly based poetics can be achieved, as all general criteria and typologies are inseparable from the universal. It follows from this that a literary theory constructed from elements that are at the same time widespread and creative of general categories, elements that are usually called invariants, is proved more valid on every occasion that these same invariants appear among literatures that have not been in regular or close contact, for example European and Asian literatures.

At the same time, as Hogan ([1997] 2010: 227) has pointed out, both comparativists and cognitivists are wary of assertions of universal humanity that have long supported "patriarchal, colonial, and other oppressive ideologies," that is, of "pseudouniversals" (225), particularly those that manifest themselves as "Eurocentric hegemony posing as universalism" (Appiah 1992: 58). In fact, it can be said that cognitive literary critics have inherited comparative literature's challenge of differentiating universals (or "invariants") from the long and insidious tradition of pseudouniversalist thinking.

Adding a new twist to this challenge today is the siren call of cognitive neuroscience. As Saussy (2015: 75) puts it, while neuroscience seems to be holding out "the temptation of an explanation of literature through brain function," the "ambitious comparatist... should be wary of filtering out the specific, idiomatic features of a text in order to make it fit within a determined schema." Interestingly, cognitive literary scholars may be uniquely well prepared for dealing with the specific and the idiomatic in the context of brain function. This is because cognitive literary theory has been shaped, since the early 2000s, by its commitment to historicist analysis (see Crane 2015; Spolsky 2015: 229-32), that is, the same commitment which has been animating the larger field of literary studies for the last fifty years. This means that cognitive historicism is one of the leading paradigms in cognitive literary studies (see Palmer 2004; Zunshine 2006; Leverage et al. 2010; Vermeule 2010; Lyne 2014; Rabinowitz and Bancroft 2014; Vincent 2015; Gavaler and Johnson 2017; Jaén and Simon 2017) and that their investigation of literary universals is informed by their attention to historically specific cultural constructions. As Ellen Spolsky (2004: viii) puts it in her preface to the coedited volume *The Work of Fiction: Cognition, Culture, and Complexity*:

> Cognitive literary theory is...well positioned to provide insights into a question that has been occluded by the well-deserved successes of the reemergent historical and multifaceted cultural studies that have proliferated after the New Criticism in the

> twentieth century. That question is this: how does the evolved architecture that grounds human cognitive processing, especially as it manifests itself in the univer-sality of storytelling and the production of visual art, interact with the apparently open-ended set of cultural and historical contexts in which humans find themselves, so as to produce the variety of social constructions that are historically distinctive, yet also often translatable across the boundaries of time and place? It is the job [of cognitive literary theory] to begin to chart the emergence, manifestation, and readability of these only temporarily stable relationships between the humanly universal and the culturally and individually specific, as coded and recorded in cultural artifacts.

The "only temporarily stable relationships between the humanly universal and the culturally... specific" are the focus of two other articles in this special issue, Haiyan Lee's "'Measuring the Stomach of a Gentleman with the Heart-Mind of a Pipsqueak': On the Ubiquity and Utility of Theory of Mind in Literature, Mostly," and my "Who Is He to Speak of My Sorrow?" Both drawon thework of anthropologist Webb Keane, who has argued that culture-specific forms of theory of mind (i. e., the evolved cognitive adaptation for making sense of people's behavior by attributing to them intentions, thoughts, and feelings) may contribute to very different ethical worldviews. As Keane (2016: 131) puts it, "[If] Theory of Mind and intention-seeking are common to all humans, how these get played down or emphasized can contribute to quite divergent ethical worlds. Elaborated in some communities, suppressed in others, these cognitive capacities appear as both sources of difficulties in their own right and affordances for ethical work."

Using a wide range of case studies—from premodern Chinese literary classics, the Sanskrit play *Shakuntala*, and a King Solomon legend, to detective fiction and the spy thriller in socialist and post-socialist China, Lee explores specific sociohistorical contexts that may encourage or suppress active exercise of theory of mind, aka mind reading, in cultural representations. Specifically, she argues that the affinity between theory of mind and narrative fiction (which has been a subject of numerous studies in the last fifteen years) "holds true mostly in modern commercial societies structured by stranger sociality, cosmopolitanism, and social mobility" but not necessarily in societies "structured by kinship sociality" (205).① In the latter, she argues, the representational project of mind reading—that is, of "understanding other minds in all their quirkiness" (221)—appears to be less salient than the project of "mind shaping," which serves "the societal goals of control, regulation, and cooperation" and may result in psychologically flat narratives that "highlight trait attributions, stereotypes, and schemata more than theory of mind" (220).

Further developing a historicist perspective on mind reading, my article builds on the work of linguistic anthropologists who suggest that different communities around the world subscribe to different models of mind, to argue that works of fiction can be fruitfully analyzed in relation to those local ideologies of mind.② My examples include English, Chinese, and Russian novels, as well as Bosavi (Papua

① For a recent study exploring the notion of community-specific models of mind reading, see Paul Dilley's (2017: 14–15) *Monasteries and the Care of Souls in Late Antique Christianity*, which suggests that "the training of thoughts practiced by early Christian monks led to the gradual acquisition of a new and particularly monastic theory of mind." Some of the key precepts of this monastic theory of mind were that the mind was both permeable and accessible. That is, monks had to learn that their cogitations arose "not only from the interior self, but also through divine guidance or demonic temptation" and that "God was aware of their private thoughts, which were also known to certain inspired saints" (15).

② For an overview of this debate in the latest *Futures of Comparative Literature* report, both in the context of the enduring concern about universalism and in relation to the new concern about the use of "'big data' in literary studies," see Heise 2017: 4, who notes, "It is unsurprising that the world literature paradigm, as one approach to globalizing the literary object of study, would be met with resistance and alternative proposals."

New Guinea) performance genres. Focusing on the opacity of mind doctrine, found in the South Pacific and Melanesia (according to which the loss of ability to keep one's feelings hidden is considered shameful), I compare cultural practices originating in communities in which people think but do not talk publicly about others' internal states, to those originating in communities in which people both think and talk about them, indeed, in which public speculation about other people's intentions is (mostly) rewarded. While we may still be a long way off from fully understanding how imaginative literature engages with a given ideology of mind, a comparatist expertise offers an immediate advantage to scholars wishing to investigate culture-specific forms of such engagement.

2 Translatability and Embodied Cognition

Karin Kukkonen's article, "Does Cognition Translate? Predictions, Plot and World Literature," proposes a cognitivist intervention into yet another issue avidly debated by comparativists: the relative importance of reading literary texts in their original languages. As Kukkonen observes, while some scholars, including David Damrosch, believe that reading in translation "makes literature as world literature available" (246), others, such as Emily Apter, stress moments of untranslatability, thus reifying the role of multilingual expertise or, at the very least, retraining our attention on the process of translation.

To see how high the stakes of this debate can get, we may want to turn to Dorothy M. Figueira's (2010) article "Comparative Literature versus World Literature." As she points out, the emergence of world literature was a boon to English departments, because it effectively changed English literature studies into "identity studies," creating attractive new opportunities for scholars who could claim "to cross spatial as well as disciplinary borders" while "not necessarily [bothering to acquire] any site-specific knowledge of languages or historical contexts" (32):

> The practicality of English departments' usurpation of the world was that they could in many institutions colonize the now discredited area studies and the smaller and therefore more vulnerable Comparative Literature programs... Most importantly, they revalorized the notion that one could responsibly read the world in translation.
>
> The question that needs to be asked then is the following: What vision of the world do these pedagogies that eschew the careful study of languages, literatures, and cultures—precisely those skills and habits that...[are] the traditional strengths of Comparative Literature—actually impart? If the rise of pedagogies of alterity pose any real threat to Comparative Literature as a discipline, it is because of the apparent ease with which their initiates can become experts. Because they do not require Comparative Literature's linguistic skills or an expert's familiarity with specific national cultures and histories, these pedagogies allow for (and even encourage) a theoretical approach that conflates individual histories and contexts. (32-33)

While cognitive literary critics do not have to take sides in the world literature versus comparative literature debate, the stark version of this debate as outlined above may remind them, ironically, of their own situation vis-à-vis other literary critics.① To work with cognitive approaches to literature, they have to develop "an expert's familiarity" with a wide range of fields in cognitive science and to keep abreast of

① See Braider 2006 for an overview, for instance, of studies resulting from "energetic pertinacity with which students of literature have turned to...visual art" (167), here, in particular, to early modern visual art.

recent developments in those fields. When they see scholars who, having not done this kind of hard homework, selectively adapt a precept or two from cognitive science and produce a reductive "cognitive" reading of a literary text, they may feel the same frustration as do comparativists who observe their colleagues from English departments "read the world in translation" and make claims that conflate "individual histories and contexts." Moreover, now that immersion in at least two linguistic environments is becoming somewhat de rigueur in cognitive literary studies, cognitive literary theorists can further sympathize with their colleagues in comparative literature who value labor-intensive expertise in "languages, literatures, and cultures."

This said, cognitive literary scholars do benefit from the global take on literature, which means that they approach the conversation about translatability from their particular angle. On the one hand, they are increasingly committed to studying literary texts in their original linguistic/cultural ecol-ogies. On the other hand, they see practices of literary translation as a richly promising subject of cognitivist inquiry. Thus Kukkonen takes as her starting point the cognitive-psychological concept of predictive processing, which "proposes that perception, emotion, and thought unfold along a feedback loop between predictions and the ways in which we constantly revise them in our exchange with the environment" (247). Using as her case studies the history of English and French translations of the Finnish epic *Kalevala*, she demonstrates that translators may decide to draw on patterns of prediction already familiar to readers in the target language or to introduce them to new predictive patterns, which may be linked to particular concepts from the source language. More often than not, such decisions depend on the historically specific "power relationships between different languages" in the "world republic of letters" (245), which means (once again) that cognitivist inquiry into translatability emerges as cognitive-historicist inquiry.

Kukkonen's argument that different languages enable "us to pay attention to different aspects of our experience" (251; which she differentiates carefully from the claim that "we think in language" [250]) is borne out in a striking way in Rita Charon's article, "Spoken Body: An *Infinite Jest* of Life, Death, and the Medical Tongue." The issue of untranslatability acquires new urgency in the context of what Charon describes as "a perilous experiment in identity manipulation" imposed on students in medical schools: through "a process hidden from them until the conversion is nearly complete, [they] are gradually forced to abandon their mother tongues and to become monofluent in the language of medicine" (263). Translation between the two, she asserts, is always inadequate.

Drawing on her experience of reading David Foster Wallace's novel *Infinite Jest* with first-year medical students, Charon focuses on aspects of embodied social cognition that are lost when medical school students undergo a "forced reeducation in the language of medicine" (264) and cease relating to patients in their native tongue. The founder and executive director of the program on narrative medicine at Columbia University Medical Center, Charon demonstrates that the cognitive-comparative perspective has the power of liberating literary studies from their nagging anxiety of social irrelevance. As she puts it, together, "comparative literature and cognitive literary studies ... can save lives" (278).

To return to the debates about reading the world in translation, have we, then, found the outer limits of translatability, rooted in the dynamics of embodied social cognition? Doctors who experience the world in medicalese lose touch with both their patients and themselves, for, as Charon shows, physicians become self-alienated through their "forced reeducation in the language of medicine" (263). This disembodied language (even if, ironically, it had been called forth to describe bodily ailments) permits no "development of affinity, shared realities, opening of permeable private worlds, expansion of autonomy, and the emergence of singular selves" (277). To quote Kukkonen, it generates no "predictive processing" that the patient and the doctor can meaningfully share (247). It seems, then, that at the very least what the cognitivist approach can contribute to the ongoing comparatist conversation about global literature is a new awareness of the body as ground zero for social cognition and hence translation.

3 Cultural Studies, Multimodality, and Social Connection

Comparatist work, writes Ursula K. Heise (2017: 7) in her introduction to the report *Futures of Comparative Literature*, "has been interdisciplinary all along: it has interfaced with art history, film studies, gender studies, history, musicology, philosophy, and translation studies." Indeed, one could argue, she observes, "that one current understanding of comparative literature revolves not so much around the study of different languages and cultures as of different media" (5).[①] In her contribution to the same report, Gail Finney (2017: 20) goes as far as to predict that the field's current commitment to "the destruction of walls and boundaries" may eventually result in the change of its name: "By 2025 a more apt term for the discipline may well be comparative literature studies," a designation that "evokes an association with cultural studies, a field to which comparative literature is increasingly indebted."

① Observe, too, the interest in cultural studies in professional organizations dedicated to cognitivist explorations abroad. For instance, the Chinese Association of Cognitive Poetics and Cognitive Literary Studies is preparing to publish the first issue of its new journal, *Cognitive Cultural Studies*, in June 2020.

Here, too, comparative literature and cognitive literary studies seem to be moving along the same trajectory, for cognitive literary theorists have considered for some time now the possibility that their field may be better represented by the designation *cognitive cultural studies*. The collection of articles *Introduction to Cognitive Cultural Studies* (Zunshine 2010a) features a variety of approaches within the field so redefined: from cognitive studies of visual art and theater to cognitive ecocriticism. Moreover, the preface to the volume emphasizes the deep compatibility between the project of cognitive cultural studies today and Raymond Williams's "original vision of cultural studies, articulated in *The Long Revolution* (1961) as exploring the relationship between 'the evolution of the human brain [and] the particular interpretation carried by particular cultures'" (quoted in Zunshine 2010b: 5).

While both fields thus acknowledge their debt to cultural studies, we may want to take a closer look at the conceptual frameworks they employ to read cultures across the "walls and boundaries" ofmedia. Are there any approaches that they already share, or may come to share in the near future?

Starting with comparativists, one is struck by the wide range of theoretical perspectives that underlie their inquiry across different modes of representation. For instance, a feminist investigation into early modern scientific discourse and visual art uncovers "the essential unity behind apparent differences in medium or form," for, "whatever the medium, women...often emerge as passive objects of visual analysis and consumption" (Braider 2006: 170). Or, to use another example, a historicist reconstruction, which refuses to read poetry and visual art as running on parallel cultural tracks, and hence isolated from each other, enriches our understanding of early modern imaginative ecologies: if "texts enable us to understand how painters *thought*, and thus the ideal content or meaning of images they produced, images help us see what the poets *saw*—the world as they imagined it, the world in which they wrote and thought as they themselves understood it" (172).

Both of these perspectives, feminist and historicist, have been crucial to the development of cognitivist epistemologies. I have already outlined the centrality of historicist thinking to the cognitivist project, as theorized in the early 2000s by Hogan, Spolsky, Mary Crane, and Alan Richardson. As to cognitive- evolutionary approaches to feminism, readers will find an important primer in the work of Nancy Easterlin, particularly in the chapter titled "Endangered Daughters" of her 2012 study, *A Biocultural Approach to Literary Theory and Interpretation*.① Also, Kukkonen (2018) explores implications of predictive processing for feminist narratology, while both Zunshine (2015a) and Lee (this issue) discuss the interplay of gender and social class in the construction of fictional characters' capacity for representing complex mental states of other people.

It seems, then, that cognitive cultural studies finds congenial a variety of paradigms espoused by comparative literature studies.② That said, what cognitive literary/cultural theorists bring to the table—especially when it comes to a critical engagement with the sister arts—

① Nancy Easterlin (2012: 248) begins with a rebuttal of the "literary-Darwinian" take on sexual psychology: literary Darwinists "glaringly" eschew in their analyses of literature "any discussion of sexual control and power, both of which are implicated in the conflicting dynamics of men and women." She then offers a reading of D. H. Lawrence's novel *The Fox*, which provides "a striking example of how a behavior 'designed' to serve evolutionary ends is finally dysfunctional for the specific psychological and relational needs of the individuals involved" (263). For a further critique of Darwinian accounts of feminism, see Hogan 2018: 22.

② For further examples of theoretical compatibility between the two fields, see discussions of their respective engagements with poststructuralism (Spolsky 2002; Heise 2017: 2; see also Charon's and Lee's respective engagement with Derridean poetics in this issue), ecocriticism (Easterlin 2010; Heise 2013), disability studies (Minich 2014; Savarese 2015), queer studies (Vincent 2015; Lanser 2017), and human rights (Anker 2012; Keen 2015).

is the sustained focus on the embodied social mind, which is multimodal and multisensory. Thus, the two articles that complete this special issue, Casey Schoenberger's "Staging Sincerity in Renaissance Italy and Early Modern China; or, Why Real Lovers Quarrel" and Elaine Auyoung's "The Unspoken Intimacy of Aesthetic Experience: Hardy and Degas," both stress multimodality of cognition while dealing, respectively, with poetry and music and with prose fiction and visual arts. What their analyses imply is that a critical conversation that crosses representational boundaries is not merely a critical fad (which may be known, at a particular historical juncture, by the moniker *cultural studies*). Instead, it reflects a fundamental feature of human cognition, which is not carved along the modalities corresponding, roughly, to some of our disciplinary divisions.

Conflict is at the center of Schoenberger's exploration of works of musical theater from seventeenth-century Venice and China: conflict both between the romantic protagonists themselves, Emperor Nero and Poppaea (in Monteverdi and Busenello's *Coronation of Poppaea*) and Emperor Xuanzong of Tang and Yang Guifei (in Hong Sheng's *Palace of Lasting Life*), and between what their respective audiences were asked to believe (that those protagonists were indeed romantic) and what they knew about the actual behavior of the historical figures portrayed in them (that "only a few years after crowning her" Nero would kick "the pregnant Poppaea to death" [283], and that Xuanzong would eventually order Yang's strangulation). "Scenes depicting lovers' quarrels and morally flawed characters," Schoenberger argues, "may paradoxically strike audiences as more authentically romantic because they dramatize an aspect of attachment emotions' functioning recently elucidated by cognitive science, namely, that of 'body budgeting,'" that is, "allocation of energy resources by the brain" (abstract, 281).

Body budgeting is a profoundly social process. Interacting with others—in the context of a romantic relationship but also, for instance, in the context of attending an operatic performance—involves "ceding, or agreeing to share, a degree of control over psychosomatic resources." Depending on circumstances, "the resulting vulnerability to 'emotional contagion'" may end up being detrimental to or necessary for our health (291-92). Suggesting that musical theater models body budgeting by playing up a wide range of conflicts, Schoenberger investigates some of the "affective 'ingredients'" of such multimodal conflict mongering (295). These include music and prosody (which compete with each other even as they complement each other), the uneasy balancing between what the spectators know about the protagonists and what they are made to feel on their behalf, and the evocation of "emotion concepts" (285), such as joy and envy, which are socially mediated and can thus be subject to public debate (which, in fact, happened to be the case in both seventeenth-century China and Italy, when a variety of prominent thinkers came to scrutinize the "ethical status of emotion" [282]).

A multimodal conflict (or even piling up of conflicts) is one path to social connection. Another, explored by Auyoung's article, is the production of aesthetic effects by artists and writers that seem to "transcend their chosen medium" (302). In the case of Degas, it is his ability to bring forth "paintings that seem to tell a story" (as in *The Dance Class*), and, in the case of Hardy, it is his "ability to produce novels that seem painterly" (302; e. g., *Tess of the D'Urbervilles*). Such medium-crossing representations, Auyoung suggests, prompt "audiences to supply sensory and affective content that cannot be fully represented on the canvas or the printed page," and by doing so, they allow us "to enjoy a private sense of connection to and intimacy with them and the represented scene" (303).

To explain the mechanism of this private feeling of connection (which, crucially, remains nonreciprocal, for whatever "sensory and affective" meaning viewers/readers derive from them "can never be disconfirmed"[313]), Auyoung brings together research in sociolinguistics, discourse comprehension, and empirical aesthetics. She shows that Hardy cues his readers to supply "much of their own embodied knowledge" (e. g., haptic, kinesthetic, and motor) to make sense of what he describes, thus amplifying "the asymmetry between the multimodal richness of their mental representations and the perceptual features of the printed text" (304). It is this asymmetry that "enables readers to feel as if they privately share common ground with the figures in the fictional world" (304). Degas, in turn, calls attention to spaces and bodies that can be seen only partially by viewers [prompting] them to make elaborative inferences about what is implied...They might make an inference about the implied dynamism and animation of the rooms full of moving bodies or make elaborative inferences about more local details, drawing on their social intelligence to wonder what the seated dancer in the foreground is thinking about while resting her hand on her chin. ...These inferences become the grounds for a sense of private, intimate understanding of indirect meaning that is nowhere in the external world and realized only in the viewer's mind. (311-12)

Knowing (i. e., feeling in our very body) that we understand the artist/writer's private meaning, and that this sense of intimacy cannot be taken away from us/disconfirmed, is a compelling social experience. What Schoenberger's and Auyoung's articles thus demonstrate is that a sense of social connectedness becomes more powerful when it is constructed across modalities, whether prompted by experimentation with body budgeting or with rep- resentational incompleteness. At the very least, this means that comparative literary scholars reaching out to musicology and art history may benefit from supplementing their current theoretical commitments with an inquiry into the workings of the embodied social mind.

It seems, then, that some of the core interests of cognitive literary theorists (e. g., their engagement with the difficult issue of universals, as well as their emphasis on historicizing, as they explore the dynamics of embodiment) already implicitly align them with their colleagues in comparative literature. Moreover, by casting their projects in explicitly comparativist terms, the contributors to this special issue demonstrate that both fields share the same drive: to go wider (by reaching out to other languages, cultures, representational modalities, and disciplines) in order to go deeper (by elucidating something local, particular, and unique). One hopes that this special issue will be followed by others that will bring together cognitivists and comparativists, as they seek new ways to theorize and build on this integrative drive.

Works Cited

[1] ALDAMA FREDERICK LUIS. Your Brain on Latino Comics: From Gus Arriola to Los Bros Hernandez. Austin: University of Texas Press, 2009.

[2] ANKER ELIZABETH S. Fictions of Dignity: Embodying Human Rights in World Literature. Ithaca, NY: Cornell University Press, 2012.

[3] APPIAH KWAME ANTHONY. In My Father's House: Africa in the Philosophy of Culture. New York: Oxford University Press, 1992.

[4] BRAIDER CHRISTOPHER. Of Monuments and Documents: Comparative Literature and the Visual Arts in Early Modern Studies, or The Art of Historical Tact. Saussy, 2006(a): 155-174.

[5] CRANE MARY. Shakespeare's Brain: Reading with Cognitive Theory. Princeton, NJ: Princeton University Press, 2001.

[6] CRANE MARY. Cognitive Historicism: Intuition in Early Modern Thought. The Oxford Handbook of Cognitive Literary Studies,

New York: Oxford University Press, 2015: 18-33.
[7] DILLEY PAUL C. Monasteries and the Care of Souls in Late Antique Christianity: Cognition and Discipline. Cambridge: Cambridge University Press, 2017.
[8] EASTERLIN NANCY. Cognitive Ecocriticism: Human Wayfinding, Sociality, and Literary Interpretation. Zunshine, 2010(a): 257-274.
[9] EASTERLIN NANCY. A Biocultural Approach to Literary Theory and Interpretation. Baltimore: Johns Hopkins University Press, 2012.
[10] ECKHARDT CAROLINE D. Old Fields, New Corn, and Present Ways of Writing about the Past. Saussy, 2006(a): 139-154.
[11] FIGUEIRA DOROTHY M. Comparative Literature versus World Literature. Comparatist, 2010(34): 29-36.
[12] FINNEY GAIL. The Reign of the Amoeba: Further Thoughts about the Future of Comparative Literature. Futures of Comparative Literature: ACLA State of the Discipline Report, London: Routledge, 2017:19-23.
[13] GAVALER CHRIS, AND DAN JOHNSON. The Genre Effect: A Science Fiction (vs. Realism) Manipulation Decreases Inference Effort, Reading Comprehension, and Perceptions of Literary Merit. Scientific Study of Literature, 2017, 7(1): 79-108.
[14] HEISE URSULA K. Globality, Difference, and the International Turn in Ecocriticism. PMLA, 2013, 128(3): 636-643.
[15] HEISE URSULA K. Introduction: Comparative Literature and the New Humanities. Futures of Comparative Literature: ACLA State of the Discipline Report. London: Routledge, 2017: 1-8.
[16] HOGAN PATRICK COLM. Empire and Poetic Voice: Cognitive and Cultural Studies of Literary Tradition and Colonialism. Albany, NY: SUNY Press, 2003.
[17] HOGAN PATRICK COLM. Literary Universals. Poetics Today,

1997, 18(2): 223-249.

[18] HOGAN PATRICK COLM. Sexual Identities. New York: Oxford University Press, 2018.

[19] JAÉN ISABEL, JULIEN JACQUES SIMON. Cognitive Approaches to Early Modern Spanish Literature. New York: Oxford University Press, 2017.

[20] KEANE WEBB. Ethical Life: Its Natural and Social Histories. Princeton, NJ: Princeton University Press, 2016.

[21] KEEN SUZANNE. Human Rights Discourse and Universals of Cognition and Emotion: Postcolonial Fiction. The Oxford Handbook of Cognitive Literary Studies, New York: Oxford University Press, 2015: 347-355.

[22] KUKKONEN KARIN. A Moving Target—Cognitive Narratology and Feminism." Textual Practice, 2018, 32(6): 973-989.

[23] LANSER SUSAN S. Comparatively Lesbian: Queer/Feminist Theory and the Sexuality of History. Futures of Comparative Literature: ACLA State of the Discipline Report, London: Routledge, 2017: 92-97.

[24] LEVERAGE PAULA, HOWARD MANCING, RICHARD SCHWEICKERT, et al. Theory of Mind and Literature. West Lafayette, IN: Purdue University Press, 2010.

[25] LYNE RAPHAEL. Shakespeare, Perception and Theory of Mind. Paragraph, 2014(37): 79-95.

[26] MINICH JULIE AVRIL. Disability, Losers, and Narrative Remediation. Comparative Literature, 2014, 66(1): 35-42.

[27] PALMER ALAN. Fictional Minds. Lincoln: University of Nebraska Press, 2004.

[28] RABINOWITZ PETER J, CORINNE BANCROFT. Euclid at the Core: Recentering Literary Education. Style, 2014, 48(1): 1-34.

[29] RICHARDSON ALAN. British Romanticism and the Science of

the Mind. Cambridge: Cambridge University Press, 2001.
[30] RICHARDSON ALAN. Studies in Literature and Cognition: A Field Map. The Work of Fiction: Cognition, Culture, and Complexity, Aldershot, UK: Ashgate, 2004: 1-29.
[31] SAUSSY HAUN, eds. Comparative Literature in an Age of Globalization. Baltimore: Johns Hopkins University Press, 2006.
[32] SAUSSY HAUN. Exquisite Cadavers Stitched from Fresh Nightmares. Saussy, 2006(a): 3-42.
[33] SAUSSY HUAN. Comparing Themes and Images. Introducing Comparative Literature: New Trends and Applications, London: Routledge, 2015: 68-77.
[34] SAVARESE RALPH JAMES. What Some Autistics Can Teach Us about Poetry: A Neurocosmopolitan Approach. The Oxford Handbook of Cognitive Literary Studies, New York: Oxford University Press, 2015: 18-33.
[35] SIMERKA BARBARA. Afterword: The Future of Cognitive Literary Studies. Cervantes: Bulletin of the Cervantes Society of America, 2012, 32(1): 263-275.
[36] SIMERKA BARBARA. Knowing Subjects: Cognitive Cultural Studies and Early Modern Spanish Literature. West Lafayette, IN: Purdue University Press, 2013.
[37] SPOLSKY ELLEN. Satisfying Skepticism: Embodied Knowledge in the Early Modern World. Aldershot, UK: Ashgate, 2001.
[38] SPOLSKY, ELLEN. Darwin and Derrida: Cognitive Literary Theory as a Species of Poststructuralism. Poetics Today, 2002, 23(1): 43-62.
[39] SPOLSKY ELLEN. The Work of Fiction: Cognition, Culture, and Complexity, Aldershot, UK: Ashgate, 2004: vii-xiii.
[40] SPOLSKY ELLEN. The Contracts of Fiction: Cognition, Culture, Community. New York: Oxford University Press, 2015.

[41] VERMEULE BLAKEY. Why Do We Care about Literary Characters? Baltimore: Johns Hopkins University Press, 2010.

[42] VILLANUEVA DARIO. Comparative Literature and the Future of Literary Studies. Introducing Comparative Literature: New Trends and Applications, edited by Cesar Dominguez, Haun Saussy, and Dario Villanueva, London: Routledge, 2015: 1-19.

[43] VINCENT KEITH J. Sex on the Mind: Queer Theory Meets Cognitive Theory. The Oxford Handbook of Cognitive Literary Studies, New York: Oxford University Press, 2015: 199-221.

[44] 熊沐清. 论认知诗学分析方法的多维性——以《威尼斯商人》中夏洛克一段台词为例. 认知诗学, 2014, 1(1): 3-22.

[45] ZUNSHINE LISA. Why We Read Fiction: Theory of Mind and the Novel. Columbus: Ohio State University Press, 2006.

[46] ZUNSHINE LISA. Introduction to Cognitive Cultural Studies. Baltimore: Johns Hopkins University Press, 2010(a).

[47] ZUNSHINE LISA. What Is Cognitive Cultural Studies? Zunshine. Baltimore: Johns Hopkins University Press, 2010: 1-33.

[48] ZUNSHINE LISA. From the Social to the Literary: Approaching Cao Xueqin's The Story of the Stone (Honglou Meng) from a Cognitive Perspective. The Oxford Handbook of Cognitive Literary Studies, New York: Oxford University Press, 2015: 176-196.

[49] ZUNSHINE LISA. Introduction to The Oxford Handbook of Cognitive Literary Studies, New York: Oxford University Press, 2015: 1-9.

具身社会认知与比较文学导言

丽莎·詹塞恩 著　程 鹏 译

【摘要】认知文学研究的学者们越来越意识到他们的假设和方法日益符合另一个典型的跨学科领域——比较文学。这篇关于比较文学认知方法专题的导言探讨了这两个领域之间的一致之处，概述了可能的认知主义干预，例如关于“普遍性”、(世界文学背景下的）可译性政治以及跨越媒体边界的思维实践的争论，正是这些争论使比较文学更具活力。本文讨论了认知文学和比较文学从文化研究中获得的裨益、认知文学理论家对历史语境化的努力以及对具身社会心理的持续关注。

【关键词】认知历史主义；共性；具身社会心理；世界文学；可译性

认知文学研究的学者们越来越意识到他们的假设和方法日益符合另一个典型的跨学科领域——比较文学。例如，正如卡琳·库科宁（Karin Kukkonen）(2018：244）在本专题的论文中指出，比较文学和认知文学研究“都有全球文学视角，在过去的几十年间，比较文学已经超越了欧洲的规约，进入了世界文学体系，其中跨国文学文本正不断被研究”；同样，认知文学研究“原则上把所有文学视为它的领域，因为思想和情感是任何语言或国家的文本特征”。因此，本文试图阐明这两个领域之间的一致之处，并在认知研究中提出一系列实为比较主义的解释模式。

作者简介：丽莎·詹塞恩（Lisa Zunshine），女，美国肯塔基大学的 Bush-Holbrook 教授，主要从事18世纪的英国文学与文化、认知文学研究。
译者简介：程鹏，女，安徽大学外语学院讲师，硕士，主要从事世界文学与比较文学研究。

如果我们寻找当前认知文学研究中比较主义趋势的直接学科语境，三个因素是显而易见的。首先，对英语文学的关注发生了转向。很难相信仅在十年前，文学的认知方法领域被指责为狭隘主义——“将认知理论和文学联系起来的研究往往侧重于莎士比亚和奥斯汀”（Simerka，2012：263），而认知文学研究者忧心忡忡认为这一指责不乏合理之处。随着这个领域的不断发展，它的变化之大以至于如今的研究重心时而在西班牙语和拉丁语系研究中（Aldama，2009；Simerka，2013；Jaén & Simon，2017）[①]，东亚研究紧随其后，斯拉夫研究方兴未艾。如果我们不局限于在北美发表和（或）由北美专业机构资助的文学批评，并考虑到其他国家的批评与专业趋势，这一点就特别明显。[②]

第二个因素是意识。从事文学认知方法研究的学者已经意识到，他们需要通过超越单一文学的局限，检验他们关于文学作品某些特征的普遍性主张，这些文学诉求有些是明确的，而有些是隐含的。我们知道，在人类学和心理学中关于某种特定认知模式的主张，只有当（通常是来自其他国家）不同的研究群体跟进相关研究时，才会有巨大的动力。文学分析的实践则不同：传统上，认知文学研究不依赖这种跨文化的审视。然而，假设一个特定的认知文学会受益于不同文化的检验也并不无道理。（Crane，2001；Richardson，2001；Spolsky，2001；Hogan，2003）甚至可以说，可靠的认知理论化将重视来源于数个文化传统的案例研究，而这些传统“最多只有松散

① 例如“中国认知诗学与认知文学研究会”在中国蓬勃发展。自 2008 年，该研究会一直举办国内、国际学术会议。2013 年在重庆举办首届认知诗学国际学术研讨会暨第三届中国认知诗学学术研讨会，2015 年在广州第二届认知诗学国际学术研讨会暨第四届中国认知诗学学术研讨会，2017 年在北京举办第三届认知诗学国际学术研讨会暨第五届中国认知诗学学术研讨会，2020 年在哈尔滨举办第四届认知诗学国际学术研讨会暨第六届中国认知诗学学术研讨会。欲了解更多信息，请参阅第一期“认知诗学”，特别是研究会会长熊沐清的文章以及中国比较文学文学学会认知诗学分会网站（www.cognitive-poetics.com/cn）。

② 这意味着，受过多种语言训练的研究生在选择研究认知和文学问题时具有独特的优势，而且他们应该意识到自己的优势。对心智/大脑有增无减的文化兴趣，以及致力于研究这些问题的学术网络的快速扩张，遏制了当前减少大学比较文学项目经费和取消外语需求的趋势。

的关联性”（Patrick Colm Hogan 在本专题的文章，194）。

形成认知-比较协同效应的第三个因素，是对涉及各种姊妹艺术关系、一开始认定为认知-文学探究的不断重新定位。为了对这一发展有所了解，我们希望可以超越北美学界的疆域，例如遵循关于网络“人文科学中的认知未来”的年会之学科轨迹。随着会议地点从班戈（2013）、达勒姆（2014）、牛津（2015）和赫尔辛基（2016）搬到石溪（2017）、肯特（2018）、美因茨（2019）和奥斯纳布吕克（2020），它最初对文学的关注及名称也随之而变（现在被称为“艺术与人文的认知未来”）。这意味着，实际上文学专业的学生如果参加了一次认知未来会议，将邂逅关于运动图像、表演、戏剧和舞蹈研究、视觉艺术和音乐学的小组讨论会。虽然现场有文学研究小组，但不占多数，这一切促使有抱负的认知文学理论家们在更广泛的新兴媒介领域内，看到了千丝万缕的关联和潜在的合作空间。于是他们有效地扩大了比较主义的概念基础，因为“对于有兴趣思考不同表征方式的学者们，比较文学一直是他们的家园”。

研究范围不再局限于莎士比亚和奥斯汀，致力于用不同的文学传统来检验某个特定的假设，重新思考在形成这些假设时姊妹艺术所扮演的角色——这些正是当前的一些学术趋势，同时赋予了认知主义强烈的比较观。这一视角以认知文学研究的直接专业语境作为出发点，而了解这两个领域之间亲缘关系的另一方法则为观察它们如何描述自己。

在美国比较文学协会的一份合作报告——《全球化时代的比较文学》（*Comparative Literature in an Age of Globalization*）（Saussy，2006a）中，卡罗琳·D. 埃克哈特（Caroline D. Eckhardt，2006：141）强调对比较文学“是什么”进行超越性思考的重要性；基于学术性学科为“行为和表现型现象”，她指出“比较文学至少在一定程度上可以被我们的行为所定义”。类似地，作为《牛津认知文学研究指南》的主编，我也留意到以不同的类型有什么共通之处、呈现共性作为它的本质特征——来定义认知方法的领域过于简单化了。相反，我们更关注的是把这群学者聚集在一起的过程，比如“对认知科学极为感兴趣的文学评论家和理论家”之间的持续对话，无论他们之间存在多大差异，彼此之间都有“很多话要说”。重行动而非存在，这似乎与这两个领域各自的自我认识特别相得益彰。

当我们有意识地在认知文学研究和比较文学之间所有的重叠处进行理论建构时，一个问题开始凸显。一方面，比较文学一直是包容的，苏源熙（Haun Saussy，2006 b：34）曾说，“它欢迎所有天涯海角的来客”，起到了“重构人文学科内外知识秩序的试验台”作用。这或许意味着，受到认知影响的新阐释有可能融进海纳百川的比较主义理论储备，以丰富现有的模式。从长远来看，这正是我们所希望的。另一方面，认知文学批评家是否必须有意地参与比较文学领域充满活力的争论，或者他们的认知方法是否允许他们——如果不是完全回避现有的辩论——是否可以重新构建其中的一些争论，这仍是一个悬而未决的问题。在导言的其余部分，我将如本专题的文章所表述的，重点关注关于普遍性、可译性政治及跨越不同艺术的思维实践方面的争议，概述一些可能的认知主义回应。

1 普遍性与认知历史主义

在《叙事普遍性、情感与伦理》中，帕特里克·科尔姆·霍根（Patrick Colm Hogan）指出，如果比较文学将“认知和情感科学”与叙事普遍性研究结合起来，它将为认知伦理学做出独特而宝贵的贡献。霍根（Hogan）以中国、欧洲和印度的作品及当前的文化和政治话语为例［比如在 MeToo 反性骚扰运动的语境中，利安·特韦登（Leeann Tweeden）指控艾尔·弗兰肯（Al Franken）在她睡着时，未经同意对她进行了抚摸］。霍根（Hogan）认为人们对虚构叙事以及现实生活困境的伦理回应，取决于反复出现的故事原型和相应情感价值观的特定运用（但不由其界定）。

为了解霍根（Hogan）对普遍性问题论述的利害攸关，我们也许要记住，比较文学和认知文学研究都与普遍性问题纠缠已久，它们既被普遍性的阐释潜质所吸引，又对动辄提及普遍性的内在问题极为敏感。例如，比较主义者达里奥·维拉努耶娃（Dario Villanueva，2015：16）认为：

> 因为所有的一般标准和类型都具有不可分割的普遍性，因此构建出基础坚实的诗学切实可行。而且，从普遍意义而言广泛且有创造性的元素们（通常称为不变量）构建的文学理论更合理，因为这些相同的不变量出现在没有定期接触或密切联系的文学，例如欧洲文学和亚洲文学中。

同时，正如霍根（Hogan，[1997]2010：227）所指出的，无论是比较主义者还是认知主义者，他们对长期以来支持“父权制、殖民和其他压迫性意识形态”等普遍人性的主张均持谨慎态度，这些是“伪普遍性”（225），特别是以“以欧洲为中心的霸权，伪装成普遍性”的观念（Appiah，1992：58）。实际上，可以说认知文学批评家继承了比较文学的挑战：如何区分普遍性（或“不变量”）与长期潜伏的伪普遍性思维传统。

当今这一挑战又增添了一个新的转折，那就是来自认知神经科学的警钟。正如苏源熙（Haun Saussy，2015：75）所言，神经科学尽管具备“通过大脑功能进行文学诠释的诱惑”，“雄心勃勃的比较主义者……”在过滤掉文本的特定性、惯用性特征，以符合确定的图式时更应小心谨慎。有意思的是，认知文学学者结合大脑功能来研究文本特定性和惯用性，可能恰好具备得天独厚的优势。认知文学理论形成于21世纪初，它致力于推进历史主义分析（见Crane，2015；Spolsky，2015：229-232），过去的半个世纪里这种努力也一直推动着更广阔的文学研究领域发展。这意味着认知历史主义是认知文学研究的主要范式之一（Palmer，2004；Zunshine，2006；Leverage et al.，2010；Vermeule，2010；Lyne，2014；Rabinowitz & Bancroft，2014；Vincent，2015；Gavaler & Johnson，2017；Jaén & Simon，2017），而且他们对文学普遍性的研究是通过关注特定的历史文化建构而进行的。正如埃伦·斯波斯基（Ellen Spolsky，2004：Ⅷ）在她合编的

《虚构作品的运作：认知、文化和复杂性》序言中所说：

> 在二十世纪的新批评之后，重新出现的历史与多元文化研究大量涌现，大获成功的同时也遮蔽了一个问题，而认知文学理论正好为之提供了洞见。这个问题即以人类认知过程为基础的进化建构物，尤其在讲故事的普遍性和视觉艺术的生产方面，如何与人类所处的开放式文化历史背景相互作用，从而产生了各式各样历史特色鲜明的社会结构，纵然跨越时间和地点的界限却常具可译性？（认知文学理论的）工作，正是去记载人类普遍性和文化、个体具体性之间关系的涌现、表征和可读性，拥有暂时稳定性的上述关系会被编码并收录在人类的文化产品中。

"人类普遍性与文化具体性之间暂时稳定的关系"是本专题其他两篇文章的焦点：李海燕（Haiyan Lee）的《用小人物的心灵测量绅士的胃——兼论心智理论在文学中的普遍性和实用性》以及本人的《谁在言说我的悲伤》。两文都借鉴了人类学家韦布·基恩（Webb Keane）的著作，他认为心智理论的文化特定形式（即通过将意图、思想和情感归因于人们的行为来理解行为的进化认知适应）可能有助于形成非常不同的伦理世界观。正如基恩（Keane，2016：131）所言，"（如果）心智理论和意图寻求对所有人而言是共通的，那么这些理论如何被淡化或被强调，会促成完全不同的伦理世界。这些认知能力在一些社区被重视，而在另一些社区受到压制，它们似乎既是自身困境的根源，也是伦理运作的示能。"

基于一系列广泛的案例研究——从近现代中国文学经典、梵语剧本《释迦牟尼》《所罗门王传奇》，到侦探小说和社会主义、后社会主义中国的谍战作品，李（Lee）探讨了特定的社会历史语境可能会有助或抑制心智理论（也称心智阅读）在文化表征中的积极运用。具体而言，她认为心智理论与叙事小说（过去十五年间一直是众多研究的主题）之间的密切关系"在陌生人、世界主义和社会流动构成的现代商业社会中基本成立”，但是不一定存在于“由亲属性构成的社会”（205）[①]。她认为后一种社会中，心智阅读的表征方面，即“了解怪诞背后的心智”似乎不如“心理塑造”突出，后者服务于“控制、调节和合作的社会目标”，并可能导致心理上的扁平化叙述，“突出特质归因、刻板印象和图式，而不是心智理论”。

为了进一步发展历史主义心智阅读观念，我的文章以语言人类学家的工作为基础，他们认为世界各地不同的社区认同不一样的心智模式，声称小说作品可以结合当地的思维意识形态，进行卓有成效的分析。[②]

我的举例涉及英文、中文和俄文小说，以及博萨维（巴布亚新几内亚）表演类型。聚焦于在南太平洋和美拉尼西亚发现的心智不透明学说（根据该学说，丧失隐藏自己情感的能力被认为是可耻的），我比较了仅思考但不公开谈论他人内心状态的社群文化习俗，与那些既思考又谈论他人内心状态的社群文化习俗。实际上，公众对他人意图的猜测（大部分）都会得到回报。虽然我们要完全理解富有想象力的文学如何与特定的思想意识形态相结合，还有很长的路要走，但对于希望研究此类关联文化特定形式的学者而言，比较主义的专业知识提供了立竿见影的优势。

2 可译性与具身认知

卡琳·库科宁（Karin Kukkonen）的文章《认知能翻译吗？——预

① 最近一项研究探索了特定社区心智阅读模式的概念，请参阅保罗·迪利（Paul Dilley）（2017：14-15）的《修道院和晚期古代基督教中的灵魂关怀》，该研究表明，“早期基督教僧侣的思想训练导致了一种全新的、尤其是修道院式心智理论的形成。”这种修道院式心智理论的一些关键观念是，心智既是可渗透的，也是可接近的。换言之，僧侣必须了解他们的思辨“不仅来自内在的自我，也来自于神的指引或恶魔的诱惑”，而且“上帝知道他们的私人想法，某些受启发的圣人也知道这些想法”（15）。

② 关于最新的“比较文学的未来”报告中的这场辩论的概述，参见 Heise（2017：4），无论是在对普遍主义的持久关注还是在对“大数据”在文学研究中使用的新关注的背景下，她指出，“作为一种全球化的文学研究对象的方法，世界文学范式会受到阻力和替代建议，这不足为奇”。

测、情节和世界文学》提出了一种认知主义的介入，介入比较主义者热烈辩论的另一个问题：用原文阅读文学文本的相对重要性。正如库科宁（Kukkonen）所观察到的，虽然包括大卫·达姆罗什（David Damrosch）在内的一些学者认为翻译中的阅读“使文学成为世界文学”（246），但其他一些学者，如艾米丽·阿普特（Emily Apter）则强调不可译的时刻，从而具体化了多语言专业知识的作用，或者至少，重塑了我们对翻译过程的关注。

要了解这场争辩有多重要，我们不妨看看多萝西·M. 菲格拉（Dorothy M. Figueira，2010）的文章《比较文学 VS 世界文学》。正如她指出的，世界文学的出现对英语系来说是一个福音，因为它有效地将英国文学研究变成了“身份研究”，为那些声称“跨越空间和学科边界”的学者创造了有吸引力的新机遇，同时“不一定需要（费心地获取）任何特定地点的语言或历史背景知识”（32）：

> 英语系篡夺世界的实用性在于，在许多机构中，他们可以鲸吞蚕食如今名声不佳的区域研究，以及规模较小、因而更脆弱的比较文学项目……最重要的是，他们重新确立了一种观念，一个人能可靠地在翻译中阅读世界。
>
> 那么，需要提出以下问题：这些回避对语言、文学和文化进行细致研究——那些技能和习惯……正是比较文学的传统优势——的教学法，实际上传授了什么样的世界观？如果各式各样教学法的兴起对比较文学这一学科构成任何真正的威胁，那是因为它们的初学者显然很容易成为专家。不需要比较文学的语言技能或对特定民族历史文化的专业熟稔，这些教学法允许（甚至鼓励）一种将个人历史和语境混为一谈的理论方法。（32-33）

虽然认知文学批评家不必在世界文学与比较文学之争中站队，但有讽刺意义的是，上述争辩的严酷性会提醒他们自己相对于其他文学评论家的处境。[①]要用认知的方法研究文学，他们必须培养“专家的熟稔度”，熟悉认知科学的广泛领域，并跟上这些领域的最新发展。当他们看到并未经历这种艰苦努力的学者，有选择地改造认知科学的一两条原则，对文学文本进行还原性的“认知”阅读时，他们可能会与那些目睹英语系同事“用翻译阅读世界”并将“个别历史和语境”混为一谈的比较主义者一样感到沮丧。此外，既然沉浸在至少两种语言环境中在认知文学研究中有些司空见惯，认知文学理论家们可以进一步理解认同他们的比较文学同行，后者同样重视“语言、文学和文化”领域的劳动密集型专业知识。

换言之，认知文学学者确实受益于文学的全球视野，这意味着他们用自己独特的角度对待可译性问题。一方面，他们越来越多地致力于在他们原有的语言/文化生态中研究文学文本；另一方面，他们将文学翻译实践视为认知主义探索中一个很有前途的主题。因此，库科宁（Kukkonen）以预测过程的认知心理学概念为出发点，“提出了感知、情感和思想沿着预测与方法的反馈回路展开，我们在与环境的交流中不断改进这些方法”（247）。她以芬兰史诗“卡莱瓦拉”（Kalevala）英法译本的历史为例，说明译者会使用目的语读者所熟悉的预测模式，或者用新的预测模式，这些新模式可能与源语言中的特定概念相关。通常情况下，这样的决定取决于历史上特定的“世界文字共和国里不同语言之间的权力关系”（245），这意味着（再一次）认知主义对可译性的探究显现为认知历史主义的探究。

库科宁（Kukkonen）的论点是，不同的语言使“我们能够关注我们经历的不同方面”（251）；她细致地将这一点与丽塔·卡伦（Rita Charon）文章《口头身体：对生命、死亡和医学语言的无尽玩笑》中“我们用语言思考”（250）的说法区分开来。卡伦（Charon）提出不可译性问题的紧迫性，并描述医学院的学生经历“一个危险的身份操纵实验”：通过“一个隐蔽的过程，（他们）逐渐被迫放弃自己的母语，变成一口流利的医学语言，而这一过程直到转变结束前

① 请参阅 Braider（2006），例如对“文学专业学生转向……视觉艺术孜孜不倦的执着”相关研究的概述（167），这里尤其指早期现代视觉艺术。

都不为人知”（263）。因此她断言两者（母语和医学语言）之间的翻译始终是不充分的。

卡伦（Charon）借鉴了她与一年级医学生一起阅读大卫·福斯特·华莱士（David Foster Wallace）的小说《无限笑话》（*Infinite Jest*）的经验，她着重研究了具身社会认知的各个方面，这些方面当医学生“不得不接受医学语言再教育”（264）并停止用母语与病人建立联系时则会丢失。作为哥伦比亚大学医学中心（Columbia University Medical Center）叙事医学项目的创始人兼执行主任，卡伦展示了认知-比较视角的力量，它有能力将文学研究从社会脱节的困扰焦虑中解放出来。正如她所说，“比较文学和认知文学研究……可以拯救生命”（278）。

回到关于在翻译中阅读世界的争论，那么，我们是否已经找到了根植于具身社会认知的动态中可译性的外部界限？用医学语言体验世界的医生既失去了与病人的联系，也失去了和自己的联系。因为正如卡伦（Charon）所言，医生们通过“被迫接受医学语言的再教育”而变得自我疏远（263）。这种脱离实体的医学语言（讽刺的是，它是用来描述身体疾病的）不允许“建立密切联系、共享现实、开放渗透性的私人世界、扩大自主性和涌现单一自我”（277）。引用库科宁（Kukkonen）的话，它不会让病人和医生有意义地共同面对“预测性应对处理”（247）。所以，认知主义的方法至少能为当下关于全球文学的比较主义对话做出贡献，那就是提供一种新的意识，即身体是社会认知的起点，因此也是翻译的起点。

3 文化研究、多模态和社会联系

在报告“比较文学的未来”的导言里，乌苏拉·K. 海塞（Ursula K. Heise，2017：7）写道，比较主义作品“一直以来都是跨学科的：它与艺术史、电影研究、性别研究、历史学、音乐、哲学和翻译研究交织在一起”。她评论说，的确有人可能会争辩，“目前对比较文学的理解与其说是围绕不同语言和文化的研究，不如说是围绕不同媒体的研究”[①]（5）。在同一份报告中，盖尔·芬尼（Gail Finney，2017：20）甚至预测，比较文学目前致力于“摧毁围墙和边界”，这最终可能会导致更名：“到 2025 年，比较文学研究很可能成为一个更贴切的术语，这个名称“唤起了与文化研究的联系，而比较文学正不断汲取文化研究领域的养分”。

可以看到，比较文学和认知文学研究似乎也沿着同样的轨迹在前进，因为认知文学理论家们已经思忖了一段时间，认知文化研究这个名称也许能更好地代表他们的领域。《认知文化研究导论》（Zunshine，2010a）收录了该领域内各种重新定义的研究方法：从视觉艺术和戏剧的认知研究到认知生态批评。此外，该卷的序言强调了当今的认知文化研究项目与雷蒙德·威廉姆斯（Raymond Williams）的“文化研究原始愿景”之间的深度兼容性，他在《漫长的革命》（1961）中探讨了“人脑进化（与）特定文化所承载的阐释”之间的关系以细述这一愿景。（詹塞恩，2010b：5）。

虽然这两个领域都承认来自文化研究的贡献，但我们也许更需要认真审视他们跨越媒体的“围墙和边界”来解读文化的概念框架。是否存在他们已经共用的方法，或在不久的将来可能会共同的方法？

以比较主义者为首，人们被跨越不同表征形式的探究所依据的理论观点之广泛所震惊。例如，一项对早期现代科学话语和视觉艺术的女权主义调查揭示了“媒介或形式的明显差异背后的本质统一性”，因为“无论媒介是什么，女性……通常作为视觉分析和消费的被动对象出现”（Braider，2006：170）。或者，再举一例，历史主义的重新建构拒绝在平行的文化轨道上解读诗歌和视觉艺术，认为它们彼此孤立，这一点丰富了我们对早期现代想象生态的理解：如果“文本使我们能够理解画家的想法，从而理解他们笔下画面的理想内容或意义，那么图像则帮助我们看到诗人所看到的——他们想象的

① 同理，也可以观察到美国以外致力于认知主义探索的专业机构对文化研究的兴趣。例如，中国认知诗学与认知文学研究会正准备在 2020 年 6 月出版其新期刊《认知文化研究》的第一期。

世界，他们所写作和思考的世界，正如他们自己理解的那样"（172）。

女权主义和历史主义这两种观点对认知主义认识论的发展都起过至关重要的作用。我已经概述了历史主义思维在认知主义研究里的核心地位，正如霍根（Hogan）、斯波尔斯基（Spolsky）、玛丽·克兰（Mary Crane）和艾伦·理查森（Alan Richardson）在21世纪初所做的理论化研究。关于女权主义的认知进化方法，读者可以在南希·伊斯特林（Nancy Easterlin）的著作中找到一篇重要的文章，详见她2012年《文学理论和阐释的生物文化方法》标题为"濒危的女儿"的章节[①]。此外，库科宁（Kukkonen）（2018）探讨了预测处理对女权主义叙事学的影响，而詹塞恩（Zunshine）（2015a）和李（Lee）（本期[②]）都讨论了表现他者复杂心理状态能力构建中小说人物性别和社会阶层的相互作用。

于是，认知文化研究似乎找到了比较文学研究支持的各种范式的契合点[③]。认知文学/文化理论家开启了——尤其当涉及姊妹艺术领域时——对具身社会心智的持续关注，这种具身社会认知是多模态和多感官的。因此，本专题的两篇文章，凯西·舍恩伯格（Casey Schoenberger）的《在文艺复兴时期的意大利和早期现代中国表演真诚；或，为什么真正的恋人吵架》和伊莱恩·奥扬（Elaine Auyoung）的《审美体验的无声亲密：哈代和德加》，都强调认知的多模态，分别探讨了诗歌和音乐，以及散文小说和视觉艺术。这两篇文章的分析暗示，跨越表征界限的批判性对话不仅仅是一种批判性风尚（在

① 南希·伊斯特林（2012：248）首先反驳了"文学达尔文主义者"对性心理学的看法：文学达尔文主义者在他们的文学分析中"明显地"回避"任何关于性控制和权力的讨论，这两种都与男女相互冲突的动态有关"。然后，她阅读了D.H.劳伦斯的小说《狐狸》（*The Fox*），该小说提供了"一个鲜明的例子，说明一个为进化目的而'设计'的行为，最终是如何对所涉个体的特定心理和关系需求不起作用的"（263）。关于达尔文主义对女权主义的进一步批评，请参见霍根（2018：22）。

② 与詹塞恩在《今日诗学》2020年同期发表。——译者注

③ 有关这两个领域之间理论兼容性的进一步例证，见他们与后结构主义（Spolsky，2002；Heise，2017：2；另见Charon和Lee在本期中分别与德里德诗学的交互）、生态批评主义（Easterlin，2010；Heise，2013）、残疾研究（Minich，2014；Savarese，2015）、酷儿研究（Vincent，2015；Lanser，2017）和人权（Anker，2012；Keen，2015）的相关讨论。

特定的历史节点，它可能被昵称为“文化研究”）。相反，它更反映了人类认知的一个基本特征，而并非按照大致与我们的学科划分相对应的模态。

舍恩伯格（Schoenberger）对17世纪威尼斯和中国音乐剧作品研究的中心是冲突：浪漫主义主角之间的冲突、尼禄皇帝和波佩阿的冲突（在蒙特威尔第和布塞内罗的《波佩阿加冕礼》里）以及唐玄宗和杨贵妃的冲突（在洪昇的《长生殿》里）；在他们要求各自的观众相信什么（那些主角确实是浪漫的）和他们对剧本所描绘的历史人物实际行为的了解［“在加冕几年之后”尼禄就会把“怀孕的波佩阿”踢死（283），而玄宗最终会下令赐杨自缢］之间的冲突。舍恩伯格认为：“描述恋人吵架和道德缺陷人物的场景可能会让观众觉得更真实浪漫，因为它们戏剧化了最近由认知科学阐明的依恋情绪功能的一个方面，即‘身体预算’”，即“大脑分配能量资源”（摘要，281）。

身体预算是一个深刻的社会过程。与他者的互动——在浪漫关系的背景下，但也包括观看歌剧表演的背景下——涉及“放弃或同意分享某种程度的对身心资源的控制”。根据不同情形，“由此产生的‘情绪传染’的脆弱性”可能最终对我们的健康有害或裨益（291-292）。舍恩伯格（Schoenberger）指出，音乐剧通过渲染各种各样的冲突来模拟身体预算，他调查了这种多模态冲突传播的一些“情感‘成分’”（295），包括音乐和韵律（相辅相成，也相互竞争），观众对主角的了解和他们代入主角感受之间的不稳定平衡，以及“情感概念”的唤起（285），例如快乐和嫉妒。这些概念受社会影响，因此也成为社会谈论的对象。（实际上，在17世纪的中国和意大利都是如此，当时形形色色的名流思想家都来审视“情感的伦理地位”。）

多模态冲突（甚至堆积的冲突）是通往社会关联的一条途径。奥扬（Auyoung）的文章探讨了另一条路径，即艺术家和作家似乎“超越了他们所选择的媒介”营造出的美学效果（302）。就德加（Degas）而言，是他呈现“似乎能讲故事的绘画”的能力（例如在《舞蹈课》

中），而对于哈代（Hardy）而言，是他能创作“看起来像绘画的小说的能力（302；例如《德伯家的苔丝》）。奥扬（Auyoung）认为，这种跨媒介的表征形式会有助于“观众体会无法在画布或印刷页面上充分表现的感官和情感内容”，通过这样做，使我们“能够享受到与他们和所代表的场景的私人关联和亲密感”（303）。

为了解释这种私人关联的机制［关键的一点，这种关联仍然是非双向的，因为观众/读者从中获得的任何“感官和情感”意义都“永远不会被否定”（313）］，奥扬（Auyoung）将社会语言学、话语理解和经验美学的研究综合在一起。她指出，哈代暗示他的读者融入“许多他们自己的具身知识”（例如，触觉、动觉和运动），以理解他所描述的内容，从而放大了“他们精神表征的多模态丰富性和印刷文本的认识特征之间的不对称”（304）。正是这种不对称性“使读者觉得他们私下里与虚构世界中的人物有共同之处”（304）。反过来，德加唤起了人们对空间和身体的关注，这些空间和身体只能被观众们部分看到，（推动）他们仔细地推测其中蕴含的深意……他们可能会对充满移动着的身体的房间所隐含动态和活力做出推论，或者对更多的局部细节做出细致的推断，利用他们的社交知识来猜想坐在前景中的舞者手托着下巴正在想什么。

这些推论构成了对间接含义的一种私密理解的基础，这种理解在外部世界中是不存在的，只有在观众的脑海中才能实现。（311-12）

知道（换言之，在自己的身体里感觉到）我们理解艺术家/作家的私人含义，而且这种亲密感不能从我们身上被夺走/被否定，这是一种引人注目的社会体验。舍恩伯格（Schoenberger）和奥扬（Auyoung）的文章表明，无论是身体预算实验，还是表征不完全性的实验，所导致的社会关联感在跨模态构建时都会变得更加强大。至少，这意味着涉足音乐学和艺术史的比较文学学者可能会受益，因为他们能够通过探究具身的社会心智运作来充实他们目前的理论研究工作。

似乎认知文学理论家的一些核心兴趣（例如，他们对普遍性这一难题的研究，以及他们在探索具身的动态过程中对历史语境化的强调）已经使他们与比较文学的研究者们暗中结盟。此外，通过用明确的比较主义术语表述，本期特刊的撰稿人证明了这两个领域有着相同的驱动力：走得更广（通过接触其他语言、文化、表征模态和学科）以研究更深（阐明一些地方性、特殊性和独特性的东西）。我们希望本辑专题能有更多的学者跟进，从而将认知主义者和比较主义者聚在一起，合力寻求新的方法来理论化和构建这一共同驱动力。

认知诗学本土化

后现代诗性空间，向认知诗学的转向

陈亚平

【摘要】认知过程产生出来的诗性范围，是一种对认知本身发生的来源的感受和再体验——从认知到反思认知的意识诗性，这就和通常的诠释诗学范式有了诗学跨学科上的区分。可见，《庚子杂诗》在建设一种带认知功能的诗性空间方面已经做到了，从读者解释诗，到读者自己从脑海中琢磨对诗的认知如何形成——那种国际前沿性的诗学转向。

【关键词】诗性范围；中间认知；语义场域；认知同源；原型参照

当前，史诗和长诗的界定问题还有待廓清。这个问题不仅需要这个时代客观地找到史诗和长诗叙事-话语同源、认知同源的问题出发点，还需要拒斥那些偏离。如果从审美哲学来着眼的话，长诗和史诗表述的实体世界事实上就是一个主体叙述它自身内在话语层次上的对象的多极世界。不妨比较一下原始纪颂史诗、民族传奇故事史诗、圣经史诗、民族创世史诗、英雄史诗、神话故事史诗、世系史诗、神谱雏形史诗、戏剧体长诗、民族叙事长诗、民族抒情长诗、小说式史诗和民族故事长诗……准确地说，这些长篇诗把每一个独立的诗段组合成连贯的整体，是因为在诗中，首先做到了对原始灵感的延绵开启，然后才能做到最高运思引导的内在进展，并达到附带变化的那种统一。例如，发自内心来体验赵野《庚子杂诗》长诗关键的东西，绝不只是对诗选取的重大事件题材做出比龚自珍《已

作者简介：陈亚平，四川光华学院客座教授，中国文艺评论家协会-新文艺群体评论工作专委会委员，主要从事内空间意识哲学、美学-哲学、诗学研究。

亥杂诗》[1]长诗形制更大的改变。不管从长诗的发展历史，还是从创造力能够表现的最大内容范围，长诗原则上是可以融合史诗性质的篇幅展开叙述的那种外在手段，从体式上，可以等同或接近史诗内容编排的通常比例。最重要的是，长诗比起民族传奇故事史诗，更需要合乎不可设定的多种叙述可能性的一种功能。因为不可设定的多种叙述可能性，首先意味着，有不可测的话语发生性，借助一种融合，转换出新的话语维度。它必然会改变那些体式界限凭附的唯一性和尚未存在性。它从本质上消解了体式外现和内涵之间的那种对立。

从东方和西方长诗的种类及其艺术外现的特征比较，长诗的体式有一定的不成形的故事脉络，但不以独立段落的故事、情节、情境的穿插为主要特征，全诗意象延伸的织体，基本介于抒情、叙事、泛议的平行或垂直连缀。经典史诗的体式十分直露，为体式结构特征，但不一定是合乎不可设定的多种可能性。《己亥杂诗》比起《摩诃婆罗多》[2]，后者只能说是属于原始史诗叙事类型的长诗。长诗《庚子杂诗》恰恰是介于两者之间的另一种合一文体形态，也区分了民族叙事长诗。关于这方面，我做一个严格的讨论：

1　《庚子杂诗》的变革类型，构建一种特殊长诗的诗学性

纵观东西方诗歌历史阶段的演绎，区分长诗和史诗类型所依据的原则界限从来就没有被澄清过。因为二者在组织全诗结构的基本形式上，很难有性质对立的确定性分类、界限和策略标准。记事型叙事长诗和民族史诗的经典标准，就貌似属于这一类。可是，我要说：任何经典标准的法则内部，都来源于这一法则之所以成为一个

① 清代诗人龚自珍（1792—1841）著有《定庵文集》，留存文章 300 余篇，诗词近 800 首，今人辑为《龚自珍全集》。

② 《摩诃婆罗多》是享誉世界的印度史诗，它的汉语全译本，约有 500 万字，与《罗摩衍那》并列为印度的两大史诗。

标尺的那个心灵原型。这意味着，心灵原型不管怎样预设，一定有不变的基本构建。什么是心灵原型的基本建构呢？起码要有直观的感性和认知的理性。它恰恰决定了，叙事长诗和民族史诗这二者之间，还存在一个感性（叙事-抒情）和知性（运思-判断）在根基性质的结构上永远不会变化的居中者。长诗《庚子杂诗》就是一个原型参照的范例。

《庚子杂诗》的诗学结构带有一种异质开放的特征，在继承魏晋杂诗以思绪代泛议的形制基础上，增加了类似《滕王阁序诗》《序志》《序书》和现代长诗序诗形制结合的《读〈己亥杂诗〉并致余世存》，这个不拘律体序诗和现代体序诗流例的结合方法，表面上是在索源中前修龚自珍的杂诗体式而不是元稹，但实质上，已经具有了自建的现代品质的诗学独立性。关键是，《读〈己亥杂诗〉并致余世存》从文本层次发生的渊源上，显示了《庚子杂诗》这种变式杂诗体，对语境变化而相应做出变化的特定表达方式。通过对魏晋、明清杂诗文体做形制上的分类，赵野这种变式杂诗体，我评述为：变魏晋杂诗体的随兴之感为现代杂诗体的遂深之感，变《己亥杂诗》的感讽之精密为现代杂诗体的锐思之高识；化魏晋杂诗体的际遇偶兴为现代杂诗体的奇思深辨。另外，《读〈己亥杂诗〉并致余世存》也是对《庚子杂诗》全诗首尾不脱落的长幅构架的统摄。例如：

梅花染了流行病，高调入戏
两戒河山升起巨大幻觉

汉语有灵，词气冲天而起
伟大的尘世之诗可期写成

（《庚子杂诗》序诗）

《庚子杂诗》从序诗到正诗整体的体式、体例、语体、诗歌长度的时-空织体形式，比起《酬乐天余思不尽加为六韵之作》[①]《四愁》

① 唐代诗人元稹创作的一首七言排律。

杂诗[1]、《朔风》杂诗[2]、《杂诗十二首》[3]《秦州杂诗二十首》[4]《己亥杂诗》，更具有分延的迂回和后续的引领那种自设的散体性。基本形成的格致是，《庚子杂诗》形制上以现代散体多点穿插性的杂多，来消解《酬乐天余思不尽加为六韵之作》《四愁》杂诗、《朔风》杂诗、《杂诗十二首》《秦州杂诗二十首》《己亥杂诗》律体的锁闭线性的杂一。为了十分理想地连接古今长诗的读解纽带，《庚子杂诗》人为地改变了西方古典史诗中的时空推移式的叙述视角，特别是，拿它和正统类型史诗和演变型长诗品种相比，《庚子杂诗》增加了史诗和长诗叙述手段中所少见的叙事语法。这类叙事语义代表性的特征是，把代表民族传奇的叙事表述，即事件在时间序列中产生的真实空间场景序列，夹层一样地引到长篇诗某个泛议连续体中。分析例句：

梅花染了流行病，高调入戏
两戒河山升起巨大幻觉

近来白虹贯日，望气者缄默
流光中煞星怒马鲜衣

（《庚子杂诗》序诗）

以上诗句，貌似可以感受到，“入戏”一词，对整个《庚子杂诗》篇幅展开精心预设的起承点，这是否意味着，序诗以中国式“说书开场”方式，委婉地预设了一个故事情节体系的存在？不过，概观全诗叙事和议述的构造体系，虽然存在一种时空中展开的事件序列——“梅花染了流行病”，但被诗人在接下来的句子中构造成一个由解释、评判、论究多极话语交织的递增体，让全诗表现了事件产生分解、引申出观念变化与释义延伸的新因素。析例：

①《昭明文选》卷二十九张衡《诗己·杂诗上·四愁诗四首》。
② 西晋王瓒作《杂诗·朔风动秋草》。
③《杂诗十二首》是晋宋之际文学家陶渊明的组诗作品。
④《秦州杂诗二十首》是唐代诗人杜甫的组诗作品。

打开一册旧书，修辞正派
往来其间明了和它的关系

一个隐喻后面还有一个隐喻
在脚注里找到自己的位置

（《庚子杂诗》序诗）

以上“往来其间明了和它的关系”和“在脚注里找到自己的位置”两句，明显地使作品的整体，在我们读解、想象做出转换的角度上，完全拆解了传奇史诗那个贯穿全诗的完整的故事叙述框架，由此呈现出两个或多个序列的结合体。历史上的巴门尼德残篇《论自然》[①]和这点有些相像。

我的看法是，史诗中的叙事是神魂之口的技术，它总是把自己放到人类言说中最靠前沿的那个位置中，可能是因为它孕育了现代中历数的历史和历史中切近的当代。因此，古典史诗或古典叙事性长诗，那种弥散型感官事件表现的体裁结构，在很多时候，都促进了现代自由体长诗那种弥散型内心畅想结构技巧的发展。更不可否认的事实是，在《庚子杂诗》的叙事语法中，非常明显地体现了《庚子杂诗》在和《己亥杂诗》的文体比鉴中，基本上做到了在某个穿插性的、一部分的故事穿插序列完成之尾，在其中根植一显性或隐形的观念泛议序列的成分。我指的是，诗句中交织的观念序列，从非作者的角度，被无形地组合到读者的潜见的叙述序列中。

可以判断的是，《庚子杂诗》通过对那些外在事物和内在观念有同源关联的双重叙述结构的构建，颠覆了《己亥杂诗》长诗纯粹不以外在故事穿插为中心的泛议体式结构。因此我可以预断，对现代长诗叙述形式的更大可能性来说，只要有思想最高涵盖性的超越，就有形式上任何可能存在的未现方式。《庚子杂诗》克服了《己亥杂

① 古希腊哲学家巴门尼德《论自然》残篇第一节：“πποιταί μεφέρουσιν，ὅσοντ΄ ἐπὶ θυμὸς (1) ἱκάνοι， πέμπον， ἐπεί μ΄ ἐς 。”

诗》不以外在故事、情境、情节穿插为中心的一面，但又十分客观而折中地阐扬了现代思想开放性的运思方式和动态的现代汉语句法表达方式。从细读上分析《庚子杂诗》的叙述进程，会发现，事件的发生是单线性的，只显示出它作为诗的一个表层进程。但诗中展开的运思却是多极的、立体的、交织的深层次进程。这种深层次的进程，在对诗段前后衔接性的织体中，既包含泛议性的演绎、评判、论究等穿插的行进，又包含运思性的思辨、玄悟、隐形解释等迂回的行进。正是《庚子杂诗》长诗表现出这种运思的深层次叙述话语类型，才从现代诗学和后现代主义诗学的层次上，区分了《己亥杂诗》为代表的古典泛议类型的杂诗体。因此，需要在当今诗学上引起前沿批判性思考和创造性思考的敏感点是，《庚子杂诗》不只是力图在现代诗性叙述的认识论策略上创造一种特殊的汉语词法-句法来表达其现代性质的诗化认知，还力图表现出后现代性思考方式那个多极化可能的不确定本质状况。

我负责地说，不确定的程度就是再造多极可能性的程度。《庚子杂诗》长诗叙述结构的演绎、评判、论究的穿插行进的多极化因素，就是相应的可能性叙述情节的稳定因素。例如，《庚子杂诗》诗中泛议性的演绎、评判、论究的穿插行进句：（1）泛议性的演绎：诗句沿用了从此到彼、从一般到特殊的演绎，用前提涵盖结论。如："灼灼文脉尽吸江山氤氲，朗朗星空下我们望史坐经"（《庚子杂诗》序诗第 5 首）。（2）泛议性的评判：诗句借助感性和理性的结合，引发类比性的想象，做出联想性推导，引起思考加深的迁移式飞跃。如："汉语有灵，词气冲天而起，伟大的尘世之诗可期写成"（《庚子杂诗》序诗第 5 首）。龚自珍《己亥杂诗》中只有"世事沧桑心事定"一句的泛议性的评判，与赵野《庚子杂诗》相接近。（3）泛议性的论究：诗句引出认知、观念，并对认知做出启示性的提升。如："现实太沉重，君子居易俟命，要留下温暖的说明和记录"（《庚子杂诗》序诗第 4 首）。

另外，《庚子杂诗》诗中还有运思性的思辨、玄悟、隐形解释的迂回行进句：

1.1 运思性的思辨

诗句包含便于表达思辨本身的秘密结构，特别是，从一种思想的被思和被判断本身演绎出这种内在的相互作用和相互否定的变化。因此，诗句在理性的思辨代替致思的情志这一诗学革命的层次上，形成了一种智性话语创造自我世界的那种后现代主义的“内在性”。这种内在性，我认为，也可以通过一种象征着交互性的语言来创造自我主体的思辨。因为语言的内在性是这一否定性的再造。《庚子杂诗》诗句中立足的思辨，是思想从内在上给予的超越，它高于那种只集中心思于某一方面的致思性情志。可见，《庚子杂诗》唯独立足思辨的变革，首次从杂诗的品种上相应推动了被中国诗学思想史称为“重志派”那种“写心”传统向现代的转变。如：“一个隐喻后面还有一个隐喻，在脚注里找到自己的位置”（《庚子杂诗》序诗第 4 首）。

诗句“一个隐喻后面还有一个隐喻”绝不只可从文学性层次上来读解，《庚子杂诗》包含的现代诗学意涵不只涉及文学范围。“一个隐喻后面还有一个隐喻”这句诗的意指牵涉还在于：人类共同的隐喻方法同时关系到人类普遍的哲学认知。我敢说，诗意和思辨互为条件，对隐喻的认识也基本隐含在隐喻的根基中。从本质上说，思辨和隐喻都是从本己的立足点向无限延伸的关联点过渡。从这一点看，思辨和隐喻有相像的相互支撑性。但我要问人们，又是什么动力让思辨和隐喻能够另外转渡呢？心灵语是否也存在隐喻的关系？

1.2 运思性的玄悟

诗句侧重表达一种以无为本体的自足之有的玄妙境地。我认为，无的自足基础也必然在归一的基础上才能有那个无的本根。无的体现就是无的有、空的存在，而这无的有、空的存在已经是确定的在，是有。《庚子杂诗》表达出玄学和玄悟思考的解悟本身的言说，如“偶然不可取消，过幻累积，一切有为法终会止于空”（《庚子杂诗》正诗，无题第 6 首）。

1.3 运思性的隐性解释

诗句专门设定了一种隐性的解释进程，类似于隐匿在叙述链中的渗透性评价环节。这种诗歌主体叙述者隐身充当读者视域对哲学真谛的解释，与传统杂诗的“言志”方式形成一种颠覆性的新走向，如“先知难逃被弃的宿命，最坏的可能总选择我们”(《庚子杂诗》正诗，无题第 4 首)。

值得在叙事学上前瞻追问的是,《庚子杂诗》在叙事学的语境意义上，开创了一种叙述功能和叙述语法之间相互重合的形制，这种“表层体—深层抽象—总体抽象—具体化”的叙述话语结构方式，并没有沿袭《吉尔伽美什》[①]《摩诃婆罗多》[②]《孔雀东南飞》那种纯粹化的“具体—具体—具体”那一类叙述话语主导结构。我们试着比较“具体—具体—具体”叙述话语主导结构的《孔雀东南飞》诗作体式：

> 孔雀东南飞，五里一徘徊。十三能织素，十四学裁衣，十五弹箜篌，十六诵诗书。十七为君妇，心中常苦悲。君既为府吏，守节情不移，贱妾留空房，相见常日稀。鸡鸣入机织，夜夜不得息。

再比较“表层体—深层抽象—总体抽象—具体化”合成了三个叙述话语结构方式主导的《庚子杂诗》诗篇体式：

> 少年击剑吹箫挽颓波
> 六经注我，但开变易风气
>
> 上下都是残棋，东南失忆
> 淮水飞去来王朝的新装

①《吉尔伽美什史诗》是目前已知世界最古老的古巴比伦人的英雄史诗。

②《孔雀东南飞》是中国文学史上第一部长篇叙事诗，也是乐府诗发展史上的高峰之作。

狂辞既忤逆，翰墨翻老波澜
彰显虫鱼的微言大义

诗整体保留了一部分外在故事情节“少年击剑吹箫挽颓波”穿插的纽带，但又在句子“彰显虫鱼的微言大义”里面折中地吸纳了现代运思方式的抽象—具体化表述，形成了诗的故事情节和论说情节两种不同的叙述聚合状态。同时，《庚子杂诗》没有借鉴《离骚》[①]那种纯粹化的“抽象—具体—抽象”那一类抒情主导体式。我们试着比较“抽象—具体—抽象”抒情手段主导的《己亥杂诗》诗作体式：

著书何似观心贤？不奈卮言夜涌泉。
百卷书成南渡岁，先生续集再编年。

我马玄黄盼日曛，关河不窘故将军。
百年心事归平淡，删尽蛾眉惜誓文。

罡风力大簸春魂，虎豹沈沈卧九阍。
终是落花心绪好，平生默感玉皇恩。

从长诗类型的现代性功能比较来看，《庚子杂诗》和《己亥杂诗》差异的聚焦点，也存在于类似《离骚》和《庚子杂诗》差异之间可比较的情形中。于是，《庚子杂诗》和赵野其他同类作品相比，存在一种革命性变化的转向。这就促使《庚子杂诗》的叙事结构，有必要对叙述的可能性所开启的变化前沿做出一个继承性的超越中国传统叙事的重新思考。不可否认，赵野以《庚子杂诗》为重要代表的长诗，在克服《己亥杂诗》“泛议—抒情—论理”内在结构的基础上，开创了一种“故事穿插—及事化思想情节穿插—泛议情节—结合故事穿插”的叙述结构法。这种方法，借助对故事情节截面的选择性

①《离骚》是中国战国时期诗人屈原创作的诗篇，是中国古代最长的抒情诗。

穿插，把思想观念弥散出来的评述的点、线、面变成了延绵性的让读者进一步认知的无形但能感受的思考情节。这样既可以把精心选择出的故事穿插点变成隐性的思想情节的织体，也可以把思想无形之形的组织序列变成故事凭附的载体，甚至变成故事情节本身就隐藏着思想。关键的前沿意义在于：《庚子杂诗》这种“有选择的故事穿插—及事化的思想情节和泛评—思想情节涉事化—故事穿插合一”的叙述认知方式，在肌理性的继承中，又转向性地拓展了中国传统叙事“抒情—论理”话语的形式和功能。《庚子杂诗》在很大程度上，力求古今奇思之僻，因此，这首杂诗的句法具有敏迈而气浑、致思闪缩而不谲怪、格致重厚而不冷涩的原创性。从这一点看得出赵野精思而语深的格致中既善继传统，又偏倚后创，本质上，是把握到一种把传统性渗透到后现代性的同源对应关系。如：

那手，刚刚翻开我的书页
也许扣下过母亲面对的扳机

我和刽子手使用同样语言
还要让它们分外美丽

死亡随德国一路狂奔
我统治词抵抗恶的加速度

奥斯维辛后，诗依然成立
赋格寸寸为见证作证

（《庚子杂诗》二十五《策兰祭》）

2 《庚子杂诗》的后现代诗性空间向认知诗学的转向

从人类哲学史可以发现，中国传统哲学对“思则得之”[①]“虚灵

① 参见《孟子：告子章句上》，江西人民出版社 2017 年版。

明觉”[①]的认识完全着眼于一种对主体性的开启，这恰恰就切近后现代主义显示的心灵综合自身在世界上的一切特征、对自我发生作用——那种“内在性”。我的意思是说：传统和后现代进程，都是深入一种过程本体的维度中。传统就是前后不均质的演进，因为演进由无限过程的转渡决定而来。

从《庚子杂诗》专求精义坚深的格制上看，它对魏晋律体长韵杂诗的继承性和根源性的变革是有设定方向的，明显存在一种长诗和史诗同源构造和异质界面之间，那种形成了差异的新走向。《庚子杂诗》既对应于后现代主义对自我发生作用的“内在性”维度，又有穿插故事情节和时代环境的现代认识论拓展，这两者结合，就形成一种新的兼容性整体的续现代杂诗变体。从现代诗学产生的认知根源来分析，这类现代类型杂诗表达方式的特殊变异方向，和魏晋杂诗的古典类型相比，有独特的叙述学价值和认知诗性的特定造诣。因此，对《庚子杂诗》这类化质野为灵动的变体杂诗的文本特征进行界定，需要后经典叙事时代的认知重心，向文本理解的发生来源做出转向，也需要原创更多前瞻诗学的新概念视野，包括最适用于作品系统认知的一些新研究方法。

2.1　发散且结合的诗性空间

《庚子杂诗》全诗大部分语体和句式方法是带有一定的后现代智性成分的，因为赵野十分怀疑一种假设和暂定的秩序本体，所以他不需要那些文本的本体论支撑。因此我认为，全诗在叙述的向度选择上没有选择时间性的叙述向度，而是在诗的外放性叙述列次中展现一种非均等的、各个片段交织在一起的混聚结构。这种互相没有支配关系，但又存在互相潜在介入的话语聚合空间，不是古典诗那种诗中产生画面感的视觉空间性，而是《庚子杂诗》句群段落中碰到的一个个语义环节产生的语义场界。这就造成《庚子杂诗》的论说性、泛议性、拟议性、描写性、智辨性等多重表达方式组织之间

① “虚灵明觉”见《王阳明全集》，中央编译出版社 2018 年版。王阳明，明代思想家、心学集大成者。

的位置转换，是处在间断中又合成的序列中，相当于把一个独立意向组所建立的句序转渡到下一个跨越意向组建立的句序中，只是凭借一种语义场域来做出前后的隐形连接。我认为，这本质上显现了不确定性中的暂存性那种构建—消解—构建的后现代哲学运思。应该是赵野从后现代运思中体验到的对一种或然性的看重。这一类的代表作例证如下：

洛阳城外千里无鸡鸣
皇帝下罪己诏检讨德行

二月二，龙羞于抬头
治大国若跳神，一乍一惊

天命生生不息，谁人能及
几方黄巾颠倒淋漓意

字里行间隐喻如伏兵
昨夜荧惑守户九州幽冥

（《庚子杂诗》十《读《后汉书》》）

诗句“洛阳城外千里无鸡鸣”到“治大国若跳神，一乍一惊”是包含故事元素的序列，相邻的论说元素序列“天命生生不息，谁人能及”仿佛没有做出有意识的选择，而是直接穿插到“字里行间隐喻如伏兵”这种思辨元素的序列中。这几个句子互相没有支配关系，但又存在发散、互相依赖、互相渗透的认知感应。这就成功地构建了句子各个叙述序列交互作用的不确定、变形性、偏移性、随意性……“思则得之”“虚灵明觉”的内在性空间，排斥了首尾一致的线性，体现出《庚子杂诗》这种取消因果联系、消解本体秩序的后现代原则。例如，全诗一共有四个功能单元，但各个单元之间的话语衔接都是断裂的、任意指向的，形成了全诗各个单元功能的分解式连接，让分解的过程充分体现了诗中具体到抽象、抽象到具体的关系，做出变化又有序的整合。

2.2 思想来源的认知

《庚子杂诗》更看重特殊句法和词法组织的结构形成的不易辨认性或反常性，怎样能引起读者任意译解一种超出作者原有意指的认知的发生？于是,《庚子杂诗》让读者对诗句结构和语义的感知反应，变成了读者对作者思想形成来源的臆测。属于这一类的代表作例证如下：

是夜无梦，酣睡如深海
一觉醒过世界依然

经验穷尽处，信仰升起
圣人不论六合之外

宇宙原是个完美的设计
所以该来的自然会来

万一山河大地都塌陷了
朱子说，毕竟理还在

（《庚子杂诗》十一《无题》）

诗句“是夜无梦，酣睡如深海”，直接嵌入下一句“经验穷尽处，信仰升起”，这种解散性跳跃的句子组织带有奇诡中浮思辨的无碍性和圆融性，它明显消除了魏晋、明清杂诗体遇物就述、遇事就议的易辨认性和正常感受性那种形制。例如，“是夜无梦，酣睡如深海”的故事情节，嵌入“经验穷尽处，信仰升起”泛议话语之间，就产生出介于二者之间的第三种不易辨认的中间认知性。关键的事情是，诗句“经验穷尽处，信仰升起”很容易引起读者在对“经验穷尽”的读解中产生一种推想作者“经验穷尽”这一认知来源的深入琢磨。

比如，读者会反审性地玩味存储在自己脑海中的对“经验”的看法来源和组成样式，与诗句“经验穷尽处”有什么差异。又如诗句:“宇宙原是个完美的设计”把语义的悬解点集中到以下这种读解、译解、构解的思考循环中:（1）这个感知的空间，有哪些心智形式在起推动作用?（2）这个认知是怎么在阅读中浮现出的?（3）从哪个认知的起点产生？为什么它会这样产生？

与文本的诠释性相比，最本质的差异是，这种认知过程产生的诗性范围是一种对认知本身发生的来源的感受和再体验——从认知到反思认知的意识诗性。这就和通常的诠释诗学范式有了诗学跨域学科上的区分。可见,《庚子杂诗》在建设一种带认知功能的诗性空间方面已经做到了从读者解释诗到读者自己从脑海中琢磨对诗的认知如何形成这种国际前沿性的诗学转向。例如:

> 事物要回到本来的样子
> 活着过一生，毕竟非儿戏
>
> （《庚子杂诗》十三，惊蛰）
>
> 多美的场景啊，风清物明
> 它们只要随自己的本性
>
> （《庚子杂诗》无题，十八）

在《庚子杂诗》中，上述这类诗句的出现频率很高。

2.3 历史诗转向纵深维度的推进

我的看法是，历史的诗性特质总是被相应文化的过去、现在和未来之间的诗性结构从本质性来源上决定。我们领会诗性的方式，只应该在历史维度展现的诗学根基立足。《庚子杂诗》在化解和阐扬《己亥杂诗》杜韩式神思和明清诗学“世运”“性情”范畴的律体基础上，不仅沉浸式地拓展了《己亥杂诗》咏怀中显其志、讽喻中显其诫、飘逸中见凌云豪健的文风，而且关键在于《庚子杂诗》形成了对《酬乐天余思不尽加为六韵之作》《四愁》杂诗、《朔风》杂诗、

《杂诗十二首》《秦州杂诗二十首》《己亥杂诗》弃其所短的自我运思格致。这就是：在造奇巧喻中深蕴一种李贺式至理感讽，在参悟中暗含一种李白式的刀笔鞭挞，在叙理中契合一种嵇康式的幽玄，在思辨中通达王安石式的曲致……以历史之思而高于历史之思完成了对后现代普遍境遇的思辨。这种观念中存在的历史诗性结构是由思想叙述构成的。事实上，对真正处在历史之中的一种运思进程来说，书写的历史不算是实体的历史性，最多只算是在词语上构建或重构历史。

试读例诗：

不祥的预言一个又一个
撑破空，因果素面相见

我无法想象另一层时间
我唯剩此在，泪水淋漓

苦难全接收，快乐亦是
可能的选择都仅有一次

而任地覆天翻，我只要
找回母语的气息和味道

（《庚子杂诗》三十六《无题》）

《庚子杂诗》全诗构建的历史诗学纵深是一个传统和续现代一起共存的意向系统，这是赵野对现代长诗文本思想的时代贡献。

从文体看,《庚子杂诗》构建了更有叙述纵深面的四句一节结构，即“二二四”形制组合。因为赵野更偏好句法结构带有一种内在的连接和外在的间断——对立空间性的开放。例如：

我看到汉语在废墟上哭泣
分享了它的梦想和恐惧

大雅久不作，秦朝的句法

封印一个个高蹈的亡灵

天道要求着新的叙事
苍山雪高叫：未来已来

旧世界典故出处可疑
挫败的隐喻欲重振生机
（《庚子杂诗》二十一《无题》）

这类“二二四”组合的文体形态，明显不适合融入魏晋、明清杂诗那种长于表达偶兴和随感的“二二”律体结构。《庚子杂诗》这类“二二四”组合关系的现代长篇杂诗体，更胜“二二”七言句律体一筹，因为“二二四”组合带有铺叙、插叙、论说、泛议、寓意、思辨、咏物、抒怀、论说、描绘等多个表述方式呈现的发散的纵深面，它从功能上模糊了和魏晋律体杂诗之间隐含的直接和间接的关联。这正是赵野把古典杂诗体的因果性继承，变成现代杂诗关联性转化的有意识的变革。

中国民歌意象情感表达新释：文化语言学视角

孙　毅　谢新峰

【摘要】文化语言学作为语言学多学科分支之一，以挖掘语言背后的文化动因为主。民歌是中国民俗文化的典型代表，能集中反映语言、文化和概念化之间的密切关系。本文选取部分中国民歌展开个案分析，分别运用文化语言学理论框架下的文化图式、文化范畴和文化隐喻为工具分析民歌中的意象，旨在探究民歌意象传递情感的过程及表征文化概念化的具体方式。通过考察民歌的文化概念化和语言特征因素，为深入分析民歌复杂的概念化系统开辟新视角，也为研究文化认知和语言的跨文化异同提供借鉴。

【关键词】文化语言学；民歌意象；文化概念化；情感表达

0 引　言

作为一种独特的民俗话语，民歌是一种群体性或者“地方性的集体创作”（王宏印，2014：9），可以使集体观念适应特定的或个人的目的来展示一种相对个性化和抒情化的交流。民歌有着丰富的表现主题，大致分为情感歌曲（如情歌、悲歌）、娱乐歌曲（如行会歌、学徒歌、手艺人歌）、场合歌曲（如纺纱歌、相亲歌）、仪式歌曲、

基金项目：本文系广东外语外贸大学阐释学研究院 2021 年度科研招标重点项目“约翰·济慈十四行诗的当代隐喻学阐释研究”（CSY-2021-ZD-02）的阶段性研究成果。

作者简介：孙毅，男，广东外语外贸大学阐释学研究院教授，博士生导师，主要从事当代隐喻学与认知叙事学研究；
谢新峰，男，厦门大学外文学院博士研究生，贵州师范大学国际教育学院讲师，主要从事认知语言学及应用语言学研究。

生活方式和职业歌曲（如牧羊歌、渔歌、士兵歌、流浪歌、逃亡歌），以及历史、社会和政治歌曲（Katona，2002：59）等六大歌曲主题。历经五千年的发展和完善，民歌与语言一般，记录着民俗文化的概念化过程，叙述着民间群体的具身体验、情感体验和文化体验。民歌由民间群体创造出来反映其对自己生活和周围世界的具体观念和信仰，因而有着丰富的意象和深厚的文化概念化基础。通过自然意象来表达集体化的情感和心理状态，传递深邃的隐喻含义，是中国民歌的一大特点。

受认知语言学的影响，大批国内学者已运用概念隐喻理论对诗歌中的自然意象予以解读（如周红民，2019；孙毅，2013；刘国辉，汪兴富，2010；孙毅，梁晓晶，2019；等等），而对民歌中自然意象的研究相对较少。目前，对民歌的研究思路仍以“文人创作的格局为标准模式”（王宏印，2014：9）为主，具体研究方法主要为基于主题的分类（Küllös，1991；Mona，1959），并在文体框架中定义意义生成模式（如排比、重复、矛盾、递升和夸张）（Katona，2002），即修辞手段。要突破传统研究方法的藩篱，就必须开展民歌和民间文学的跨学科研究，将民歌作为一种语言形式植根于文化概念化之中，并以一种具有相当凝聚力的方式表征文化概念化进行论述。从文化概念化视角分析民歌中的自然意象，有助于探索和挖掘民歌中的文化元素，进一步了解文化概念化对民歌语言使用的影响。鉴于此，本文运用文化语言学的理论框架，以中国民歌为研究对象，分析其通过意象传递情感的方式及表征文化概念化的特点，试图为解读民俗文学作品提供一个全新的诠释视角。

1 理论框架：文化语言学

作为语言学的一门多学科分支，文化语言学（Cultural Linguistics）探索语言和文化概念化之间的联系（Palmer，1996；Sharifian，2011），侧重考察具有文化基础、用人类语言进行编码和交流的概念化。“文化语言学”一词最早是由认知语言学领域的奠基人之一 Ronald

Langacker 在强调文化知识和语法之间关系的声明中开始使用的。Langacker（2008：81）认为："当意义被确定为概念化的时候，所有层次的认知都是具身的（embodied），而且是蕴含于文化中的（culturally embedded）。"Palmer（1996：3）也认为，认知语言学可以直接应用于语言和文化的研究，这是因为"语言是基于意象的语言符号的游戏"，而且这种意象是文化建构的。以文化语言学（Sharifian，2011，2015，2017）形式出现的多学科语言和文化研究已经"从语言认知方法所强调的个人认知和语言之间的关系转移到了语言、概念化和文化之间的关系上"（Sharifian，2011：3）。

文化语言学理论把语言视为"一个复杂的适应系统"（complex adaptive system），融合来自认知科学的"分布式认知"（distributed cognition）和"多施事动态系统理论"（multi-agent dynamic systems theory）等概念，强调在社会和文化背景下研究语言。文化语言学在文化概念化的基础上提出话语研究的综合视角，涉及文化、认知-语义、语法甚至语言单位的各个层面。语言的各种特征和层次，从形态句法特征到意义（包括语义意义和语用意义）再到语篇，都能对文化图式、文化范畴和文化隐喻所体现的文化概念化进行实例化（见图 1）。同时，语言在文化概念化的形成过程中扮演着双重角色。一方面，语言互动为语言使用者提供空间来构建其具身体验的意义，促进文化概念化的形成；另一方面，语言结构和语言使用借鉴并反映文化概念（Sharifian，2003）。因此，文化建构的知识或文化知识

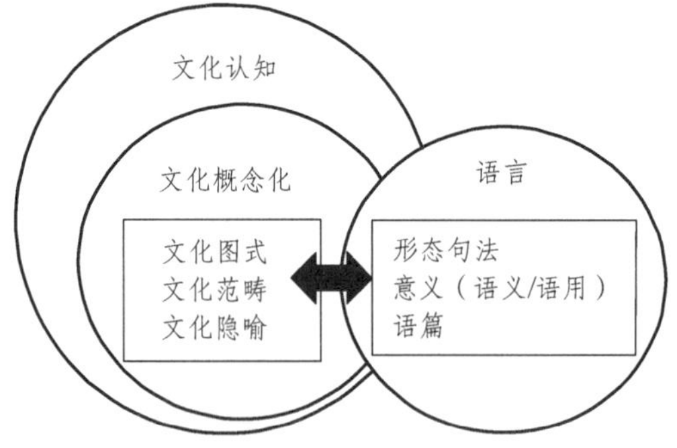

图 1　文化语言学的理论与分析框架（Sharifian，2017：3）

为语言使用者提供了共享语境，成为给定群体认知自然和认知世界的共同前提。另外，对语言本体的研究对理解文化概念化以及最终理解与语言和语言变体相关的文化认知亦具有重要意义。

文化概念化是文化语言学的核心概念，传达文化群体对生活、环境、宗教等方面的认知和信仰（Sharifian，2015），在文化隐喻、文化图式和文化范畴中得以体现。文化隐喻、文化图式和文化范畴具有密切联系，文化图式为概念化提供结构，文化隐喻将包含丰富文化图式结构的文化范畴设定为源域进行相应映射和拓展，进而形成文化概念化。文化语言学以文化隐喻、文化图式和文化范畴为基础，建立了一个适合民间文学研究的分析框架，不仅探讨民歌的语言特征和文化概念化特征，更重要的是探讨具体语言特征和概念化背后的文化动因。理解复杂的民歌需要以大量的语言事实为基础，进行广泛而深入的实证研究。这意味着需要采用自下而上的方法，从动态发展的视角考察语言和文化的关系。再者，与概念化相关的民歌特征包括文化隐喻、文化图式和文化范畴，形成一个特有的文化体系，在不同的表征维度中，可以捕捉到民间群体对情感的独特态度。从这种意义上讲，文化语言学理论及其分析框架适合用于研究具有文化基础的民歌。

2　中国民歌意象及情感表达

借助奇特意象来表达抽象的情感是诗词和民歌创作的共同特点。因此，在传统的诗词研究中，研究者大多集中在对意象进行审美特征和文化探源的阐释（余渭深，董平荣，2003：5），分析时常借用“托物言志”“触景生情”“情景交融”等词语来强调“意”和“象”之间的联系，却较少在文化层面探讨二者融合的深层原因。鉴于此，本文从文化语言学的视角出发，探讨中国民歌意象的选择及其情感表达的文化内因。因为文化范畴是由文化建构的识解范畴，主要反映在人类语言的词汇中（Sharifian，2017：4），在中国民歌中不具有普遍规律，所以本节将重点分析中国民歌意象依靠文化隐喻和文化图式传递情感和表征文化概念化的方式。

2.1 通过文化隐喻传递情感

身体在人类概念化中的作用受到了认知科学的广泛关注。一个主要的研究链，或称“具身链”（e. g., Lakoff & Johnson, 1980, 1999; Johnson, 1987），探索了许多使用身体作为源域的概念隐喻。例如，概念隐喻“心乃情绪之基座”（The heart is the seat of emotions）反映在英语中，“心”是情感中心的文化概念化。思维源自身体与环境的互动，即身体及其所处的环境会影响甚至决定人们的认知（刘立辉，2019：3）。因此，“具身化的隐喻不仅仅来自身体内部，然后表征在个体的头脑中，而是在很大程度上来自文化世界定义的身体互动”（Gibbs，1999：155），不同的文化对身体和具身体验的概念化不同，为身体的各个部位和器官及其功能赋予不同的价值和意义。本文结合下例进一步阐述一种常见文化隐喻类型——具身化的文化隐喻。

折杨柳歌辞（二）

腹中愁不乐，愿作郎马鞭。
出入擐郎臂，蹀坐郎膝边。

这首民歌是由南北朝时期的《折杨柳歌辞》第二首。该民歌先以“腹中愁不乐”直抒胸臆，凸显了汉语身体部位术语和文化概念化之间的关系。在汉语中身体部位和内脏在表达情感上占据了中心位置，如“愁肠百结、捶胸顿足、肝胆相照和满腹辛酸等”都是以身体部位表达情感或感受的丰富例证。“腹中愁不乐”的歌词正是建立在千百年来中国文化以内脏喻情感的深厚文化根基之上的语言表征。其次，该民歌引出马鞭意象。马鞭是北方游牧民族生活中的主要用具，出入帐篷和席地而坐是其典型的生活方式。女主人公以马鞭刚健之意象抒女子温婉之柔情，将看似矛盾的二者完美地融合在一起，使整首歌听起来颇具南方吴声西曲之韵味。这种融合是南北朝时期民族大融合的具体写照。彼时，民族错居加强了各民族之间的交流与融合，社会经济条件和生活环境的变化改变了他们的文化认知，形成了不同的文化概念化。“愁不乐”点出女子与心爱之人的离别，满腹愁怨，所以希望成为心上人的马鞭，进出帐篷可以缠在其手臂上；席坐于地时可以休憩在他膝边。在民歌中描述这些用具和生活方式不仅反映了牧民对生活实践的具身体验，也由此反映了整个游牧民族群体的文化认知基于其生活经验的特点。

动物是民歌传递情感的另一类重要意象。马、鱼、雁等在文化隐喻的构建中往往作为源域去理解丰富的情感。Geeraerts（2010）指出，认知语言学特别关注语境的四个元素：词汇、话语使用、意义和社会语境。其中，意义和社会语境两个要素与文化语言学理论支柱之一的文化隐喻的关系更为显著。Geeraerts 认为，意义是通过概念化来理解的，是百科全书式的，以经验为基础，且每个经验都具有文化性；同时，概念隐喻又是意义构建的机制。因此，文化与隐喻的关系是不可分割的。社会语境是指语言的社会文化性质及其与情境认知的关系，也指其在不同语言、文化和话语中的变体。《鸿雁》这首民歌正是意义和文化隐喻及社会语境和民族文化相结合的具体体现。

鸿　雁

鸿雁，天空上，对对排成行；
江水长，秋草黄，草原上琴声忧伤。
鸿雁，向南方，飞过芦苇荡；
天苍茫，雁何往，心中是北方家乡。
鸿雁，北归还，带上我的思念；
歌声远，琴声颤，草原上春意暖。
鸿雁，向苍天，天空有多遥远；
酒喝干，再斟满，今夜不醉不还。

《诗经》中“鸿雁于飞”塑造了鸿雁南飞、思念家乡的意象，影响深远。中国文化中鸿雁传书的典故，描述鸿雁春来北国，秋去南方，在千百年来的往返途中传递着无数的故事与情感。通过对江水、秋草、鸿雁成排飞行、草原琴声等意象的描写，这首现代蒙古族祝酒歌向读者勾勒出一幅具有丰富隐喻特征的自然图景。与自然相关的隐喻系统凸显了民间群体对自然的认知，固化于民间群体的文化认知中，形成一种相对稳固的、凝聚着群体文化特征的心理结构表征（阎志芬，2000：88）。鸿雁主要繁殖于我国东北和内蒙古地区，是这些区域民间群体文化认知中固有的一部分。鸿雁因季节变化而迁徙的属性从源域投射到靶域中远行之人的属性，以民间群体对自然界动物的具身体验为具体内容充实民间群体文化中关于思乡的认知，传递远行之人对家乡的眷恋。

枯鱼过河泣

枯鱼过河泣，何时悔复及！
作书与鲂鱮，相教慎出入。

与《鸿雁》相比，《枯鱼过河泣》更能在文化上体现某一群体文化的特殊性。因为隐喻除了具有跨文化差异外，在同一文化内部也会呈现不同程度的差异和变体。同一文化内部的差异可表现在社会、区域、民族、风格、亚文化、历时性和个人维度。因此，任何隐喻性分析都应该同时考虑身体和文化元素，以正确地解释隐喻性映射背后的概念化。Sharifian（2017）认为，在构建隐喻的经验基础时，身体和文化之间的互动包括两个阶段：在第一阶段，概念隐喻选择了那些基于身体体验的经验，有助于理解和激发两个不同经验领域之间的隐喻映射。因为所有人都拥有相同的身体构造，所以无论人们的背景如何，第一阶段对每个人应该都是一样的。在第二阶段，这种基于身体的经验被文化信息过滤、调整和修改。因此，结果不是普遍的，而是具有文化特殊性的。《枯鱼过河泣》正是体现了渔民这一特殊群体在一个特定历史环境下构建文化隐喻的一首民歌。

《枯鱼过河泣》讲述一条枯鱼过河时不禁伤心痛哭，写信给同伴，告诫它们出入要谨慎。这首民歌只交代枯鱼写信告诫同伴，并未解释自己为何哭泣、为何后悔，给读者理解该民歌的情感表达造成一定的困难。只有结合该民歌创作时渔民群体的生活实践，才能够解读出渔民自比鱼干，告诫同伴出入要谨慎的意思。鱼被渔民捕获并制成鱼干是渔民群体共有的文化认知，渔民利用隐喻将这一文化认知投射到其生活实践中，暗指在动荡的东汉末年人们宛如任人宰割的鱼肉，灾难可能随时降临。对《枯鱼过河泣》情感表达的这一解读验证了 Sharifian（2008）的观点：文化认知是一个群体所共有的一套信仰和价值观的认知系统，但又有其特殊性。文化隐喻是异质分布的（heterogeneously distributed），即文化群体中的一些成员比其他成员对某一文化模式了解更深。文化群体间的差异来自每个次文化群体都可能产生自己独特的文化认知机制，以不同目的来展示各自的信仰和思想，代表其文化概念化（Sharifian，2011）。因此，某些与潜在文化隐喻相关的子隐喻只有通过对文化群体的信仰、风俗和实践的广泛了解才能得到解释。同时，民歌中的文化隐喻以生产生活实践为基础，表明了特定社会条件对文化群体在思想和行动上的要求，决定着与情感有关的行为模式和语言表达的文化可接受性。

2.2 通过文化图式传递情感

除了从文化隐喻的角度解读民歌意象之外，文化图式也是分析民歌意象传递情感的重要手段。文化图式包含意象图式、情感图式、事件图式、识解图式、角色图式和命题图式等众多图式，用以记录“文化群体对行为的信念、规范、规则和期望，以及与经验各组成部分的相关价值”（Sharifian，2017：12-13）。中国民歌中最典型的图式是意象图式。这是因为农民的朴素认知来自其对环境最初始的具身体验，而农作物又是农民在劳作过程中最频繁接触的植物，饱含着他们丰富的具身体验、情感体验和生命感悟。这也使得植物意象成为中国民歌中最常见的意象之一。

赤日炎炎似火烧

赤日炎炎似火烧，野田禾稻半枯焦。
农夫心内如汤煮，公子王孙把扇摇。

农民群体在劳作过程中频繁而精细地体验着情感，建构了意象图式，即“群体心中容易想象的、象似性的和约定俗成的意象”（Palmer，1996：66）。意象图式是人类普遍共有的具有认知、推理、隐喻能力的一种大脑模式，常被用来理解和分析概念隐喻的生成。例如，“向下”（downward）表达悲伤（grief）、成熟（maturity）、遮蔽处（sheltered place）或保佑（blessing）等意思。《赤日炎炎似火烧》前两句“赤日炎炎似火烧，野田禾稻半枯焦”，描写天上骄阳似火，酷热难耐，地上庄稼被晒得枯焦，处于奄拉的状态，呈现“向下”（downward）的意象图式。这两句歌词描绘了民间群体对植物形态及其动力程序的基本感知。但是，语言和认知的关系是“身体—大脑—文化”三位一体的，文化认知需要置于社会文化起决定作用的语境中才能得以理解（Hamper，2005）。因此，该民歌的后两句将农民内心“如汤煮”和王公贵族“把扇摇”两种生活状态进行对比，自然环境中“弯曲”（bending）的属性被投射到社会环境中阶级压迫及其所导致的“悲伤”（grief）属性，体现了文化群体特殊性对隐喻在文化概念化过程中的制约。

民歌也经常借用情景来表达情感（Kóczy，2011），遵循原因、情感、控制、失控、行为反应的情感图式（Kövecses，1990）。具有文化特性的情感图式（emotion schemas）将某一情感或情感状态与特定活动、参与者以及其他相关因素联系起来（Sharifian，2011），将情感概念化为状态、事件、行动和活动（Kövecses，2000）等一系列图式结构。因此，植物意象通常都被放在诗节开篇位置创设情景，以隐喻的方式“设定”或“投射”其后的情感信息（Ortutay，1982），从而在整体上构成一个完整的情感图式。

涉江采芙蓉

涉江采芙蓉，兰泽多芳草。
采之欲遗谁？所思在远道。
还顾望旧乡，长路漫浩浩。
同心而离居，忧伤以终老。

古人素有以花草赠亲朋的传统，既表达对亲朋的关怀、思念等情感，又传递美好祝愿。这些具有文化属性的植物意象影响着民间群体的情感表达方式及语言使用特征。《涉江采芙蓉》中的荷花、兰草和香草都是古人寄托情怀的常规意象。该民歌通过对采莲这一事件的图式化描写来传达女子的情感。先描写女子在江中泽畔采集荷花和兰草的欢快画面；接着通过自问自答指出采摘的花草要送给的人身在远方；最后道出两人虽“同心”却要“离居”，只能“忧伤以终老”。“欢快地采芙蓉—无法送与心上人”的图式结构表明了女子忧伤情感的图式化过程，即该情感产生的原因和行为反应，流露出“良辰美景奈何天，赏心乐事谁家院”的幽怨之情。该民歌将女子因无法和心上人相聚所致的悲伤情感寄托在这些文化意象之上，以语言为载体委婉地表达了其文化概念化。

需要注意的是，人们的情感体验会因所处文化的不同而存在差异。首先，这是由于人们在体验这些情感时的确切感受不同。更重要的是与这些感受相关的特定文化场景（事件图式）不同。人们无法通过观察个体来了解农民的真实心态，而是通过在“环境—个人”关系中观察他们，其中“环境可能意味着自然（他们所处的物理环境）或社区（他们所在的社会环境）”（Tomori，1935：87）。因所处环境不同，事件图式在一个文化系统中具有多种规约化模式，如婚礼事件模式（Mandler，1984）。圆月是中国婚礼事件文化认知模型中象征圆满婚姻状态的自然意象之一。同时，在中国的文化认知模型中，不同形态的月亮也常与不同事件相关联，被赋予不同的情感和文化内涵。例如，一钩新月，可联想到稚嫩的初生事物；一轮满月，可联想到美好的团圆生活。因此，月亮意象被文人墨客赋予了丰富的情感，具有极强的象征意义和深厚的文化底蕴。

望　月

高空月儿将奴笑，
高不高低不低挂在树梢，
明不明暗不暗把奴来照。
休笑我来休来照，

你我不差半分毫，
缺的日子多，
圆的日子少。

《望月》将月亮的升降、光线和形状等要素与恋爱中男女约会的场景结合在一起，构建起与月亮有关的事件图式。合时，“人约黄昏后，月上柳梢时”，月亮是相爱之人花前月下的见证。以前，月亮刚升上树梢，照着女子和心上人。而现在，月亮“高不高低不低”“明不明暗不暗”表明时间与之前完全一致，不同的只是月下只剩女子一人。望着月亮就像月亮在嘲笑自己一样，显露出女子对月亮的埋怨。离别时，“人有悲欢离合，月有阴晴圆缺”，月亮是相爱之人互寄相思的寄托。歌词第二句中女子对月亮发起反击，月亮你也不要嘲笑我，你我一样，都是缺的日子多，圆的日子少。通过对月亮位置、亮度和形态等相关要素的描写，与之相关的事件图式不断发生变化，女子的情感也在望月、怨月和讥月的过程中依次加深，把女子的苦苦相思在对月亮的怨忿中表现得淋漓尽致。

民歌中的情感表达还可以从识解图式的角度进行解读。Sharifian（2011）认为，作为文化概念化基础的一般图式应该通过识解图式来实施。识解图式是指那些在文化群体间形成的话语类型中优先使用的、约定俗成的识解操作，包括认知参照、视角选择、注意力、空间背景等认知活动。研究表明，民歌中的概念模式以独特的形式存在，现实的物理空间是其他虚构或非即时事件的基础（Sharifian，2011）。过去的、投射的、期望的或不可能的未来事件都在民歌中得到表征。这种识解图式的一个关键特征是，现实和虚构是由突出的自然实体连接起来的。这些自然实体作为空间连接器，使二者能够进行传递。因此，情感就以一种间接的态度表达出来，不露声色地将读者的注意力从外部环境转移到个人问题上来，但情感的表达始终十分隐蔽。

在识解包括情感在内的生命情感过程时，自然界中的各种意象都可能成为民间群体的认知参照点。民歌运用注意力驱动法引导读者在空间中做主观运动，即概念化者对空间运动的心理模拟，其目的要么是在心理空间上疏远或者接近心仪之人，要么是引出或消除负面情感。例如，民歌《青青河畔草》先写景，由远而近，从园外草色收束到园内柳烟，再汇聚到园中央伫立在高高楼上的女子。在心理上所覆盖的空间路径经过一些具有隐喻意义的地标和区域，通过语言元素进行实例化。注意路径主要通过空间指示语（spatial deixis），尤其是远端指代体现（Kóczy，2017）。因为它们指向有界区域或容器类型的实体，定位了注意力传递到的进一步场景。该民歌共有“河畔”“园中”“楼上”“当户”四个空间指示语。其中，“园中”和“楼上”代表两个容器实体，“河畔”处于花园有界区域之外，“当户”则处于高楼有界区域之内。通过注意路径的转换，该民歌创设了女子心爱之人远在他方而自己独锁楼头的现实物理空间。“昔为娼家女，今为荡子妇”道出女子身份的今昔对比，多舛的命运并未改变。这些自然实体成为空间连接器，将现实和虚构、过去和现在连接。空间维度的隔离叠加时间维度的对比，增强了女子哀愁，令篇末流露出的闺怨显得分外感人。

青青河畔草

青青河畔草，郁郁园中柳。
盈盈楼上女，皎皎当户牖。
娥娥红粉妆，芊芊出素手。
昔为娼家女，今为荡子妇。
荡子行不归，空床难独守。

在民歌的创作过程中，经过精心设置的自然景观被特别阐释为情感情景。其中最典型的例子是元散曲《天净沙·秋思》，仅用一系列名词短语的简单陈列就创设了悲凉的情景。类似地，《敕勒歌》前六句从宏观着眼，对平川、大山、天空和四野做静态勾勒，通过陈列代表自然意象的名词描绘出四周环境，意境壮阔雄伟。名词短语提供了认知参照，读者根据参照点的变化进行心理模拟，创设出一个与物理空间类似的心理空间。虽然在语言层面，名词的陈列是一种静态的表达，但在读者的心里却是动态变化的。在这个空间中，牛羊在草原上吃草的场景体现了敕勒族人独特的审美情趣，体现了其对故乡的依恋之情。

敕勒歌

敕勒川，阴山下，
天似穹庐，笼盖四野。
天苍苍，野茫茫，
风吹草低见牛羊。

3　中国民歌意象表征及情感传递的特点

意象和情感是民歌解读的两大要素。一方面，情感体验是通过意象来传递的，民歌的显著特征之一就是通过对自然的初始形象的意象隐喻来传达个人情感（Erdélyi，1961）。另一方面，民歌中的意象被认为是一种特殊阐述形式的情感场景（Kóczy，2017），能在几个抽象层次上同时表征（Kövecses，2000）。因此，意象可以是较为复杂的自然场景，也可以是自然现象的简单参照，读者可以根据意象在不同隐喻场景中的作用来观察它们。在某个特定群体文化中，自然意象及其结构和时间特征形成一个连贯的文化概念化系统。但是，将自然领域中的具体意象应用于情感等抽象领域并非自动，而是受到文化制约的。完全相同的自然意象在不同群体的文化认知中可以传递不同的情感。在中国民歌的文化概念化过程中，最典型的建构机制就是文化隐喻和文化图式，其意象表征和情感传递有以下几个特点。

（1）空间在民歌意象的隐喻表征中占主导地位。

隐喻是民歌通过意象表达个人情感的重要手段。运用大量的自然意象，民歌将自然作为源域映射众多抽象思想，而空间在隐喻表征中占据主导地位。从物理角度来说，这是因为自然意象作为实体，存在于空间维度；自然意象或注意力需要在现实或虚拟空间中运动，并在这一过程中生成意义。从认知角度来说，空间感知是人类共有的一种具身体验，而且它也适用于包括时间在内的其他各种认知领域（Zlatev，2007）。这有利于民歌中的意象文化概念化，成为民间群体共享的文化认知。从语言的角度来看，在自然意象的不同语义属性中，指示物理空间的语言在传递抽象思想方面起着核心作用。Levinson（1983）指出，指示现象是语言和语境之间的关系反映在语言自身结构中的最明显的方式。换言之，它是利用了话语的物理、社会、文化环境以及语言使用者的人际关系的一种识解操作（Tátrai，2010）。指示语还具有重要的话语功能，说话者通过使用指示性表达，使听话者将注意力转移到所述事件的某些方面，并从说话者提供的有利位置进行观察。这使得对物理空间的心理模拟成为可能。常见的指示语可以分为空间指示语、时间指示语、人称指示语、社交指示语和话语指示语（Levinson，1983）。在指示物理空间的语言中，最常用的当属空间指示语。例如，《青青河畔草》中“河畔”“园中”“楼上”“当户”四个空间指示词有效地指引读者注意力的转移，从远处的景物收束到楼上的女子。

更为特殊的情况是，部分民歌如《敕勒歌》，将一组名词或名词短语放在歌词前半部分来创设场景或建构心理空间。这种创作手法与概念整合理论建构心理空间的方法有所不同。根据概念整合理论，心理空间的建构往往借助介词短语、副词、连词、主谓结构等心理空间建构语（周晨阳，林正军，2019：47-48）。尽管中国民歌中的这些名词或名词短语看似缺乏认知基础、没有实质关联，但是却巧妙地利用名词间模糊的空间关系建构起一个场景，借以解决感知和方向问题。从认知的角度来看，这是因为名词所描述的事物在空间中具有物理扩展和存在位置（Langacker，1991）。同时，在特定条件下，不同名词（如有定名词和无定名词）可将其所指对象描述为实际物体或虚拟物体（Langacker，2008）。自然意象的这种语言表征方式给概念化者一种不确定感，增加了不断发展变化的场景的隐喻潜力，凸显了中国民歌独特的文化概念化方式和语言魅力。

（2）情感的传递依赖意象的文化隐喻。

农民群体文化认知的一个基本内容是其对情感的态度（Kóczy，

2017)。然而，在分析农民群体如何在民歌中传递情感时面临着两个问题：情感如何在隐喻中得到反映和表征？情感-自然映射是如何被农民群体的文化认知所驱动的？

首先，情感在民歌中的隐喻介于规约隐喻和诗意隐喻之间。新颖性是诗意隐喻的一个普遍特征（Lakoff & Turner，1989）。尽管民歌中传递情感的隐喻是约定俗成的，不具有新颖性，但是由于文化隐喻异质分布的特点，它们可用于反映次文化群体文化认知的文本中表征诗意隐喻。例如，《枯鱼过河泣》就体现了枯鱼意象在某些民间群体文化认知中的新颖表达。同时，因其不需要相当大的脑力努力就能被具有相同文化认知的民间群体所理解，它们又可以表征规约隐喻。对于民间群体而言，思乡之情是家乡的景色（Homesickness as scenery in hometown）。鸿雁、江水、秋草、草原、芦苇荡等场景是蒙古族人所思念的家乡；而敕勒川、阴山、天空、草原、牛羊等场景表现了敕勒族对故乡的热爱和眷恋。其次，民歌将实体领域的自然意象投射到抽象领域的情感范畴并非任意的，而是以民间群体相同的具身体验和“每个人都能理解的原始抽象来建构情感”（Stoll，1957：173），以直接和基本的方式发挥作用。因此，民歌不会通过描述自然意象来表达强烈分化的个人思想和情感，而是只表达民间群体共有的、集体性的情感认知。例如，月亮意象在中国民歌中常被用来传递爱情的甜蜜或痛苦。通过这种方式，自然意象经过文化图式、文化范畴和文化隐喻形成了一个具有显著群体文化特征的文化概念化系统。

（3）意象的图式化表征是解读民歌的重要手段。

图式是语言表征中几种约定俗成的图式化模式的概括性表述。民歌中包括许多图式，其中最常见的有意象图式、情感图式、事件图式和识解图式四种，这几种图式同时也是解读民歌的重要手段。意象图式是容易想象的、传统的象似性意象（iconic images），并且是与具身或社会经验明显相关的认知结构或理解模式（Palmer，1996）。民歌中的自然意象在很大程度上依赖于与空间有关的意象图式。例如，路径图式经常被用于各种目标驱动的抽象图式。《鸿雁》中“向南方，飞过芦苇荡”和“北归还，带上我的思念”两句点明了鸿雁迁徙的路径，也表明了歌者希望与鸿雁一起返回故里的目的。这一路径的描述是受歌者内心强烈的愿望驱动的。情感图式是理解情感的重要手段，也是探索民歌的基本要素。情感概念由情感图式实例化（Sharifian，2003）。正如 Palmer 所说的，“情感是目标驱动的意象（goal-driven images）的复杂组合，控制着情感状态和场景，包括话语场景”（Palmer，1996：109）。因此，民歌主要通过场景呈现情感状态（Sharifian，2011）。这些带有文化烙印的场景影响文化群体表达情感的方式和语言，使得情感图式可以在描绘各种主题的场景中识别。例如，《涉江采芙蓉》《青青河畔草》两首民歌就是通过创设场景冲突投射情感冲突，使读者体会到哀怨的情感图式产生的过程的。事件图式指事件发生的程序或过程，归纳出民歌最古老的层级常出现在与特定场合或与仪式有关的民歌中。花前月下本是描述男女相会的场合，但《望月》中只剩女子一人与月亮对话，相思之情油然而生。识解图式涉及心理空间、空间背景、参照点（认知参照点与主观运动）、视角选择等认知活动。这些认知活动是作为文化概念化基础的一般图式实现概念化的根本途径（Sharifian，2011）。对《青青河畔草》和《敕勒歌》的解读正是借用了识解图式中的认知参照点和心理空间两种识解操作完成的。

另外，角色图式即关于社会角色的知识，是人们期望处于特定位置的人做出相应的行为（Nishida，1999）。民歌表达特定的道德准则，限制着性别角色图式的行为规范（Kóczy，2017），体现在男性和女性在隐喻场景中的具身体验和他们的行为中。在匈牙利民歌中，女性角色被隐喻性表征为一个静止的实体，而男性角色是一个动态的主体，试图以各种形式接近静止的实体（Kóczy，2017）。但在中国民歌中，性别角色的使用则截然不同。在中国民歌中，女性角色多处于显性地位，而男性角色则处于隐性地位。《折杨柳歌辞》《涉江采芙蓉》《青青河畔草》《望月》《上邪》等民歌都是以女性口吻表达其对恋人的思念或对爱情的向往。虽然这些民歌有可能是创作者借女性角色而作，但是从女性视角表达文化群体对自然环境或社会事务的观察是中国民歌的一个独特叙事视角。

4 中国民歌意象文化概念化的形成

民歌是民俗文化的重要组成部分，是民间群体语言特征和文化概念化的具体体现。民歌意象文化概念化的形成受诸多因素影响。在文化语言学者看来，民歌意象的文化概念化主要是建立在民间群体特定的习俗和规范基础上，清楚地反映了民间群体在情感、爱情和婚姻等个人事务方面受到的道德限制。通过对中国民歌意象的具体解读发现，影响中国民歌意象文化概念化形成的因素主要体现在以下三个方面。

第一，社会、文化和经济因素奠定了民歌中文化概念化形成的文化基础。文化概念系统具有具身基础，文化认知模型的概念单元（conceptual units）是由经验驱动的结构，是直接或间接生活经历的产物（Gibbs，2006；Johnson，1987）。个人先验知识，如隐喻认知，在民间群体交流过程中形成，受社会、文化和经济因素制约。而个人先验知识又可形成共享的经验，使概念单元具有能被使用相同语言或拥有相同概念单元的话语群体所理解的意义（Kövecses，2017）。因此，民间群体生活的集体经验是群体成员对生活环境的集体感知，以传统农耕社会的生产生活环境为基础，决定着民间群体文化认知的概念化形式及与情感有关的语言表达的文化可接受性。另外，文化认知是一个复杂的适应系统，存在于语言群体成员间的跨时空互动中（Kövecses，2017）。文化概念化系统不是由大量通过框架结构对概念的静态表征组成，相反，它是一个动态且不断发展的系统，表征生活在社会、历史和物理环境中的一个民间群体以统一的方式理解其经历。

第二，文化隐喻依赖并影响着文化概念化。一方面，文化隐喻依赖组成民间群体世界观的文化概念化和源自跨文化映射的跨域概念化。作为概念系统的文化为隐喻表达的使用提供了概念语境（Kövecses，2017），成为隐喻产生的默认前提条件。这不仅揭示了民间群体成员如何将自己的经验应用于隐喻的概念化，而且揭示了他们对自然的总体看法。然而，农民们碎片化的世界观在民歌中并不是以直接的方式展示出来，而是隐藏在复杂的、模糊不清的隐喻性意象中。因此，自然意象需要借助一个连贯的文化概念化体系，其中源域、靶域及其映射分别平等地表征民间群体的文化概念化。另一方面，隐喻允许知识从已知领域映射到与之相关的社会和心理等未知领域，从而进行概念化并建构文化认知模型（孙毅，周锦锦，2020：19）。由于文化隐喻具有异质分布特征，每个文化群体都可能借助意象的文化隐喻来展示其信仰和思想，形成各自独特的文化概念化。《折杨柳歌辞》《枯鱼过河泣》《鸿雁》等民歌都在一定程度上验证了隐喻概念化的跨语言和文化的多样性（Kövecses，2005）。

第三，语言实例化文化概念化。语言形式和结构特征代表了民间群体在文化认知史某个阶段上的积极洞察。例如，“柳”与“留”发音相近，语音层的属性特征投射到语义层，建构起“挽留”的语义特征，形成了柳树、柳枝、柳条等意象在民歌和诗词中有关“送别”的文化范畴。尽管文化范畴只反映在人类语言的词汇中，但是这一现象说明，“在语言中，各种语言单位——从语素到语篇结构——通常都会实例化蕴含在文化系统和世界观中的概念化”（Sharifian，2011：112）。这也意味着概念隐喻相关的表达并非每次都涉及从一个域映射到另一个域的在线认知过程。一些概念隐喻只是“僵化”的概念化，语言使用者并未特意去搜寻这些表达的文化根源，或在使用它们时掺杂任何概念映射。在这种情况下，概念隐喻更类似于一种相对固定的文化图式，引导人们思考并在此基础上理解某些经验领域。

如上所述，中国民歌意象的文化概念化是具身体验、文化体验和语言使用三者有机互动的产物。在分析民歌时，研究者不仅要考虑民歌所具有的集体性、抒情性、口授传统等各种话语类型学属性，而且要考虑自然意象所关涉的文化概念化、个体/群体经验、空间结构、语义属性和隐喻性等问题。

5 结 语

民歌作为一种由农民群体创作的独特的文学作品，通过自然意象表达情感和心理状态，反映民间群体对自身生活环境和自然界的思想和信念，并深深植根于文化概念之中。本文在文化语言学视阈下分析了民歌中的意象及其传递的情感，探索民歌意象的概念特征及其表现文化概念化的形式。综合考虑到语言的文化认知语义、语法属性甚至话语特征，为民间文学研究形成一个合适的分析框架。本研究证实，民歌运用大量意象的目的不是单纯地描述事物或景物，而是利用民间群体对意象的具身体验（尤其是空间体验）和文化体验抽象出文化图式，与文化隐喻一起传递出不同的情感。与此同时，民歌语言和结构模式也是民歌意象文化概念化实例化的重要手段之一，主要在文化范畴维度得以彰显。

参考文献

[1] Z ERDÉLYI. Adatok a népköltészet szimbolikájához. Ethnographia, 1961 (72): 173-199, 405-429, 583-598.

[2] D GEERAERTS. Recontextualizing grammar: Underlying trends in thirty years of Cognitive Linguistics // T Elzbieta, C Michal, L Wiraszka. Cognitive Linguistics in action: From theory to application and back. Berlin, New York: De Gruyter Mouton, 2010: 71-102.

[3] R GIBBS. Taking metaphor out of head and putting it in the cultural world // R Gibbs, G Steen. Metaphor in Cognitive Linguistics, Amsterdam: John Benjamins, 1999: 146-166.

[4] R GIBBS. Embodiment and cognitive science. Cambridge: Cambridge University Press, 2006.

[5] B HAMPER. Image schemas in Cognitive Linguistics: Introduction // B Hamper. From perception to meaning: Image schemas in Cognitive Linguistics. Berlin, New York: De Gruyter Mounton, 2005: 1-14.

[6] M JOHNSON. The body in the mind: The bodily basis of meaning, imagination and reason. Chicago: The University of Chicago Press, 1987.

[7] I KATONA. Szépen szóló madáka. Népdalaink szöveges üzenete.

Budapest: Masszi Kiadó, 2002.

[8] J KÓCZY. Az erdő konceptualizációja a magyar népdalokban. Magyar Nyelv, 2011 (107): 318-325.

[9] J KÓCZY. Cultural conceptualizations of RIVER in Hungarian folksongs// F Sharifian. Advances in Cultural Linguistics. Berlin, New York: Springer-Verlag, 2017: 223-245.

[10] Z KÖVECSES. Emotion concepts. Berlin, New York: Springer, 1990.

[11] Z KÖVECSES. Metaphor and emotion: Language, culture, and body in human feeling. New York, Cambridge: Cambridge University Press, 2000.

[12] Z KÖVECSES. Metaphor in culture: Universality and variation. Cambridge: Cambridge University Press, 2005.

[13] Z KÖVECSES. Context in Cultural Linguistics: The case of metaphor // F Sharifian. Advances in Cultural Linguistics. Berlin, New York: Springer-Verlag, 2017: 307-323.

[14] I KÜLLÖS. The messages of a repertory investigation: The quantitative stylistic analysis of Csángó folksongs // A Koiranen. Finnish-Hungarian Symposium on Musik & Folklore research. Tampere: Tampereen yliopiston kansanperinteen laitos, 1991: 15-21.

[15] G LAKOFF, M JOHNSON. Metaphors we live by. Chicago: University of Chicago Press, 1980.

[16] G LAKOFF, M JOHNSON. Philosophy in the flesh: The embodied mind and its challenge to western thought. New York: Basic Books, 1999.

[17] G LAKOFF, M TURNER. More Than Cool Reason: A Field Guide to Poetic Metaphor. Chicago: University of Chicago Press, 1989.

[18] R LANGACKER. Foundations of cognitive grammar (Volume II: Descriptive application). Stanford, California: Stanford University

Press, 1991.

[19] R LANGACKER. Cognitive grammar: A basic introduction [M]. Oxford: Oxford University Press, 2008.

[20] S LEVINSON. Pragmatics. Cambridge: Cambridge University Press, 1983.

[21] J MANDLER. Stories, scripts and scenes: Aspects of schema theory. Hillsdale: Erlbaum, 1984.

[22] I MONA. Népdalszöveg rendszerezés és népdalszöveg tipológia. Ethnographia, 1959 (70): 563-578.

[23] H NISHIDA. A cognitive approach to intercultural communication based on schema theory. International Journal of Intercultural Relations, 1999, 23 (5): 753-777.

[24] G ORTUTAY. Magyar néprajzi lexikon V. Budapest: Akadémiai Kiadó, 1982.

[25] G PALMER. Toward a theory of cultural linguistics. Austin: University of Texas Press, 1996.

[26] F SHARIFIAN. On cultural conceptualizations. Journal of Cognition and Culture, 2003, 3 (3): 187-207.

[27] F SHARIFIAN. Distributed, emergent cultural cognition, conceptualisation, and language // R M Frank, R Dirven, T Ziemke, et al. Body, Language, and Mind (Vol. 2): Sociocultural Situatedness. Berlin, New York: Mouton de Gruyter, 2008: 109-136.

[28] F SHARIFIAN. Cultural conceptualizations and language: theoretical framework and applications. Amsterdam, Philadelphia: John Benjamins Publishing Company, 2011.

[29] F SHARIFIAN. Cultural Linguistics // F Sharifian. The Routledge handbook of language and culture. London and New York: Routledge, 2015: 478-492.

[30] F SHARIFIAN. Cultural Linguistics. Amsterdam: John Benjamins, 2017.

[31] B STOLL. Közösségi költészet — népköltészet. Megjegyzések a XVII. századi kéziratos szerelmi lírához. Irodalomtörténeti Közlemények, 1957 (62): 170-176.

[32] V TOMORI. A parasztság szemléletének alakulása: A parasztság szemléletének és eszméltségi fokának lélektani vizsgálata. Szegedi: Szegedi Fiatalok Művészeti Kollégiuma, 1935.

[33] S TÁTRAI. Áttekintés a deixisről. Magyar Nyelvőr, 2010 (134): 211-232.

[34] J ZLATEV. Spatial semantics// D Geeraerts, H Cuyckens. Handbook of cognitive linguistics. Oxford: Oxford University Press, 2007: 318-350.

[35] 刘国辉，汪兴富. 论诗歌意象建构的认知途径：象似性与隐喻性表征. 外语教学，2010，31（3）：24-27.

[36] 刘立辉. 艾略特的个人故事和公共叙事——一种具身认知视角. 认知诗学，2019（1）：1-10.

[37] 孙毅. 人体隐喻的多义路向推演——从“头（head）”说起. 东北师大学报（哲学社会科学版），2013（5）：121-124.

[38] 孙毅，梁晓晶. 崔致远诗歌意蕴的当代隐喻学重构与新释. 东疆学刊，2020，37（3）：108-114，128.

[39] 孙毅，周锦锦. 认知隐喻学畛域中汉英自我概念隐喻意涵重塑. 外语研究，2020，37（4）：13-21.

[40] 余渭深，董平荣. 合成空间与中国古典诗词意象. 外语与外语教学，2003（3）：4-6.

[41] 王宏印. 中国古今民歌选译[M]. 北京：商务印书馆，2014.

[42] 阎志芬. 古典诗歌意象的叠加与民族文化传统的积淀. 中南民族学院学报（人文社会科学版），2000（4）：85-88.

[43] 周晨阳，林正军. 艾米莉·狄金森死亡概念的认知建构. 认知诗学，2019（2）：46-55.

[44] 周红民. 认知视域中汉诗意象的文化属性和可译性限度. 外语研究，2019，36（4）：74-79.

基于图形-背景与脚本理论的蔡伸思妇词认知诗学解读

姜　洁　　邹志勇

【摘要】本文主要运用认知诗学的图形-背景理论鉴赏《菩萨蛮》《小重山》及部分蔡伸思妇词典型性词作，运用脚本理论提炼出蔡伸思妇词爱情脚本。首先，概述蔡伸家世、仕历与研究现状，提出两大认知诗学理论：图形-背景理论和脚本理论。其次，运用图形-背景理论分析以《菩萨蛮》和《小重山》为主和部分典型性思妇词的诗句。最后，运用脚本理论提炼出蔡伸思妇词“离别-相思-构想重逢”的爱情脚本，建立帮助读者理解蔡伸思妇词情感意蕴的认知结构，进而为认知诗学本土化以及读者运用该理论解读中国古典诗词提供借鉴。

【关键词】认知诗学；蔡伸；思妇词；图形-背景；脚本

0 引　言

宋词是中华文化的瑰宝，以其精妙典雅的体式、高度凝练的语言艺术为世人称道。南渡时期的宋词，题材视角更是以多元化的特征示人。蔡伸词虽被定义为南渡词人作品，但其词体选择多为小令、次为慢词，精妙洗练。但是，蔡伸词思想内容较集中于咏怀、爱情、思妇，与南渡时期大家作品相比略显促狭；因而文学史家和批评家对其人其作着墨不多，对于蔡伸的具体作品亦尚待深入挖掘。

作者简介：姜洁，女，辽宁师范大学文学院硕士研究生，主要从事认知诗学、唐宋文学研究；
邹志勇，男，辽宁师范大学文学院副教授，硕士生导师，主要从事中国传统文化及中国古典文学的教学和科研研究。

思妇题材诗肇始于先秦时代，直到《宋书·乐志》引用建安时期曹丕的《燕歌行》，“思妇”才确指思念远行丈夫的妇人。随着历史的变迁、以思妇为文学创作题材的文学作品的不断累积，逐渐演变成一种诗歌艺术题材的传统。据中华书局 1965 年 6 月第一版唐圭璋编《全宋词》所载，蔡伸词共 176 首。笔者认为，关于蔡伸的思妇词的界定需要满足如下条件：第一，词中的第一人称是一位女性。但是宋词常常出现“代言体”，因此思妇词的记叙、描写和抒情均以女性的视角而非男性的视角；第二，词的题材倾向是女性怀念远行的恋人/丈夫，抒发的思想感情是别时的恋恋不舍、别后的无限思念、追忆往昔以及相思的怅然情绪。有鉴于此，笔者分析得出蔡伸思妇词共 31 首。

本文撷取蔡伸《友古词》中思妇题材词作，旨在实践文学批评新方法，对蔡伸思妇词进行微观的典型性文本的批评、宏观提炼思妇题材词的认知结构，验证认知诗学理论对蔡伸思妇词研究的可行性和可能性，进而为认知诗学本土化、为中国古典诗词的批评与阐释提出新视角，以及为读者更精准地理解和欣赏中国古典诗词提供启发。

1 蔡伸研究现状与认知诗学内涵

1.1 蔡伸家世、仕历与研究现状概述

蔡伸，字伸道，号友古居士。今福建省仙游县人。宋哲宗元祐三年（1088）生，徽宗政和五年（1115）登进士第。绍兴二十六年（1156）十月卒，年六十九。祖父蔡襄，字君谟。北宋名臣，文学家、书法家、茶学家，谥号忠惠。父亲蔡旻“终宣义郎，开封府工曹，累赠少傅……少傅早世，三岁鞠于外氏”（蔡戡，1997：86-87），由此可知蔡伸由外祖父文彦博家抚养。外祖父文彦博，字宽夫，汾州介休人。今存《潞公文集》。其人“忠直亮，临事果断，皆有大臣之风”（脱脱，1997：10264）。蔡伸从政后不同流合污，坚守气节，或受其外祖家教育影响。蔡伸子嗣情况详见李戡的《大父行状》，以其长子湍和次子洸较为有名。蔡伸的孙辈中，长孙蔡戡最为著名，其有《定斋集》二十卷等著作传世。

根据对蔡戡《定斋集》卷十四的《大父行状》和周必大《周文忠公集》卷六十三中的《中大夫赠特进蔡公神道碑》的参照分析，可简要梳理出蔡伸的仕历（见表 1）。

表 1　蔡伸仕历

宋哲宗元祐三年（1088）	出生
徽宗政和五年（1115）	登进士第，担任辟雍正，调任太学，官职变动担任西京博士
宣和年间（1119—1125）	出任潍州北海县知州，任期届满后，担任徐州通判
建炎初	担任顿递官，不久任神武右军； 担任参赞官，曾劝降反贼，后任真州通判； 授予滁州知州官职，罢免后主管台州崇道观
绍兴九年（1139）	起任徐州知州，调任德安府知州
绍兴十一年（1141）	担任和州知州，后为浙东安抚司参议官
绍兴二十六（1156）年十月	去世

关于蔡伸词的研究，大约开始于 20 世纪 80 年代，只有相隆本（1980：89）学者的《“风雨送春归”句最早见于蔡伸词》论文考证词句出处；2000—2010 年出现了郭姗姗和潘俊峰（2010）的期刊论文《蔡伸词灵活多变的叙述艺术》，主要就蔡伸词的叙述特征进行了研究；2011 年至今，通过哈尔滨师范大学赵婷婷（2012）的论文《蔡伸〈友古词〉研究》了解到蔡伸词未受到词学家太多重视以及受学者研究关注度较低的现状；苏州大学何抗（2012）的论文《蔡伸及其词研究》大致总结了蔡伸的生平，并结合文本分析了词作的情感内涵和生命体验；李璇（2016）的三篇期刊论文《蔡伸家世和词集版本流传考》《论蔡伸的〈友古词〉创作》《蔡伸与向子諲词作优劣论辩》分别就追溯蔡伸家世、词作版本考证、文学比较研究等角度展开了研究；郭珊珊（2017）的《“千古恨悠悠，长江空自流”——蔡伸咏怀词浅析》是结合作品具体分析其咏怀词。

其中，多数论文的研究方法为就历史和文献对词人及文本进行推测和考证、比较研究不同作家文本以及结合文本中某类题材进行具体分析。因蔡伸属于地域性文人，相关文献残缺，有价值的文献十分有限，这就给研究的开展带来了较多困难。

1.2 认知诗学内涵与图形——背景理论、脚本理论

认知诗学起源于 20 世纪 70 年代。其概念率先由以色列学者 Reuven Tsur 提出、后来发展的一种全新解读作品的工具，被学者广泛运用到撰写文学批评的文章中。其广义定义是运用认知科学研究成果、文艺理论，坚持以文本为导向、以文学阅读为研究目的，同时关注制约文本与阅读效果的信息处理过程或心智运作机制的一门新兴交叉学科，是“阐释学的一种形式”（Peter Stockwell，2002：65）。

作为由多种科学理论和学科研究方法交汇而成的一门交叉学科，认知诗学研究方法鲜明地体现着与认知语言学、认知文体学和认知叙事学联系紧密的特点，因而狭义可将其定义为由文学和语言学结合而成的新学科（熊沐清，2008：209）。它在力图回答历来文学研究所关心的热点问题的同时，努力建构自己的文学理论和文学批评理论体系，实现了对以往语言学与文学结合的一次本体论意义上的提升，因而对文学和语言学研究都具有一定的借鉴作用。

文章选用认知诗学诸多系统化理论中的两个：其一，运用图形-背景理论对蔡伸思妇词中的典型性文本尝试批评，深入探讨蔡伸思妇词意境生成过程；其二，运用脚本理论分析、提炼总结蔡伸思妇词的爱情脚本，有助于读者宏观地把握蔡伸思妇词的认知结构。

2 基于图形-背景理论的蔡伸思妇词解读——以《菩萨蛮》《小重山》为例

2.1 基于图形-背景理论的《菩萨蛮》解读

杏花零落清明雨。卷帘双燕来还去。枕上玉芙蓉。暖香堆锦红。

翠翘金钿雀。蝉鬓慵疏掠。心事一春闲。黛眉颦远山。

（《菩萨蛮·杏花零落清明雨》）（唐圭璋，1965：1014）

词体在五代以后，进一步确定了以小令为主的文本体式。题材取向以柔情为主，审美规范以婉约为美。但是，小令的体制很短小，容量有限。一首多则五六十字，少则二三十字。这让小令文体在情感的抒发上受到一定的限制。因此，小令普遍在清丽淡雅或艳丽婉约的词风特点上，还有蕴藉深厚的艺术特色、寄情于景的表现手法。

在这首小令中，作者为我们描绘出了一幅早春闺阁景色的画卷，刻画了一个独处闺中的女子慢慢梳妆的动态，勾勒出女子的肖像和女子起床梳洗时的娇慵姿态，暗示了人物孤独寂寞的心境。第一句，描写杏花在淅淅沥沥的春雨中飘落的动态的画面。“杏花”和“雨”皆是动态的。其中，杏花相对形状比较小，所以“杏花”与“清明雨”构成了凸显与被凸显、衬托与被衬托的图形与背景的关系。奠定了这首词的伤春、哀愁的感情基调。第二句中的“卷帘”是静态的，在本句是背景；“双燕”则是动态的，而且形状较小，引人注意，因此构成了本句的图形，以静衬动地凸显并勾勒出第二幅画面——卷帘飞燕图。此外，结合这首词的整体意境看，此句还运用了反衬的手法，以“双燕”来反衬思妇的落寞孤独。第三句运用了借代的修辞手法，“玉芙蓉”代指思妇，她有如芙蓉一样鲜妍姣好的容貌。这句词的图形-背景的体现方式是拓扑空间方位：“玉芙蓉”与“枕”是附着的关系，不随着人的视角的改变而变化。第四句的“暖香”“锦红”代指带有温度和香气的绸缎被，这句词在嗅觉和视觉体现的图形-背景关系，用暖香气味作为背景，突出了环境的宁谧温馨，带有慵懒、暧昧的色彩；绸缎被则是背景，勾画出思妇清晨懒起的状态，与之相似的诗句还有“南窗月满，绣被堆香暖”（《清平乐》）、“鸭炉香尽锦屏中”（《虞美人》）。第五句的“翠翘”和“金钿雀”都是做工精美的女子的发饰，此句中图形-背景的体现关系则是意象叠加，中国诗词讲求一种含蓄蕴藉之美，观察者不需费力地细致刻画女子的妆容和工具，通过叠加的意象，就可以揣测出思妇的生活品质的高雅和精致。只通过意象的叠加，而非详细说明，能够留给读者无限想象的空间。第六句描写了思妇梳妆慵懒的动作，与前一句一笔带过地对她的首饰的特写相呼应。思妇晨起梳妆，看似情绪低落，让她慵懒提不起精神化妆的原因是思念着的人不能现时一睹她的美丽，也反映出了思妇的心境和内心的寂寞空虚。末两句交代出了思妇慵起梳妆的个中缘由——有心事。而她的所思所想则是观察者不可窥测的，只能借着发现她眉头皱着，像远处的小山般线条起伏而表现出些许愁绪。图形-背景关系则是借助形容词来体现，"颦"是形容词，意为皱眉，反映出思妇孤独的心境，进而抒发出绵渺的思念和淡淡的失落情绪。

这首词全篇内容是写在清明雨天，一个女子早晨自慵懒迟起至无心梳妆的过程。结构清晰明了，作直线型之描叙。此词抒思妇孤独落寞情绪，写闺怨之情。虽被"心事"一词略微点破，但仍然能通过环境描写，通过思妇起床前后一系列的动作、首饰，留给读者去揣摩其内心的隐秘的空间。而这首词中，图形-背景也是通过其变化和移动全方位地进行展现的。读者在阅读过程中，图形和背景不断形成、发生动态变化：从雨中飘落的杏花到窗帘边翻飞的燕子、懒起的思妇、香气温暖的绸缎被、她华丽的首饰，再到思妇心不在焉地梳妆，眉头微蹙地在凝神思念，最终在作者的引领下，归结到"思妇"这一图形。作者用精巧的小令，给读者描绘出了一幅层次感和动态感极强的图画。

2.2 基于图形-背景理论的思妇词《小重山》解读

又如：

楼外江山展翠屏。沆沆虹影畔，彩舟横。一尊别酒为君倾。留不住，风色太无情。

斜日半山明。画栏重倚处，独销凝。片帆回首在青冥。人不见，千里暮云平。

(《小重山·楼外江山展翠屏》)（唐圭璋，1965：1012）

这首《小重山》则是一首中调，词风体现了婉约派的特色：内容为送别词，侧重儿女风情；结构精巧、音律和谐，带有一种含蓄蕴藉之美。

首句描绘出一幅阔大的景色，楼外的山峦如翡翠屏风一样迤逦排开。介词短语中的名词，根据它们的形状大小、动态或者静态、所属关系等特征进行分析，一些作为图形，另一些则作为背景。在这句词中，“江山”与“楼”形成了图形与背景的关系，因为“外”使它们形成了拓扑空间方位关系（梁丽，陈蕊，2008）。观察者在楼里，是近景；像翡翠屏风似的“江山”，是远景。根据透视现象中近大远小的特点，“江山”因其距离远，所以视觉体积面积小，更能够被突显。第二句描写出彩虹淡淡的影子，映照着横卧水面的一叶彩舟。此句体现的图形-背景关系是投影空间方位，图形和背景都会随着观察者视角的变化而变化。“彩舟”相对于“虹影”来说，面积、体积小；根据空间大小的联想特征来说，前者为图形，后者为背景。而且“舟”虽在词句中是静止状态，但它相对于彩虹而言在概念上是可移动的。所以可确定“舟”为图形。与这句相似的图形-背景体现方式还有“沙上寒鸥接翼飞”（《浣溪沙》）、“征帆初落桥边”（《清平乐》）。其中，“彩舟”“寒鸥”“征帆”皆是图形，都有着体型小、可移动的特点，而“虹影”“沙上”“桥”背景则相对静止。第三句交代叙写的是送别筵席，描写的是女子倒酒的动作。第四句是抒女子离别时依依不舍之情，表达出女子离别时的留恋、伤感和不舍的愁绪。第五句描绘了太阳渐落，在山腰处熠熠生辉。这句词中并未出现动词和方位词，是通过形容词体现图形-背景关系。描绘太阳即将落山，光线越来越黯淡，女子与恋人也快要分别了。越发显出环境的悲凉，透露出女子在别离时依依不舍的心境。“明”字使“半山”和“斜月”构成图形-背景关系，也刻画了思妇的不舍、留恋和无可奈何的怅然情绪。通过形容词的使用而体现的图形-背景关系，对这首词的整体意境形成有所助益。第六句勾勒出一幅思妇画槛远望图，这句词的图形-背景关系是通过投影空间方位来体现。女子的恋人乘舟远行，她站在楼台上倚着从前经常眺望的栏杆处目送恋人离开。第七句描绘出一个天际行舟图卷：行舟是动态的，而且相对于江水来说体积和形状小而作为图形。青冥指天空，形容船犹如航行在广阔无际的蔚蓝的天空中，看不到尽头。“片帆”作为可以移动的图形，

“青冥”做它浩渺旷远的背景，图像随着观察者的视角转变而变化中，营造出了一种悠远空灵的意境。末句写出女子远眺恋人却见不到他的身影，只能看到向晚的天边的云，仍然宁静地在天边停伫。与唐代诗人钱起的“曲中人不见，江上数峰青”（彭定求，1960：2651）。有异曲同工之妙。以景结情，袅袅余音成为构成全篇整体的关键一环。“人不见”与前文的“留不住”，虽然重字，但其意义和抒发的感情却相应和。词的前面大部分篇幅着力抒写离别时所见之景和哀伤之情。结尾描写恋人离开，画面上只有天边停伫的云。这极其省净清丽的画面，给读者留下了思索回味的广阔空间：思妇哀怨之情或已融入了绵绵不绝的江水，或化作了天边的两三朵暮云，给人们留下空灵的遐想。图形-背景在这首词中的对意境的作用则是能够让读者精准地把握这些图形和背景之间的关系——凸显与被凸显、衬托与被衬托，从而更好地领会作者想要表达的情感情绪与诗歌的意境。

从对以上两首在词体式、意境营造、情感抒发等方面皆具有典型性的蔡伸思妇题材词进行解读可知，词中的“图形”与“背景”之间存在独特的关系：凸显与被凸显、烘托与被烘托。图形-背景理论来源于认知科学，后由心理学家建设并发展而形成的一种认知理论。学者 Stockwell 提出的理论阐述了文学同样具有图式：文学的图式不但具有异于其他艺术形式中图式的特征，而且是带有不断建构性的。因此，图式理论不仅完全可以用来对文学作品特别是诗歌这类文学体式进行分析和研究，尤其是分析诗歌的意境营造中更是有优势。

刘勰便在《文心雕龙·隐秀》中率先运用“境”的概念来评论嵇康、阮籍的诗，可作为文学意境论的萌芽。唐代王昌龄的《诗格》中直接出现了“意境”概念。但他当时的意思，只是指诗境三境：“诗有三境，一曰物境；二曰情境；三曰意境。”（薛富兴，2000：31）中国文学所特有的“意境”是“诗意”和“画境”的结合。

大多数的意境都是通过诗词中意象之间的图形-背景关系体现的。因此，在图形-背景理论视阈下进行文本分析，有助于理解和感知意境。如“落日归云，寒空断雁”一句开篇点明了节令，勾勒出日暮下秋日中的南国景致。“落日”和“云”“天空”和“雁”构成了互为映衬的图形与背景的关系。秋天景色本来就是给人一种萧瑟凄凉之感，落日相对于云来说是动态的，大雁在辽阔的空中盘旋也显得格外醒目，衬托出秋天的南国景色更加旷远、萧瑟。天空辽阔，残照如轮，所以更加凸显。在这里，被突出的“落日”和“断雁”也是词人孤寂落寞情绪的传达载体，图形和背景的相互映衬下，不仅精准地描绘了秋日的景象，而且表达出作者的孤独的深切感受，还营造出了孤凄悲凉的意境。

图形-背景的空间组织认知原则也是构成诗歌意境的重要手段（彭定求，1960：2651）。蔡伸思妇词中意境的营造大多通过不断变化、不断建构的图形-背景不同关系，营造出词作整体空间上的美感。如“碧桃溪上蓝桥路”“鸭炉香尽锦屏中”“玉箫吹凤怨，惊起楼中燕”等，其中的方位关系对烘托诗的整体意境起了关键的作用。

一切文学文本描绘的都是处在一定的时间和空间内的事物，可以说时间和空间既是诱发词人有所感发的写作动因，又是构筑“意境”的本质手段，同时起着意境营造的积极作用。蔡伸在进行思妇词艺术构思和意境创造的过程中，无处不流露着时间和空间意识。如“回首当时云雨梦，两难忘”“物是人非空断肠，梦入芳洲路”等把对时间的感悟和情绪投向对往事的追忆，体现了一种绵绵不绝的相思愁绪；如“宝钗鸾镜会重逢，花里同眠今夜月。月华依旧当时节，细把离肠和泪说”描写的是期盼重逢和团圆但却不可得，体现了一种因物是人非而营造出的含蓄凄黯、惆怅绵远的意境；又如“楼前流水悠悠，驻行舟”“柳下朱门傍小桥”皆是开头句子，分别作为词后句的大背景。词人勾勒出自然环境，点明地点，“流水”“行舟”“朱门”“小桥”相对于“楼”和“柳”来说都是图形，它们的关系通过方位词“前”“下”和动词“傍”体现出来。前句中动静结合、静中有动，动中有静。图形与背景相呼应，让人感受到自然风景的动态美，构成一幅简约明丽的图画。

综上，诗歌中体现的图形-背景关系对思妇词意境的营造有重要意义，但其仍要结合全篇的语境和词作中具体语句进行具体问题具体分析。研究蔡伸思妇词中的图形-背景应先把握词句中的方位词。小令和慢词虽笔墨不多，但其意境之所以形象生动、具有表现意识，就在于它的图形-背景不断建构、不断生成而形成了一种时空结合。

3 蔡伸思妇词爱情脚本

在认知诗学理论中，脚本是每个读者个体在一定的社会、文化的影响之下，从心智方面协调某些特定的情境而建立并且不断变化和改变的能够帮助人们理解话语的认知结构。对于属于婉约派的蔡伸思妇词，可以通过分析相关文本提炼思妇词的脚本。每一首词中的主人公的心境、情绪、经历的爱情故事不尽相同，爱情叙事的发展、情感情绪的抒发与传达都各有其动因。在分析过程中，可以尝试从文本的话语中那些明显的提示（意象）与读者或听者处理这些提示所依赖的脚本之间的关系中得到解释。蔡伸思妇词诸多篇章中的爱情和思妇思念产生的动因不同，由此而传达出的正面或负面情感情绪也不同，但大体上也是有其共性可追溯的。

蔡伸思妇词的脚本较为简单集中，与其创作视野、选用的词体限制叙事抒情等特点有关。其脚本的变化主要是基于每篇思妇词中抒情、景色描写、人物刻画方法之间的不同排列组合。而在景色描写中的意象冷与暖、喜与悲，在抒情语句中表示喜怒哀乐强烈情感的感叹句和在人物刻画方法中选取的形容词，则是提炼脚本过程中最明显的提示。

蔡伸的思妇词在抒情方法分为两类：一是间接抒情类；二是直抒胸臆类。第一类词的情感抒发大体步骤是人物描写和景色描写的交错构成，没有出现能够表达词人强烈情感的词汇和语句，而情感的抒发大多蕴含于环境与人物的刻画中。例如《减字木兰花·多情多病》中，上阕首句和第二句即形象肖像、动作描写刻画了一个相思成疾的思妇形象，借形容词“愁”精准地点明。第四句是景色描写，“零落桃花”美景正在消失，也暗喻思妇的容颜渐老。下阕皆是对思妇的动作描写，仍然借助形容词“愁”另外是“强”，思妇为了排遣心中的孤独和哀伤，看着窗帘外透过燕子的剪影开始弹奏。末句她弹奏的是《幽兰操》，幽怨感伤而哭泣。这首词与《减字木兰花·锦屏人醉》异曲同工，皆体现的是“景色描写—抒发情感—人物描写—抒发情感”的抒情步骤。上阕首句和第二句是细节描写与环境描写，锦屏人代指闺中女子，她外出时沉醉在氤氲着温暖香气的春天景致中。第三句、第四句是景色描写，是女子乘舟所见。下阕第一句、第二句、第三句皆是女子登楼眺望思念恋人的动作描写。末句通过细节刻画了思妇蹙眉哀愁的神情。

第二类词为直抒胸臆类。《卜算子·春事付莺花》的尾句“若是真心待于飞，云里千条路”是闺中思妇的无奈感叹，意中人能不能和她相守，就要看他的选择了；如《惜奴娇·隔阔多时》这首慢词更为典型，全篇是以抒情为主，开篇感慨分别时间长、距离山高水远连相见说话都很难，抒强烈的思念之情。下阕慨叹雪夜寒冷，抒发了思妇孤寂悲凉的心情以及与恋人长相厮守的期盼，情感抒发较为直率。

因其题材为思妇词，预设即恋人已经离开，主要描写思妇怀人和抒发相思之情的。所以蔡伸思妇词的爱情故事脚本几乎不会涉及“初遇”“钟情”“欢会”这三类。排除单一地抒发情感的少量词作，蔡伸思妇词的爱情脚本通常遵循如下发展步骤：由“离别⇌相思—构想重逢”构成的爱情步骤可以说隐现在绝大多数思妇词作里。这样不仅词人在选用描写、抒情受限的词体的情况下，通过意象的精准选择、形容词和表达强烈情感词句的恰当安排而略去其中的很多细节，仍然能传达出动人的情感情绪。而且读者在欣赏蔡伸思妇词时，参照这一脚本，设想出词人因词体而不得不略写的情节，以达到一个合理的理解。三个步骤即为主要步骤，但可以循环往复、改变顺序地出现，构成各有不同的精致的爱情故事。

4 结 语

通过运用图形-背景理论，对以《菩萨蛮》《小重山》为代表的蔡伸思妇词以及部分典型性篇章的语句尝试进行批评，分析出词作中的图形与背景之间存在多层的关系，进而阐述图形-背景对词作意境生成和词情感抒发的影响。从宏观角度，运用脚本理论提炼出蔡伸思妇词“离别⇒相思—构想重逢”基本爱情脚本，有助于读者在欣赏作品时更精准地把握蔡伸特定类型词作传达的情感意蕴，填补文本因体式限制而存在的空白。此外，认知诗学理论与文本批评方法，为中国古代诗歌批评开拓了新路径与范式。但是需要将认知诗学本土化，必须寻找适合文本的理论与路径，方能精巧地展现中国诗歌之美。如果说蔡伸思妇词中的相思最为凝练的表达是“一生怀抱，为君牵役”，那么新型的文学理论在中国古代诗歌批评中的实践、将认知诗学本土化的尝试也将如此牵系并启迪怀抱热忱、立志融汇中西进行学术创新的学者们。

参考文献

[1] P STOCKWELL. A Stylistics Manifesto// S G Csábi. Zerkowitz. Textual Secrets: The Message of the Medium. Budapest: Eotvos Lorand University, 2002: 65.

[2] 郭姗姗，潘俊峰. 蔡伸词灵活多变的叙述艺术. 鸡西大学学报，2010（6）：122-123.

[3] 郭珊珊. “千古恨悠悠，长江空自流”——蔡伸咏怀词浅析. 安徽文学，2017（3）：24-25.

[4] 何抗. 蔡伸及其词研究. 苏州：苏州大学，2012.

[5] 李璇. 蔡伸家世和词集版本流传考. 湖州师范学院学报，2016（1）：48-52.

[6] 李璇. 论蔡伸的《友古词》创作. 唐山师范学院学报，2016（1）：90-95.

[7] 李璇. 蔡伸与向子諲词作优劣论辩. 闽江学院学报，2016（7）：1-5.

[8] 梁丽，陈蕊. 图形-背景理论在唐诗中的现实化及其对意境的作

用. 外国语，2008（7）：31-37.
[9] 彭定求. 全唐诗. 北京：中华书局，1960：2651.
[10] 蔡戡. 大父行状. 定斋集卷十四//丛书集成续编. 台北：新文丰出版公司，1997：86-87.
[11] 唐圭璋. 全宋词. 北京：中华书局，1965：1012.
[12] 唐圭璋. 全宋词. 北京：中华书局，1965：1014.
[13] 相隆本.“风雨送春归”句最早见于蔡伸词. 齐鲁学刊，1980（6）：89.
[14] 熊沐清. 语言学与文学研究的新接面——两本认知诗学著作述评. 外语教学与研究 2008（7）：299-305，321.
[15] 薛富兴. 东方神韵——意境论. 北京：人民文学出版社，2000：31.
[16] 脱脱. 宋史：卷三百二十. 北京：中华书局，1997：10264.
[17] 赵婷婷. 蔡伸《友古词》研究. 哈尔滨：哈尔滨师范大学，2012.

口译产出的深层认知加工图式模型建构

贺一舟

【摘要】口译产出的深层认知加工图式模型建构一直是学界关注的热点问题。运用实证研究法，从90名学生中抽取46人对其进行一个学期的“图式”训练，实验结果表明：图式训练对于提升口译产出质量具有明显作用，训练内容中空间政治意识和百科知识训练对提高口语产出质量效果作用突出，加强对学生的图式培训和分类归纳有利于提高学生的图式积累；根据实验目的建构口译产出前、中、后三个阶段的图示模型，揭示口译产出过程中大脑深层图式加工机制，为进一步提高口译质量和改进口译教学提供参考。

【关键词】口译产出；深层认知加工模型；产出质量；图式模型建构

1 引 言

自20世纪80年代以来，认知语言学成为语言习得研究的显学，认知语言学从大脑的神经机理和心理体验层面揭开了语言认知过程中大脑信息加工的深层工作机制，大大提高了语言习得的效率。口译产出的深层认知加工模型建构一直是口译研究的热点问题。目前对口译的认知语言学研究主要有以下几个学派。法国著名口译研究专家丹尼尔·吉尔（Daniel Gile）提出的口译认知资源分配理论认为，口译活动中原语信息听辨、信息意义的表征与理解、信息暂时贮存、译语组织与计划、译语信息表达与监控处理环节都是控制性

基金项目：本文系江西省教育厅科学技术研究项目“口译产出的深层认知加工图式模型建构”（GJJ191065）的阶段性研究成果。

作者简介：贺一舟，副教授，硕士研究生，主要从事外语教学研究。

加工过程，而成功的口译则是各个环节彼此协调、相互配合的结果（张威，2013：36）。“释意理论”（Deverbalization）的代表人物巴黎高级翻译学院（ESIT）达尼卡·塞莱斯科维奇（Seleskovitch）和勒代雷（Lederer）两位翻译学家和口译专家创立的“释意理论”（又称交际与释意理论）认为，口译最重要的是传送意义，译员不应受到原语的词句和句子结构的约束，这些表层结构只是口译中意义表达的指路信号，而不是意义本身（张洁，2013：110-111）。在心理语言学语言信息加工理论的基础上，Gerver（1976）和 Moser-Mercer（1997）等人提出了同传的心理信息加工模型，这些模型显示口译中信息接收、信息解码与编码、译语产出等各个阶段都有缓冲存储区（临时性存储），都在工作记忆中发挥作用并且不断从长时记忆中得到信息反馈（张威，2013：36）。Setton（1999）提出了口译研究的认知与语用理论，该理论认为，口译认知加工过程的核心是口译员要在工作记忆系统中建立并不断修正包括口译情景（situation）与话语（discourse）在内的心理模型（mental model）（张威，2013：37）。国内学者吴文梅教授对口译的认知加工模型进行了比较深入的研究。

2 理论基础

图式是认知语言学研究中的一个非常重要的概念。近年来，图式理论为口译深层认知加工模型建构提供了新的研究视角。图式（Schema）一词最早起源于格式塔心理学，意为“完形”“整体”（李琴，2020：54）。瑞士著名心理学家皮亚杰（Jean Piaget）认为“图式是指动作的结构或组织”（左承沫，周玉琨，2020：73）。J. Malley 等认为“图式是长时记忆中信息储存的一种方式，是围绕一个共同题目或主题组织起来的大型信息结构。图式的典型结构是按层次组织，使信息子集归入更大，包容更广的概念之中”（Malley，1990：232）。这里的概念就是图式。人们想要建立对于新知识的正确理解，关键在于新的知识能否匹配已知的概念与经历，即知识图式（胡大为，冯宇豪，2017：90）。图式可以分为语言图式、内容图式和形式图式三种。语言的编码、解码都依赖已有的语言图式、内容图式和形式图式，输入的语码必须与这些图式相匹配，才能完成语码处理过程，即语码的接受—解释—重组—内化（张戈，2015：152）。口译产出就是译者在接受口译材料之后如何利用已有图式激活大脑中存储的图式进行意义产出的过程，在这一过程中，图式发挥着至关重要的作用。“口译过程中的每一个环节——理解、意义形成和表达，都为口译信息处理图式模型的构建提供可靠的理论基础。”（王湘玲，胡珍铭，2011：108）倪蓉认为，图式具有三种特性：可增长（accretion），在旧图式上增加变量；可调整（tuning），修改现存图式；可重构（restructuring），建构全新的图式（倪蓉，2004：50）。也就是说，图式是可以经过训练得到优化和改善的。模型是指通过主观意识借助实体或者虚拟表现、构成客观阐述形态、结构的一种表达目的的物件（该物件并不等于物体，不局限于实体与虚拟、不限于平面与立体）。模型有实体和虚拟模型两种，虚拟模型又分为虚拟动态、虚拟静态和虚拟幻想三种，本研究中的图式模型属于一种静态虚拟模型。目前国内把图式理论运用到二语习得的研究还比较少见，运用到口译的研究更是少之又少。究竟如何利用图式理论理解口译产出的深层认知加工过程？对译者进行图式训练能否提高口译产出水平？可否建构口译产出的图式加工模型为口译训练提供科学依据？这些问题是目前口译产出研究中的新话题。

3 实验设计

3.1 研究问题

随着国际交流的日益频繁，口译的重要性日益凸显。提升口译产出质量是口译研究和口译教学亟须解决的重要课题。但是，在日常的教学和培训中，教师的口译训练比较盲目，缺乏科学理论指导，学生对口译产生畏惧心理，原因在于学生对大脑信息加工机理不明，训练者无从着手，受训者不知所措，口译产出质量低下，译后不知如何总结，口译人才培养缓慢，无法满足对外开放与国际传播的需要。如何进行科学的口译训练？如何消除口译者的心理焦虑？能否建构口译训练的图式模型提高口译训练的质量？究竟如何利用图式理论理解口译产出的深层认知加工过程？对译者进行图式训练能否提高口译产出水平？可否建构口译产出的图式加工模型为口译训练提供科学依据？这些都是口译工作者和口译训练者的困惑。

3.2 研究目的

运用图式理论，分析口译产出的大脑深层加工机制，利用图式理论建构口译产出的深层认知图式模型，科学指导口译认知过程，改革口译培训和教学方式，提高口译产出质量，培养国家急需的高层次口译人才，为提升中国文化软实力和国家形象提供强大的人力支撑和技术供给。

3.3 研究内容

通过实验研究、对比研究和行动研究，考察图式训练对于提高口译产出质量的有效性。把口译图式训练过程图式化，建构口语产出的深层认知图式模型，从口译活动前，口译过程中输入、记忆、产出三个过程，以及口译产出后三个环节对口译产出作深层次的图式建构。为口译产出的大脑加工机制和语言神经的运行机理提供科学解码，运用图式模式科学高效训练口译译员，提高口译产出效率。

3.4 研究方法

（1）实验研究法。从 90 名学生中选择 46 名口译参赛选手作为受试对象，通过 4 个多月的训练，观察其赛前的图式积累，赛中的图式激发、记忆整理、图式筛选与口译产出，以及赛后的图式归类。运用对比方法，区别经过图式训练和未经过训练学生的差别，证明图式运用在口译训练中的效益。同时，对受试对象口译前后和口译过程中进行图式模型建构，期待揭开口译过程中和口译前后受试对象的口译图式模型，为今后的口译训练提供理论指导。

（2）对比研究法。对比研究是把一组具有一定相似因素的不同性质物体或对象安排在一起，进行对照比较；通过综合比较它们在构造方面的差异、在性质方面的不同，得出这种物体或对象某性质是由哪些因素造成的。本研究采用实验组和对比组的数据比较，以及受训前后口译产出质量变化对比，直观真实反映差别，分析产生差别的原因，证明图式训练和图式模型建构对提高口译水平和质量的科学性。

（3）行动研究法。行动研究是指在自然、真实的教育环境中，教育实际工作者按照一定的操作程序，综合运用多种研究方法与技术，以解决教育实际问题为首要目标的一种研究模式。在本研究中，让受试对象和对比组学生进行为期4个多月的图式训练和常规训练，通过行动研究体现差别，归纳成长发展规律，找出差别产生的原因，以图式模型的形式展示出来，直观真实地揭示口译过程中大脑的图式加工机制，运用行动研究，思路清晰，逻辑严密，体现研究的真实性与科学性。

3.5 实验过程

实验前对 90 名学生进行一次口译测试，记录其基础成绩，作为实验数据的参照。从 90 名学生中随机抽取 46 学生培训模拟参加某项口译比赛。经过为期 4 个多月（将近一个学期）的图式理论与图式模型讲解和实战培训，发现 46 名受试学生的口译成绩得到大幅度的提高。而对比组的 44 名学生在进行常规的课堂教学后做同样的竞赛试题，成绩提升幅度较小，少数学生甚至出现负提升（侧面证明了语言磨蚀现象的存在）。实验结果表明：运用图式理论对学生进行口译强化训练，增加平时的图式积累，教会学生科学进行图式归类整理，分析口译产出过程的大脑信息加工图式机制，指导学生准确记录核心信息，由下而上激发大脑储存的图式结构，形成中介思维，由上而下激发大脑图式，选择性地形成目的语言，口译产出质量明显提高。指导学生每次测试（比赛）后须再次进行图式整理。经过反复训练，学生大脑中存储的图式结构日益丰富，为下一次的口译工作储备丰富的图式资源。实验结果证明，受试群体口译成绩提升幅度较大，口译产出质量显著提升，实验效果良好。实验证明图式是可以进行训练进行优化的。

受试组训练的主要内容和方法如下（如图 1 所示）：

第一，让学生收听或者观看 VOA、BBC、CGTN 中的国际新闻报道，最初采用慢速版，逐渐过渡到常速版，要求学生重点关注国际政治形势、科技进步、医疗、体育、财政等信息，帮助学生对于热点话题如人工智能（artificial intelligence）、克隆技术（cloning）、物联网（IOT）、欧盟（EU）、脱欧（departure from the European Union, Brexit）、纳米技术（nanotechnology）、全球变暖（global warming）、精准扶贫（targeted poverty alleviation）、能源危机（energy crisis）、水资源短缺（water shortage）、非洲贫穷（African poverty）、中东地区动荡（unrest in the Middle East）、朝鲜去核（denuclearization of North Korea）、诺贝尔奖（Nobel prize）、人类攻克癌症（man conquers cancer）、阿尔茨海默病（Alzheimer's disease）、糖尿病（Diabetes）、跨境旅游（transnational tourism）、出国留学（studying abroad, oversea studying）、乡村旅游（rural tourism）、民宿（homestay）、学术造假（plagiarize）、器官移植（organ transplant）、太空行走（space walk）、中美贸易冲突（Sino US trade conflict）、人类命运共同体（community of common destiny for all mankind）等有大致了解，帮助其关注相关话题报道，培养其时代感。

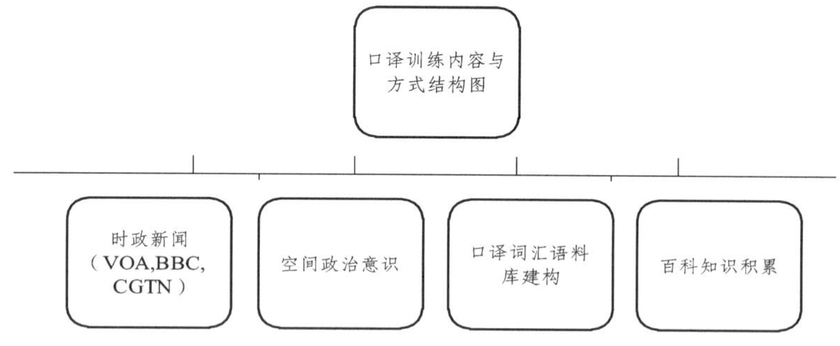

图 1　口译图式训练内容与方式结构

第二，培养学生的空间政治意识。口译中很多材料会涉及政治事件，因此平时要加强培养学生的空间政治意识。如了解全世界主要国家的英文名称、主要城市及最近发生的大事等，帮助学生在脑海中构建空间政治地图，形成大脑中的空间图式，如标志性建筑、该国的总统、首相或者总理的英文名字等，这样学生就很容易激发相关的图式信息，口译产出的质量和效率将大大提高。

第三，为学生建立口译词汇语料库。由于口译材料涉及的领域广泛，词汇量要求特别大，一旦遇到陌生新词学生有可能反应不过来，从而产生口译失误。因此，在教学中帮助学生构建热点话题、科技新词、网络流行语语料库，积累强大的词汇语料系统，让学生在口译过程中能够快速刺激大脑图式系统，不至于产生词汇盲点和知识性卡壳。

第四，丰富学生的百科知识。百科知识包含天文地理、网络新闻、日常口语话题等知识。百科知识在口译产出中能够为学生提供许多潜意识的判断能力，更能丰富学生的大脑图式内容，避免产生一些信息的误判和盲区，提高口译者的反应能力和大脑灵敏度。

3.6 数据统计与分析

表 1　46 名受试学生两次成绩对照及提升幅度

学生编号	学生分类	初试成绩（满分 100 分）	赛题成绩（满分 100 分）	提高分数（分）	提升幅度（%）
No.1	受试组	67	92	25	37.3
No.2	受试组	64	90	26	40.6
No.3	受试组	61	88	23	37.7
No.4	受试组	63	87	24	38.1
No.5	受试组	57	78	21	36.8
No.6	受试组	60	74	14	23.3
No.7	受试组	58	80	22	37.9
No.8	受试组	63	84	21	33.3
No.9	受试组	55	74	19	34.5

续表

学生编号	学生分类	初试成绩（满分100分）	赛题成绩（满分100分）	提高分数（分）	提升幅度（%）
No.10	受试组	62	77	15	24.2
No.11	受试组	57	76	19	33.3
No.12	受试组	64	80	16	25
No.13	受试组	61	75	14	23
No.14	受试组	60	67	7	11.7
No.15	受试组	55	73	18	32.7
No.16	受试组	54	66	12	22.2
No.17	受试组	57	65	9	15.8
No.18	受试组	64	77	13	20.3
No.19	受试组	57	68	11	19.3
No.20	受试组	46	63	17	30.4
No.21	受试组	62	88	26	41.9
No.22	受试组	52	74	22	42.3
No.23	受试组	53	66	13	24.5
No.24	受试组	57	69	12	21.1
No.25	受试组	41	59	16	39
No.26	受试组	38	56	18	47.4
No.27	受试组	65	78	13	20
No.28	受试组	66	79	13	19.7
No.29	受试组	61	66	5	8.2
No.30	受试组	64	71	7	11
No.31	受试组	59	74	15	25.4
No.32	受试组	47	59	12	25.5
No.33	受试组	63	82	19	31.2
No.34	受试组	44	58	14	31.2
No.35	受试组	54	76	22	40.7
No.36	受试组	45	67	22	48.9
No.37	受试组	57	78	21	36.8

续表

学生编号	学生分类	初试成绩（满分100分）	赛题成绩（满分100分）	提高分数（分）	提升幅度（%）
No.38	受试组	66	79	13	19.7
No.39	受试组	51	69	18	35.3
No.40	受试组	54	77	23	42.6
No.41	受试组	62	75	13	21
No.42	受试组	48	65	17	35.4
No.43	受试组	36	55	19	52.8
No.44	受试组	45	61	16	35.6
No.45	受试组	44	59	15	34.1
No.46	受试组	37	58	21	56.8

表 2　44 名对比组学生成绩对比表

学生编号	学生分类	初试成绩（满分100分）	赛题成绩（满分100分）	提高分数（分）	提升幅度（%）
No.1	对比组	71	66	−4	−5.6
No.2	对比组	66	65	−1	−1.5
No.3	对比组	63	63	0	0
No.4	对比组	68	67	−1	−1.5
No.5	对比组	60	59	−1	−1.7
No.6	对比组	55	57	2	3.6
No.7	对比组	48	44	−4	8.3
No.8	对比组	49	50	1	2
No.9	对比组	54	56	2	3.7
No.10	对比组	43	44	1	2.3
No.11	对比组	56	57	1	1.8
No.12	对比组	62	65	3	4.8
No.13	对比组	55	58	3	5.5
No.14	对比组	47	49	2	4.3
No.15	对比组	66	69	3	4.5

续表

学生编号	学生分类	初试成绩（满分100分）	赛题成绩（满分100分）	提高分数（分）	提升幅度（%）
No.16	对比组	60	64	4	6.7
No.17	对比组	49	48	−1	−2
No.18	对比组	52	55	3	5.8
No.19	对比组	48	50	2	4.2
No.20	对比组	61	64	3	4.9
No.21	对比组	60	65	5	8.3
No.22	对比组	45	49	4	8.9
No.23	对比组	56	57	1	1.8
No.24	对比组	61	60	−1	−1.6
No.25	对比组	44	46	2	4.5
No.26	对比组	57	57	0	0
No.27	对比组	62	64	2	3.2
No.28	对比组	43	45	2	4.7
No.29	对比组	56	55	−1	−1.8
No.30	对比组	29	31	2	6.9
No.31	对比组	49	47	−2	−4.1
No.32	对比组	62	65	3	4.8
No.33	对比组	61	64	3	4.9
No.34	对比组	56	57	1	1.8
No.35	对比组	60	62	2	3.3
No.36	对比组	45	48	3	6.7
No.37	对比组	54	52	−2	−3.7
No.38	对比组	49	51	2	4.1
No.39	对比组	50	49	−1	−2
No.40	对比组	47	49	2	4.3
No.41	对比组	61	64	3	4.9
No.42	对比组	56	55	−1	−1.8
No.43	对比组	44	47	3	6.8
No.44	对比组	51	57	6	11.8

实验数据分析：经过 4 个月的训练，受试组成员的成绩最高提升 26 分，最低 6 分，平均提高 16.8 分，提升幅度最高达 56.8%，最低达 8.2%，平均提升幅度为 31%。对比组学生中，经过常规的口译课程教学，最高提高 6 分，提高最大幅度为 11.8%，甚至出现 12 人负增长和 2 人持平，平均提高 1.2 分，提升幅度为 2.9%。无论从提高分数还是提高幅度进行比较，都会发现图式训练对改进口译产出质量是有效的（如表 2 所示）。运用 SPSS 统计学软件分析了对比组和受试组的参赛前成绩及参赛试题成绩。相关样品 t 检验分析，对比组 p 值为 $0.260>0.05$，表示成绩差异不显著。受试组 p 值为 $0.0008<0.05$，表示成绩差异显著。由此证明图式训练实验的效度较高（如表 3 所示）。

表 3　受试组与对比组口译成绩变化情况

组别	人数（人）	口译提升最低成绩（分）	口译提升最高成绩（分）	口译提升平均成绩（分）	口译提升最低幅度（%）	口译提升最高幅度（%）	口译提升平均幅度（%）
受试组	46	5	26	16.8	8.2	56.8	31
对比组	44	-4	6	1.2	-5.6	11.8	2.9

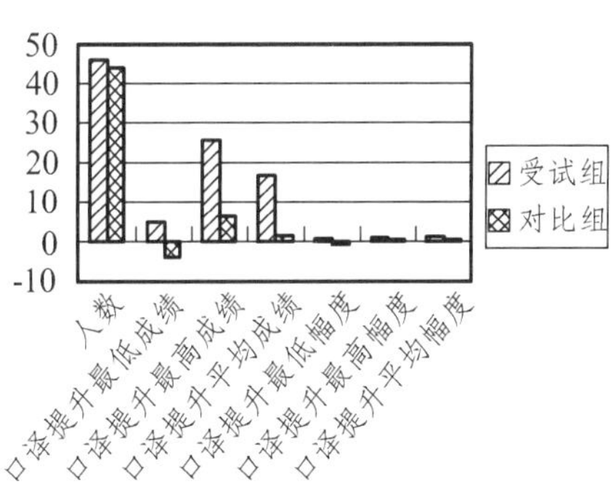

图 2　受试组与对比组口译成绩变化情况柱状图

首先，由于学生的分组是采用随机抽取方式，保证了实验的可信性和公平性；其次，两组学生进行同一份试卷的测试，保证了数据分析的可靠性。在实验中，我们运用图式模型对受试组学生进行针对性的口译训练，增加平时的图式积累，教会学生科学进行图式整理与归类；在训练时，指导学生对数据，重大政治、经济事件，目前比较流行和时尚的话题给予关注，引导学生分析口译产出过程的大脑信息加工图式机制，准确记录核心信息，由下而上激发大脑存储的图式结构，形成中介思维，由上而下激发大脑图式，选择性地形成语言，口译产出顺利完成。测试（比赛）后再次进行图式整理。实验结果证明：受试群体口译成绩明显提高，口译产出质量显著提升，实验效果良好；而对比组的学生，我们只进行常规的口译课程教学，发现成绩提升幅度较慢，有个别学生甚至出现负增长。这充分证明了常规的口译训练效果明显次于图式训练。因此，口译产出的深层认知加工图式模型建构对于指导口译强化训练具有明显的作用，研究具有实用性价值。

3.7 图式运用效果对比分析

以上数据分析证明了图示训练对于口译产出质量提高的有效性，为了深入分析受试群体和对比组学生的成绩差异究竟体现在哪些方面，笔者对两组学生进行了跟踪调查，发现受试组学生在听力技巧、把握口译材料大意、笔记整理和语言输出四个方面明显优于对比组学生。对比组学生普遍反映，有很多话题他们从未听过，所以无法把握语段大意，或者即使听懂材料内容，也抓不住核心内容，信息在大脑中一闪而过，无法激活大脑图式结构，笔记内容凌乱，翻译时支支吾吾，效果比较差，少数学生太长时间不经过强化训练和口译实践，还会产生语言磨蚀现象，出现成绩负增长的现象。对比显示，多让学生进行音频、视频材料输入，关注社会热点问题，并分类整理，加强图式训练，有助于改善和拓展受试者的图式结构，提高图式加工速度和质量，是比较科学的口译教学方法。这一对比也进一步证明了图式训练和图式模型建构对于提高口译产出质量的科学性（如表 4 所示）。

表 4　受试组与对比组口译过程中的能力素养对比

学生分组	听力水平	捕捉能力	速记能力	概括能力	组织能力	反应速度
受试组	较好	强	要点清晰	强	强	快
对比组	较差	较弱	凌乱	弱	弱	慢

4　口译产出的深层认知加工图式模型建构

4.1　赛前图式训练模型建构

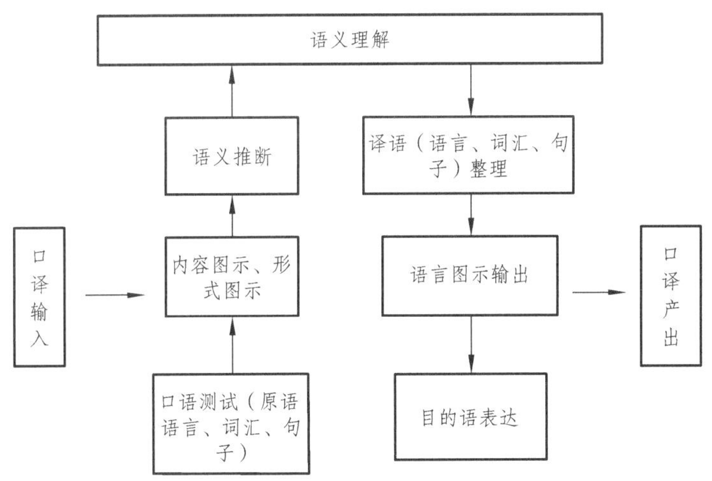

图 3　图式模型 1

这是测试前的一个图式训练模型图，体现了教师教学中对学生进行口译训练主要三种形式：音频、视频、文字，训练的内容涉及很多方面，主要包括时政新闻、经济、文化、医药健康、科技前沿等内容，重点强调学生对数字、重要术语、重大事件、核心词汇等的强化训练，旨在帮助学生在大脑中更新丰富形式、内容和语言三种图式，优化学生大脑中的图式结构，为口译产出做准备。根据前面的论述，图式是可以不断丰富和优化改进的，所以对学生进行图式训练有科学依据，实验数据也证明了其科学性。

4.2　口译产出中大脑的深层认知加工图式模型

该模型从左至右表示输入和产出过程的流程图，左边由下至上表达比赛起初图式加工是由下至上的过程，由口译测试过程中学生听到或者看到的原语词汇，句子等材料组成，大脑听到这些原语信息之后会刺激大脑中的图式，主要是内容和形式图式，经过大脑加工，快速对原语材料进行语义推断，进入理解阶段；这时候口译开始进入产出阶段，大脑中的图式与新输入的图式进入理解阶段之后，开始由语言图式指导如何进行词汇和句子的组织表达，产生通顺可理解的目的与表达，口译产出完成。口译产出时，图式的加工路径是由上至下的，起到监控和调节作用。

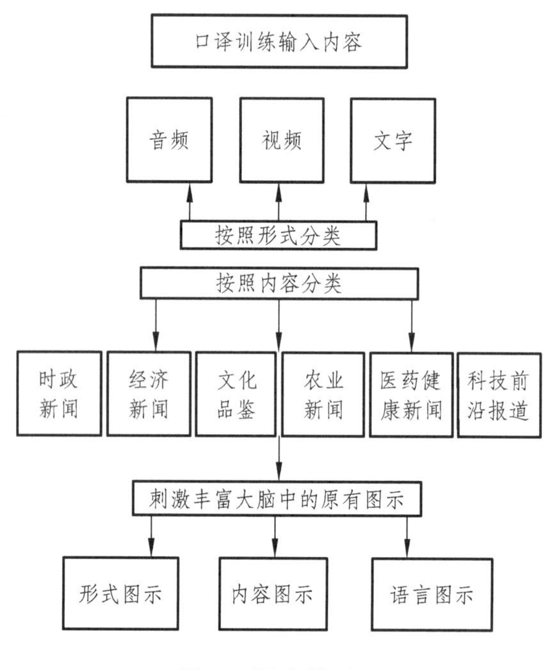

图 4　图式模型 2

4.3　口译训练后或者竞赛后图式变化模型图

该模型中，最小的圆圈表示口译产出过程中真正运用的图式，中间较大的圆圈表示大脑已经存储的图式，最大的圆圈表示口译产出后形成的新的图式结构。这一变化表示，平常进行的图式训练和口译测试越多，积累的图式就会逐渐增加，下一次提供工作和能够激活的图式增多，口译产出质量逐渐提高，充分证明了进行图式积累的重要性，也证明了进行有目的图式训练，对于提高口译产出水平是有效的。也说明了图式是可以增长、调整和重构的。图式训练对于口译产出的作用是毋庸置疑的。

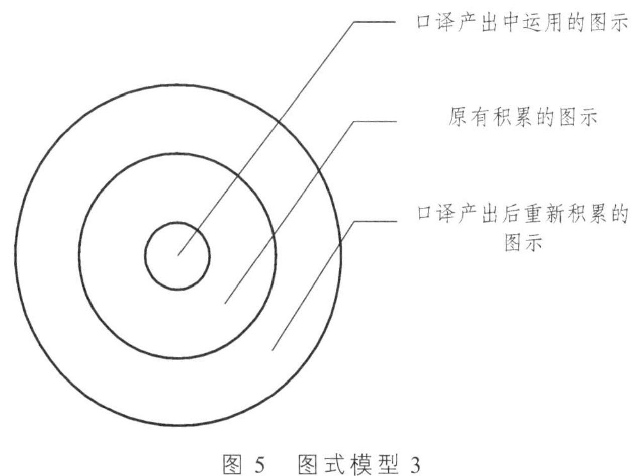

图 5　图式模型 3

4.4　口译产出过程中图式循环模型图

该模型直观地揭示了口译员在进行口译时的图式工作模式，口译信息刺激大脑的语言中区，迫使大脑中的图式苏醒，经过图式加工，大脑对输入语言进行理解，语言图式开始指导大脑进行目的与的转化，产出比较流利的目的语，口译完成。这一过程充分显示了图式在口译输入与产出中的工作机制，为口译训练和口译教学提供比较科学的指导。平时训练应该加强图式训练过程，有针对性地输入，帮助学生建立丰富的高级的图式结构，为新的口译产出提供丰富的图式储备。

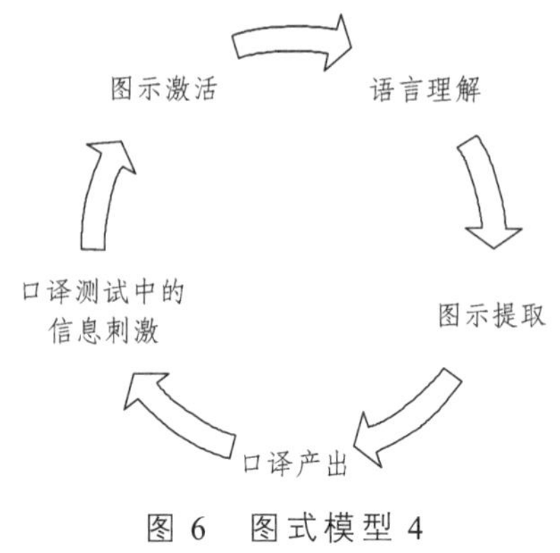

图 6　图式模型 4

5　结　语

口译产出能力是口译者的核心技能，是检验口译人才核心素养达成的重要指标，对于培养国家当前紧缺的口译人才，提升中国国际形象具有重大的实践价值。将图式理论应用于口译研究，不仅可以彰显图式理论在口译研究中的强大生命力，也能为图式理论的应用开拓新的研究领域。口译产出深层认知加工的图式模型建构将为口译出产提供认知心理学的理论阐释，解密口译过程中大脑信息处理的深层加工机制，为口译产出能力培养提供科学依据，为充分挖掘人工智能、有效开发大脑的语言信息处理能力提供理论支撑与导向，对于培养国家急需的高级口译人才，提升国家对外传播能力，加强国际交流，提升中国国家形象，以及落实“一带一路”建设和文化软实力建设都将发挥重要作用。

参考文献

[1] O’ MALLEY. Learning Strategies in Second Language Acquisition. Cambridge: Cambridge University Press, 1990.

[2] 胡大为，冯宇豪. 图式理论下本科口译进阶课程的教学改革研究. 教育教学论坛，2017，（45）：90-91.

[3] 李琴. 基于图式理论的英语语篇教学实践. 江苏教育，2020，(1)：54-57.

[4] 倪蓉. 图式理论对英语听力教学的启示. 上海理工大学学报(社会科学版)，2004，26(4)：49-52.

[5] 王湘玲，胡珍铭. 口译认知过程中信息处理模型的图式诠释. 湖南大学学报(社会科学版)，2011，25(5)：107-110.

[6] 张戈. 图式理论视域下的汉英会议口译研究. 新疆大学学报(哲学人文社会科学版)，2015，43(4)：151-156.

[7] 张洁. 释意理论及其对情境建构教学模式的启示. 西华大学学报，2013，32(2)：110-113.

[8] 张威. 口译认知加工机制的理论述评. 天津外国语大学学报，2013，20(1)：33-39.

[9] 左承沫，周玉琨. 基于图式理论的旋转类动词的类型研究. 大学教育，2020，(3)：73-67.

从《葬花吟》的英译本看“焦点-背景”阐析的重要性

栗霞　于欢

【摘要】认知诗学里的焦点-背景理论有助于增强诗歌赏析的层次感和透彻性，是诗歌赏析的重要方法之一。本文以“焦点-背景”的阐释为基本出发点，从焦点-背景层次递进、背景信息隐现虚化以及焦点-背景的相互渗透三个层面对中国古典诗词《葬花吟》原文以及大卫·霍克斯和杨宪益、戴乃迭的译文进行试探性分析，表明了“焦点-背景”阐释在诗词翻译中的重要性。

【关键词】诗词翻译；焦点-背景理论；《葬花吟》

0 引　言

《葬花吟》是《红楼梦》中为数不多的长篇诗歌，也是曹雪芹精心创作以表现林黛玉性格的重要作品（姜克滨，2017：45）。目前针对《葬花吟》文本的语言研究主要集中于对诗中所体现的文化意象从概念隐转喻等角度进行认知解读以及翻译传播，如潘华菊（2014）对《葬花吟》三种英译版本进行了比较，分析译本中的翻译策略和手段在激活源语和目的语图式方面的效果；吴淑琼，杨永霞（2020）

基金项目：本文系内蒙古工业大学翻译学科团队重点项目（ZD202045）；内蒙古自治区“十三五”规划项目“MTI教师职业化发展路径研究”（19WY14）的阶段性成果。

作者简介：栗霞，女，内蒙古工业大学教授，硕士，主要从事认知语言学、应用翻译理论与实践研究；
于欢，男，内蒙古工业大学外国语学院硕士生，主要从事认知语言学研究。

基于认知识解解析了杨宪益译本和大卫·霍克斯译本的认知翻译过程，从而揭示译者、原文和读者之间的多重互动关系。目前在中国知网上以“《葬花吟》”和“焦点-背景”为关键词进行检索发现暂时没有学者从焦点-背景理论视角赏析《葬花吟》原文及其英译本，但《葬花吟》整首诗歌是通过借助描写晚春时节落花的景象来表达诗人的内心世界，因此在整首诗中注意力焦点的转换以及背景信息的烘托对理解原诗作者的思想尤其重要。基于此，本文以“焦点-背景”的阐释为基本出发点，从焦点-背景层次递进、背景信息隐现虚化以及焦点-背景的相互渗透三个层面对中国古典诗词《葬花吟》原文以及大卫·霍克斯和杨宪益、戴乃迭的译文进行试探性分析，以探讨诗词翻译过程中对“焦点-背景”阐释的重要性。

1 焦点-背景理论

国内学者对“figure”这一术语的翻译看法不同，本文支持部分学者的观点，将其译为“焦点”，一方面是因为其更能体现认知语言学中的突显观，如将其译为“图形”，则语义中所带有的注意力信息会被相对淡化；另一方面，焦点-背景这一观点起源于心理学，最初用于人们对图形的感知中。丹麦心理学家鲁宾（Edgar Rubin）最早于1915年提出了图形从背景中分离的基本心理现象，通过实验描述了焦点和背景之间的关系并证实了人类视觉感知凸显（perception prominence）的存在，随后被完型心理学家应用于知觉组织研究。在认知语言学框架内，焦点（figure）是具有完整结构，在知觉者认知中由于突显而“前景（foreground）”的部分，是注意的焦点；而背景（ground）在认知中突显程度相对较低，是被“后景（background）”的环境。因此，“图形”这一术语和认知语言学中所体现的焦点还稍有不同，因此本文选择“焦点”也是为了区别于心理学术语中的“图形”。

认知语言学家将焦点-背景理论广泛应用于语言学研究，如Langacker（1991：282-278）“界标”的概念对表示空间位置关系的介词如 in、up、out 等以及小句进行了研究；Talmy（1996）详细描述了焦点和背景并分别列举了其联想和定义特征。

国内学者更多地将焦点-背景理论与认知诗学结合，应用于对文学作品的研究。如匡芳涛、文旭（2003）探讨了焦点-背景分离原则在语言空间结构和时间事件结构中的现实化，进而增强该理论的认知解释力；汪珍、胡东平（2011）利用焦点-背景理论作为基本的认知原则，研究《鲁迅小说选》英译本中隐喻的凸显和句式转换，为文学译本的传播提供参考；缪海涛、陈龙宇（2020）基于焦点-背景理论对中国山水诗歌意象的认知功能进行解读，从而传递了中国山水诗歌特有的认知功能意义。

2 《葬花吟》原诗及其英译的认知分析

本文基于焦点-背景理论，对《葬花吟》原文以及大卫·霍克斯和杨宪益、戴乃迭的英译本（以下简称“霍译”“杨译”）从焦点-背景的层次递进、背景信息的隐现虚化以及焦点-背景的相互渗透三个角度解读《葬花吟》中“焦点-背景”信息中蕴含的诗人以及译者的思想，并阐述“焦点-背景”信息在诗词翻译中的重要性。

2.1 焦点-背景的层次递进

落花，作为唐代诗人的惯用诗歌意象，成为渲染忧愁情绪而普遍存在的主体。[①]在描述落花的过程中，作者难免会通过各种具有中国特色的意象词汇实现其意境。在原文中，作者曹雪芹通过焦点和背景的层层递进，展现出一种动静结合的情境，全方位地呈现出一种真实可感的景象。

原文 1：花谢花飞花满天，红消香断有谁怜？游丝软系飘春榭，

① 原文是视角转换的一个连贯性的动作，曹雪芹最开始以“花”切入，将“花”作为焦点，“天”作为背景；在第二句中，将“游丝”凸显为焦点，“春榭”作为背景，无论是从焦点的角度还是从背景的角度都是一个视野的缩进、注意力画面的压缩，在层次上有递进的感觉，进而为下文“闺中女儿”这一焦点的出现以及下文因情绪的压缩而抒发惆怅哀婉的感情进行铺垫。

落絮轻沾扑绣帘。

霍译: The blossoms fade and falling fill the air, of fragrance and bright hues bereft and bare. Floss drifts and flutters round the Maiden's bower, or softly strikes against her curtained door.

杨译: As blossoms fade and fly across the sky, Who pities the faded red, the scent that has been? Softly the gossamer floats over spring pavilions, Gently the willow fluff wafts to the embroidered screen.

原文传达的意境是花儿已经枯萎凋残，风儿吹得它漫天旋转。褪尽了鲜红颜色，消失了芳香，有谁对它同情哀怜？柔软的蛛丝儿似断似连，飘荡在春天的树间。漫天飘散的柳絮随风扑来，沾满了绣花的门帘。

大卫·霍克斯的译文在意义表达以及形式上取得了不错的效果，其将两句的焦点作为主语，将第一句的背景作为宾语，将第二句的背景具体化为地点状语，在句式上仅将背景信息后置，产生了递进的感觉。杨宪益夫妇的译文则选择将焦点信息放于句子中作为不同的成分而呈现焦点和背景的递进。在第一句诗中，将焦点和背景信息放置于以连词连接的小句中，主要凸显了后半句诗，即"who"的感受。在第二句诗中，则将焦点和背景信息提至主语和宾语的位置，在形式上同样产生了递进的感觉。

简而言之，霍译只改变了背景信息的位置，而杨译则同时改变了焦点和背景信息的位置。二者相比也产生了不同的效果。霍译符合原文所描绘的动态画面，"花谢花飞花满天"当中，"花"作为焦点在"天"这一背景中呈现出相对动态的图景，而"游丝软系飘春榭"当中，"游丝"相对于"春榭"背景呈现出相对静态的图景，因此，译文中将"天"作为宾语可以更好地体现出"花"与"天"相互动的动态画面，将"春榭"作为地点状语则符合漫天蛛丝儿似断似连、飘荡在春天的树间这一相对静态的图景。而杨译则相对缺少动静结合的感觉，而更多突出的是"人"在诗中环境下的感受，译文更多地带给读者身临其境的感受。可见，在翻译过程中，可以通过对原文焦点和背景信息的层次判断，从句法结构的角度再现原诗所展现的意境，进而达到形式或功能上的对等。

2.2 背景信息的隐现虚化

如著名的人脸花瓶实验，在通常情况下，人们不可能同时注意到脸和花瓶。“人们就是在焦点和背景之间的转换过程中完成对信息的感知、注意、识别和理解。”（梁丽，赵静 2005：116）但是在对信息的感知过程中，人们可能会因关注焦点的持续变化而淡化背景信息，如缪海涛、陈龙宇（2020）在对柳宗元的《江雪》进行分析时，提到诗中情境对焦点和背景进行的虚化。

原文 2：杜鹃无语正黄昏，荷锄归去掩重门；青灯照壁人初睡，冷雨敲窗被未温。

霍译：At twilight, when the cuckoo sings no more, the Maiden with her rake goes in at door. And lays her down between the lamplit walls, while a chill rain against the window falls.

杨译：Dusk falls and the cuckoo is silent; Her hoe brought back, the lodge is locked and still; A green lamp lights the wall as sleep enfolds her, Cold rain pelts the casement and her quilt is chill.

原文描述的是杜鹃泣尽了血泪默默无语，愁惨的黄昏正在降临的场景。诗中女子扛着花锄忍痛归去，紧紧地关上重重闺门；清冷的灯光照射着四壁，人们刚刚进入梦境。轻寒的春雨敲打着窗棂，床上的被褥却依旧冷冰。[①]虽然整句诗的总体背景是黄昏时段，刻画了一种静态的富有整体感的画面，但是在整个语境下却呈现出动态的参与感，并通过视角注意力的不断变化，更使得整个画面呈现出一种动态。在这样一种静态的画面下，作者通过将背景信息虚化，从而凸显关注的焦点，最终凸显画面的动态感。原文中，以“杜鹃”作为焦点的信息被凸显为焦点，“黄昏”被视为背景，紧接着以“荷锄”这一动作的发出者作为焦点，而淡化了背景信息。在“荷锄归

① 对原文意象的描写来源于古诗文网《葬花吟》译文及注释。

去掩重门”中很难找到相对应的背景信息，虽然作者没有描述，但是可以推测出此时的背景信息依旧为“黄昏”。作者通过将焦点信息从“杜鹃”向“女子”的过渡，给人以视觉拉近放大的感觉，令诗中的主体更为突出，背景信息则被相对虚化。在下半句诗中，分别以“青灯”“人”“冷雨”“窗”以及“被”作为焦点，同样背景信息却难以区分，实际上在这种视角不断转变的情况下，背景信息的凸显便不是那么重要。从整体上看，作者勾勒这样的画面实际上是要突出黛玉内心的不安，外界“黄昏”这一背景就仿佛是她的命运，而选择去忽视背景也对应她对自己命运的反抗，进而再通过视角的不断变化表达林黛玉对自己身世与爱情的双重感叹。

在大卫·霍克斯的译文中，通过三个介词短语展现背景信息，且将“at twilight”这一短语置于句首，首先奠定了全句的背景信息，为后文背景信息的虚化做铺垫，其次将“杜鹃无语”这一信息处理为 when 引导的时间状语从句，在内容上可以更加凸显全句主语“the Maiden”，相对于原文而言，将“杜鹃”处理为背景虽然淡化了画面的动态感，但增强了林黛玉的内心活动，给人以杜鹃为林黛玉哭泣的感觉；在焦点的选择上，霍译选择将“女子”与“冷雨”作为主语进行凸显，使人不自主地联想二者之间的关联，进一步增强了冷雨所营造的冰冷的意境与林黛玉悲剧命运发展之间的关系。

杨宪益夫妇的译本中，将第一句的背景信息提至句首，作为对于读者关注度更高的焦点信息，从而在目标语当中隐去与背景有关的信息，从而使原诗所渲染的气氛更强烈。杨在翻译这两句诗的时候，将主要意象作为焦点置于主语的位置，注意力焦点的不断转换可以体现出女主人公内心思绪的杂乱物化到外部世界。

由此可见,《葬花吟》所勾勒的画面中存在背景信息虚化的情况，但实际背景信息又以隐现的形式存在，所以可以透过隐现的背景信息去探寻诗句中所要抒发的情感以及诗中人物的性格特点。在翻译过程中，针对背景信息的隐现虚化，可以将译文中的背景信息前景化，从而与后文的焦点信息建立同一性联系；针对具有多焦点的诗句，可以选择相对淡化部分焦点，将重要的焦点信息进一步凸显，从而强调二者之间的联系。

2.3 焦点-背景的相互渗透

梁丽、陈蕊（2008）提到了唐诗中焦点和背景的相互映衬不仅可以准确地描绘诗歌所要表达的意象，而且可以用于表达作者的深切感受。由于人们的注意力似乎难以找到集中的焦点，但是在意象中似乎又能够感觉到注意力在不断转化，因此就产生了焦点和背景的相互渗透。

原文 3：昨宵庭外悲歌发，知是花魂与鸟魂？

霍译: Last night, outside, a mournful sound was heard: but neither bird nor flowers would long delay.

杨译: Last night from the courtyard floated a sad song—Was it the soul of blossom, the soul of birds, Hard to detain, the soul of blossom or birds?

原文描绘了不知院外什么地方传来一阵阵悲凉的歌声。在这样一幅画面中很难区分什么是焦点，什么是背景。“悲歌发”是主人公的听觉感官，虽然眼前无人，却听见了悲凉的歌声。女子眼前无“人”，自然“人”不可能成为画面的焦点，因此也就不可能是焦点。然而，从女子的思绪上看，诗文的焦点和背景其实是相互渗透的：庭外是女子最开始注意力集中的地方，可以视为焦点，而随着悲歌的到来，庭外的焦点信息被淡化为背景信息，此时歌声作为新信息，吸引了女子的注意力，此时在女子的想象之中，自然会想象出在庭院外的某处，必定是有人或者其他生物发出这样悲惨的声音。这样看来，其实女子的注意焦点在于心中所想的庭院外的某个人或者某种生物，那就是焦点，其余的全景即“庭外”便成了背景。

在霍译的版本中，大卫·霍克斯也将“悲歌”作为主语突出，而背景信息则是通过空间方位词而体现。在对后文的处理中，霍译将女子心中的“花魂”和“鸟魂”实体化，也作为焦点凸显，将女子心中的意象外化，表面上是在“哭花”，而实际上林黛玉是在“哭己”，从而为《葬花吟》增加了叙事的成分，声音不再是抽象的概念和一闪即逝的诗歌意象。因此，在翻译过程中，译者可以将导致焦点和背景相互渗透的虚拟化感知通过实词名词等形式进行外在物化，从而凸显出原文中所要表达的真实情感。杨译则较好地贴合原文的意象构建，开始以“庭外”作为焦点，“悲歌”以宾语的形式作为背景；与霍译不同的是，杨译并没有将“花魂”和“鸟魂”实体化，而是以疑问句的方式在形式上与原文相匹配。

3 结 语

本文以《葬花吟》原文以及大卫·霍克斯和杨宪益、戴乃迭夫妇的译文为例，基于焦点-背景理论的认知视角，对中国古典诗词进行解读。研究发现：首先，《葬花吟》中焦点和背景信息存在一定的层次感，通过焦点和背景层次凸显，可以呈现出动静结合的画面。在翻译过程中可以选择从句法结构的角度再现原诗所展现的意境，从而达到形式和功能上的对等。其次，通过背景信息的隐现虚化，可以实现静态画面的动态参与感，在翻译过程中，可以将背景信息前景化，从而凸显后文焦点信息；针对具有多焦点的诗句，可以选择相对淡化部分焦点，而将重要的焦点信息进一步凸显，从而强调二者之间的联系。最后，焦点和背景有时会相互渗透，从而表现诗人以及诗中主人公的视线和思维。在翻译过程中，可以将导致二者渗透的虚拟化感知外在物化，从而凸显出注意的焦点。这种焦点-背景的互动和动静的结合使得诗人能够在有限的语篇内营造出多重意象，带领读者领略不同的意境，感同身受，实现中国古典诗词特有的认知功能意义。

参考文献

[1] R W LANGACKER. Concept, Image, and Symbol: The Cognitive Basis of Grammar. Berlin: Mounton de Gruyter, 1991.

[2] L TALMY. Towards a Cognitive Semantics (Vol Ⅰ). London:

Addison Wesley Longman Limited, 1996.
[3] 姜克滨. 从落花到葬花——论《葬花吟》的诗意预叙. 红楼梦学刊，2017（6）：45-58.
[4] 匡芳涛，文旭. 焦点-背景的现实化. 外国语，2003（4）：24-31.
[5] 梁丽，赵静. 焦点/背景理论在句法分析中的作用. 华中科技大学学报（社会科学版），2005（2）：116-119.
[6] 梁丽，陈蕊. 焦点/背景理论在唐诗中的现实化及其对意境的作用. 外国语（上海外国语大学学报），2008（4）：31-37.
[7] 缪海涛，陈龙宇. 基于焦点-背景理论的中国山水诗歌意象的认知功能解析. 外国语文，2020，36（6）：80-84.
[8] 潘华菊. 从图式理论角度论《葬花吟》英译. 长春师范大学学报，2014，33（03）：71-72.
[9] 汪珍，胡东平. 焦点-背景理论下颜色隐喻的英译研究——以《鲁迅小说选》两个英译本为例. 西南交通大学学报（社会科学版），2011，12（03）：30-36.
[10] 吴淑琼，杨永霞. 认知识解视角下《红楼梦·葬花吟》不同译本的翻译策略对比研究. 外国语文，2020，36（5）：119-126.

认知文体批评

论福斯塔夫“混合”的想象

余雅萍

【摘要】福斯塔夫爵士是莎士比亚在历史剧《亨利四世》中塑造的最复杂的人物形象之一。他时善时恶，时而机智幽默，时而又贪婪怯懦。然而每一性格的呈现都有他丰富而活跃的想象力作前奏。本文尝试以认知科学中的概念混合理论剖析福斯塔夫的想象——想象虚构的自己，想象过去与未来以及想象缺席的权威，解析其想象背后的“混合”机制——身份的混合，时间的混合及从“有”到“无”的混合，以此跳出“善恶”二元论的框架，展现福斯塔夫“恶”之表象背后的复杂人性。

【关键词】混合；福斯塔夫；想象

0 引 言

福斯塔夫爵士（Sir John Falstaff）是莎士比亚（William Shakespeare）在历史剧《亨利四世》（*Henry IV*）中塑造得最复杂的人物形象之一。恩格斯认为他“给前台表演的贵族的国民运动提供了宝贵背景”（1972：585）。美国著名文学批评家哈罗德·布鲁姆（Harold Bloom）在《西方正典》（*The Western Canon*，2004）中说，在各种对福斯塔夫的评价中，他“最喜欢萧伯纳的‘昏庸可恶的老怪物’，我认为，这一评价也是因为萧伯纳私下已意识到，他在机智上无法与福斯塔夫相比，所以不能带着常有的轻松赞赏自己的心智

基金项目：本文为 2017 年国家社科基金重点项目“戏剧表演和观赏的认知研究”（17AWW006）的阶段性成果。

作者简介：余雅萍，女，浙江大学外国语言文化与国际交流学院博士研究生，主要从事英美文学研究和文学认知批评研究。

而鄙薄莎士比亚”（2015：40）。福斯塔夫的机智令萧伯纳自叹不如。布鲁姆继而总结道：“莎氏从福斯塔夫起就在想象性写作的功能（这就是如何对他人言说）之外加上了如今占据主导或许也更沉郁的诗艺训诫：如何对自我言说”（2015：40）。由此可见，让福斯塔夫人物形象大放异彩的正是伴随他言说时异常丰富的想象。而“想象”作为文学文化领域的关键词，已经渐渐地受到21世纪认知科学的青睐。在《想象——文学和认知的交集》（*Imagination: Literary and Cognitive Intersections*，2015）中，美国浪漫主义评论家艾伦·理查德森（Alan Richardson）将想象分为三个层次：第一层次的想象是视觉或其他感知系统所接收到的意象；第二层次的想象涉及在心理空间对各种信息进行混合（blend）；第三层次的想象是大脑的“默认模式”（default mode），包括对过去的回忆，对未来的展望，心灵理论等（2015：226）。碎碎念的福斯塔夫，时而对他人言说，时而又转为对自我言说，他的想象和他的言说，已经到了不可分离的地步。言说时伴随的想象包括对虚构身份的想象、对过去未来的想象以及对缺席权威的想象。吉尔斯·福柯尼耶（Gilles Fauconnier）和马克·特纳（Mark Turner）在《我们的思维方式》（*The Way We Think*，2002）中提出了概念混合理论（conceptual blending theory，简称CBT）。他们认为，混合由两个或多个输入空间投射到一个混合空间进行意义的建构，因此混合意义包含的信息和结构来自两个及以上的空间（Fauconnier & Turner，2002）。本文用概念混合理论细细推敲福斯塔夫的想象，发现它呈现出以下三种形式：身份的混合、时间的混合以及从“有”到“无”的混合。在“混合”机制作用下的想象挑战读者的认知，给读者带来了特殊的审美体验，让福斯塔夫成为世界文学宝库中极其鲜明生动、有血有肉的艺术形象，且具有很高的美学价值和不可抗拒的艺术魅力。

1　以身份混合虚构自我

福斯塔夫言说时伴随着其对虚构身份的想象。《我们的思维方式》第十二章节为“身份和角色”（“Identity and Character”）。福柯尼耶和特纳提出，我们对于自我的认识是建立在概念混合（conceptual integration，也作 conceptual blending）的基础之上的。在所有人类思维技巧中，最基本的便是对两种身份的混合，就像我们常说的“如果我是你，我就会……”。因此，某些具有影响力的人物就是通过概念混合的方式进入我们的生活，和我们的身份混合在一起的（2002：249-268）。福斯塔夫通过将自己与他人的身份混合，虚构出一个伟大的自我，这点和哈姆莱特有几分相似。哈姆莱特在第二幕第二场跟幼时好友罗森格兰兹和吉尔登斯吞谈玄说理时感叹自己只要不做噩梦，即使是生活在果壳里，也照样可以想象自己是拥有无限空间的国王（《莎士比亚悲剧选》，2001：221）。福斯塔夫这个整日游荡毫无作为的破落户有着和哈姆莱特类似的想法，即整天幻想着自己是生活在无限空间里的国王或亲王。在第二幕第四场，胖乎乎的小人物福斯塔夫当上了演员，扮起了“国王”和“亲王”，虽演技蹩脚，但其想象和模仿的能力，绝对让人拍手称好。他小心翼翼地维持着自己和亲王之间的“友谊”，不时拿自己开玩笑来取悦亲王以博其一笑。他又趁着演戏的机会调侃亲王，赚回些许尊严。福斯塔夫这个蹩脚的三流演员演起了自己心仪的一流角色，由此产生了戏剧性混合。这种戏剧性混合让亲王产生一种认知错觉。不知道是该笑还是该哭，该把他的话当真而责备抑或只是当作玩笑一笑了之。读者看福斯塔夫，也好似雾里看花，全然看不透他心里所想。艾米·库克（Amy Cook）认为莎士比亚创造了一个个具身的、虚构的世界，需要我们用具身认知的视角去解读同样是具身的人物角色。混合空间就像是准备好了道具、人物以及剧本的舞台，等待着演员的即兴表演（2006：83）。福斯塔夫在听到亲王“你就权充我的父亲，向我查问我的生活情形”的建议时，立刻就回复“我充你的父亲？很好。这一张椅子算是我的宝座，这一把剑算是我的御杖，这一个垫子算是我的王冠”（《莎士比亚历史剧选》，2001：132）。此时的福斯塔夫自身即是混合的结果。他作为演员，部分表征他所演的人物——国王，因此“宝座”“御杖”“王冠”得即刻到位。部分代表他本身，一个现实中的无业游民，只有“折凳”“铅剑”“秃顶”（现实情境可从亲王的话语中推断），来自两个心理空间的信息混合后，呈现在亲王及同伴面前的福斯塔夫既不完全虚构，也非全部真实，这种似是而非的状态成就了他非凡的魅力，甚至产生了一种非常滑稽的喜剧效果，给这正统严肃的历史剧增添了别样的韵味。

虽然情感的表演和情感本身并不是一回事，但是女人看到死去的丈夫时的反应却给演国王的伶人表演抒发情感提供了参考（Cook，2006：93）。在这一点上，福斯塔夫可谓深谙此理，在想象虚构的自己时，不仅准备好各种匹配的道具，还为自己情感的表演做了充分的铺垫。“好，要是你还有几分天良的话，现在你将要被感动了。给我一杯酒，让我的眼睛红红的，人家看了会以为我流过眼泪；因为我讲话的时候必须充满情感。（饮酒）我就用《坎拜西斯王》的那种腔调。”（《莎士比亚历史剧选》，2001：132-133）在福斯塔夫看来，唯有在酒精刺激之下酝酿出的情感，才能助其进入国王的角色，体味他内心满腹的悲哀和对未来继承人深深的忧愁。

在身份混合的过程中，最体现难度的是作为演员的福斯塔夫在“国王”和“亲王”两个角色间的灵活切换。从高高在上的国王亨利四世，到放纵叛逆的亲王哈尔，福斯塔夫在两个角色之间的瞬间变换看似游刃有余。从“听我的话。各位贵爵，站在一旁”到“启禀父王，我从伊斯特溪泊来”，再配合作为演员的福斯塔夫滑稽的形象，让人不得不感慨这臃肿不堪的躯体里居然藏着如此灵活善于变通的灵魂。亲王哈尔借着自己扮演的角色——国王亨利四世道出了对福斯塔夫的真实评价，他是“充满着怪癖的箱子”“塞满着兽性的柜子”“水肿的脓包”“庞大的酒囊”“堆叠着脏腑的衣袋”“填着腊肠的烤牛”“道貌岸然的恶徒”“须发苍苍的罪人”“无赖的老头”“空口说白话的老家伙”……这一连串的符号把哈尔心中荒淫放荡、为非作歹的福斯塔夫形象地展示在观众面前。这也预示着福斯塔夫并不如愿的结局，他注定当不上大人物，如贵人般过清清白白的生活。因为他手头能帮他实现如此愿望的唯一筹码——“好朋友”哈尔，也是非真实的，即他所谓的友谊关系也纯属虚构。虽然这并非哈尔对福斯塔夫首次调侃，然而这么赤裸裸的评价却是头一遭，这让福斯塔夫非常紧张。此时他扮演的亲王急忙替他开脱，“不，我的好陛下；撵走皮多，撵走巴道夫，撵走波因斯；可是讲到可爱的杰克·福斯塔夫，忠实的福斯塔夫，勇敢的福斯塔夫，老当益壮的福斯塔夫，千万不要让他离开你的哈利的身边；撵走了肥胖的杰克，就是撵走了整个的世界”（《莎士比亚历史剧选》，2001：135）。当下的福斯塔夫是福斯塔夫和亲王哈尔混合的结果，一方面，福斯塔夫是演员，他扮演的亲王哈尔想在国王面前为福斯塔夫塑造一个正面的形象，以扭转国王对他混迹于三教九流的不良印象；另一方面，福斯塔夫又代表的是自己，他此刻得不断强调自己对亲王哈尔的有用性以保全自己的未来。福斯塔夫的想象完成了实与虚、明与暗、显与隐的空间转变。在表演舞台的横向角色穿梭中始终纵向贯穿着自身不确定的定位，从演绎他者（国王与亲王）的摇摆中跳向生死未卜的自我。福斯塔夫的命运就在这十字交叉中进行着，也暗示着他最后“不能如愿”的结局。这个“十字”意象，是哈姆莱特式的踟蹰，也是人生的十字路口及生命的十字架。福斯塔夫思维跳跃的同时，观众已经再一次在似是而非的状态中迷失了。然福斯塔夫在“国王”与“亲王”这两个角色间的灵活切换，这出色的“表演”终究是为了保全作为福斯塔夫的“自己”。

2 以时间的混合想象过去与未来

福斯塔夫的想象同时也体现在时间的维度上。处于当下的福斯塔夫在想象时总不忘翻过去的旧账，绘未来的蓝图，是过去和未来的福斯塔夫在时间维度上混合的结果。这和国内学术界对福斯塔夫的评价大相径庭。翻译家方平先生在人民文学出版社 2001 年版《莎士比亚历史剧选》前言中对福斯塔夫如此评价：“……这里非常形象化地表明了这个自我欺骗的人既没有过去，也没有未来，像一切没落阶级一样，他只为眼前而活着。（《莎士比亚历史剧选》，2001：5）”18 世纪英国著名文学评论家塞缪尔·约翰逊（Samuel Johnson）认为,“没有一个人的心灵是置于当下的,大多用于对过往的追忆和对未来的期许”。约翰逊为人脑的这种自然倾向起了个很动听的名字,叫作“想象”(1968:22)。佛教中称之为“冥想”,而神经科学家把它叫作大脑的“默认模式”(Richardson,2015:230)。研究者对于默认系统在大脑中的作用尚存争议,但是有一点得到了一致的认同,即便是在休息时,人脑也处于异常活跃的状态,或回忆过去,或展望未来,或做白日美梦,或猜度他人行动,且很多白日美梦都指向未来。福斯塔夫并非没有过去也没有未来,很多他的自我言说中充满着对过去的忏悔和对未来的各种幻想和期许。“想象过去和未来”为福斯塔夫的空间思维拓展出了一个时间维度,福斯塔夫的“想象”更是对这一角色有限空间的刻画之突破。“要是我做起大人物来,我一定要把身体长得瘦一点儿;因为我要痛改前非,不再喝酒,像一个贵人一般过着清清白白的生活(《莎士比亚历史剧选》,2001:184)。”对于过往,他显然带有忏悔之意,“痛改前非”是他跟日日纵酒的过往诀别的坚定信念,甚至可以不再触碰他的心头之好——酒。他想象中未来的自己在形象、地位等方面皆产生翻天覆地的变化。“大人物、贵人”作为符号限定了这个身份的必要条件,即“瘦、清白”。可见在福斯塔夫心目中,大人物是瘦的、清白的,而绝不如他那样胖的、酗酒的。这些符号不仅仅否定了他自己颓唐的过去,也否定了他迷醉的当下。因为从过往到如今,他既不瘦,也不清白,又酗酒无度。因此他对未来的期许完全寄托在戒酒上面,似乎象征着恶魔的酒,一旦离开了他,他便可以变瘦,变清白,变贵人。虽然这些对未来的想象看似是不切实际、海市蜃楼般的自我欺骗,但是白日梦式的想象更能体现人物现在所处生活环境中的窘迫和无奈。这个部分否定自己过去和现在的人,把一切希望都寄托在可能会改变自己命运的亲王“哈尔”身上。他想依仗着亲王的崛起,当上大人物。

福斯塔夫在时间维度上的想象也体现在他对生死荣誉的思考上。既然想象着自己有美好的未来,福斯塔夫断然不肯轻易抛却生命,坦然面对死亡。因而他在死亡面前必然多了一份怯懦,少了一份洒脱。人死后，生前的功名利禄、美妻娇妾终将在秋风荒冢里化作烟尘。即便是战场上挥斥方遒的英雄豪杰，在死亡来临的刹那也难免流露出恐惧的眼神，更何况是福斯塔夫这样一个长久以来游离在主流社会之外、不务正业、流落江湖的破落户。印度当代哲学家乔德哈里认为人对死亡的恐惧源于以下三方面："首先，死亡是种痛苦的经验，一个垂死的人，通常要经历巨大的痛苦。其次，死去之后万事皆空，我们生前孜孜以求的享受、荣誉、名位、财富等等，一切将化为乌有。第三，我们将被周围的人忘却，因此失去我们的骨肉和亲朋挚友。"（1981：139）这正印证了福斯塔夫关于"荣誉和死亡"的哲学性思考。"那两个字荣誉又是什么？一阵空气。好聪明的算计！谁得到荣誉？星期三死去的人。他感到荣誉没有？不。他听见荣誉没有？不。那么荣誉是不能感觉的吗？嗯，对于死人是不能感觉的。可是它不会和活着的人生存在一起吗？不。为什么？讥笑和毁谤不会容许它的存在。"（《莎士比亚历史剧选》，2001：173）所以为了远离死亡，他躺倒在战场上装死。为了远离死亡，他把中世纪视为比生命还贵重的荣誉抛却一边。达马西奥（Damasio）在《笛卡尔的错误：情绪、推理和人脑》（*Descartes' Error*，1994）一书中提出"身体回路"的概念，它是经由身体流通信息的系统，用于改变人在特定环境下的身体状态，如恐惧、顿悟等。身体状态的认知表征能识别外部变化，即使没有发生在自己身上也好似亲身经历一般（1994：100）。福斯塔夫想象着在战场上死去的人，就好似自己也死去了一次，经历了一次可怕的临死前的心灵激荡。虽然得到了荣誉却也因此丧失了生命。这迎来送往中反映出一个悖论：在战场上，他这般身份的人，是选择生命与恶名还是选择死亡与荣誉？在想象死亡的过程中，福斯塔夫感受到了极大的恐惧。对死亡的恐惧和向生的欲望已经完全超越了中世纪封建骑士眼中至高无上的荣誉。既然人们生前孜孜以求的荣誉、财富等一切在死后都将化为乌有，为何还要为这些即将归为虚无的东西搭上宝贵的生命？福斯塔夫也像哈姆莱特一样，在生死面前曾有过"生存还是毁灭"式的思考。两者在面对未知的死亡时都产生了恐惧感。哈姆莱特在第三幕第一场中有这样的内心独白："谁愿意负着这样的重担，在烦劳的生命的压迫下呻吟流汗，倘不是因为惧怕不可知的死后……"(《莎士比亚悲剧选》，2001：236）而福斯塔夫虽鲜有如此崇高和深刻的思辨，但从他仅有的几句关于荣誉和死亡的话语中，我们也窥探出福斯塔夫哲学式的想象。在死亡面前灵魂的怯懦和望而却步是共通的人性，是对不死的未来一种侥幸的期许。约翰逊博士赞扬莎士比亚，说他笔下人物的言行都受到人皆不能免的普遍激情的影响，而此时约翰逊首先想到的那种逃避死亡意识的激情（布鲁姆，2015：171）。这和国内很多批评家的观点显然是相异的，如"荣誉感的彻底丧失，充分说明封建道德在他身上完全解体了——不仅封建道德，一切的道德观念在这个人身上都不存在了"(《莎士比亚历史剧选》，2001：5）等。布鲁姆将福斯塔夫逃避死亡的行为归因于人皆不能免的普遍激情，因而假使以此作为判断福斯塔夫道德败坏的唯一依据显然失之偏颇。

3 以"有"和"无"的混合想象缺席的权威

福斯塔夫对王者身份的幻想和对过去未来的想象中，都存在一个虽缺席但又在场的权威。权威的隐现揭示了人的思维过程中"有"和"无"的混合机制。福柯尼耶和特纳认为，人类总是在假装、模仿、撒谎、幻想、欺骗并且提出各种假设。我们的精神生活惯于依赖我们的反事实（counterfactual）思维。这种思维的主要认知机制就是概念混合。总之，我们生活在一个反事实的动物园里，充斥着各种现实中缺席的事物（2002：217-248）。福斯塔夫在和人对话时频频出现意义停顿、思维间隙。这停顿和间隙恰恰是在言说的中央，比言说更具表现力。殷企平教授在《阐释三境界：外国文学教学的艺术之路》一文中提出阐释的第二境界，即"此处无声胜有声"，也就是中西诗学都常常提到的"沉默"或"无言"的境界（2012：152）。张隆溪教授也引用苏轼的诗句对"无言"的境界做了非常生动而形象的阐释："欲令诗语妙，无厌空且静。静故了群动，空故纳万境。"

（2006：233-234）针对这种现象，库克则试着从认知的视角再现了从“物”到“无”、从“话语”到“无言”的思维过程（2006：83-99）。这几种诠释有异曲同工之妙。实然，沉默无言并非思维的静止，而是活跃思维的外在伪装。沉默处恰恰是能引发思维高潮的间隙，这个认知过程是极为复杂的。福柯尼耶和特纳认为混合是对思维间隙的衔接，它不仅是语言的功能；它证实我们将信息从两个及以上的心理空间映射到混合空间构建混合（2002：241）。虽然福斯塔夫没有完全处于沉默状态，但是他在对他人进行言说时存在大量瞬间的意义停顿与思维间隙。在第二幕第二场，抢劫过路商客前，有这样两组对话，构思非常巧妙。

> 盖兹希尔：咱们抢到了这笔钱，大家可以发财了。
> 福斯塔夫：大家可以上绞架了。
> 亲王：各位听着……
>
> 波因斯：杰克，你那马就在那篱笆的后面，你需要它的时候，可以到那里去找它。再见，不要退却。
> 福斯塔夫：如果我得上绞架，想揍他也揍不着了。
> 亲王：奈德，我们化装的物件在什么地方？
>
> （《莎士比亚历史剧选》，2001：115）

两组对话的共同之处在于：福斯塔夫在言说时出现意义的脱节和断层，像是对他人言说，又像是对自我的言说。如若是对他人的言说，我们找不到他人回应他的任何符合逻辑的话语。如此我们只能将此看成是他自我言说时无意义的喃喃之音。然而这些言说真的是无意义的吗？莎士比亚这位善于摆弄语言的大师，怎肯随意浪费笔墨，让无用的辞藻占据篇幅?我们可将福斯塔夫的言说看成经他多重心理空间混合后的产物：一些原本存在的内心想法，在思维的混合机制的作用下输出的内容。来自输入空间 1 的信息“抢劫国王的钱发财”和来自输入空间2的信息“国王的财产神圣不可侵犯”混合成“抢了国王的钱便是侵犯了国王的财产”后最终通过语言输出，其直接带来上绞架面对死亡的后果。其他人没有经历类似的思维建构过程，因而无法与他产生共情。在整个抢劫团伙中，福斯塔夫最具危机意识，然而心理混合空间里有一个缺席的在场掌控着一切。它是不在场的、外在世界的中心——国王。国王的角色看似不在场，但在福斯塔夫眼里，他却高高在上，不可侵犯。国王成为不在场的在场也是莎士比亚时代父权社会的权威法则的体现。福斯塔夫的矛盾在于，一方面他处处流露出对至高法则唯命是从；另一方面，他又时时想要挑衅权威。他每一次的心理建构过程都是标榜道德正义的国王和注重当下享乐的人性之间的艰难博弈。缺席的国王无处不在，他不仅参与建构了福斯塔夫和亲王间的关系，同时他也是福斯塔夫对未来幻想中不可缺的对象等。这个不在场却胜似在场的国王始终占据福斯塔夫的心理空间，因而造就了前言不搭后语、自欺欺人、滑稽无底线的福斯塔夫。因国王不在场的在场，福斯塔夫对亲王亦步亦趋，点头哈腰，怕他“就像怕一头乳狮的吼叫一般”，全然不敢在他面前豪气地嚷嚷“我要像打一条狗似的把他打个半死”(《莎士比亚历史剧选》，2001：156)。因国王不在场的在场，福斯塔夫在亲王面前的每一言说都是心理空间混合的复杂结果。虽然在抢劫过路客商时临阵脱逃，然而还是想着在亲王面前树立绿林好汉的美好形象。他的话语让被言说者不知其所云，一会儿是“两个”假想敌，随即变为“四个恶汉向我冲了上来”，继而便是“我举起盾牌把七个人的剑全挡住了”“我刚才告诉你的这九个穿麻衣的人”“这十一个人中间就有七个人倒在地上”，这些数字和一开始的“我一个人跟他们十二个人短兵相接”又存在较大出入。这些看似矛盾的言语，暗指思维的断层。然细观这些数字，层层叠加，前一数字参与了后一数字的心理建构过程，正如福柯尼耶和特纳所说，概念混合的过程可以重复进行，前一次混合的结果可以进入下一次混合的输入空间(2002：279)。由此每一个新数字的产生都是旧数字参与混合的结果，直至达到福斯塔夫想象的极限。虽然是小贵族出身，然而福斯塔夫从没站在正义的一方当过好汉。但在想象中，他可以将自己塑造成英雄的形象，从战胜两个假想敌到与十二人短兵相接的过程中完成了自我英雄形象的建构。为了建构绿林好汉的伟岸形象，福斯塔夫在言语时出现了暂时的混乱，这也可能是因为他的言语对象不同，对绿林好汉的定义和要求各一，导致他面对不同听话者时不得不安排不同的言语，以维护自己的完整的绿林好汉的主体形象。当然福斯塔夫活跃的思维活动并非无人知晓。亲王哈尔绝非愚昧无知，这在第一幕第二场他的独白中清晰可判，“我完全知道你们，现在虽然和你们在一起无聊鬼混，而是我正在效法着太阳，它容忍污浊的浮云遮蔽它的庄严的宝相，然而当它一旦穿破丑恶的雾障，大放光明的时候，人们因为仰望已久，将要格外对它惊奇赞叹”（《莎士比亚历史剧选》，2001：101）。大智若愚的亲王对福斯塔夫的思维了如指掌。为他日后崛起做铺垫的小人物该有的小伎俩或正是他在福斯塔夫身上找到闪光的点。

4 结　语

莎士比亚笔下的大胖子福斯塔夫在伦敦东市的“野猪头酒店”演绎着属于他自己的故事，在这个故事里他是绝对的主角，连声势煊赫的帝王将相都成了他的配角。他出身贵族却流落江湖，他英雄末路却幻想变成大人物，他屡遭讽刺却阿 Q 式地挽回自己的面子。这个穷极无聊的人物身上体现出没落的封建贵族阶级的虚荣心和优越感，因此荣耀的过往标签和山穷水尽的当前境遇产生极大反差时，福斯塔夫选择了想象。在他的想象世界里，他绝不是道德败坏的混蛋，而是有着高贵血统的爵士。在他的想象世界里，他的拦路抢劫是一种无罪且又高尚的职业。在他的想象世界里，他长得仪表堂堂，体格魁梧，有一副愉快的容貌，一双有趣的眼睛和一种非常高贵的神采。在他的想象世界里，荣誉就是一阵空气，而活着是一种更为积极的入世哲学。布鲁姆说，“萨缪尔·约翰逊博士令人感动地认识到，福斯塔夫表现了‘最讨人喜欢的性格，即永远无忧无虑’。约翰逊始终非常需要这一性格，他喜欢把自己描述成福斯塔夫，年老而无忧无虑，有着逐渐衰退又无时不在的活力”（2015：173）。而这活力正是基于孩童般的想象力之上的。福斯塔夫的想象伴随着他对他人的言说和对自我言说的整个过程。福斯塔夫的想象过程是一个以概念混合为基础的思维建构过程。因此对福斯塔夫的诠释和理解不能只停留在文字的表面。解析其想象背后的“混合”机制——身份的混合，时间的混合及从“有”到“无”的混合，能帮助读者跳出“善恶”二元论的框架，展现福斯塔夫“恶”之表象背后的复杂人性。

参考文献

[1] COOK AMY. Staging Nothing: Hamlet and Cognitive Science. Substance, 2006 (2): 83-99.

[2] DAMASIO R ANTONIO. Descartes' Error: Emotion, Reason, and the Human Brain. New York: Avon, 1994.

[3] FAUCONNIER GILLES AND MARK TURNER. The Way We Think: Conceptual Blending and the Mind's Hidden Complexities. New York: Basic Books, 2002.

[4] JOHNSON SAMUEL. Selected Essays from the “Rambler”, “Adventurer”, and “Idler”. New Haven: Yale University Press, 1968.

[5] RICHARDSON ALAN. “Imagination: Literary and Cognitive Intersections” The Oxford Handbook of Cognitive Literary Studies. New York: Oxford University Press, 2015: 225-244.

[6] 布鲁姆. 西方正典：伟大作家和不朽作品. 江宁康，译. 南京：译林出版社，2015.

[7] 陆扬. 死亡美学. 北京：北京大学出版社，2006.

[8] 马克思恩格斯全集：第 29 卷. 北京：人民出版社，1972.

[9] 宁平. 我国近 25 年莎士比亚历史剧研究述评. 辽宁师范大学学报（社会科学版）：2004（6）：86-89.

[10] 莎士比亚. 莎士比亚历史剧选. 朱生豪，译. 北京：人民文学出版社，2001.

[11] 莎士比亚. 莎士比亚悲剧选. 朱生豪，译. 北京：人民文学出版社，2001.

[12] 殷企平. 阐释三境界：外国文学教学的艺术之路. 外国文学，2012（1）：147-154.

[13] 张隆溪. 道与逻各斯. 冯川，译. 南京：江苏教育出版社，2006.

显性情节中的反战叙事和隐性进程中的人性与理性的冲突
——海伦·邓莫尔《围困》中的战争创伤叙事

杨　康　　刘胡敏

【摘要】海伦·邓莫尔的历史小说《围困》（*The Siege*，2001）一发表就获得了英国柑橘文学奖，对这部小说的解读和批评大多关注小说对真实历史的刻画和对战争的控诉。本文通过文本细读，将关注点放在小说中看似微不足道的情节和叙事上，意在揭示小说显性情节下的反战主题背后有一条关于人性与理性冲突的隐性叙事进程，并探讨这条叙事进程如何与显性情节发生作用。作者通过显性情节和隐性进程再现了战争给人们精神世界带来了循环性创伤，本文指出只有直面人性和自我，而不是一味追求理性，才能打破这种循环，治愈创伤，真正走出战争的伤痛。

【关键词】反战叙事；人性冲突；显性情节；隐性进程

0　引　言

英国著名诗人海伦·邓莫尔不仅以诗歌闻名，其创作的小说也颇受好评。她的历史小说《围困》一经发表，就获得了英国柑橘文学奖，并迅速进入英国畅销书的榜单前列。这部小说主要讲述了列

基金项目：本文系国家社科基金项目“新世纪英国战争小说创伤叙事和伦理反思研究”（19BWW076）的阶段性成果。

作者简介：杨康，男，广东外语外贸大学英文学院硕士研究生；
刘胡敏，女，广东外语外贸大学英文学院教授，博导，主要从事英美文学、创伤文学和希腊罗马神话研究。

宁格勒围困战中，安娜及其家人在困境中求生的故事。在小说的显性情节中，作者表达了对战争的控诉，流露出对主人公安娜坚韧、冷静、勇敢等品质的赞扬。然而，小说中还存在与反战主题无甚关联的一些情节和叙述，如安娜对已逝母亲的怀念、安娜父亲与情妇的故事、苏联政府的极权统治等，这些看似与主题无关的叙事是小说的另一条隐性叙事进程。这条隐性叙事进程聚焦个人在极端环境下的脆弱和无力，刻画个人在极端环境下的挣扎和抗争，凸显人性和理性之间的冲突，展现了个人内心世界所遭受的创伤，整体上和显性情节起到互为补充、相互照应的作用。也只有把握了这条隐性进程，才能避免对小说的单一解读，全面把握《围困》这部小说的文学张力，全面理解潜藏在小说表层下的创伤叙事。

1　冲破城市和精神的双重“围困”：显性情节中的反战主题

作为一部具有浓厚反战色彩的历史小说，《围困》并没有把笔墨放在战场的血腥和残酷上，而是用冷静客观的笔调刻画了列宁格勒围困战中普通人所面临的求生困境、伦理困境、精神危机和创伤体验，表现了战争的残酷和破坏性，凸显了反战的主题。这部作品总体可以分为三个部分。第一部分主要描述战前安娜一家在母亲死后的生活日常。第二部分是小说的主体部分，描写了战争突然爆发后安娜一家以及城内的居民所面临的种种生存危机。第三部分叙述了在城内居民大批死亡后，物资供给不再紧张，活下来的人们有了生存的希望，而战争的阴霾似乎即将过去。本文将按照这三个部分，对显性情节所反映的反战和隐性进程表现中人性与理性冲突的相互作用进行探讨。小说的标题是“围困”，这一标题本身有着特殊的语境和丰富的含义。放在具体的战争背景下，这一标题显然指的是围困战中被封锁的列宁格勒以及城中的居民所面临的生存资源匮乏和与世隔绝的困境。在这样的物资封锁中，人们为了生存只能各自为营，在怀疑和猜忌中一步步走向自我孤立和自我隔绝，人与人之间的联系被切断，原本物质层面的围困也逐渐变成了精神层面的围困，战争的恐怖在其对人性的摧毁和破坏中得到了进一步的体现，显性情节下的反战主题也因此得到了强化。

1941年，德国单方面撕毁了和苏联的互不侵犯协议，对列宁格勒进行了长达900多天的封锁，城中居民面临着物资不足和信息隔绝的生存困境，小说正是设置在这样的历史背景之下，主要讲述安娜及其一家人是如何在这样的环境下想方设法获取生存资源的。封锁初期，安娜的父亲自愿参军，安娜则在父亲好友玛丽安的帮助下，照顾尚未成年的弟弟。有了玛丽安带来的各种物资和钱财，三人能够勉强生存。然而随着战事加剧，列宁格勒被进一步封锁，城中物资供应更加紧张，安娜的父亲也因意外受伤被遣返回家，安娜不得不采取各种非常手段获取必要的生存资源，如冒着被空袭轰炸的危险到城外挖菜、在空袭烧毁的房子里寻找物资以及把父亲珍贵的藏书作为燃料取暖等。在没有尽头的封锁中，生存变成了生活的全部目标和意义，人们在物质意义上的围困中陷入了生存的困境。

在求生动力的驱使下，人与人之间的信任也逐渐崩塌，城市的“围困”变成了精神上的“围困”。当物资紧缺到一定程度时，城内的生存似乎已经成了一种零和博弈，猜忌和怀疑也随之而来，不管是排队领取物资时小心翼翼生怕有人抢走自己的物资卡，还是走在回家路上提心吊胆，害怕有人搭话询问，这些警惕旁人的行为说明人们在敌军封锁期间形成了各自围困的精神孤岛，敌人已经不仅仅是纳粹的士兵和军队，周围互相抢夺生存资源的普通人也成了潜在的敌人。曾经的朋友、邻居甚至是亲人，似乎都在这场生存的零和博弈中成了自己的对手，生存的压力将人们割裂开来。然而人们内心深处又害怕这种分裂，因为他们生存下去的最大信心，恰恰来自他们对人与人之间联结的依赖：他们始终坚信，城外的政府和人民没有抛弃城内坚守着的人们，这一点也是他们赖以生存下去的最后一丝希望。可是当城内人互相警惕和自我隔绝的时候，这种信仰也失去了存在的根基，城内的人们也因此生存在一种精神围困的矛盾当中，矛盾的一端是对生存的渴望和人性的抛弃，另一端却是对他人的依赖和共存的信念，物质上的封锁逐渐转变成精神世界的围困。作者对城市被“围困”以及居民精神被“围困”的描写也构成了小说的显性情节，这一条显性情节揭示了战争的残酷，表达了作者强烈的反战情绪。

在这种精神围困中，城中的人们也不得不面临各种各样艰难的伦理选择。安娜看到邻居的孩子营养不良，纠结是否应将自己的物资补给分给他们。如果分了，家人的营养得不到保障，弟弟本就瘦弱，很可能因营养不良而生病；但如果不分，邻居的孩子可能因为营养不良死去，而且本就孱弱的邻居也很有可能支撑不住随孩子而去。安娜的父亲也同样面临着生死的抉择，如果他活着，一副病体的他只是这个家庭生存的负担，但如果他死了，无疑会给失去母亲的安娜和卡雅带来又一次巨大的精神打击。守城的指挥官也不得不在两难中决定城内物资补给的份额，如果他选择削减本就低于生存线的补给份额，就相当于通过居民的死亡来缓解物资的紧张。但如果他不减少份额，本就不足的物资也难以维持，结果还是会有很多居民因此活活饿死，居民死去只是早晚的问题而已。作为一个守城的指挥官，他有最大限度优化资源配置的责任，但作为一个尚有良知的普通人，他却要受到杀人所带来的良心拷问。这种进退维谷的艰难选择，是小说中几乎人人都要面对的困境。正如小说最后提到的，“人人不提，但人人都心知肚明，他们的生存是以其他人的死亡为代价的”，（170）[①]当生存变成一种零和博弈的时候，这样的选择便难以避免。这种人与人之间的对立和割裂，这种个人即为孤岛的精神状态，恰恰是“围困”二字的最好注脚，是对残酷的战争最有力的控诉和谴责，反战的主题也在对这种精神围困的刻画中得以彰显。

但是小说没有简单停留在对这种双重围困的刻画，更着力展示了人们最终冲破围困的努力：安娜和其他女工共同劳作，相互扶持，彼此信赖；安德鲁伊和安娜在生存困境的考验之下反而建立了深厚的感情。即使是陷入生存“零和博弈”的城中居民，也始终有着自

① 文中只标注页码的引文均引自 *The Siege*，引文均为本文作者自译。

己不可逾越的底线，即使他们对生有着强烈的渴望，也不会为了生存而选择投降，反而是竭尽所能地反抗。他们着力修建战壕，为可能的强行攻城做迎战的准备，更在城内埋下各种陷阱和地雷，这样即使列宁格勒被占领，也能在最后关头给予敌人一次“自杀式”的打击。如果说城市和精神的双重围困源自个人对生存的追求和生存资源困乏的矛盾，那能让人们冲破这种围困的不仅有人们内心深处对人与人之间联结的信任和重建，更有人们心中视死如归的抵抗和牺牲精神，这种内在的坚守和信仰让城中的居民在绝望的处境中也没有放弃对未来的希望。因而在小说的显性情节中，战争的残酷无情反而凸显了人们的坚韧与顽强。小说不仅仅是对战争进行控诉，更着力于展现人们内心世界的挣扎与抗争。外在世界的无情和内在世界的坚守形成了一种对比，在凸显战争残酷的同时，也流露出对人性光辉的讴歌与赞美，小说的反战思想因而有了更深的层次。

2　理性背后的创伤：隐性进程中的创伤叙事

然而，仅仅用“冲破围困”的反战思想来解读《围困》这部小说是远远不够的。如果说这部作品近乎冷酷的冷静笔调可以看作作者为了客观地反映战争而有意为之，那么其他一些看似细枝末节的无关情节则很难用这一理由加以解读。不管是小说中字里行间对地理环境差异的强调，还是对安娜追梦失败和无奈的叙述，抑或是对父亲郁郁不得志的刻画，这些似乎都和反战的主题没有很强的关联性。这说明，在反战主题之下，小说还存在一股与之并行甚至先行于这一主题的叙事动力，只有找出这种动力，才能把这些看似无关的情节统一在一起，更为全面地把握小说的叙事动力，挖掘作者的创作意图。

针对这种显性情节下隐藏的叙事动力，申丹教授提出了“隐性进程”的概念。她指出，“在不少叙事作品中，存在双重叙事进程，一个是情节运动，也就是批评家们迄今所关注的对象；另一个则隐蔽在情节发展后面，与情节进程呈现出不同甚至相反的走向，在主题意义上与情节发展上形成一种补充性或颠覆性的关系”（申丹，2013），而这种隐藏在显性情节背后的叙事运动就是叙事的隐性进程。

通过文本细读可以发现，在反战主题情节发展的背后的确存在一股先于这一主题的隐性叙事进程：从父亲与其情妇被时代抛弃的痛苦和无奈，到安娜母亲死于产后并发症，小说中的人物经历了种种难以预料、不可控制的事情，他们的命运似乎被一种神秘而不可控的力量所控制，而战争则是这一系列随机事件中最令人痛苦的。在这条隐性进程中，值得关注的不仅仅是战争本身，而是在种种极端的环境和际遇之中人们内心世界所发生的改变，以及这种改变背后的精神创伤。在小说的显性情节中，读者能看到人物内心中的坚守，在隐性进程中，人们的精神世界却经历了人性和理性的冲突，遭受了失语的创伤。在战争的影响下，人们被迫选择了一种近乎冷漠的理性，人的本性受到了压抑，这种压抑和冲突带来的创伤构成了隐性进程中创伤叙事的主要动力。

正如聂珍钊所说，理性是“人在特定环境中的正确认知和价值判断”（聂珍钊，2014：252），理性的选择看似是人自主做出的抉择，但抉择的理性与否在根本上却依赖于“特定环境”，而人性却是“人作为人而非兽存在的本质属性”（聂珍钊，2014：271），是人本身的一种属性。也正是因为理性实际上在很大程度上受到环境的制约，而人性却是人自身的一种特质，理性也必然会在某种特定情形中和人性及人的本能产生矛盾，而这种矛盾恰恰就是安娜和安娜母亲理性显得“冷漠”的原因：她们极力克制自己心中痛苦、恐惧、不满等各种消极的情绪，压抑自己近乎本能的冲动，时刻保持客观和冷静，并根据她们所处的情形做出她们认为正确的选择。这种压抑和克制在某种程度上促成了精神的麻木与失语，带来了潜藏在理性下的创伤。

从隐性进程的角度来看，“围困”这一标题就已经暗示了造成失语性创伤的原因。这里的“围困”并非仅仅指战争背景下个人所面临的精神孤岛的困境，更是指个人在各种极端环境和非常境遇下的孤独无助和脆弱无力的状态。在这种状态下，周围环境的压力似乎形成了一种包围和吞噬的暗流，将个人裹挟在不可控制的困境之中。

“围困”因而营造了一种对比的关系：个人处于一种被孤立包围的状态，这种状态下人是渺小和无力的，个人的选择在很大程度上被抑制，而能够生存在这种极端环境中的人也往往有一种近乎冷漠的理性，然而这种理性是以自我沉默和自我失语的精神创伤为代价的，这一点在小说的主要人物身上得到了印证。

小说的开头主要讲述了战前安娜一家的生活。从反战主题的角度来看，这些内容似乎可有可无。但如果从隐性进程的角度进行考量，小说开头的内容实际上已经为全书奠定了冷峻、客观的基调，并揭示了贯穿小说始终的创伤叙事动力。与一般文学作品中的母亲形象不同，安娜的母亲首先是一名冷静沉着、思维缜密的学者，其次才是一位负责、理智的母亲。在工作中，她的严谨认真受到了同事们的一致好评，对客观事实的强调和对实证方法的重视也让她在医学科研事业如鱼得水。这份理性不仅仅停留在工作中，更延伸到了她的日常生活之中。即使是在照顾自己的女儿时，她也时常用一种带着疏离的温情来应对女儿的诉求，用一种进行科学研究的方法态度来处理和他人的亲密关系。甚至到了她生产大出血、生死攸关之际，她也能十分冷静地按铃呼叫护士，用冷静客观的语调报告自己的情况，“以免吓到护士”（8）。可以看到，理性在某种程度上已经抑制了安娜母亲正常的情绪表达，而这种理性也并非全然出自她个人的抉择，她的工作、社会对女性的规训，包括丈夫潜在的不忠行为，都对她产生了巨大的影响。她并非天生理性，而是“不得不”用理性去应对生活的一切。

然而这种理性的背后实际是创伤应激障碍的一个重要症状。赫尔曼提到，“有时逃脱不掉的危险处境可能引发的不只是恐怖和愤怒，吊诡的是，也可能出现超然的冷静状态，此时恐怖、愤怒和痛苦都消散不见了，事件还在不断进入意识中，但宛如已和它正常的意义脱钩了”（Herman，1992；31）。这说明，小说许多人物身上所体现的理性实际上不仅仅是一种被迫选择，更是一种精神上的麻木和精神创伤的体现。在这种精神状态下，真实的情感表达被麻木的理性压抑，个人也因而陷入一种精神失语的困境之中。在这种麻木和失语中，战争与死亡似乎变成了日常，人们也似乎逐渐“习惯了”这种生活，一切都显得“正常”起来（31）。

这种“被迫理性”和创伤应激障碍所带来的麻木在安娜身上体现得更为明显。母亲的去世和父亲的消沉深深影响了安娜，使她被迫成熟，原本极度依赖母亲的她现在只能在睡梦中重回母亲的臂弯。当她醒来，她必须承担起照顾弟弟和父亲的责任。有着绘画天赋的她似乎也失去了对生活中美的敏感，对现在的她来说鲜花的价值远远不及院子里种的土豆，因为这些蔬菜才能提供弟弟成长所必需的“营养和维生素”（2）。即使当父亲为了鼓励她，安排她去给曾经的名演员画肖像，她也仅仅沉浸在短暂的喜悦中。即使当她用一个艺术家特有的细腻和感性去照顾托儿所的孩子时，也会被批评过于“感情用事”（16）。丝毫不在意孩子的感受、只懂得套用教育理论的院长对她颐指气使。适合照顾孩子的安娜只能做一名临时工，适应政治环境的院长却能如鱼得水。可以说，安娜的生活从来没有掌握在她自己手中，她的一切都是特定环境下无奈的选择，家庭的不幸和社会的腐败完全压抑了她所谓的个人意志，而她能够生存下来也恰恰因为她继承了母亲的性格，由感性被迫走向了近乎冷漠的理性。即使她内心深处仍然有着对浪漫和温情的渴望，现实的重担却早已经剥夺了她选择和表达的权利，她也因此和母亲一样被迫陷入了精神麻木和精神失语的创伤之中。

从反战的显性情节来看，小说开头部分人物的相关经历似乎并不能体现小说的主旨思想，但实际上这一部分已经为全书奠定了一个压抑、肃穆的基调和氛围，这与后面对战争期间城中居民在困境中苦苦挣扎的痛苦生活实际上也有着共通之处，这一共通之处在隐性叙事进程下则更加明显。从创伤叙事的角度来看，安娜与其母亲在人性和理性的冲突中走向冷漠理性的过程实际上是一个精神世界被隔绝、被失语的过程，这一过程实际在某种程度上剥夺了她们表达自我情感诉求的本性，她们的理性实际上是创伤应激障碍的体现。

在隐性叙事动力之下的创伤叙事中，小说开头也并非与后文割裂，而是与其一脉相承，共同展示了个人与环境之间的关系、人受环境影响所发生的改变和被迫做出的抉择、这种抉择中被压抑的人性和情感以及这种压抑所带来的精神创伤。正如作者在采访中所说，小说并非为了“回顾历史”，而是试图展现人们在这样特殊的历史环境下复杂且不断变化的“内在世界”（McCrum，2021），揭示战争背景下个人在人性和理性之间的痛苦抉择。因此，在小说的开头部分，小说反战主题下的显性情节似乎还未完全运作，小说的隐性叙事动力就已经先行于这一显性情节开始发挥作用，暗示了小说另一个潜藏的主题：残酷的战争中人性和理性的冲突以及这种冲突所带来的失语性创伤。

3 理性和人性的冲突：小说的双重叙事进程

小说主体部分的笔墨主要放在战事突然爆发后城中被围困居民的求生经历和困境。结合前文的论述不难发现，这一部分的隐性进程和显性情节实际上呈现出两种相反的走向。显性情节中，人们在战争所带来的困境中艰难求生，最终冲破了城市和精神的双重围困，小说从战争所带来的绝望走向了重生的希望。但在隐性进程中，生存却是以被迫选择理性及其所带来失语的精神创伤为代价的。人们冲破围困的时刻，恰恰是这种精神麻木和精神失语最为严重的时候。小说在对未来的希望中结尾，希望之下却隐藏着战争所带来的难于言说的精神创伤。

小说开头的部分为展开营造了一个“山雨欲来风满楼”的压抑氛围，虽然安娜会用“我们和德国之间存在协议”（21）这件事来安慰自己，相信战争不会爆发，但是许多人都隐隐地感到了战争的逼近，并用诸如“情势”“近况”（21）等语焉不详的措辞来隐藏自己对战事的恐惧，而战争也的确在民众惶惶不安的情绪中突然爆发了。从显性情节来看，这是为了用民众内心没有言说的恐惧来渲染战事的恐怖和残酷，而从隐性进程来看，这种言语上的逃避实际上也是某种程度的失语，是过去战争所带来的精神创伤的体现，而这种失语也在安娜父亲身上得到了最好的体现。安娜父亲是一位十分有才华的作家，他曾经也大受欢迎，但现在他所创作的故事因为不够“社会主义”、不够“积极向上”而失去了发表的机会，就连作家协会的成员也直接指出，时代已经变了，“作家也要做出相应的调整”（3）。然而安娜的父亲不肯屈从于大环境，固执地遵循之前创作的准则，写出来的作品既没有得到同僚的认可，也没有受到大众的欢迎，甚至连自己的女儿都直言不喜欢他的故事，他也只能将自己的作品束之高阁，不再试图去发表自己的作品。而细读他的故事不难发现，他的作品中最重要的就是对过去战争经历的隐喻式再现，“冬天将军和饥饿将军的争辩”表现了战争的残酷，并说明战争不仅摧残人的肉体，更能在对肉体的折磨中逐渐摧毁人的精神，也正是这种对战争的恐惧让他在列宁格勒封锁初期忍不住对着图库佐夫的雕像祈祷，祈求像他这样的英雄能够再度出现，“拯救人们于水火之中”（29）。社会大环境对这种故事的否定实际上说明不仅仅个人会主动选择逃避和失语来应对创伤，整个社会意识其实都在逃避战争历史、主动失语。民众告诉自己不该沉溺于过去，而是应该着眼当下，全身心地投入社会的建设，人们的这种“理性”也是一种对自身表达和精神诉求的压抑。然而，不管是过去战争经历所带来的精神创伤，还是这种选择性“失语”所带来的创伤，在战争可能爆发的时候，又不可避免地被重新唤醒，人们心中恐惧的不仅仅是即将到来的战争，更是过去战争历史留下的伤痛与折磨。对创伤的逃避、对创伤重现的恐惧以及人性和理性冲突所带来的精神性失语，构成了隐性进程中重要的创伤叙事动力。

在围困战的初期，安娜及许多居民被强制征募去修建防御工事，他们没有像样的工具，没有足够的食物，他们中的许多人甚至是“不知道战争为何物的孩童”（40）。卡蒂亚也是小说中为数不多的直接丧命于战争炮火之下的人物之一。在战争爆发前，她本是学校的优等生、“温室里的花朵”，过着平静安稳的生活。而当战争爆发，她被送来修建工事，天真的她似乎意识到了战争的可怕，但她的心态却仍旧停留在从前的生活。当许多人尝试去适应围困之下的生活，对这种劳作“习以为常”的时候，卡蒂亚却说出了“有人会因为我的学习成绩，因为我读博的理想，甚至因为我定做的漂亮裙子杀了我”（32）。这样看似荒唐不已的话也反映出她害怕的不是战争本身，而是被战争剥夺的生活和逝去的过往。最后她被空袭中倒塌的房屋砸中，当场丧命。从反战的主题来看，她的死亡说明了战争的残酷和恐怖，战争能够在极短的时间里给社会带来巨大的破坏，对人的精神造成极大的摧残。而从隐性进程来看，卡蒂亚的死亡并非全然是一个悲剧，她对过去的沉溺也可以看作她对自我情感最直接、最本能的追求和表达。从这一角度来看，没有像其他人一样强迫自己保持冷静理性的卡蒂亚反而做到了精神上的某种自由。尽管这种自由以逃避甚至死亡为代价，但她的死亡意味着她在精神世界中得到了发声的权利和自由，她不像其他人一样强迫自己适应战争所带来的剧变，更从未压抑自己真实的情感诉求和表达。她的死亡实际上是自我的一种选择，这一点也和卡蒂亚临死前露出“天真的微笑”形成了呼应（48）。对卡蒂亚来说，要生存意味着选择压抑自我情感的理性和精神失语的创伤，死亡反而是精神和身体的真正自由。

而恪守理性的伊芙根尼亚则和脆弱的卡蒂亚形成了鲜明的对比。与其他人不同，伊芙似乎完全不需要适应的过程就能应对战争带来的困境。面对指挥官的呵斥和刁难，她不卑不亢；在挖壕沟的时候，她卖力地工作；当休息的时候，她也不会去操心战争，而是抓紧休息的时间。似乎无论处于什么样的环境，她都会努力适应，泰然处之。甚至当人们因担心空袭而骚动时，也是她站出来宽慰所有人“只要你有好的心态，就能应对不知道什么时候会来的空袭”（148）。正是她的这份从容和镇定让人们短暂地平息了下来，也正是这份冷静和镇定、这种主动适应环境的心态和能力，增加了伊芙生存的概率。从显性情节来看，伊芙身上所体现的理性是人们冲破双重围困必需的选择。但从隐形进程来看，伊芙的这种理性是以隐藏自己内心真实的恐惧、不安和无助为前提，强行让自己适应环境的抉择。她越显得理性和冷静，内心的情感遭受到的压抑和克制就越强，失语性精神创伤和创伤应激障碍所带来的精神麻木也就越来越严重，这也是为什么看起来坚强冷静，甚至有些冷酷的伊芙会在安娜面前控制不住自己的情绪，“痛快地哭一场”，然后安慰自己“一切都会好起来的”。精神的麻木和失语只是一种对创伤经历的逃避，并不能真正治愈创伤，因而在合适的契机之下，这种被压抑的情感就会自然而然地爆发。与安娜和安娜母亲一样，在选择理性的同时，伊芙也经历了失语性的精神创伤。

随着战事推进，围困战进入胶着阶段，德国军队通过交通封锁和空袭轰炸的方式试图彻底摧毁列宁格勒。在物资极度匮乏的情况下，守城指挥官在处理补给分配份额的问题时陷入了两难：一方面，削减份额实际上是以支撑不下去的部分人的生命换取另一部分人生存的希望，相当于变相杀人；另一方面，增加份额则意味着如果封锁没有被打破，全城的人都会死掉，这无疑是一种极大的冒险。在反战的显性情节中，这一伦理两难显然是战争所导致的结果。而从隐性进程来看，这一抉择本身反映了作者对人性和理性冲突的思考，这一点在指挥官处事的方法和态度中更为明显。在这种极端的情况下，无论指挥官做出什么决定都可能会造成灾难性的后果，不论是城中人们大批死亡，还是周围同事对他的指责，抑或战争结束后政府可能对他进行的审判，都是他将来可能面对的问题。然而当他下令削减补给份额时，他却清楚地明白他“不得不”这么做（50），他的选择从来不是源于自己的意志，而是种种外在因素决定的结果。正是因为明白这一点，明白自己所处的被动位置，他才会始终强调“数据”的重要，不管是各种物资的数量，还是人员的伤亡，在他的眼中都只是用以决策参考的信息而已。在显性情节中，指挥官的进退两难是战争直接导致的。在隐性进程中，这样抉择却体现了理性和人性的碰撞，选择理性而压抑人性的指挥官在同僚眼中显得“没有人的情感”（151），但实际上一切都是不得已为之，人性的本能让他在被迫做出杀人的抉择时心怀愧疚和不安，而对环境的认知和判断却让他不得不放下这种情绪，做出理性的抉择。活生生的人也在这种人性和理性的冲突中变成了可以计算的数字，本该有着自主意识和情感的人在环境的压力和近乎冷漠的实事求是中逐渐异化。指挥官也强忍内心的挣扎，在其他人面前始终保持客观和冷静，从未在其他人面前将自己真实的情感宣之于口。在这种精神压抑之下，他也同样经历了失语性的精神创伤，战争也正是通过这种伦理困境给人们的精神世界带来了巨大的折磨和苦痛。

到了围困战的后期，这种人性和理性的交锋也更加明显和残酷。当父亲因为伤痛和营养不良死去后，碍于人力紧张和极度严寒不便出门的天气，他的尸体不能火化。与沉湎于伤痛的玛丽安不同，安娜在面对父亲的死亡时，第一时间出现的却并非伤心和不舍，而是她埋藏在心底近乎算计的考量：幸亏父亲死在月初统计生存人口之后，这样安娜家还可以多领一个人的补给份额来保证她弟弟的营养。这也是为什么当安德鲁伊问安娜自己死去后，安娜是否会像玛丽安陪着她父亲那样陪着自己，安娜的第一反应是否定的。在安娜看来，人死之后只是一团没有意义的“冻肉”（159）罢了，生者更应该关注当下的事情。这样近乎冷漠的理性继承自安娜的母亲，但是也离不开环境的影响和塑造。从显性情节来看，这是战争对人性的摧残，对生存的渴望压倒了人与人之间情感的联系。但从隐性进程来看，恰恰是这份冷漠的理性和对环境的适应能力让安娜能够在困境下幸存，也是这份理性让她更加痛苦。不管是她在睡梦中对逝去母亲的追忆，还是她将自己的补给分给邻居，抑或是她想方设法照顾好尚不懂事的弟弟，都说明安娜在秉承绝对理性的同时，也从来没有放弃过她本性中善的那一部分，而她所谓的理性也是以抑制自己真实情感为前提的。因此随着封锁的延长，人性和理性的冲突会始终存在，而为了生存走向冷漠理性所带来的精神失语性的创伤也会一直存在。

小说结尾部分是围困战的后期，这一部分反战思想表达的力度有所减弱，并和隐性进程产生了一定的冲突。在列宁格勒封锁中，尽管有大批人死去，幸存下来的人心中却有了生的希望。尽管封锁并没有解除，但是现有的物资补给已经能保证城中的幸存者起码不会死于饥饿。只是所有人都心知肚明，他们的生存是以其他人的死亡为代价的。然而结尾的部分对这一点并没有过多强调，而是似乎在尽力渲染一种充满希望的氛围：安娜及其一家在劫后余生的释然中散步，安娜的弟弟也找到了玩伴，伊芙干劲十足地在小园子里松土种菜，就连曾经醉心政治斗争的邻居也对出身知识分子家庭的安娜改变了看法。战争虽然没有过去，但人们已经熬过了最难的那一个寒冬，所有人带着希望努力地生活着。从这一点看，小说显性情节中的反战思想完成了从绝望始、以希望终的过程。

然而，从隐性进程来看，重要的不是人们重拾希望应对困境，而是幸存者本身对待困境采取的态度。从这一点来看，战争虽然很快就会结束，人们所经历的精神创伤实际上并没有消失。在小说结尾部分，有一个场景颇值得读者关注与思考：一群男人走过伊芙的院子，看见她在卖力地松土和播种，并被她身上所流露的生命力和韧性所吸引，不禁看呆了。他们觉得，像这样的女人，“看起来似乎能够永远这样劳作下去”（175）。尽管这一段描写只是一带而过，显得不那么重要，但实际上有重要的特殊含义。通过比较可以发现，作者在结尾部分重点描述的幸存者都是在封锁战中努力求生、保持理性和从不放弃的人，而那些沉湎于过去、不愿意做出改变的人，比如卡蒂亚、玛丽安和安娜的父亲，都因不能应环境的变化做出理性的选择而死去。这也说明，这种生存的希望并没有冲淡战争对人们精神世界的影响，生存下来的人已经习惯用这种近乎冷漠的理性去应对普通的生活，被压抑的情感和精神麻木的状态实际上是创伤应激障碍的持续，这种精神失语性的创伤也会伴随这种“理性”的生活方式一直存在。

小说结尾处所展现的希望背后，更是隐藏着创伤伤痛再度复发的因子，这一点在小说最后一句话的隐性叙事进程中得到了印证：当有人看见安娜、安娜恋人和安娜弟弟在一起散步时，还以为他们是一家三口，但“他们不是，当然不是”（176）。从显性情节来看，这句话显得稍显突兀。但从隐性进程来看，这句话别有深意。这三个人能在一起生活只是环境和一系列机遇共同作用的结果，很大程度上也是获取生存资源和维持生存所做出的理性抉择，他们之间的关系当然也可能随着环境的变化而发生改变，所以他们“当然不是”一家三口。这一点在围困系列的第二本小说《背叛》也得到了印证：

在冷战时期，安娜一家在不得已的情况下被卷入了政治斗争，猜忌、试探和背叛不仅让他们身陷危险之中，也让他们在战争中建立起来的感情和联系受到了挑战和动摇，他们很有可能因为充满斗争的政治环境“不再是”一家人，人性、理性、真实和谎言的碰撞也预示着失语性创伤的重现。因此，《围困》小说的最后一句话非但不突兀，反而延续了全文的隐性进程，成为一条隐性的叙事线索，将这股叙事动力引向了它的续作，人性和理性也将陷入新的矛盾和斗争之中。把小说的开头和结尾联系起来看，不难发现，小说中的创伤叙事实际上是处在一个循环的过程之中：潜藏—唤醒—复现—潜藏，创伤也远远没有结束，下一个新的循环也即将到来。

4 结 语

与传统的战争创伤叙事不同，《围困》并没有将重点放在战场的血腥和暴力，也没有试图再现宏大的战争场面，而是更加关注战争背景下个人内心世界所经历的苦痛与挣扎，小说看似平淡的叙事背后恰恰是对个人精神世界变化的真实再现。《围困》中的战争创伤叙事通过显性情节和隐性进程中展现了丰富的文学张力，两条叙事进程也呈现出相互补充又相互冲突的关系。显性情节中，战争的残酷突出了环境对人的巨大影响，而人们最后也冲破了城市和精神的双重围困，经历了一个从绝望走向希望的过程。而在隐性进程中，人们的精神世界所遭遇的打击和创伤并没有随着战争的结束而消失。战争让人们被迫面对人性和理性的冲突，这种冲突所带来的创伤可能随着战争的结束潜藏起来，却又会在新的战争到来之时被重新唤醒，陷入一个新的循环之中，小说的开头和结尾之间的呼应也印证了这种战争创伤的循环，《围困》的战争创伤叙事也在这种循环中有了更深刻的意义。正如刘胡敏（2020）所说，“战争的创伤不是经历过战争和士兵的‘专利’”，在战争创伤的循环和复现中，即使是没有经历过战争的普通人同样会在创伤经历的“移植”中经历创伤的苦痛。只有直面创伤，直面内心，而不是一味地选择“理性”，才能打破这种循环，真正地治愈创伤，走出战争的伤痛。

参考文献

[1] HELEN DUNMORE. London: Penguin, 2001.

[2] JUDITH HERMAN. Trauma and Recovery. New York: Basic Books, 1992.

[3] ROBERT MCCRUM. “The Siege is a novel for now”—— Helen Dunmore talks about fact, fiction and the contemporary in the historical. https: //www. theguardian. com/books/2001/jun/10/fiction. [2021-02-28].

[4] 聂珍钊. 文学伦理学批评导论. 北京：北京大学出版社，2014.

[5] 刘胡敏. 论帕特·巴克战争小说中的创伤书写. 当代外国文学，2020（2）：48-54.

[6] 申丹. 何为叙事的“隐性进程”?如何发现这股叙事暗流?. 外国文学研究，2013（5）：47-53.

无法抹去的民族创伤记忆
——《纳粹军官的犹太妻子》中犹太身份的背弃与建构

周 雅　刘胡敏

【摘要】《纳粹军官的犹太妻子》是英国犹太作家伊迪斯·汉恩·比尔关于自己在犹太大屠杀期间惨痛经历的自传。回忆录主要讲述了大屠杀期间比尔为躲避纳粹迫害，伪造身份嫁给纳粹军官的故事。同时，叙述中暗藏了一条犹太人的民族身份认同感由弱到强的完整线索。第二次世界大战爆发前，许多欧洲犹太人受同化主义影响，对犹太文化了解甚少。二战后，战争年代的犹太民族似乎在集体创伤记忆中找到了民族身份的联结，重拾了对民族身份的认同感。这部自传是20世纪犹太人对民族身份由背弃至回归的缩影，作者通过讲述自己在二战期间的真实经历展现了大屠杀给犹太民族带来的精神和肉体的双重创伤，同时通过二战前后犹太身份认同感强弱的对比揭示了创伤记忆之于犹太身份重构的意义。

【关键词】大屠杀；创伤记忆；身份；背弃；建构

基金项目：本文系国家社科基金项目“新世纪英国战争小说创伤叙事和伦理反思研究”（19BWW076）的阶段性成果。

作者简介：周雅，女，广东外语外贸大学硕士研究生，主要从事英美文学和现当代文学研究；
刘胡敏，女，广东外语外贸大学英文学院教授、博导，主要从事英美文学、创伤文学和希腊罗马神话研究。

0 引 言

英国犹太作家伊迪丝·汉恩·比尔 1914 年出生于奥地利维也纳，并在那儿度过了愉快的青年时期。随着二战爆发，德国纳粹发动了惨无人道的种族清洗运动，比尔美好的青年生涯就此结束。纳粹剥夺犹太人的财产，捣毁犹太教堂，强迫犹太人参与奴役劳动。1941 年，比尔被迫前往德国北部的劳动营劳动，1942 年她被遣返维也纳，并借助雅利安朋友玛格丽特·但纳的身份前往慕尼黑，开始了自己的“潜艇”（U-Boat）生涯。在慕尼黑比尔遇到了德国军官维纳·弗特，在向后者坦白自己的真实身份后，两人结婚，并生下一个女儿。二战结束后，比尔选择重申自己的犹太人身份，并与维纳离婚。晚年时，在女儿的催促下，比尔根据自己在大屠杀时期的亲身经历写了这本回忆录《纳粹军官的犹太妻子》。这本回忆录所记录的不仅是二战期间比尔个人的创伤经历，她的创伤经历也是大屠杀给整个犹太民族造成的集体创伤记忆的缩影和代表。大屠杀期间，比尔为了生存被迫隐藏自己的犹太身份，战后又选择恢复原来的身份。她对身份的困惑体现了转型时期犹太人共同的身份困惑。本文将结合二战期间的历史背景，通过文本细读剖析犹太人在大屠杀前后对民族身份认同感的变化，揭示大屠杀给犹太民族带来的巨大的肉体和精神创伤，以及创伤记忆对犹太身份重构的意义。

1 同化之殇——解放时期犹太身份的背弃

《纳粹军官的犹太妻子》的前三章主要聚焦于纳粹发动大屠杀前比尔在维也纳的青年生活。少年时期的比尔过着无忧无虑的生活，“在维也纳上小学的时候，我觉得整个世界都来到这个城市。我坐在阳光明媚的咖啡馆，喝咖啡、吃蛋糕，享受无与伦比的交谈”（比尔等，1999：17）。比尔的父母恩爱，两人从不争吵，一家人过着和睦的家庭生活。比尔一家的幸福生活是当时犹太人深度参与西方世俗社会的缩影，然而犹太人为了获得这种幸福生活所付出的代价却是背弃自己的文化。在描述自己的青年时代时，比尔常会提到“同化”这个词，甚至称自己为“彻底同化的维也纳犹太人”（27）[①]。比尔出生于1914年，而19世纪至20世纪初在犹太历史上被称为“解放时代”（李晔梦，2017：138），同化思潮席卷犹太人生活的每个城市，维也纳在当时是犹太人参与德国文化并引领其发展的城市象征。根据米尔顿·戈登（Milton Gordon）在《美国生活中的同化》中对“同化”所下的定义，他认为“同化”是一个连续的过程，第一步就是文化适应，即少数群体对主流文化价值观的吸纳（戈登，2015：189-191）。当时的维也纳是犹太人高度同化，融入德国社会生活的典型城市，在维也纳，犹太人不仅是文化的消费者，也是文化的制造者。历史学家汉斯·康（Hans Kohn）曾说：“世纪之交的维也纳，大部分知识分子都是犹太人。”（Rozenblit，1984：2）犹太人抱着极大的热情参与社会文化建构，融入社会生活。比尔在回忆那段暴风雨前的平静时也一反该书惯有的灰色语调，热情洋溢地赞美自己的同胞对于西方文化的贡献：“我们有的是才智和时尚。我们的城市是高雅的‘多瑙河的女王’‘红色维也纳’，我们拥有社会福利和工人住房政策，弗洛伊德、赫茨尔、马勒等天才在这里酝酿、迸发他们的灵感，创造心理分析学、锡安主义、社会主义、改革、复兴。他们在这里绽放光芒，照彻全世界。”（27）二战爆发前的近半个世纪是犹太人高度同化、为城市贡献智慧的缩影，不仅文人名流走出封闭的宗教圈，许多普通人也开始接受西方理性的启蒙，融入外界世俗文化。

比尔的青年生活同样备受同化主义的影响，她几乎不曾有机会学习犹太文化。比尔成长于一个犹太文化氛围并不深厚的家庭，她父亲开的餐馆不遵循犹太规则，家里的规矩也是如此。1928年，由于通货膨胀，父亲卖掉了餐馆，替曾经的雇主管理本地唯一一家守

① 文中只标注页码的引文均引自《纳粹军官的犹太妻子》，翁海贞译，新星出版社2005年版。

持犹太食物教规的宾馆。据比尔回忆，有一天一个高瘦的男子走进父亲管理的宾馆吃早餐。“他的头发金黄，一身奥地利外省人的打扮，身穿皮短裤，头戴斜插岩羚羊毛的提洛尔省传统边帽。”（25）父亲并未认出这位男子是犹太人，断定他走错了地方。然而当这位男子摘下帽子，换上犹太人的传统帽子，站起身作餐前祷告时，父亲才笑着说：“我看，连犹太人也分不出谁是犹太人了。”（25-26）犹太人朝着同化的方向越走越远也就意味着犹太人放弃了越来越多的民族特点，从而将自己彻底融进西方文化中，“连犹太人也分不出谁是犹太人”。在同化主义的影响下，不少维也纳犹太人同化的步伐愈发激进，他们以犹太身份为耻，甚至通过改宗、接受洗礼来逃避犹太身份。少年时期的比尔虽然周六会被送到犹太教堂上儿童礼拜课但因为家里的帮佣是天主教徒，不敢走近犹太教堂，所以比尔和妹妹们很少去，几乎不曾学任何东西。由此我们可以看出当时维也纳的犹太人已经在各方面高度融入了当地人的生活，逐渐背弃了自己的传统文化。同化主义为犹太民族虚构了一个世界大同的美梦，沉浸在梦里不愿醒来的犹太人满怀热情地参与当地人的文化生活和经济消费，放弃了自己的饮食习惯、服饰风格，甚至是语言宗教，逐渐丧失了对自己民族的文化认同感。

然而这是否意味着西方人已经完全接受了犹太人呢？显然没有。戈登认为文化同化只是同化的第一步，真正的同化，即融合（fusion）只有在居住国当地人完全接受少数群体并且两个群体间有大量通婚的情况下才能发生（戈登，2015：253）。当时的维也纳并不具备这样的环境。以比尔父亲所开的宾馆为例，比尔认为父亲的宾馆即使是一个天堂一样的地方，但也有不尽如人意的地方。这个宾馆是象征意义上的维也纳，无论怎样同化，维也纳永远不可能是犹太人真正的故乡。歧视性的规定始终在提醒着犹太人，他们与非犹太人之间有一层无法超越的文化隔膜，譬如宾馆所在的地方不允许犹太洁食屠宰法，直到比尔的父母成年时犹太人才被允许在维也纳城定居，他们的祖辈只能在远离维也纳的偏远乡村定居（27）。同化主义将犹太人置于一个十分尴尬的境地：一方面，相对宽松的社会环境使得犹太人开始厌恶自己的民族身份，渴望融入西方社会，并在一定程度上取得了成功；另一方面，各种歧视性的规定又时刻提醒他们不可能融合，西方社会从未真正准备好接受他们。犹太人流散的历史决定了根植他们血液之中的无家可归感，屈居在他人故乡的犹太人无时无刻不在面临着两种文化身份的割据和困惑感。在这种文化同化过程的撕裂中，犹太人丢失了自己的文化和宗教。1941年，身处阿什尔斯莱本劳教营的比尔和其他犹太人想要一起庆祝光明节。然而她们一群人中无一人会说祷告。比尔感叹道："我们竟然完全不懂自己的文化、自己的礼拜仪式！这就是我们在维也纳的同化生活的遗产。"（121）

可悲的是，丧失了自己民族特性的犹太人却无法真正剥离自己的民族身份，比尔在回忆自己的青年生活时尽管充满怀念，但敏感的她已经觉察出同化主义所暗藏的谎言与无能。"在一个反闪族的国家，每一代犹太人都承受身为犹太人的负累，却不曾被赋予犹太人的力量——教律学习、祷告、团结的社区。我们不会讲意第绪语或希伯来语，我们对犹太上帝没有深刻的信仰，我们既无波兰哈西德教派严谨的信仰，也无立陶宛犹太法典学者深奥的知识。我们没有自由的美国人的勇敢——你要记得这一点。并且，当时还没有以色列国，没有沙漠之军，没有一如其他国度的国度。"（27）同化主义不仅没有达到最初的目的，反而将犹太身份变成了每一个犹太人不得不背负的负累。为了不被视作异类，犹太人最大限度地隐藏起自己的民族身份，试图摆脱"他者形象"，然而却陷入了一个两者皆不可得的鸿沟。"解放时期"的犹太人一方面想摆脱犹太身份，却无法真正剥离，另一方面想融入西方社会，却始终没有真正被接纳。

2 犹太大屠杀——身体记忆与精神创伤

正当犹太民族沉浸在同化主义的温床之时，二战爆发，希特勒对犹太民族的暴行升级，揭开了同化风潮的残忍面纱，并给犹太民族留下了不可磨灭的创伤。回忆录第四至第十章详细记录了二战爆发后比尔的悲惨遭遇。与“解放时期”犹太人主动摆脱传统宗教的束缚、接受西方理性的启蒙不同，犹太大屠杀以一种更为激进暴力的方式延续了解放时期的同化主义，解构犹太人的民族身份。

纳粹对犹太人的暴行可大致分为两类。第一类是奴役犹太人的身体和谋杀他们的性命。历史上有六百万犹太人死于大屠杀，奥斯维辛集中营的惨案令世人震惊。比尔最挚爱的母亲是早期受害者，在被盖世太保从维也纳运到灭绝营的六天后遇害。即使是在大屠杀中侥幸活下来的很多幸存者也遭受了无法逆转的身体伤害。在前往慕尼黑遇到自己未来的纳粹军官丈夫之前，比尔还曾被发往芦苇种植场以及劳动营为纳粹分子做苦工。比尔在芦苇场时每天从清晨六点劳动到中午，接着从下午一点到傍晚六点。她一周工作六个全天，半个星期天。“很快，全身的肌肉和关节抽筋、肿痛。我的骨头酸痛、头脑发昏。”（82）在劳动营劳动时，十三个月里每周劳动八十小时，却只能被分配仅供充饥的食物。那时，比尔的男友裴比会给她寄一些面包，寄到之时面包早已不新鲜，可比尔和其他女工们却视之为美味：“我们感恩地啃咬 14 天前的陈面包。我们用湿布包裹面包，让面包软化，像小老鼠似的一丁点一丁点地啃。”（111）由于长期的营养不良和劳累过度，许多女工生理失衡，连月经都停了。劳动营的监工每隔一段时间就会提高工作定额，为了完成工作，比尔的“指尖残破，被纸板磨得血肉模糊。”（114）

在劳动营时，除了与裴比通信外，比尔无法接触到外界信息，然而集中营的残暴还是传到劳动营的女工耳中，她们听说看守都是施虐狂，琢磨出各种非人的折磨方式，惩罚体力不支的人，让她们每天活在担惊受怕中。在离开劳教营之后，比尔返回维也纳并在雅利安人朋友的帮助下成功伪造了自己的身份前往慕尼黑，并在那儿遇到了德国军人维纳，随后与之结婚，开启了自己委作潜艇（U-Boat）的生活。在扮演恭谨、温顺的雅利安妻子时，比尔表面看似平静而沉默，内心却风起云涌——神经紧绷，情绪起伏，精神压力巨大。她总是失眠，并且时时刻刻担忧，因为她“必须显露无忧无虑的样子“(185)。大屠杀带给比尔的后遗症不仅是虚弱的身体，还有无尽的失眠和焦虑。即使是在大屠杀结束后的许多年，那些幸存者身上的编号和无意识的身体记忆也无时无刻不提醒着她大屠杀的存在。

第二类暴行则是从意识形态上无视犹太人的存在，并通过让自己的政策正当化来确保任何德国士兵都不会萌动恻隐之心。当时的许多犹太人为了保住性命，不得已选择改宗或伪造证件来隐藏自己的犹太身份。纳粹发动大屠杀旨于在历史上彻底抹杀犹太人的存在，通过种族清洗达到净化的目的。纳粹对犹太人的非人行径可以看作一种民族身份对另一种民族身份的倾轧。芦苇种植场的监工常会宣讲:“某些种族的用途就是给其他种族劳动。这是自然的法则。这就是为什么波兰人为我们德国人劳动，法国人为我们德国人劳动。今天你们为我们劳动，明天英国人也要为我们劳动。”(83)纳粹通过将犹太人贬为次等民族来构建自己民族血液中的虚假优越感，并将自己的非人行径美化为自然的法则。比尔在阿什尔斯莱本工作时一位重要的商界领袖去世，犹太人被命令不能去悼念。一位犹太女孩莉丽解释道:“他们若看不见我们，就可以装作不知道我们的存在。”(119-120)比尔当时觉得莉丽太偏激，直到晚年写作这部回忆录时才领悟到这名犹太女孩话中的真理:“他们采取各种措施，确保当地的德国人永远看不见我们。或者即便看见了，也无须承认我们的存在。又或者即便承认了我们的存在，他们仍可以说，我们活得还不错，从而永远不会产生任何负罪感或萌发恻隐之心。”(120)

在扮演雅利安人妻子的生活中，比尔将真实的自我压抑在心灵的最深处，她这样形容自己的潜艇生活:“我觉得自己被活埋，被活埋与沉默之中，被活埋的大洋深底。”(247-248)战前沉浸在天下大同的同化美梦中的犹太人在大屠杀暴行中察觉到了德国人与生俱来的对外族人的仇恨。比尔这样写道:“一直以来，我们早已习惯将他们对犹太人的仇恨称为‘偏见’，多么文雅多么委婉的词汇。

事实上，他们对我们的仇恨与他们的宗教一般古老。他们对我们的仇恨与生俱来，他们在必然仇恨我们的教育之中成长。德奥合并一开始，那层庇护着我们免与他们仇恨的文化薄膜，便尽然褪落。”（56）与温和的同化主义不同，大屠杀以暴力的方式试图消灭犹太民族，通过肉体谋杀和精神洗脑来使犹太人厌恶自己的犹太身份。同化主义对犹太民族的民族性来说是一次温和的消解，而大屠杀则是暴力的解构。

杰弗瑞·亚历山大（Jeffery C. Alexander）在《创伤：社会理论》（*Trauma：A Social Theory*）（2013）中提到，当个人与集体共同遭遇了痛苦的经历，并在意识上留下了难以磨灭的影响，文化创伤便发生了（Alexander，2013：6）。它不仅与个人的身份认同有关，同时也与集体的身份认同有关。犹太大屠杀给犹太民族的集体意识留下了永恒的文化创伤，这种创伤的症状之一就是身份危机。在种植场时为了躲避纳粹的迫害，比尔天真地想要通过改信基督教来改变自己的命运。“这个办法曾经被视为简直不可思议，被视为无耻地背叛自己的父母和文化。而今看来却是十分合理的策略。”（98）她渴望能够暂时剥离自己的犹太身份，去享受一个普通人的权利——和裴比组成一个家庭。而后在慕尼黑生活的许多年里，比尔必须彻底抹杀自己生来禀赋的个性，将自己从蝴蝶退化成蛹。直到德国战败，比尔无须继续伪装时，她感觉自己仍是一艘潜艇。“她没有立即浮出水面。这需要时间，很长时间。永远。”（259）大屠杀的残酷暴行使幸存者需要花费余生来重构二战期间被压抑和丢弃的自我，她渴望有人记得真正的她，可当胜利来临时，似乎犹太人自己也不再记得如何做一个犹太人。战后犹太身份重建是犹太民族共同面临的选择，是治愈创伤的必经之路。

3　直面创伤——犹太身份的重构

《纳粹军官的犹太妻子》的高潮内容主要聚焦于比尔伪造身份后

的潜艇生活。然而尽管如此，比尔依然在前三章花了不少篇幅陈述二战爆发前自己在维也纳时的青年生活。笔者认为，比尔这样安排旨在为全文暗藏一条完整的犹太认同意识的线索，而比尔犹太人认同感由弱变强的转折点正是大屠杀事件。因此本书的意义绝不囿于揭露大屠杀给犹太民族留下的精神与肉体的双重创伤，也就是说作者并未沉溺于描述痛苦，让下一代的年轻人背负着犹太民族的创伤历史前行，战争结束后如何平息身份危机和寻找生活意义也是作者想要表达的重要内容。比尔将创伤与身份重构联系起来，从而挖掘民族创伤之于犹太身份重构的意义。对于犹太人来说，直面创伤和治愈创伤的过程就是身份重构的过程。

首先，犹太民族在大屠杀带来的创伤记忆中找到了同胞的联结和信任。本书的第十一至第十四章讲述了二战结束后比尔的选择与生活。比尔选择重申自己的犹太身份，并参加了一个名为“法西斯受害者”的组织。里面全是像她一样在大屠杀中设法以某种方式活下来的人。“得知自己并非孤单一人，对我来说极为重要。我们看着彼此的面孔，不需一言，便懂得彼此的故事。我屡次去维也纳寻觅却愈发难以找到的东西——不再说谎，不再躲藏，不再恐惧，渴望有人理解——终于在‘法西斯受害者’中间找到。”（265）此时的比尔比任何时候都渴望回到犹太人身边去，这块共同的“伤疤”成为犹太人相认的记号，只有和拥有同样经历的族人在一起，她“不可言说”的故事才得以被“倾听”。

1948 年苏联企图吸纳比尔为东德安全部密探，比尔拒绝后失去了苏联人的信任，只得逃亡英国。在那段暗中安排逃离的日子，比尔经常需要带着女儿安吉拉排队数小时来获取各种证件。尽管女儿极为懂事，只是偶尔哭闹，但是推着婴儿车穿越满街的废墟让比尔身心疲惫。有一天，比尔在路上偶遇了一位犹太士兵，比尔向他谈起带女儿排队的困难，士兵立即让比尔把女儿放在他那里，比尔欣然同意，只因士兵是犹太人，她不相信犹太人会伤害她的孩子。由此可见，拥有同样民族创伤记忆的犹太人在战争年代对自己的族人有着独一无二的信任感，这种信任感源于对自己族人的认同，更深层次是对自己民族身份的认同。此时的比尔已经不再是战前背负着民族的苦难在同化教育中成长起来的维也纳小女孩，她享受着自己族人的善意，也尽自己所能帮助自己的族人。

正如阿伦·雷·伯格所说："大屠杀是犹太身份的关键。"（Berger，1985：93）在无数次接受犹太人的帮助、感受族人的善意之后，比尔写道："你看，总会有奇迹出现。光明节的一支意第绪歌曲、广播里一位英国拉比的祷告、火车上或者街头某人的善意，都会提醒我，无论我隐藏得多么虚假，不论恐惧驱使我在自我否认之中堕落得多么深，犹太人始终是我的族人，我始终属于他们。"（293）大屠杀给犹太民族留下了无法治愈的创伤记忆，创伤记忆却又恰好成为重构身份治愈创伤的起点。饱受苦难的犹太人内部分享着无法与外人言说的创伤经历，个人记忆汇聚成集体记忆，铸成了犹太民族独特的民族记忆。

其次，大屠杀事件带来的二战难民安置问题直接推动了以色列合法建国，为犹太民族提供了除流散和同化之外的另一个选择。历史上，战后犹太人的身份重构之路主要有两条，分别是汉娜·阿伦特（Hannah Arendt）所代表的激进启蒙路线和肖勒姆（Gershom Scholem）所倡导的温和启蒙路线。前者秉承德国传统，强调用理性的态度分析和看待犹太人的一切问题；后者在遵从德国理性和严守犹太教的两种极端中寻求文化复国主义为中间道路，认为根本的复国应是对犹太传统的精神性回归（高晓倩，2020：25-32）。比尔重构犹太身份的方式与肖勒姆所提倡的文化复国主义不谋而合。从纳粹分子手中死里逃生的比尔在经历了这一场浩劫后真正认可了自己的犹太身份，并在 1984 年移居以色列，"终于来到犹太人中间，生活在自己的国家"（297）。在比尔小的时候，父亲从未教过她如何做一个犹太人，经历大屠杀后，她选择送女儿去犹太学校，将她培养为犹太人。因此大屠杀记忆不仅使得犹太人对犹太民族性产生了认同和归属感，即肖勒姆所说的精神性回归，还加速了犹太复国主义的进程，为流散或同化的犹太人提供了另一条出路。

除了在战后选择重申犹太身份，并回到自己的国家生活之外，晚年的比尔还通过写作来重构身份和治愈创伤。有学者认为，大屠杀的目的是要糟践犹太人，然后屠杀他们，然后通过抹掉他们的记忆第二次毁灭他们（申劲松，2010：111-118）。我们知道，战争创伤最明显的症状就是失语，大屠杀幸存者失去了与外界沟通的能力，他们无法讲出自己的故事，或是沉溺在过去的创伤碎片中，只能对现实发出只言片语，又或是对自己的故事缄口不言，期待沉默和遗忘最终抚平创伤。然而创伤会折磨着受创主体，使其即使在远离创伤多年后仍然受困于过去，无法与现实构建起有机互动。1957 年，比尔在与维也纳犹太人弗雷德·比尔结婚后，两人只对彼此讲过一次自己如何从纳粹分子手里逃生的故事，之后的 30 年来他们不再提起这些恐怖的事件。比尔渴望将这些记忆深埋心底，“让过去堆积，漂流而去，犹如海难的残骸，期望这些残骸最终会沉默，被遗忘”（297）。这种应对方式在大屠杀幸存者中十分常见，创伤的难以言说性使得外部世界与大屠杀亲历者之间形成了一个真空地带，受创主体无法言说，外部世界进而对这一历史事实进行否认。长久的“不可言说”最终可能会导致记忆的忘却，而受难记忆则会进一步对犹太民族内部的自我身份认同产生致命的解构。因此，尽管比尔出于保护机制长久以来不愿回忆自己的创伤经历，她仍然选择在晚年完成这部回忆录，让世界看到犹太人的苦难历程并感受犹太人的内心创伤。

二战后欧洲对于犹太大屠杀的消极反应实际上是这场浩劫的余震，否认这一历史事实就等同于否认犹太人的存在。正如前文提到纳粹抹杀犹太民族性的重要方式之一是在精神上视他们不存在，在前往慕尼黑前，好友丽瑟尔曾告诫比尔：“你看，你要记着，伊迪丝，不许谈论犹太人，再也没人提起他们。一个字都不许提，人们憎恨听到犹太人这几个字。”（137）二战结束后，世界依然不想听到犹太人这几个字，他们想埋葬这个大屠杀的故事。作为亲历残酷大屠杀的幸存者之一，比尔明白大屠杀事件对犹太民族的意义，以及将故事延续下去对年轻一代犹太人坚守犹太性的意义。大屠杀记忆应以这样一种“缺失的在场”存在于每一个犹太幸存者的心中（申劲松，2010：111-118）。而犹太民族作为大屠杀伤痛记忆的载体有必要将这种集体创伤记忆印刻在脑海中，铭记并告诫后人不要再延续这样的苦难。

罗利和查沃斯（Rowley&Chavous）认为：“种族身份认同是对于种族意义和其重要性等方面产生的态度和信念。”对于拥有犹太民族身份的人而言，自大流散（Diaspora）以来所经受的种种苦难已经成为溶解在民族血脉中的集体记忆，化作一条维系民族性的精神纽带，是不可忘却的。而与此同时，受难者对于苦难记忆的坚守也是在反向加深那些怀揣民族信仰、坚守民族身份的犹太人的身份认同。（赵艺瞳，2020：72）标记着犹太人之存在的正是“残骸一般的过去”，而每一代犹太人也将背负着这段经历负重前行。在同化主义中成长起来的比尔在大屠杀的洗礼下蜕变成最坚毅的犹太人，她在本书的末尾写道：“我拒绝‘融进当地文化’这种游戏，我开始送女儿上犹太学校，将她培育成犹太人。”（297）

比尔通过讲述自己的故事以及对于犹太身份的坚守超越了创伤“不得不说”与“难以言说”的悖论，实现了从灾难记忆中的“康复”。正如阿伦·雷·伯格所说：“铭记和讲述大屠杀故事是一种仪式：是犹太人存在的标杆和对与上帝所签盟约之确定。”（Berger，1985：64）或许赋予战争任何正面意义都是不道德的，但是去歌颂人类在战争面前展现的尊严，去铭记人类对自己身份的坚守——即使这种身份是负累——却是光荣的。大屠杀事件和无处不在的大屠杀记忆某种程度上成了犹太民族寻求身份认同中最稳定也是最血淋淋的支点，它挑战着人类的良心，衡量人类的道德，诉说人类的悲剧，成为所有犹太人在高度物质化的世界对抗同化风潮的武器。

4 结 语

《纳粹军官的犹太妻子》详细刻画了二战时期纳粹分子给犹太民

族带来的苦难与创伤，然而作者并不局限于描述创伤，还旨在从创伤中发现治愈创伤重构身份的途径。比尔通过展现二战前后犹太人民族身份认同感的强弱对比揭示了大屠杀之于犹太民族身份构建的意义。西方价值体系的崩塌引导了大部分犹太人的回归传统，呼应了犹太正典《托拉》中展现的宗教母题：受难和重生（高晓倩，2020：25）。犹太人在创伤中开启了身份重构之路，坚定了建立一个自己的国家的决心。晚年时期，作者还选择在写作中反向加强自己的民族身份。西奥多·阿多诺（Theodor W. Adorno）曾说："奥斯维辛之后，写诗是野蛮的。"（1983：34）创伤的不可言说性以及大屠杀的残暴程度使得文学好似溃烂伤口上的一个创可贴，写出来就已经是美化。然而对于犹太作家来说，大屠杀文学的意义或许不是见证，而仅仅只是叙述本身。犹太人的故事将代代相传，引导寄居在他人故乡的犹太人回归故土。犹太作家比尔的自传是20世纪犹太人对民族身份由背弃至回归的缩影，作者通过讲述自己在二战期间的真实经历以及战后选择恢复犹太身份揭示了大屠杀给犹太民族带来了精神和肉体的双重创伤和大屠杀创伤之于犹太身份重构的意义。

参考文献

[1] ADORNO W THEODOR. Prisms. MIT Press, 1983.

[2] ALEXANDER, C JEFFREY. Trauma: A Social Theory. John Wiley & Sons, 2013.

[3] BERGER L ALAN. Crisis and Covenant: The Holocaust in America Jewish Fiction. State of University of New York Press, 1985.

[4] ROZENBLIT L MARSHA. The Jews of Vienna, 1867—1914: Assimilation and Identity. Suny Press, 1984.

[5] 高晓倩. "艾希曼审判"之争背后：战后犹太集体的身份重构之路. 中国文学研究，2020（03）：25-32.

[6] 李晔梦. 同化主义语境下欧洲犹太知识分子的身份困惑——以卡夫卡为个案的考察. 郑州大学学报（哲学社会科学版），2017（04）：138-145.
[7] 米尔顿·M. 戈登. 美国生活中的同化. 马戎，译. 南京：译林出版社，2015.
[8] 申劲松. 从马拉默德短篇小说《湖畔淑女》看“大屠杀”与犹太身份的构建. 国外文学，2010（02）：111-118.
[9] 伊迪斯·汉恩·比尔，苏珊·德沃金. 纳粹军官的犹太妻子. 翁海贞，译. 北京：新星出版社，2005.
[10] 赵艺瞳.《湖畔女郎》：“凝视”理论视域下的犹太伦理身份认同. 华中师范大学研究生学报，2020（02）：70-73.

情感研究

西方瘟疫叙事中的情感书写

龙　丹

【摘要】笛福的《瘟疫年纪事》、雪莱的《末世一人》和加缪的《鼠疫》分别作为18世纪、19世纪及20世纪西方瘟疫叙事的代表性作品，在西方瘟疫叙事传统中占有重要的位置。三部作品都刻画瘟疫袭击导致的人类情感的变化，并以此映射西方社会某个时代的情感结构，反映了文学家对时代弊病的反思与批判。笛福在《瘟疫年纪事》中着力刻画的恐惧反映了18世纪英国中产阶级的焦虑；雪莱在《末世一人》通过鼠疫袭击前后盛世与末世的对比建构并解构了盛行于19世纪英国的人类中心主义骄傲；加缪在《鼠疫》中以鼠疫隐喻生存于荒诞的现代世界中人的流放感，并提倡通过共同体的建立进行抵抗。三部作品分别以瘟疫书写时代，反映了文学家对人的使命、人的本质、生存的意义等永恒命题的思考。

【关键词】瘟疫叙事；情感书写；《瘟疫年纪事》；《末世一人》；《鼠疫》

自古希腊历史学家修昔底德记录公元前430年的雅典瘟疫以来，瘟疫一直是西方文学家书写的对象，他们不仅再现瘟疫对个人和社会造成的灾难，而且以瘟疫为隐喻书写时代的寓言。英国现实主义作家丹尼尔·笛福的小说《瘟疫年纪事》（*A Journal of Plague Years*，1722）、英国浪漫主义女作家玛丽·雪莱的小说《末世一人》（*The Last*

基金项目：重庆市社科规划项目“英文期刊《天下月刊》的中国话语建构与传播”（2021NDYB141）和国家社会科学基金重大项目“认知诗学研究与理论版图重构”（20&ZD291）的阶段性成果。

作者简介：龙丹，女，四川外国语大学期刊社副教授，博士，主要从事英美文学研究。

Man，1826）及法国存在主义作家阿尔贝·加缪的小说《鼠疫》（*The Plague*，*1947*）都通过书写瘟疫而描绘了不同时期的西方社会缩影。三部作品分别从现实主义、浪漫主义、存在主义等不同的范式书写瘟疫的爆发，三部作品都着力刻画瘟疫袭击后人类的情感反应——惊恐、悲伤、绝望、自责、耻辱、流放感等，并以此映射时代的主流情感结构：18世纪英国中产阶级的焦虑、19世纪英国启蒙主义者的骄傲、20世纪西方现代人的流放感等。

西方资本主义工业社会的后现代发展，科学技术对人类身体极限的突破与挑战，恐怖袭击与反恐战争对人类身心造成的创伤，传染病、艾滋病、癌症等对人类生命和生活方式的改变给西方批评理论提出新的课题，在此背景之下，情感日益成为诸多学科和跨学科领域的分析重心（Clough，2007：1）。"情感转向"这一概念源自2007年Clough & Halley的同名新书（*Affective Turn*），2010年Gregg & Seigworth出版《情感理论读者》（*Affect Theory Reader*）[①]，2011年Patrick Hogan出版《情感叙事学》（*Affective Narratology*），同年《今日诗学》（*Poetics Today*）推出情感研究专刊。2015年美国现代语言协会会刊*PMLA*推出题为"情感"的专刊，试图回答情感与教育、情感与性别、情感与种族的关系，研究情感的认识论、美学、道德、政治意义等。文学研究的情感转向探究叙事与情感的关系，即情感如何引导叙事以及叙事如何作用于读者的情感。霍根在《情感叙事学：故事的情感结构》提出"故事情节由情感系统主导"（Hogan 2011：1），"故事的主要部分都是情感系统的产物"（Hogan

① Gregg & Seigworth勾勒当代西方情感研究的八种方向：人类与非人类本质的差异；cybernetics、人工智能、机器人、生物信息、生物工程研究中，生物与非生物之间的情感差异；文化研究、哲学研究；心理学研究；属下研究研究权力如何规范身体以及身体对规范的服从与溢出；偏离语言学转向，研究前语言、元语言、语言外的区域如何与身体感官（触摸、味觉、嗅觉、节奏、动感、运动神经系统）互动，同时继承语言学转向的结构论，在更广泛意义下定义社会和文化。对情感（emotion）的历史化研究，关注情感/激情的传播，包括社会环境（atmospheres of sociality），群体行为，情感的感染、身份认同的问题；情感的科学研究。苏珊妮·基恩（Suzanne Keen）梳理了当代西方心理学、哲学、神经科学、进化生物学、法学、人类学、历史学、社会学、语言学、计算机科学等出现的情感研究。

2011：2）。历史研究者关注历史与情感的四个论题：历史上的人如何体验、表达、运用情感，经济、政治、文化、性别等因素如何塑造情感，个人和集体情感如何影响历史以及情感在历史上的变迁（赵涵，2020：133）。

西方瘟疫叙事作品日益进入读者的视野。这些作品生动刻画瘟疫造成的情感反应，包括恐慌、焦虑、绝望、羞耻、孤独、流放感等，瘟疫及其伴随的死亡威胁激发的极端情感很容易在读者心中引起共鸣。瘟疫叙事对情感的细致描绘不仅再现瘟疫引发的个体情感，更是以此映射时代的情感结构，反映了作者对时弊的反思与批判，对人的本质、生存的意义、人类命运等问题的思考。

1　瘟疫的现实主义书写——建构焦虑

笛福在《瘟疫年纪事》中再现了1665年伦敦瘟疫出现、蔓延、肆虐、消退的全过程，详细地刻画瘟疫的传播路径、患者的症状、伦敦各区的死亡人数、政府和个人的抗疫措施等。叙事者H. F. 称1665年为“悲惨之年”“恐怖的时期”，称伦敦为“悲惨的城市”，认为伦敦人经历一场“恐怖的劫难”（笛福，2013：174）。笼罩着整部作品的是深入灵魂深处的惊恐、哀伤、绝望乃至疯癫，笛福用文字勾勒出有声的画面，让瘟疫患者及其家人的哀号与尖叫在读者“耳边萦绕回响”（同上）。对瘟疫受害者情感的逼真书写不仅再现了1665年瘟疫对伦敦社会造成的灾难性影响，也映射了18世纪英国中产阶级的焦虑。

笛福用现实主义的白描手法呈现瘟疫袭击下伦敦城的恐怖。他不厌其烦地在小说多处附上伦敦97个教区每周的《死亡数字统计表》，呈直线上升的死亡数字拨动读者的心弦，曾经无比珍贵的生命此时退化为数字，统计表上数字的增加与瘟疫的破坏力成正比，也与故事中的伦敦居民以及故事外的读者的恐惧心态成正比。1665年6月，伦敦西区死于瘟疫的人数上升到每周68人左右，西区的上层人士开始惊慌，他们带着家眷和仆人乘马车“蜂拥出城”（笛福，2013：

39)。到了8月，单是克里普尔盖特教区就有886人死于瘟疫。8月的第3周，伦敦总死亡人数已高达5319人。英国皇室早已搬走，整个伦敦似乎变成一座空城（50)。无处可逃的伦敦人犹如惊弓之鸟，如坐针毡，唯恐瘟疫之灾下一秒降临在自己头上，“悲叹和哀伤挂在每一张脸上”（51)。9月，有报道称一夜之间死去3000多人（270)，每周的死亡数字直逼4万（277)，伦敦城内外一片“荒芜枯寂，人们处在最可怕的慌乱之中”，甚至“到了绝望的地步”（266)，“人们在灵魂的极度痛苦中孤注一掷，而对死亡的恐怖就挂在人们的脸孔和表情上”（367)。被感染的家庭门上画上红色的十字，门口站着守卫，禁止屋内的人外出。醒目的红字与患者身上的肿块和溃烂之处一样，是瘟神的面孔，它也成为伦敦人背负的沉重负担，其本意是警示人们远离瘟疫源，却增加了他们的恐惧。曾经熙熙攘攘的街道变得荒芜凄凉。瘟疫期间的孕妇和初生婴儿最为悲惨，瘟疫年死于分娩的孕产妇以及婴儿的数量较前一年翻了一番，1664年是647人，而1665年增至1242人。有的妈妈死于瘟疫后，活着的婴儿还在吮吸她的乳房，有的婴儿因为哺乳被感染，不幸夭折。

笛福诉诸听觉意象，描述瘟疫引发的恐惧情绪。小说字里行间充满了声音的意象，无论是患者的，还是女人的、孩子的声音，都是可怕的、撼人灵魂的、令血液发冷的。黄昏时分，在伦敦的每一条街道，呻吟、悲鸣、哀号、尖叫、咆哮、哭喊、忏悔声汇成一股强大的恐惧气流，在城市上空回旋激荡，令人失去求生的欲望，失去理智。伦敦变为地狱。患者“在灵魂和肉体的惨痛之中大声疾呼”（77)，他们发出的“呻吟和嚎叫常常将我的灵魂刺穿”（143)。患者家庭的悲惨“是难以言表的，而通常正是从这类屋子里，我们才听到最为凄惨的悲鸣和嚎叫”（106)。

女人发出的可怕的尖叫和哀号响彻整个伦敦，也响彻整部小说。从街道两旁的窗户里发出的哀号声令路人动容：“妇女和孩子的悲号响彻屋子的门窗……连世上最刚强的人听着也会为之心碎”（51)。当H. F. 经过劳斯伯里的土地拍卖市场时，头顶的窗子猛然打开，“有个女人发出三声吓人的嚎啕，接着是一种最难以效仿的强调哭喊道，哦！死亡，死亡，死亡！而这让我猝然惊恐起来，连我的血液都发冷了”（141）。贝尔胡同里，男主人出于恐惧把自己给吊死了，“我能听到女人和孩子们发了狂一样在屋子里尖叫着跑来跑去”（142）。一位单亲母亲发现女儿大腿内侧“那要命的标记”后，以吓人的模样尖叫起来，“这既不是尖叫，也不是哭喊，而是那种恐惧，攫住了她心魄”（107）。小说中多处提到女人的哀号，这是叙事者在劳斯伯里的惊恐经历的强迫性重复，瘟疫的恐惧以声音的形式侵入他的记忆，如鬼魅般挥之不去。作者用文字创作了一首瘟疫悲怆曲，真实、形象地传递瘟疫对受害者造成的身心伤害、对幸存者造成的心理创伤，直击读者的感官，在他们心里留下恐怖、哀伤的情感。

笛福在作品中反复强调语言再现瘟疫时显得苍白无力，更加深了恐怖的程度：“难以言表的无胜惊恐”（53）、“那确实是非常、非常、非常的可怕，此类情形非语言可以表达”（113）。弥留之际的人发出的哀鸣，幸存者发出的惊恐之声，笼罩在伦敦上空的恐惧的气流令叙事者感到文字的无力：“但愿我能让人读起来如闻其声，正如我觉得现在我听到的那样，因为这声音似乎仍在我耳边萦绕回响。”（174）在瘟疫面前，不仅语言显得苍白，叙事者也意识到任何书写的策略都是欠缺的，他反复地思考：“要向读者更为生动地描述那些时刻的悲惨，或是让他更圆满地理解那种复杂纠结的苦难，还能够怎么说呢？”（274）瘟疫造成的惊恐一直对抗、逃逸、否定文字再现。语言作为人类文化的社会建构物，与自然、疾病、人类体验相比是后来者，瘟疫袭击下人类的情感体验超出了语言言说的范围，整部小说对惊恐、恐慌、悲痛、绝望、悲惨到家、吓死人等词的反复使用仍然无法言说瘟疫造成的人类惊恐情感的强度。

笛福似乎比同时代的人更加警觉瘟疫可能带来的影响，这或许源于他对 1665 年瘟疫的童年记忆。他早在 1709、1712 年就在《评论》（*The Review*）期刊上发表文章反对英国支持瑞典与波兰、瑞典、俄罗斯等国的战争，担忧战争会滋生、传播瘟疫。1720 年，法国马赛暴发瘟疫，直逼英吉利海峡，似乎笛福最担心的事情终究会发生。他随即在 *The Daily Post*、*Applebee's Journal*、*Mist's Journal* 等多本期刊上发表文章，警告世人瘟疫可能从马赛传播到英国。时任英国首相沃尔波尔（Robert Walpole）1722 年 2 月宣布重新颁布《隔离法案》（*The Quarantine Act*），但迫于部分商人和自由主义者的压力，沃尔波尔政府不得不放松隔离法案的实施。显然这令笛福非常不满，他在 1722 年推出两本瘟疫叙事作品，即小说《瘟疫年纪事》和小册子《为瘟疫做合适的准备》（*Due Preparations for the Plague*），在后者中他同样提及 1665 年伦敦瘟疫，并直接对读者说教，大谈应对瘟疫的措施。在小说《瘟疫年纪事》中，笛福毫不避讳其书写目的就是引起读者对瘟疫的重视："要做到把这些时刻准确地描述给那些没有看见过的人，告诉读者什么是随处可见的真正恐怖，那就必须给他们的心灵以恰切的印象，让他们充满惊讶。"（51）事实上，笛福的担忧不是没有根据的。1665 年瘟疫共计夺走 7 万人的性命；14 世纪黑死病（1348—1370）杀死英国 1/4 到 2/3 的人口；此后鼠疫反复袭击英国，尤其是 17 世纪，据统计每隔 15 到 20 年伦敦就会爆发一次鼠疫（Gilman，2009：32）。笛福似乎担心健忘的英国人忘记历史的惨痛教训，因此谱写了一首悲怆交响曲。小说中种种惊恐的意象、回旋在伦敦上的尖叫声和哀号声在读者脑海中留下深深的印记，必定会让他们更加重视眼前的威胁。

凯瑟琳·米勒（Miller，2016：18）发现 1665 年伦敦瘟疫引发了与瘟疫相关的印刷品的爆炸式增长，反映了英国人对瘟疫叙事的病态迷恋及时代的焦虑。笛福在《瘟疫年纪事》中营造恐慌和悲伤的气氛，其根本原因在于担忧法国瘟疫蔓延至英国后会破坏其经济秩序。正如笔者在另一篇文章（龙丹，2020）中谈到的，H. F. 的鞍具商身份是笛福别有用心地设计的，他代表 18 世纪正在兴起的英国中产阶级。当瘟疫袭来时，H. F. 拒绝逃离伦敦，称买卖、货物、仓库、房子、仆人等是"我在世上的全部所有"（40），这种视财富高于生命的原则正是笛福重商主义的真实映照。他在《完美的英国商人》(1726)中为英国商业高唱赞歌，称商业不仅改变个人命运，更是英国的立国之本。贸易不仅支撑英国国内的开支，并为海外扩张建立了基础。他称“商业是人们积攒财富和改善家庭的最现成的方式，是体面的人和上好的家庭涉足的领域”。商人承担战争的费用、支付国债、支撑政府的信用。他甚至宣称“英国的伟大不在于战争和征服……而完全在于商业，在于在国内发展我们的商业并向国外延伸……”，他称商业是英国殖民扩张的基础：“正是由于商业，在未知的土地上进行了新的探险，在无人居住的岛屿和未开垦的美洲大陆建立了新的移居地和种植园，设立了新的居住区并形成了新的征服。”(舍尔曼，2019：275-276)然而，瘟疫一旦蔓延，会造成劳动力不足、原材料短缺、海外贸易通道受阻、海外市场竞争力下降。正如小说所写，由于伦敦瘟疫肆虐，英国出口的商品被海外消费者拒绝，其竞争对手荷兰随即占领了市场，从而导致英国个人失业、经济萧条。笛福早年经商，做袜子批发，进口酒、香烟和其他商品。他也多次破产，对经济危机带来的灾难性后果深有体会。尽管他对商人大加赞赏，称他们为新时代的新英雄(Richetti，2015：30)，但瘟疫造成的经济萧条令英雄无用武之地。

1665年瘟疫后，次年伦敦又遭遇大火。在笛福看来，两场灾难之后建立起的新秩序中，幸存下来的H. F.所代表的中产阶级成为中流砥柱，他们承担历史的使命重建伦敦，通过发展贸易实现富国强国的理想，而阻碍这一理想的障碍之一就是当时科学无法防控的瘟疫，因此他在《瘟疫年纪事》中极力书写恐惧的情感，直击读者的心智，以此敲响警世钟。事实上，笛福在小说中建构的恐惧不仅作用于18世纪的英国普通读者，这一情感也沉淀至瘟疫叙事传统中，无论是《鼠疫》中尖叫的妇人还是《末世一人》中的尖叫，都令读者想到笛福笔下被惊吓得失去神智的妇女和那萦绕在耳边的哀号。

2 瘟疫的后浪漫主义书写——解构英国启蒙者的骄傲

玛丽·雪莱的小说《末世一人》想象人类在2092年亡于一场鼠疫的故事。小说开篇再现了启蒙时期英国的盛世景象，字里行间流露出叙事者作为英国人的骄傲，然而这种骄傲的情感很快随着瘟疫在英国的蔓延被解构。鼠疫造成的末世景象令叙事者反思西方启蒙思想家津津乐道的西方文明的精髓，尤其是其西方中心主义思想。小说通过盛世与末世的鲜明对比，通过骄傲到羞耻的情感逆转，犀利地批判盛行于19世纪英国的骄傲，向英国人敲响警世钟。

自18世纪法国启蒙运动以来，西方哲学思想日益聚焦人的主体性，这令西方人因生而为人感到骄傲，笛卡尔的“我思故我在”、《哈姆雷特》中“人是宇宙的精华、万物的灵长”、康德的“人是目的”等思想反映了18、19世纪人类主体性的高涨，知识分子和艺术家庆祝人从宗教的束缚中获得解放。17世纪科学的兴盛和18世纪启蒙运动无限地增大了西方人的信心。培根在《崇学论》中提出“知识就是力量”，主张人类通过科学驾驭自然，将人类与自然的关系定位为征服与被征服。笛卡尔提出“我思故我在”为哲学第一原理，认为世间一切事物都有可能是错觉，唯有那个“进行思维的我”是任何怀疑论者都无法推翻的（罗素，2018：93）。启蒙思想家相信理性和教育可以让人摆脱不成熟状态，康德认为启蒙的精髓就是号召人们运用理智脱离不成熟状态（Kant，1949：132）。理性经过启蒙运动的洗礼被置于曾经属于上帝的圣坛，人类摆脱神对人的束缚之后将理性的枷锁套向了自然。康德提出“人是目的”，把人的目的当作绝对价值，称人是“自然界的最高立法者”，主张“理智的法则不是理智从自然界得来的，而是理智给自然界规定的”（康德，1996：593）。

《末世一人》的上篇把上述启蒙思想家的骄傲再现得淋漓尽致，具体表现为作为英国人的骄傲、作为人类知识传承者的骄傲、作为自然征服者的骄傲。小说开篇，生活在乡村的孤儿弗尼似乎具有与生俱来的“英国中心主义”思想，虽然他食不果腹、衣不蔽体，却莫名地为英格兰感到自豪，称其领土面积不大，但从精神力量的角度来看，它远远超过了人口更多、领土更宽广的国家（Shelley，1996：7）。显然这里人口更多、领土更宽广的国家是指欧洲其他国家，也泛指东方国家。不仅如此，他时常在高地上鸟瞰平原和山脉，想象他的族人在领土上劳作，把故土当作宇宙的中心：“此时那个点于我成为世界的中心，这个星球上的其他成为寓言，不费吹灰之力就遗忘了他们的存在。”（7）在弗尼的认知中，英国与其他国家相比具有绝对的优越性，这种优越性尤其体现在其文化的先进性上，而其他国家则被置于不重要的边缘，因而英国被认知为欧洲乃至世界的中心。雪莱以孤儿弗尼之口表达这一英国中心主义思想，披露其毫无根据、荒谬、幼稚，增加了反讽的效果，揭露19世纪流行于英国集体无意识的狂妄自大。19世纪的英国在资本主义工业发展和帝国主义扩张两个方面处于鼎盛时期，随着经济收益和海外殖民地的增加一同膨胀的是英国人的自我意识，这弥漫在英国人的集体文化中，连生活在乡村的孤儿弗尼都潜移默化地内化了这一思想，甚至滋生了“英国例外”的幻想。小说中，当瘟疫袭来时，英国人认为瘟疫是发生在土耳其等东方国家的，因此欧洲是安全的；即便欧洲其他国家已经出现瘟疫时，英国人仍然笃信英国不会被传染。

《末世一人》中的叙事者不仅因身为英国人而骄傲，更是为西方人文知识大唱赞歌，其自豪感跃然纸上。小说中的温莎伯爵艾德里安被塑造为人文知识的化身，通过青年弗尼对他的赞美与臣服，雪莱再现了19世纪西方人文主义者的盲目自信。孤儿弗尼因缺乏关爱和管教曾锒铛入狱，对社会充满仇恨。但这一切却因艾德里安的出现发生了逆转。弗尼被艾德里安驯服，后者成为他的精神导师。弗尼解释道，艾德里安让他臣服的不是他的地位，而是他的活泼、智慧和仁慈，他渊博的知识、崇高的哲学（20）。在艾德里安的指导下，弗尼踏上了精神启蒙之旅，他如饥似渴地阅读西方哲学、文学、诗学、修辞经典，并欣喜地发现自己在这些知识的指引下发生了蜕变，他称“所有我看到的东西都有更深层次的意义”（23），“我似乎转变成另一个人”（24）。人文知识启发了弗尼的心智，开发了他的潜力，优化了他的道德，改变了他的命运，弗尼惊呼这是一个奇迹。人文知识的启蒙让他变得自大：“我的视野扩大，我对整个人类的倾向和能力开始感兴趣。国王被称为他的臣民之父。突然我似乎变成了人类之父。”（120）弗尼认为启蒙思想充盈了他的灵魂，升华他的思想，让他踏上人类启蒙的高速公路并成为世界公民，他相信自己将要拥有不朽的荣誉。

如西方18世纪启蒙思想家一般，掌握了知识的弗尼把自然当作其征服的对象，《末世一人》第一卷构建的第三种骄傲的情感即为自然征服者的骄傲。小说中，人被称为创造者，而自然被当作人的臣子：“确实，唯有人的头脑创造了一切对人类而言好的、伟大的东西，而自然本身仅仅是他的首席部长。”（7）自18世纪以来，西方主流的哲学和科学思想把自然当作人类征服的对象，西方人对自然的认识以人为出发点，认为自然的存在以人为目的，因此对待自然的态度主要是工具主义的。接受人文主义启蒙的弗尼赞美人类对自然的占有：“啊！愉快的地球，愉快的地球人！上帝为你建造了庄严的宫殿，啊，人！你值得拥有你的住所！看看我们脚下郁郁葱葱的地毯，头顶蔚蓝的苍穹；大地生产、孕育了一切，天堂的踪迹囊括一切。”（58）在他看来，造物主让地球如此美丽，物产如此丰富，均因为人类值得拥有这一切：“如果他不好，为什么会这样？我们需要房子庇护我们度过四季，看看给我们提供的原材料；树木枝繁叶茂；平原上堆满岩石，形状各异、斑驳多样”（59）。在弗尼的眼里，人因为拥有灵魂、思想、想象力而比其他物种高贵，人几乎被升华到与上帝同等的地位，变得无所不能：“人类意志是无所不能的，能磨钝死亡的利剑，抚平疾病的温床，拭去痛苦的眼泪。”（60）

玛丽·雪莱在《末世一人》的上篇形象地建构了英国人的骄傲、西方人文知识传承者的骄傲、自然征服者的骄傲，其目的并非为这种骄傲唱赞歌，而是为下文埋下伏笔，随之在小说的后两篇对这一英国骄傲进行解构，以瘟疫这一特殊的情节设置和末世的惨象对其进行颠覆，发人深思。正如芭芭拉·约翰逊（Johnson 1993：265）所言，《末世一人》开篇赞美英格兰实则赞美人，赞美人类在思想上的掌控力，歌颂人类独立于世、处于自给自足的中心，但随着小说的进程，这种神秘、自大的人类肖像逐渐被解构。玛丽雪莱借叙事者之口要求人类“阅读你的堕落”。

小说中，叙事者弗尼的妹夫、英国护国公雷蒙德被批评家称为拜伦式的英雄。玛丽·雪莱设计了他在希腊战争中丧生的情节，这解构了西方中心主义者的骄傲。雷蒙德认为希腊与土耳其的冲突是文明与野蛮的对抗，他宣称自己要引领希腊这个年轻、充满活力的国家去追求自由与秩序（117）。这种把东方与西方的差异扭曲为野蛮与文明的冲突的偏见反映了19世纪盛行于英国乃至欧洲的西方中心主义思想及种族偏见和文化谬误，爱德华·赛义德等批评家在21世纪揭露这种刻板印象背后的殖民权力阴谋。玛丽·雪莱领先于时代地戳穿了这一谬误的虚假性，她在小说中揭露所谓文明的使命不过是西方人为自己无法抑制的征服欲寻找的借口而已，激励雷蒙德去征战的最大动力是他的虚荣心，他希望自己的墓碑上刻着“君士坦丁堡征服者”。雪莱借弗尼之口表达了对殖民战争的控诉：“我低头看到尸横遍野的大地，为自己的族群感到羞耻。”（141）不仅如此，白人征服者雷蒙德最终丧生希腊战场，丧生于瘟疫中，丧生于希腊公主埃瓦德妮的诅咒中：“我把自己出卖给死神，唯一的条件就是你会随我而去——火、战争、瘟疫，合力将你毁坏——啊，雷蒙德，你无处可逃。”（142）阿伦·理查森指出小说暗指瘟疫来自东方——非洲，象征殖民他者对帝国中心的集体复仇，与自西向东的殖民扩张和掠夺相反，瘟疫自东向西，将帝国主义者吞噬（Melville，2007：844）。Bewell（2009：307）称《末世一人》为第一部也是最后一部英国帝国主义史，小说揭露了殖民主义将带来的可怕后果。小说中，雷蒙德的死亡揭开了瘟疫蔓延的序幕：“猎户死于森林，农夫死于玉米地，渔夫死在自家鱼塘”，英国人不得不仓皇逃跑。“英国例外”论被击破，伦敦人也如“东方蛮族”一样丧生于瘟疫之下，他们被迫认清自己的本质——“我们是什么，地球的居民，居住在这无限空间的芸芸众生中最不值一提的？”（181）

在西方的瘟疫叙事传统中，瘟疫往往被当作上帝惩罚人类的某种手段。玛丽·雪莱继承并修正了这一传统，把瘟疫当作来自自然的惩戒，她借弗尼之口指出：“自然，我们的母亲，我们的朋友，转向威胁我们。她简单地显示，她允许我们给她制定律令，制服她的力量，但她只需要动一动手指，必定让我们颤抖。”“她可以拿起地球，抛向空中，生命灰飞烟灭，人类和他的努力付之东流。”（183）自18世纪法国启蒙运动以来，西方人因为征服自然、改造自然的能力而沾沾自喜，他们利用科学技术随意开采自然资源，破坏原生环境，危及动物生存，对此他们不仅没有丝毫悔恨之意，反而歌唱自己作为征服者的无限荣光。雪莱领先时代地意识到，这种无节制的滥用自然资源必定导致灾难性的后果，她通过瘟疫的隐喻勾勒一幅末世景象，希望对世人敲响警世钟，要求人们正确认识自己在宇宙中的位置，敬畏自然，她在小说中指出，人类不是造物主，不是万物的使用者，不是生死的掌控者，更不可能永垂不朽（181-2）。

《末世一人》与英国浪漫主义文学的关联是显而易见的，有研究者指出小说中的主人公均是以英国浪漫主义诗人为原型的：弗尼和妹妹是华兹华斯式的乡村兄妹，艾德里安是雪莱式的人文主义者，雷蒙德是拜伦式英雄。小说中，弗尼夫妇与他们的朋友在湖区过着惬意的生活，吟诗作画，歌颂橡树、夜莺、湖泊，生活富足而甜蜜。这几乎是对湖区诗人生活的真实再现，令读者联想华兹华斯兄妹与柯勒律治在格拉斯米尔的诗意生活。在小说的结尾，作为末世一人的弗尼与动物亲近，重新回归自然。这一主题似乎与华兹华斯等浪漫主义诗人对工业革命的批判、对自然的尊重相似。休姆曾批判浪漫主义对人类潜力的非理性自信，他指出，“一切浪漫主义的根子就在这里：人，个人是可能性的无限的储藏所”（Hulme,

2000：5）“浪漫主义混淆了人性与神性的东西……它模糊了人类关系的轮廓，引入了属于非人类的完美”（Hulme，2000：11）。在这一点上，显然玛丽·雪莱与休姆的观点是相似的，她在小说中背离浪漫主义诗歌传统，不仅解构了人类的自大，而且建构了自为存在的自然。

在《末世一人》中，人类灭亡之时，其他生物却安然无恙，这进一步解构了人类中心的宇宙观，表明自然并非如康德等人所言的以人类为目的而存在。普拉齐认为瘟疫的破坏性意味着作者对浪漫主义意识形态、政治理想及性别思想的批判（Plug，2003：160）。埃尔默认为小说不仅批判了浪漫主义理想，甚至对人类这一概念给予致命一击，认为它不是固定的，也不是无可改变的，而是会变化、会犯错的（Elmer，2009：359）。卢梭在《论人类不平等的起源》中指出动物应该享有自然权利，因为他们与人类一样有感官，因此值得同情对待（Hutchings，2007：186）。但玛丽·雪莱笔下的动物不仅不需要人类保护，反而比人类更强大，与自然维持更好的关系，有更强的免疫力。把自己当作万物主宰的人类想当然地认为地球会因为人类遭遇的灭顶之灾感到悲痛：“你没感到地球震动发出痛苦的吼声，空气中孕育着尖叫与嚎哭，——都宣布人类的末日吗？”（249）但事实上，“这些都没有伴随我们的坠落”。春光依旧灿烂：新绿含苞待放，鲜花开满大地，绿叶在和煦的春风中跳动，溪流唱着歌曲流动，大海风平浪静；小鸟在森林中醒来，黑色的大地涌出足够的食物。“死神仅仅眷顾人类。”（216）浪漫主义诗人善于把诗人的情感投射到自然中，或赞美自然触发了内心的灵感，从而产生崇高感，激发诗人的想象。但玛丽·雪莱犀利地解构了这一点，她认为自然是自在自为的存在，并不与人类共情，她甚至不无夸张地指出，人类的灭亡似乎并不影响地球的生态和谐。雪莱揭露人类在茫茫宇宙中如蜉蝣，其居所若蚁丘，但人类却被自己的盲目自大遮蔽了双眼，如井底之蛙一般把自己当成宇宙之王。这种盛行于19世纪的骄傲自大必将招致横祸，因此她以预言者的身份想象人类灭亡的末世惨状，彼时人类的政治制度、文化传统、荣誉与光辉都将不值一提："英格兰，杰出者的摇篮、智者的学院，你的孩子已离去，你的荣光已褪去！你，英格兰，你是人类的胜利，是造物主的眷顾……但他给的光辉已消散，再也无法重现。"（256）

在传统浪漫主义诗歌对自然的建构中，自然通过语言的媒介被再现，但语言所蕴含的社会意识形态将自然简化为符合人类利益和人类认知、人类目的的话语建构物（Huchings，2007：190）。但在玛丽·雪莱的笔下，关于人类末世的寓言撰写在树叶上并隐藏在洞穴中，人类需要解读树叶、洞穴等传递的来自自然的讯息，才能理解自身的命运，可见意义的产生不是从语言到自然的单向过程，而是语言与自然的相遇，自然的物体和过程有能力打乱、修正人类对自然做出的话语阐释。从这个意义上而言，雪莱对人类骄傲的解构甚至超越了英国浪漫主义诗歌对当代英国文化的批判，她在解构人类的骄傲时也将浪漫主义诗人在自然面前的自大一并解构了。

《末世一人》可以被看作对英国浪漫主义文学的戏仿，小说人物以浪漫主义诗人为原型，并再现19世纪英国启蒙者乃至浪漫主义诗人生而为人的骄傲。《末世一人》又可被读作一部宏大的悲剧，其主人公是大写的人类，其致命的性格缺陷即骄傲，骄傲招致其命运的逆转，导致自然的审判，他们的地位从造物主般的崇高堕落到蜉蝣和蝼蚁般的低贱，人类的情感从骄傲转为自责。雪莱以敏锐的观察力、犀利的笔触、惊骇的末世场景敲响警世钟，警醒世人回归文明的源头，反思人性的本质，正确对待人与自然的关系。

3 瘟疫的存在主义书写——抵抗流放感

法国存在主义作家加缪在小说《鼠疫》中书写被鼠疫围困在城内的阿赫兰人对抗鼠疫的故事。在小说的卷首，加缪引用丹尼尔·笛福的话"用别样的监禁生活再现某种监禁生活，与用不存在的事表现真事同等合理"。这一引言似乎为读者和批评家解读小说提供了某些提示，“别样的监禁生活”显然是指小说中因为鼠疫被隔离在城内、与外界切断联系的阿赫兰人，“不存在的事”当然是指小说中虚构的鼠疫事件。那么“某种监禁生活”是什么呢？有评论家认为这是指法西斯战争给人类造成的困境（柳鸣九，2004：110）。加缪在其他地方谈到《鼠疫》时指出，“我试图通过鼠疫来表达外面所遭受的窒息以及我们所经历的受威胁和流放的环境。同时，我还把这种表达推广到总的生存概念上。《鼠疫》将描述那些在战争中经历思考、沉默和精神痛苦的人的形象”（柳鸣九，2004：110）。从这一段话来看，似乎鼠疫是隐喻战争的，1940 年，被德国法西斯占领的法国民众过着监禁的生活。但其意义又不止于此，它也是作者对人类“总的生存概念”的存在主义反思。正如加缪在小说开篇所写，阿赫兰是“个纯粹的现代城市”，“当代人全部如此”（2）。此外，小说的结尾指出，“可鼠疫究竟是怎么回事？那就是生活，如此而已”（271）。有研究者指出，鼠疫的意义是三重的：字面意义的、时代意义的和绝对意义的，显然第三种最为重要，“表现了人的基本现实是非理性的、荒谬的，时刻面临死亡威胁的情况下，所应采取的态度和行动”（刘雪琴，1992：68）。因此，我们认为，通过想象鼠疫带给人类的痛苦，加缪的意图绝不仅仅在于表达法西斯战争带来的颠沛流离，而是形象地描绘西方现代人遭遇生存困境时其内心的孤独、无助感，这些困境可能是战争、环境恶化、流行病肆虐、精神荒芜、心理创伤等造成的。加缪创作的目的并不止于揭示现代生活的荒诞性，而是积极地思考寻求意义的方法，他通过小说主人公里厄医生等人自发的抗疫行为呼吁现代人团结一致、积极抵抗客观世界中不可抗的因素，在命运共同体中寻求生命的意义。

荒诞命题贯穿加缪一生的创作，是“在他创作历程中充分、完整而有力的展现”（柳鸣九，2004：106）。加缪认为“荒诞是在人类的需求与世界的非理性的沉默这两者的对抗中产生的”（柳鸣九，2004：108），柳鸣九称这种对抗为断裂：“人类对理性、和谐、永恒的渴求与向往与自然社会生存有限性之间的‘断裂’，人类的奋斗作为与徒劳无功这一后果之间的断裂”（柳鸣九，2004：108）。由于客观世界不随人类的意志和行为改变，事物的发展不以人类的意愿为转移，人类因此感到疲惫、厌倦、失望、无助，感到愿望无法实现，努力也不能改变现实。有研究者称“荒诞”与“反抗”是加缪哲理中最重要的两个支柱（余乔乔，2002：73）。的确如此，加缪揭示现代生活的荒诞性，将世界的本质暴露在世人面前，其目的是号召人们进行反抗。加缪要求人们先觉醒，继而反抗：“义无反顾地生活，穷尽现有的一切，知道自己的局限，不为永恒枉费心力。”（郭宏安，2013：72）正如《西西弗神话》中的国王一样，“如果说这神话是悲壮的，那是因为它的主人公是有意识的”（余乔乔，2002：73）。西西弗国王深知他推上山的巨石会再次滚落下来，明白自己无论怎么努力也无法打破命运的诅咒，但他仍然坚持抵抗，他幸福感的获得在于与命运抗争的过程。

加缪在《鼠疫》中也勾勒出现代世界的荒诞，小说开篇用灰暗的色彩勾勒出不友好的城市生存环境：“毫无色彩”（加缪，2013：1）、“毫无臆想”（2）、“缺乏活力”（3）、“生活面貌都很平庸”（3）、“人们感到厌倦”（2）。鼠疫袭击后的城市更是失去颜色和愉悦的情感：“鼠疫肆虐中的酷日扑灭了一切色彩，赶走了一切欢乐。”（96）阿赫兰城的居民们在理性的节制下按部就班地过着乏味的生活，在光秃秃的环境中以平庸的节奏沉沉睡去。城里的人重复着毫无意义的生活：矮老头朝街上的猫吐唾沫，老哮喘病人把几颗鹰嘴豆倒来倒去，号称要写书的格朗每天重复修改着那句关于女骑士骑马的句子……加缪用鼠疫象征与人类社会断裂的外在世界，因鼠疫囚禁在阿赫兰城的人们被剥夺记忆、希望、生命以及生存的意义，他们被无助、孤独、绝望、忧虑、疲惫等情绪包围，加缪称这一系列荒诞的感觉为流放感：“在这个骤然被剥夺了幻想与光明的世界里，人感到自己是一个局外人。这是一个得不到解救的流放，因为人被剥夺了对失去的故土的记忆和对福地乐土的希望。这种人与生活，演员与布景的分离，正是荒诞的感觉。”（柳鸣九，2004：109）

加缪着力描写流放感在时间和空间上的表现：“鼠疫带给同胞们

的第一个感觉是流放感”，“那时刻不离我们心田的空虚，那确确切切的激情，那希望时间倒流或相反，希望时间加快飞逝的非理性的愿望，那刺心的记忆之箭，正是这种流放感”（60）。流放感是一系列情感的综合，包括对当下囚禁环境的无助感，与亲人朋友离别的孤寂感，既有追忆往事时的遗憾与悔恨，又有对不可期的未来的不实幻想与不敢轻易幻想的矛盾心态。流放感是时间和空间的双重折磨。首先是时间对人们的流放。人们感受到时间的漫长，他们必须学会与时间妥协，放弃掌控时间，因为对过去、现在和未来，他们都无能为力：“他们对当前心急如焚，对昔日水火不容，而且自身又前途渺茫。”（62）沉浸在记忆中的“放逐犯”往往感到深切的痛苦和悔恨，回忆变得遥不可及；而对亲人团聚的未来的幻想又被无情的鼠疫击碎，但当下的生活又因为鼠疫的肆虐而惨不忍睹，因此未来不可期。往前看、往后看都只会徒增痛苦与无助，人们猛然意识到自己变成了世界的流放犯，他们强迫自己低着头，谨小慎微，他们犹如停在深渊、飘浮在半山腰，“被遗弃在没有方向的日子里和毫无结果的回忆中”（61）。

流放感还意味着空间对人类行为和情感的阻隔。阿赫兰被比作“铁窗”（62），限制人们的行为，尤其是像记者朗贝尔一样被困于城内的外乡人。鼠疫在他们与家乡之间竖起了一道高墙，“他们受困于空间，而且时刻碰撞到阻断他们避难的鼠疫灾区与他们遥远家乡的堵堵高墙”（62）。整座城市“气氛阴郁，死气沉沉”，“热得像蒸笼”（27），恐惧、焦虑、空虚、孤独令本来令人窒息的环境难以忍受，但他们无法逃离，他们每次试图逃离都被高墙反弹回来，流放感加剧。更糟糕的是，他们还给自己建了一堵心理的围墙，拒绝与当下的外在世界交流，沉浸在对家乡的思念、对家人的追忆中，回忆遥不可及的土地、丘陵、树木和女人。“他们固执地抱住自己过分逼真的幻象不放”（63），这些幻象不仅不能带来心理安慰，反而使他们变得敏感，失去对情感的掌控：“要么无缘无故地感到痛苦，要么无缘无故地怀抱希望。”（64）这些外乡人对阿赫兰没有感情，这里不承载他们的记忆，城市的未来也不包含他们，他们就像“失落的幽灵”（93），被失落感吞没，而流放感让时间停住了脚步，让流放者在孤立的空间中永恒地漂浮着，被思念、恐惧、无助、空虚、孤独、绝望等情感吞噬。

关于面对荒诞的办法，加缪的态度是积极的，他既反对自杀，也不同意寄希望于来世，而是主张坚持奋斗、努力抗争（柳鸣九，2004：109）。研究者都达成了共识，即加缪的荒诞主义哲学重点之一是反抗，在 1951 年推出的《反抗者》一书中，加缪甚至提出了“我反抗故我在”的哲学（柳鸣九，2004：113）。然而，反抗具体以什么形式进行才能有效则鲜有人论述。似乎西西弗国王的执着与对命运的藐视就是答案。柳鸣九（2003：63）曾指出：“在《鼠疫》中，关于人应该如何面对荒诞的哲理，显然比加缪以前任何一部作品都表现得明确、清晰、有力度。”这一“明确、清晰、有力度”的抵抗策略包括对共同体寄予的希望和期待。小说的叙述者反复使用“同胞”“我们全体同胞”（96）等词，不仅旨在将彼此孤立的阿赫兰人团结起来，将叙述者与小说中其他人物关联起来，更是从情感上邀请读者加入这个特殊的共同体，共同寻求现代生存的意义。遭遇鼠疫袭击的阿赫兰象征广义的现代城市，小说中书写的流放感并非个人的体验，而是一种共同情感：“原本属于个人的感情，比如，和心爱之人的离情别绪……都突然变成了整城居民的共同感情。”（57）自发组织的卫生防疫队将人们从压抑的流放感中拯救出来，个人不再是孤岛，而是与相同命运的人因相似的情感和相同的行为形成共同体。加缪通过小说人物塔鲁揭示鼠疫的隐喻，他指出“人人身上都潜伏着鼠疫”（223），稍不留神就会把鼠疫传染给别人。这是指个人主义盛行的现代社会中，专注于个人的欲望往往危害他人。因此，小说提倡应该永远站在受害者一边，像医生一样维护生命，以共同体对抗“鼠疫患者”。当恶劣的外在环境抽干了生命的意义时，拒绝做“鼠疫患者”，维护生命是人类必须采取的抵抗行为。

小说中的人物均不是以个体存在，作者在人物称呼上强调他们的职业，如医生里厄、公务员格朗、记者朗贝尔、旅行者塔鲁，还有门房、神父、法官等，这似乎赋予他们某种集体的身份，以个体寓言共同体的命运。“再也不存在个人的命运了，只有鼠疫这个集体的经历和休戚与共的感情”（146），人们唇齿相依。鼠疫的爆发把阿赫兰人凝结为一个与鼠疫对抗的整体，更多清醒的人加入抗疫共同体，包括曾经只关心自己家人安危的法官奥东、曾经一心想要逃离阿赫兰去寻找妻子的记者朗贝尔等。但他们非常清楚，抵抗不一定有效，其意义仅仅在于抵抗本身以及抵抗这个行为滋生的共同体情感，“我们所有的人都吃着同样的流放饭，等待着同样毫无把握而又激动人心的团聚和太平”，耐心与执着是他们的共性：“同样的顺从，同样的坚忍，既无尽期，又无幻想。”（161）

加缪鼓励现代人对抗生存环境的荒诞，而幸福感和生命的意义在于抵抗的过程，他借主人公里厄大夫之口呼吁：“只有疯子、瞎子或懦夫才会放弃斗争”（108），里厄最先识别鼠疫的症状，他对这个强大的敌人有清醒的认识，知道自己的任何行为都可能无法阻挡鼠疫的蔓延。当鼠疫消退，全城人都沉浸在胜利的喜悦中时，他非常冷静地意识到，鼠疫是不可能消灭，将来某一天，它会“使人们再罹祸患”（273）。尽管如此，他从未放弃抵抗，他全力以赴地照料每一个病人，减轻他们的痛苦，或者陪伴他们走到生命的尽头。城里其他人也在他的引领下自发组建志愿者防疫队，甚至连记者朗贝尔也放弃了逃出城的计划，与阿赫兰人一起面对流放。他们意识到，即使鼠疫“意味着无休无止的失败”，但“这不是停止斗争的理由”，他们应该“全力以赴去同死亡作斗争”（110）。在这里，每位防疫志愿者都成了那位西西弗国王，他明知自己费力推上山的石头必将滚下来，还是坚决地重复这个行为，因为抵抗不可抗因素的行为本身产生了意义。《鼠疫》表明：“人在反抗中证实了自己的价值，摆脱了孤独感，找到了团结、友爱和幸福。”（余乔乔，2002：75）

小说表明，尽管这些卫生防疫组织的志愿者们冒着生命危险在帮助他人，共同对抗死敌，但这种抵抗行为不能被当作英雄主义，因为以这样那样的方式斗争是唯一需要做的事，是“顺理成章”的事，“这个道理并没有什么可赞扬之处”（115）。在加缪看来，通过对抗给本来荒诞的生活赋予意义，这行为本身是存在的一部分，是人在当下必须采取的行动。因此，他拒绝对此大加讴歌，这种对英雄主义的低调陈述反而凸显出其在人类共同体中的普遍属性和自然属性，人们明知不可为而为之，通过采取行动消解荒诞社会的流放感。同时，作者表明，英雄主义应该居于次要位置，不能超越人们追求幸福的正当要求，而人们自发组织的对鼠疫的抵抗正是他们找回幸福的努力，因此，它仅仅是自然、自发、普通的、私人的行为，不应该用慷慨激昂的陈词加以赞美。

将阿赫兰人囚禁、致无数人死亡的鼠疫不仅仅象征法西斯战争，也是象征更广泛意义的现代人的生活困境。小说中着力刻画的流放感可以用来概括人类社会面临的诸多困境，如塞缪尔·贝克特的戏剧《终局》中寸草不生的自然环境与残缺的人类肉身，如彼得·汉德克戏剧《卡斯帕》中被语言和文化规训弄得四分五裂的西方现代主体，如美国作家德里罗小说《坠落的人》中的形体艺术家对“9·11”事件的强迫性重复操演等。传染病、生态环境恶化、资本主义的恶性竞争、强权政治、恐怖袭击、宗教冲突……日益使得人类文明危机重重，就如面临鼠疫的阿赫兰人。然而，《鼠疫》表明，“人在面对恶的时候，应该正视恶，承认恶，战胜恶；恶虽败而不能绝迹，人虽胜而不能止步，幸福总是存在于相对之中”（53）。更为重要的是，当人拒绝做“鼠疫患者”，拆除阻隔个体沟通的高墙，形成互助的共同体，以抵抗共同敌人为目的，以尊重生命为目的，就能给荒诞的客观世界赋予意义。

4 结 语

2020年新冠肺炎在全球范围内的暴发，逐渐改变了人们的生活习惯和思维方式，对瘟疫、病毒、死亡、生命等的关注定义着普通人的生活和情感。瘟疫叙事书写瘟疫的发生与蔓延、对人类社会造成的危害以及人类的应对措施，但瘟疫叙事的意义又不仅仅在于瘟疫本身，具体的瘟疫作品承载着再现历史的使命，作品精心设计的情节、人物、意象表达特殊的人类情感，有力地再现时代的精神。笛福的《瘟疫年纪事》、雪莱的《末世一人》、加缪的《鼠疫》通过对瘟疫的想象，分别从现实主义、浪漫主义和存在主义的不同视角刻画了瘟疫袭击给人类带来的恐惧、羞耻、流放感等情感，以此映射西方社会不同历史阶段的主流情感，具体表现为 18 世纪英国中产阶级的焦虑、19 世纪英国启蒙思想家的骄傲、20 世纪现代人的存在主义荒诞。三部作品以真实或虚构的瘟疫作为书写对象，通过瘟疫与人的关系反思人的存在、人的本体、人的意义等问题，就人与他人、人与其他生物、人与自然、生命与死亡等永恒的主题做出探索。

参考文献

[1] BEWELL ALAN. Romanticism and Colonial Disease. Baltimore: John Hopkins University Press, 1999.

[2] CLOUGH PATRICIA, JEAN HALLEY. The Affective Turn: Theorizing the Social. Durham: Duke University Press, 2007.

[3] ELMER JONATHAN. Vaulted Over by the Present: Melancholy and Soveignty in Mary Shelley's The Last Man. Novel, 2009, 42(2): 355-359.

[4] GILMAN ERNEST. Plague Writing in Early Modern England. Chicago: the University of Chicago Press, 2009.

[5] GREGG MELISSA, GREGORY SEIGWORTH. The Affect Theory Reader. Durhm & London: Duke University Press, 2010.

[6] HOGAN PATRICK COLM. Affective Narratology: The Emotional Structure of Stories. Lincoln & London: University of Nebraska Press, 2011.

[7] HUTCHINGS KEVIN. Ecocriticism in British Romantic Studies. Literature Compass, 2007, 4(1): 172-202.

[8] JOHNSON BARBARA. The Last Man //Audrey A. Risch, Anne K.

Mellor & Esther H. Shcor. ed. The Other Mary Shelley: Beyond Frankenstein. Oxford: Oxford UP, 1993: 258-266.

[9] KANT IMMANUEL. The Philosophy of Kant. Carl J. Friedrich ed., New York: Random House, Inc., 1949.

[10] PLUG JAN. Borders of a Lip: Romanticism, Language, History, Politics. New York: State University of New York Press, 2003.

[11] MELVILLE PETER. The Problem of Immunity in The Last Man. SEL, 2007, 47(4): 825-846.

[12] MILLER KATHLEEN. The Literary Culture of Plague in Early Modern England. London: Palgrave Macmillan, 2016.

[13] RICHETTI JOHN. The Life of Daniel Defoe: A Critical Biography. Malden, Massachusetts: Blackwell Publishing, 2015.

[14] SHELLEY MARY. The Last Man. Ontario: Broadview Press, 1996.

[15] 阿尔贝·加缪. 鼠疫. 刘方，译. 上海：上海世纪出版股份有限公司，2013.

[16] 丹尼尔·笛福. 瘟疫年纪事. 许志强，译. 上海：上海译文出版社，2013.

[17] 丹尼尔·舍尔曼. 西方文明史读本. 赵立行，译. 上海：复旦大学出版社，2019.

[18] 郭宏安. 新中国 60 年的加缪小说研究. 当代外国文学，2013（2）：71-78.

[19] 康德. 任何一种能够作为科学出现的未来形而上学导论. 庞景仁，译. 北京：商务印书馆，1996.

[20] 刘雪琴. 反抗的人生——论加缪的《鼠疫》. 外国文学研究，1992（4）：62-69.

[21] 柳鸣九. 论加缪的创作. 学术月刊，2003（1）：57-66+112.

[22] 柳鸣九. 论加缪的思想与创作. 当代外国文学，2004（2）：98-115.

[23] 龙丹，杨莉鸽.《瘟疫年纪事》的创伤叙事研究. 外国语文，

2020（5）：40-47.

[24] 罗素. 西方哲学史（下卷）. 马元德，译. 北京：商务印书馆，2018.

[25] 余乔乔. 加缪作品中的荒诞哲理. 中国社会科学院研究生院学报，2002（4）：72-75.

[26] 赵涵. 当代西方情感史学的由来与理论建构. 史学理论研究，2020（3）：133-148.

以“感知力和激情”认知荒野

——论瑞克·巴斯的雅克山谷叙事

邱小轻

【摘要】瑞克·巴斯在虚构叙事里时常强调自然界的神奇，其实，他在非虚构叙事中也不断使用神奇一词描写他所移居的雅克山谷，并强调用感官和心灵去感知与感受荒野及荒野万物。本文结合生态学家、人类学家兼哲学家戴维·爱布拉姆关于人与万物相连以及用身心去感知自然万物的观点，研读巴斯对雅克山谷的纪实性叙事。巴斯对移居雅克山谷的感性书写，对该山谷的神奇的全身心感受，以及与动物相遇时对彼此内心活动的感性描写，充分说明荒野的神奇，荒野万物的灵性与感性，以及人类可以用感知力和激情认知荒野。

【关键词】瑞克·巴斯；荒野；神奇；感知力；激情

0 引 言

瑞克·巴斯（Rick Bass）是美国当代非常活跃的环境作家或曰自然作家。[①]自 1987 年夏天起他一直居住在美国蒙大拿州最西北的

基金项目：本文系 2020 年度国家社科基金重大项目“认知诗学研究与理论版图重构”（20&ZD291）的阶段性研究成果。

作者简介：邱小轻，女，广东外语外贸大学英文学院教授，硕士生导师，主要从事叙事学、现当代童话改写、美国当代自然书写研究。

① 瑞克·巴斯多数时候被归为自然作家，比如安·罗纳德（Ann Ronald）的文章“Kingdom，Phylum，Class，Order：Twentieth-Century American Nature Writer”［Western American Literature. 1999, vol. 33（4）：384-402］、瑞克·巴斯等作家共同书写的文章“The Rise of Nature Writing：America’s Next Great Genre?［Bass R. et al., Manoa. 1992, 4.2（Autumn）：73-96］等。司各特·斯洛维克（Scott Slovic）则将巴斯的作品归为环境文学（in Rick Bass’s Brown Dog of the Yaak，1999：137）。鉴于巴斯 30 多年来创作的虚构与非虚构叙事大多带有鲜明的环保主题，而且他本人是个环保积极分子，因此本文倾向于称他为环境作家。

雅克山谷。该山谷常年居住人口约 150 人，隶属林肯县，北边与加拿大接壤，南边是库特奈河，东边是巨大的人工湖库卡努萨湖，西边是爱达荷州的高山（Bass，2008：121）。他常年在荒野砍柴、徒步、采摘野果野菜、钓鱼、打猎等。当然，写作是他的生活重心。面对雅克山谷这个新住所，他说："它[住在雅克山谷]让我感觉舒服。"（feel right；Bass，1996：21）可见巴斯与雅克山谷的密切互动，以及对感知力的强调。

戴怀尔（Jim Dwyer）认为巴斯的虚构书写具有独特的魔幻现实主义色彩，对自然的描写"几乎超现实"，作品呈现出种种"怪异、野性、神奇的形象与事件"（in Weltzien，49，50）。他的虚构作品的确给人魔幻现实主义的感觉。以《熊的神话》和《天空、群星、荒野》两个中篇为例，前者存在大量关于育空荒野（the Yukon，位于加拿大西北，延伸至北极圈内）的细致描写，还叙述了人物极其敏锐的感官功能和各种动物般的言行举止；后者既有对巴斯的故乡得克萨斯州西部荒野万物的生动描写，又着力叙述了多种动物的奇特或奇异行为。

这些所谓"魔幻现实主义"元素在巴斯的非虚构叙事中亦大量存在。正如汉特（Richard Hunt）指出，"神奇""神秘""谜"（magic/wonder/mystery）这些词语在巴斯的非虚构著作如《九英里狼》《迷失的棕熊》《雅克的棕色犬》《新的狼群》等出现次数递增，认为这些字眼是理解巴斯 20 世纪 90 年代末以来的作品的关键（in Weltzien 105，117）。事实上，除了《雅克的棕色犬》，巴斯其他关于雅克山谷以及他在该山谷的个人经历的非虚构叙事，包括《冬季》（*Winter*，1991）、《雅克之书》（*The Book of Yaak*，1996）、《野生湿地》（*The Wild Marsh*，2009）、《我为何来到西部》（*Why I Came West*，2008）、《我的爱犬柯尔特》（*Colter*，2000）等，若借用戴怀尔的话，均充满"怪异、野性、神奇"元素。巴斯作为一名严肃作家，他清楚知道虚构与非虚构叙事之间的界限。

因此，有必要审视巴斯在非虚构作品中如何书写荒野的神奇与神秘，以及如此书写的意义。本文结合生态学家、人类学家兼哲学家爱布拉姆（David Abram）关于人与万物相连以及用身心感知自然万物的理论主张，回答以下三个问题：巴斯如何书写他对雅克山谷以及自然万物的认知？这样的书写揭示了荒野与自然万物的什么特性？巴斯如此书写的意图又是什么？

1 感知与感受感性的非人类自然

爱布拉姆以亲身实践和大量事例指出人类与非人类自然能够进行有效沟通，人与万物相连，非人类自然与人类一样具有情感和感知力。他的两部专著，即《感性的魔力：不止人类的世界里的感知与语言》（*The Spell of the Sensuous: Perception and Language in a More-Than-Human World*，1996）和《成为动物：地球宇宙学》（*Becoming Animal: An Earthly Cosmology*，2010），均富有感染力地论证了人类用身心去感知非人类世界的可能性与卓越成效。在《感性的魔力》一书，他指出现代科学忽视了人类的日常生活体验，而他认为这种主观体验恰恰对认知世界具有重要作用，因为科学家本人也是生活在一个不完全确定的主观世界里。因此他有意用具身体验来揭示人类亲身参与自然界，从而感知自然万物的惊人效果（Abram，1996：29，195）。他强调参与性感知（participatory perception），强调联觉或曰通感（synaesthesia），认同庞蒂的现象学语言观，指出万物均拥有表达潜力（Abram，1996：43，45，56）。在《成为动物》一书，他继续阐发，强调人类的动物性以及地球的感性，认为尊重万物的不可知或万物具有一定神秘性与不确定性，其实是在呼唤我们回到身体里面（Abram，2010：1，66-67）。他为地球众多生物被忽视而鸣不平，认为把感性的地球视为附属空间来贬低、征服、避开等的习惯性观点极其有害，认为语言不只为人类拥有，而是生机勃勃的地球的一个特性，认为语言的首要功能不是再现周遭世界，而是让人类参与到这个世界，彼此进行认真、深入交流，他还认为人类与其他物质共享一种由身体直接感知的语言，该语言比人类词语更古老、更深刻（Abram，2010：3，4，8，9，173-74）。此外，与物质女性主义理论家巴拉德（Karen Barad）所持的万物以内在互动的方式相连且相互依赖的观点相类似（Barad，2007：140），爱布拉姆也认为人类只是生物圈的一分子，跟万物纠缠而密切互动（Abram，2010：68）。

巴斯对荒野以及万物的看法与爱布拉姆的高度契合。他充分肯定万物互联："自然的一切织成一张网，万物相连"（Bass，1996：73）；认为"没有绝对的独立，所有独立都是相对而言"（Bass，2009：10）。他强调雅克山谷的地方精神，称其为"一个精神处所"。（Bass，1996：63-64，1999：93）。与爱布拉姆相似，他也强调感觉/感受本身，以及用身心去了解自然的有效性与重要性。他指出，电子与微观电子时代不断侵蚀着我们的感官，使我们的感知变钝，难以参与到真实世界中。（Bass，1992：76）他认为科学有野性的一面，但它严守边界，以至于无法接触到神奇与神秘。（Bass，1996：57）与爱布拉姆一样，巴斯也非常关注自然界的语言，会躺在草地上"倾听……棕熊的音乐，狼的音乐，麋鹿的音乐，青蛙的音乐"（Bass，1996：84）；也会想象"冰川将如何以冰的爪子在石头上写下自己的词语、自己的句子、自己的故事"（Bass，2008：70）。

"感觉（到）""感受""感知（力）"（sensate/sentient/sentience）等表示身心感受的词语是巴斯作品的高频词，可以说是理解其作品的一个关键，在其 30 余本著作里，无论是虚构还是非虚构叙事，也不论是早期作品（20 世纪 80 年代中至 90 年代末），还是 21 世纪以来的各种文类书写，均时常描写人在荒野时依靠各种感官来了解周遭世界，一直强调感知力是了解和理解荒野万物的途径。他如此描写雅克山谷幸存的 14 处没有开通公路的荒野片区的感性特征："这是一处具有上帝痕迹之地——仍有上帝的气味、感觉、视野、味道以及声音——永远鲜活"。（Bass，1996：113）他甚至说："拥有感知力和激情"是达到生物意义上完美的两个首要步骤（Bass，2008：8）。值得注意的是，当被问及如何在虚构与非虚构两种不同创作风格中转换时，他说："我能真真切切感觉到什么时候可以动笔创作虚构作品"（Bass & Johnson，1998：144）。可见他对"感觉"的重视程度。

2 受到神秘力量的感召

巴斯认为是神秘力量把他召唤至雅克山谷。《我为何来到西部》开篇就说这是“一个爱情故事”（Bass，2008：1）。当然，这是指发生在他与雅克山谷之间的爱情。因此，这本讲述他爱上并一直爱着雅克山谷的书，充满激情和各种美妙情感。他以感性语言解释了自己为何从美国南方（密西西比州）万里迢迢来到与加拿大接壤的遥远西北一角：他相信两个相隔千里的人与物之间存在“灵气的化学反应，存在某种意识，或者令人战栗的前意识”，使他冥冥中受到“召唤”（summons），从南方跨越中西部，来到人烟稀少的西北部（Bass，2008：10）。

他还具体说是顺从内心指引，与女友（后来成为他的妻子）驱车离开密西西比，一路往西往北，最终来到雅克山谷，“在那第一眼、第一种气味、第一次触摸中，就知道自己爱上了它，知道在生物上达成了与它合拍的欲望”（Bass，2008：7）。巴斯至今觉得来到这个蓝色山谷仍然是“一个谜”，当时是一种“奇怪、突然蠢蠢欲动的感觉向我们袭来”，于是离开了密西西比（Bass，2008：35）。这也验证了爱布拉姆的观点，即尊重万物具有一定神秘性与不确定性，这样的认识其实是提醒我们遵从内心的感觉与感受（Abram，2010：1，66-67）。事实上，即使在密西西比州的野外工作八年，他也努力满足身心需求：“投身周遭世界中，填满所有感官[需求]”（Bass，2008：26）。

其实，从教育背景看，巴斯是典型“理工男”，大学主修的是地质生物学专业。从工作经历看，毕业后从事的是与专业对口的石油地质学家。但是，相较于科学，他更喜欢艺术，认为艺术源于强烈感情，介于科学世界与精神世界（the world of the spirit）之间，跟随小溪、小江、江河（Bass，1996：37）。对艺术做出如此感性认识，的确符合他以身心去感知自然万物的一贯主张。

自然作家罗纳尔德（Ann Ronald）发现，自然作家会依据其教育背景来描写、分析、思考自然世界，从而形成一套独特思维方式；

她还发现，这些自然作家的教育背景以及在荒野逗留或居住的原因与时长，均会反映到他们的自然书写中。（Ronald，1999：390）她依据叙述者与所述主题的距离（主观性与客观性、亲密程度、激情等），把自然作家分为六类，由于巴斯已经在西北部扎根，罗纳尔德认为可以将其从“移民”作家转成“居民”作家。（Ronald，1999：391，398）巴斯自 1987 年移居雅克山谷，至今已有 30 多个年头，可谓合格的“居民”作家。诺纳尔德认为作家所属类型会决定他们对所描写的地方的坦率程度、真实程度、主客观性、真实性以及地方感，指出一个自然作家了解的第一手材料越多，在一个地方驻留的时间越长，其笔下的风景就会变得愈加熟悉且愈加神秘。（Ronald，1999：391，394）

的确，地质学出身的巴斯会特别关注地质变迁（如长篇小说《曾为沧海之处》）、岩石的特性（如短篇《岩石的生命》以及同名短篇小说集）、万物的变化（如变形（metamorphosis）一词在虚构与非虚构作品中均不时出现）等；由于兼具“移民”和“居民”作家身份，其荒野描写细致中透着好奇与赞叹，荒野充满神秘感，人在荒野中不断感知气候、各种动植物以及矿石等所散发出来的力量，显示出来的神奇或者神秘感。

3 感受雅克山谷的神奇

戴怀尔研读巴斯的虚构叙事时发现，其 20 世纪 90 年代创作的一个主题是“自然世界在物质与精神层面的统一”，相较以前的作品，能更好将神话融进故事中（Weltzien，69）。的确如此。巴斯不仅书写荒野可见的物质层面，也强调其不可见但可感知的精神层面，此外还认为自然与神话密不可分。比如，神话一词以及神话概念在《熊的神话》里表现得淋漓尽致。男女主人公均不时想起流传久远的熊的神话，并对该神话有着不同理解；相较之下，女主人公已经将神话融入自己的生活，认为半辈子的生活如同熊的神话，既神秘又真实，神秘是因为生活中发生了许多她无法掌控的奇妙事情，而之所以真实，是因为她认识到生活存在不可捉摸之处，唯如此才显得珍贵，值得继续（邱小轻，2020：92-93）。

关于神秘，巴斯认为不应视其为知识的敌人而去攻破它，因为这样做其实伤害了神秘的保护层，使得位于神秘下面的知识受到伤害或改变（Bass，1996：6-7）。换句话说，巴斯认为神秘包裹着知识，或者说，神秘本身就是知识，值得我们好好欣赏和感受。爱布拉姆对人类认知的有限性论述可以佐证巴斯对神秘的见解："我们的身体嵌入感官场所，我们只能从自己的有限视角和有限场所体验事物，这注定任何确定、清楚的知识一定会被一层不肯定包裹，从而变得神秘。"（Abram 273-274）

巴斯发现雅克山谷充满奇迹，甚至觉得神奇是我们人类赖以生存的所在（Bass，1996：6-7）。尽管这片47.1万英亩的荒野在外人看来毫不起眼，甚至丑陋，连巴斯也多次坦诚这是一处"奇怪、黑乎乎、湿漉漉、不好客的地方"（Bass，1999：11），"对许多到访者而言，真不是一个美丽的山谷"（Bass，2008：62），其本质是"生物性的荒野，而非娱乐性的荒野"（Bass，2009：5）。但对巴斯而言，无论是日常起居还是艺术创作中，他均发现有某种无形力量或某个东西在推动着他。在谈及为何热爱雅克山谷寒酷的冬天时，他说"我们内心有某个东西热爱着冬天"（Bass，1996：18）。这个不可名状的东西究竟是什么他并不知晓，只能感觉到它的存在。在谈及写作虚构叙事时，他觉得"似乎这些故事均从这些树林穿过我而递送给读者"（Bass，1996：9）。他似乎只是自然与人类之间的一个中介。更多时候，他用具体的东西来描写对自然界的感受和与自然界的联结。他认为每个人的身体内部都存留着"荒野的血液节奏"（blood-rhythms of wilderness）（Bass，1996：12）；认为人类需要荒野万物所展示出来的种种力量和气质："百合花、蕨类、苔藓、蜉蝣的力量……池塘和河流的阳刚之气，石头的阴柔之美"（Bass，1996：xvi）。因而，他会"跳进土地的深处"（Bass，2018：17），而且把所有感官充分打开，使整个人处于迷幻中，近乎催眠状态。（Bass，2008：38）这种感知万物力量和气质的方式，正是爱布拉姆强调的参与性感知（Abram，1996：43）。

而最让巴斯感到雅克山谷的神秘的时节是隆冬一月。他发现这时候人的感官变得超级灵敏，坚信这种超级灵敏现象有一天能得到科学解释。在《野生湿地》一书他叙述了一连两天碰到的三起奇异事件。第一起发生在一个阳光灿烂的下午，他驱车回家路上，疲惫中无来由冒出非常想见到一群火鸡的念头，没想到这些至少在 25 英里之外才能见到的火鸡在他往前行驶不足 1 英里后真的出现在了上空！第二起发生在第二天，他和朋友驱车上山滑雪，来到不可能有动物出没的高处时，突然渴望见到一只猞猁或山猫，没想到走到拐角处时一只小山猫就站在路中央！第三起发生在当晚，他写信给一个朋友，谈论起他们都喜爱爱丽丝·门罗的短篇，没想到第二天打开邮箱居然收到这个朋友的来信，信中细数了他俩喜爱门罗短篇的原因和程度！（Bass，2009：36-37）。

诚然，这种超乎寻常的感官体验可以被视为对自然的超现实主义描写，从而将巴斯的写作风格归为“魔幻现实主义”（Dwyer，2001：50），或者“环境魔幻现实主义”（Bergmann，2017：553）。但是，上述这些关于雅克山谷的神秘的具体描写均为巴斯本人亲身经历，收录在其非虚构著作中。他还将神秘视为一种知识来欣赏和感受，认为自然“比我们大得多，我们无法完全了解。我们只是它的一部分而已”。（Bass，1996：47）此外，他在接受采访时也强调雅克山谷的神奇和生活的奇妙（Bergmann，2017：553）。因此，将巴斯的感受视为真实更合乎情理。

4 感应自然万物的情感

上面几节着重讨论了巴斯对雅克这片荒野的真实感受，那么他又是如何感知荒野中的万物呢？自从来到雅克山谷，巴斯感觉（feels like）住在这里的人们跟周围万物的生命周期更吻合（Bass，1996：15），觉得“自己与河流、石头、鹿拥有的共同点，如同跟人拥有的共同点一样多”（Bass，2008：17）。他还相信快乐可以转化，可以让森林里所有的人与物一同感受到，并让彼此相连（Bass，2009：118）。这充分契合爱布拉姆的人与万物相连的观点。（Abram，2010：68）

1995年和2017年受访时，他强调人类与动物能彼此感知。（Stobb 101）鉴于当今大多数人跟自然界处于疏离脱节状态，他明确表态，会在必要时使拟人手法成为“故事一部分”或“故事中我们那部分的一部分”（Cazajous-Augé 2）。可见拟人手法可以展现动物自身的情感与反应。不少学者从不同学科证明拟人化的积极作用。新物质主义重要代表人物班尼特（Jane Bennett）认为拟人化可以“培养我们对物质力[即物质施事能力]的敏感性”，“使我们与物质产生共鸣”，避免人类中心论（Bennett 119-120）。物质生态批评家奥伯曼（Serpil Oppermann）持相似看法，认为拟人手法既展示生命多样性又使我们认识到物质组成的共同特点（唐建南 122）。

因此，巴斯用代词“他”或“她”指代动物，打猎时会循着动物留下的足迹往前走，认为这些足迹反映了“动物们的思维状态”（Bass，2008：42）。在《雅克之书》专门用一个章节“四只郊狼”讲述了他与郊狼的近距离接触。当他在一座高山上对着位于山坡的一头公牛叫喊时，他惊奇地发现居然是一头郊狼回应了他的叫喊，这头郊狼“好奇地抬头看着他”，当他再次叫喊时：

> 这头郊狼——矮小、浅灰色但接近银色——舔了舔他的嘴唇，仿佛在卡通片中，然后蹦蹦跳跳跑出树林，顺着傍晚的风沿着光滑的岩石往上走……当他离我四十码时，蹲坐下来嚎叫。我对着他嚎叫，然后开始尖叫。他应和着，又开始朝我走过来——有时呈直角式，似乎想离开，但只要我尖叫，他又重新调整方向，朝我径直走过来。他一路走到我跟前。当看到我蜷缩着小小身躯躲在岩石里，受到惊吓，抬起一条腿跑开了。但我发出奶牛、麋鹿般的呜呜声，或者人类悲伤的声音，又甚或是郊狼的呜呜声——所有悲伤的声音听起来都一样——虽然他转身要跑开，但又

无法自拔，没能离开。

……

我蜷缩成一团，像一头小麋鹿，作出跛脚动作，交替发出麋鹿和郊狼的声音。他坐着，黄绿色的眼睛明亮尖锐，微笑看着我，似乎高人一等——似乎在笑我的窘迫。我坐着，回看他，继续发出呜呜的悲伤声音：极为短暂的一瞬间无数事情在我们之间传递——电子的东西，新时代的东西，情感与脑电波，在我们相距五英尺的范围内相互碰撞。我们在相互理解，在交流，就像两位老朋友穿越遥远距离互通信件。郊狼在笑话我同时扮演着那么多不同东西，而我笑话他居然如此不同、如此勇敢地坐在我这个带着步枪的人身旁。

……

（Bass，1996：29-30）

巴斯如此细致地描写了跟一只郊狼的偶遇。他先后模拟奶牛、麋鹿、郊狼的叫声以及悲伤时人与动物会发出同样的呜呜声，以引起郊狼的注意并与之交流。他发现郊狼对这种声音迅速做出回应，以为他是同伴，等到发现蜷缩在岩石间的他不是同伴时，想走开却又被他继续发出的呜呜声吸引住，于是两者坐着对视，巴斯惊讶发现郊狼并不害怕他手中的步枪，感觉与郊狼就像老朋友般顺畅交流。有意思的是，后来当他试着用人类的语言跟郊狼交流时，郊狼马上跑开了（Bass，1996：31）。自此，无论他在原地如何重复之前的呜呜声，这只郊狼再也没有出现。这似乎表明，人类的语言破坏了他们之间的信任。人类欲跟动物交流，必须使用动物所用的语言，努力模仿他们的声音。巴斯正因为这么做而获得了郊狼的信任。

这并非他唯一一次用身心去跟动物交流。当两只郊狼在追赶他的两只家犬过程中碰到他时，他发现这两只郊狼停了下来，“站着不动，智慧的脸上显露出困惑和犹豫”，“他们的心在告诉他们继续追赶下去……但我能看到他们的想法在改变，他们身体的一部分说不要再追赶，而另一部分却在说，继续追赶，越过他，赶快越过他”（Bass，1996：35）。巴斯对他的爱犬柯尔特的叙述情真意切。《我的爱犬柯尔特》这部书的副标题“我曾拥有的最好的狗的真实故事”就可感受到巴斯的浓浓爱意。他不时以柯尔特的眼光看世界；看着柯尔特，他的心会燃烧；在他眼里，柯尔特像一朵绽放的玫瑰，美丽动人。（Bass，2000：31，62，146）

巴斯觉得可能因为在群山里居住了很长时间，自己已经成为群山一分子，他还能听到群山对他说话，要他放慢环保的步伐：“现在对我悄悄说，*平和*，或者，*平静下来*”（Bass，2008：128；原文的强调）。巴斯用身心感知到了群山的语言，呼应了爱布拉姆的语言观，即人类与其他物质共享一种由身体直接感知的语言。（Abram，2010：173-174）

5 结　语

巴斯认为，一旦我们人类忘记愤怒，忘记狂喜，我们变得没那么感性，然后不再感性，那么我们会随着荒野的消失而迷失，我们会变得没那么有人性。（Bass，2008：99）可见人类保持感知力和激情的重要性。

巴斯在《雅克之书》中发出这样的感慨：“这是一场内战，如果人们对土地没有尊重感，那么又怎能要求土地对人们尊重呢？”（Bass，1996：112）即使在近年出版的纪实性著作《旅行的盛宴——与美国最好的作家在路上及共餐》（*The Travelling Feast：On the Road and at the Table with America's Finest Writers* 2018），我们看到他心目中的最好作家，许多都致力于环境书写，包括皮科克（Doug Peacock），斯奈德（Gary Snyder），洛佩兹（Barry Lopez），威廉斯（Terry Tempest）Williams。他本人沿着梭罗、利奥波德等前辈自然作家保护荒野的足迹（Bass，1996：72），一直身体力行，积极投身环保运动。仅以 20 世纪最后 10 年为例，他在各大报纸杂志一共发表了 50 余篇呼吁保护雅克山谷尚未通路的那片荒野的文章，然而，令人遗憾的是，没有一块石头或一小块土壤得到保护（Bass，1999：87）。尽管如此，他仍然奔走在环保的崎岖山道上，仍然继续以感性语言书写人与荒野的动人故事，以身心感觉、感受、感知荒野万物来彰显荒野的神奇与神秘，自然万物的灵性与感性，人与万物相连、同为地球生物圈的一分子，以此提醒我们重新审视人与自然的关系。

参考文献

[1] D ABRAM. The Spell of the Sensuous: Perception and Language in a More-Than-Human World. New York: Vintage Books, 1996.

[2] D ABRAM. Becoming Animal: An Earthly Cosmology. New York: Vintage Books, 2010.

[3] K BARAD K. Meeting the Universe Halfway: Quantum Physics and the Entanglement of Matter and Meaning. Durham & London: Duke University Press, 2007.

[4] R BASS. et al.. The Rise of Nature Writing: America's Next Great Genre?. Manoa, 1992, 4 (2): 73-96.

[5] R BASS. The Book of Yaak. Boston and New York: Houghton MifflinCompany, 1996.

[6] R BASS. Brown Dog of The Yaak: Essays on Art and Activism. Minneapolis: Milkweek Editions, 1999.

[7] R BASS. Colter: The True Story of the Best Dog I Ever Had. Boston and New York: Houghton Mifflin Company, 2000.

[8] R BASS. Why I Came West: A Memoir. Boston and New York: Mariner Books, 2008.

[9] R BASS. The Wild Marsh. Boston and New York: Houghton Mifflin Harcourt, 2009.

[10] R BASS, K C JOHNSON. What the Woods Would Expect of You: An Interview with Rick Bass // S Griffiths, K Kehrwald. Delicious Imaginations: Conversations with Contemporary

Writers. West Lafayette: Purdue University Press, 1999: 142-149.

[11] CAZAJOUS-AUGÉ CLAIRE. An Interview with Rick Bass. Transatlantica, 2016 (1): 1-9.

[12] A RONALD. Kingdom, Phylum, Order: Twentieth-Century American Nature Writer. Western American Literature, 1999, 33 (4): 384-402.

[13] STOBB BILL. The Wild Into the Word: An Interview with Rick Bass. Interdisciplinary Studies in Literature and Environment, 1998, 5 (2): 97-104.

[14] O A WELTZIEN. The Literary Art and Activism of Rick Bass. Salt Lake City: The University of Utah Press, 2001.

[15] 邱小轻. 从新物质主义视角看《熊的神话》对人与非人类自然的后人文书写. 当代外国文学，2020（4）：88-94.

[16] 唐建南. 物质生态批评——生态批评的物质转向. 当代外国文学，2016（2）：114-121.

依恋与悲怆

——认知历史主义视阈下《英格兰，英格兰》的情感认知解读

蒋勇军

【摘要】依恋是一种人与人、人与物，乃至人与社会的亲密关系，理应产生愉悦的情感，而依恋的危机、疏离或缺失则会产生相反的情感效应。依恋的情感效应受情感系统的支配，同时也受到具身、社会、文化和历史等因素的影响。朱利安·巴恩斯小说《英格兰，英格兰》中主人公玛莎·科克伦的童年个性的培养、怀特岛上的爱情与权力之争乃至最后返回怀特岛不同程度地承受了依恋的疏离、危机和缺失。怀特岛也是对英格兰的重构，与其说是一种对“英国性”的怀旧情怀，不如说是对历史的依恋，是对依恋缺失的一种认知重构。认知是具身的、历史的，历史也是具身认知的，认知历史主义视阈下《英格兰，英格兰》中的依恋系统激发出一种悲怆的情感。

【关键词】朱利安·巴恩斯；认知诗学；情感；认知历史主义

0 引 言

至少从柏拉图和亚里士多德时代起，情感就被看作文学和文学体验的重要组成部分，但在 20 世纪的大部分时间里，文学的情感在

基金项目：重庆市教委规划项目“朱利安·巴恩斯小说的认知历史主义批评研究”（21SKGH146）和四川外国语大学校级科研项目“朱利安·巴恩斯作品的情感认知研究”（sisu202111）的阶段性成果。

作者简介：蒋勇军，男，四川外国语大学期刊社编辑，博士，主要从事认知诗学、认知文学研究、外国语言学及应用语言学研究。

很大程度上被忽视了；直到 20 世纪末和 21 世纪初，情感才开始受到文学研究的再次关注（Richardson，2016）。随着情感理论和情感科学的发展，情感认知研究将推动文学的情感探讨。“过去几年，情感认知是一个与认知科学关系越来越密切的重要话题”（Ong et al.，2017：84）。“情感认知”（affective cognition）泛指通过具身认知获得的主观感受或评价。这个术语最早由萨·斯塔茨（Sara Staats）和马乔里·斯达森（Marjorie Stassen）在 1985 年发表的《希望：情感认知》（Hope：An Affective Cognition）一文中提出。他们没有对该术语做具体的界定，但从文章内容可知，情感认知的含义广泛，涵盖了希望（hope）、快乐（happiness）、悲伤（sadness）、忧愁（unhappiness）和绝望（hopelessness）等情绪。“情感认知”是当前国外文学与情感研究中的一个核心术语。它受依恋系统、性欲系统等情感系统的支配，同时又与社会、文化、历史密切相关。

朱利安·巴恩斯（Julian Barnes）打破了小说与其他体裁之间的藩篱，《福楼拜的鹦鹉》（*Flaubert's Parrot*，1984）、《10½章世界史》（*A History of the World in 10½ Chapters*，1989）、《英格兰，英格兰》（*England England*，1998）、《豪猪》（*The Porcupine*，1992）和《红衣男子》（*The Man in the Red Coat*，2020）等小说中的历史书写融合了虚构和历史，将现实与虚构、历史人物与虚构人物交织在一起，通过多种方式重构过去或历史，融合了现实主义和后现代主义的创作手法，形成独具个性的巴恩斯式历史书写。他的历史书写“根据真实的历史事件改编的小说这并不是什么新鲜事，但无疑是当下的文学潮流”（Guppy，2000/2001：57）。莱格特（Bianca Leggett）认为巴恩斯的历史书写受到拒绝妄想和追求真理的意识驱动，是他抵制历史相对主义的一部分，他对历史叙述表现出渴望承认客观真理的不确定性却坚持我们无论如何都要相信它这种对立的观点。“这种尝试在方法论层面，试图超越文化和生物的二分法，在认识论层面，就相当于在客观现实主义和文化相对主义之间走一条折中的道路”。（Richardson，2010：3-4）

对于小说《英格兰，英格兰》的研究，国内外主要探讨了其中的国家身份、记忆、真实与虚构、英国性等问题（Bradford，2011；Romero，2011；Head，2006；Nünning2001；罗媛，2010；王一平，2014/2015；

李颖、李会芳，2020 等）。如罗梅罗（Betsabé Navarro Romero）（2011）把小说置于历史语境中考察后，认为《英格兰，英格兰》讽刺了国家身份的人为塑造；黑德（Dominic Head）（2006）认为巴恩斯试图在怀特岛（Isle of Wight）上复制主题公园来建构"英国性"；王一平（2014）认为"怀特岛国是通过各种拼借而来的，无历史性，是空洞'历史的缝合与转换，并利用大众传媒等进行自我塑形，才完成了对这一新民族国家意识形态的整合与统治"（84）。鲜有人探讨《英格兰，英格兰》中的情感意蕴。本文尝试在认知历史主义的视阈下，从情感认知的层面探讨《英格兰，英格兰》历史书写中记忆与依恋对小说主人公玛莎·科克伦（Martha Cochrane）的身份构建中的悲怆情感。

1 《英格兰，英格兰》嬉闹中的历史重演

"历史书写元小说"（historiographic metafiction）是一种后现代文学体裁，它依赖于小说中融入的历史文献。历史与虚构的融合依赖心智的模拟，最终形成一个心智意象。"巴恩斯的作品例证了后现代主义对历史真实性的怀疑，并结合了典型的当代嬉闹。他的作品中包含了历史人物以及改编的文学作品、互文参考、跨越体裁边界……不仅陈述了传记写作和历史真相之间的关系，还颇为有趣地回答有关记忆的问题、寻找过去触手可及的方法以及改变过去的观点以适应现在的倾向"。（Stott，2011：12）这种形式创新"提升了读者对基于事实的历史、传记或文献虚构的认知要求，这种虚构的元小说制造了不确定性，却仍力求真实性"（Stott，2011：63）。这与历史主义和新历史主义有很大的不同，既不同于历史主义的客观论，也不同于新历史主义的相对主义立场。因此，巴恩斯式的历史书写虽然是历史的重演，但他行走在客观历史与虚无历史之间，符合认知历史主义的历史观。①

① 认知历史主义的历史观请参阅理查森（Alan Richardson）的《神经的崇高：认知理论与浪漫主义时期的文本》（*The Neural Sublime: Cognitive Theories and Romantic Texts*）中的第一章"绪言：认知历史主义"（"Introduction: Cognitive Historicism"）。

《英格兰，英格兰》是一部历史书写元小说。“英格兰在世界上的作用就是扮演一个衰落的象征，一个道德和经济的稻草人。”（55）巴恩斯认为，当代英国存在自由市场完全主导的倾向，常常为了别人的消费而推销自己和模仿自己的倾向，对旅游收入的日益依赖。《英格兰，英格兰》是这个国家当今模样的一个花哨、滑稽、极端的版本（Guppy，2000/2001：55）。怀特岛的主题公园复制历史，剔除民族历史不光彩成分，提供高品质休闲、高档消费和其他商品。为迎合顾客消费的需要，历史都可以随意篡改。岛上有的几乎都是早些时期的物品的复制品。这些虽然是复制品，但更胜过原件，再现了英格兰的历史和文化。在新的环境中复制历史，效果却令人满意，“这件复制品和‘原件’一样受到游客的欢迎”（217）。绝大多数受访者认为复制品完美，没有必要去博物馆欣赏“原件”了。岛国是“乌托邦式”的家园，没有犯罪，没有司法体系和监狱，也没有政府，只有一个没有选举权的总督，因而没有选举和政客，是一个理想的“和平的王国，一种新型的国家，一章未来的蓝图”（243）。然而，无论这些物品如何与原件相似，但都不是真实的历史，回避了真相的问题。

“历史是一个壮汉”（178），历史上的传奇故事几乎完全是男性。然而，岛上对历史人物的性别取向进行了篡改，罗宾变成了女性大盗，演绎新罗宾汉传奇。“逍遥帮”变成了一群“仙女组合”，并加入了同性恋等元素，因为“同性行为在不作道德评判的背景下是一种历史常态”（181）。里面的服装怪异、活动仪式化，并积极招募男同性恋和少数族裔的人。这些扭曲历史的做法让马克斯博士难以接受，“感觉遭受了职业生涯中前所未有的侮辱”（182），并提出辞职。因此，怀特岛上对历史的重演“遗忘了历史”（Guignery，2006：59），变成了一场历史闹剧。历史应该是一个严肃对待的问题，但在怀特岛上，“历史被保存了下来，但以一种极其简单的方式，而且纯粹是为了旅游也就是经济目的”（Guignery，2006：59），历史的重演变成了嬉闹。

《英格兰，英格兰》质疑了历史的真相和真实性，岛国的历史是复制而来的，真相难以寻找，真实性受到质疑。小说中唯一的真实时刻（Guignery，2006：114）和获得真相发生在复制的约翰逊博士“向她弯下腰，喘息着，喃喃低语，她突然感受到的真相是他的痛苦是真实的。其真实性来自与世界的真实接触”（262）。这里的真相不是事实，而是情感的真实，这种真实是与现实世界真正接触后的情感反应。岛国上的世界是复制的世界，岛上过着与世隔绝的生活，很难获取历史的真相。唯一可以信赖的是已死去的人。人类如鲜花般生命短暂和绚丽，岛国犹如“没有花瓶和水”的鲜花。岛国是基于历史基础上的改进，看似一切都是真的，其实“一切都不是真的”（264）。

怀特岛主题公园犹如幻想，看似真相而非真相。保罗和玛莎袭击总督的农民起义的表演看似更加真实，但历史被挪用、被再造、被复制，乃至被粗化。个人的信仰已丧失，“看看英国发生的事情。古老的英格兰。它什么都不信了。嗯，它现在还是得过且过。它还运作良好。但它失去了严肃性”（285）。怀特岛是主题游乐公园，里面的历史复制品主要是迎合经营的需要，虽然运作良好，却丢失了信仰。“小说中的每件事和每个人都是对令人怀疑的记忆和怀旧之物的伪造，往往是一种讽刺。因此，巴恩斯……毫不留情地强调，他的同行们隐含或忽略的意义：英国性是一种空洞的幻想。”（Bradford，2001：93）历史在怀特岛上重演，第一次是闹剧，第二次是悲剧。

2 玛莎的记忆与依恋身份建构

格林布拉特（Greenblatt，1980：9）认为，自我塑造不考虑文学和社会生活之间的明显差异，跨越了文学人物角色的创造、自我身份的塑造、被自己控制的力量所塑造的经验、塑造其他自我尝试的界线，这会让我们获取特定文化中复杂的意义互动，他强调自我塑造的历史性和文化特性。《英格兰，英格兰》如同巴恩斯之前的小说《伦敦郊区》《凝视太阳》，采用传统叙事的时间顺序，主要是以玛莎·科克伦（Martha Cochrane）回忆自己的生活为线索。第一部分为“英格兰”，主要讲述玛莎追忆青少年的成长，她喜欢拼图游戏，对宗教和记忆持怀疑态度。第二部分“英格兰，英格兰”提出了一种幻想：媒体大亨杰克皮特曼爵士和他的同事将怀特岛变成一个巨大的主题公园，起名“英格兰，英格兰”；岛上复制了英格兰最著名的历史建筑、网站和数据。岛上的项目是一个巨大的成功，而英格兰却遭遇了极度的衰退。第三部分是“安格利亚”，故事发生在几十年后一个现在被称为安格利亚的村庄，“英格兰，英格兰”大陆则变成了一潭死水。它被描绘成一个神秘、受排斥、惯犯少的国家，没有境外势力的影响。

小说中有两条线索，一明一暗。明线是玛莎讲述自己从年少到年老的生活故事，是对自己一段有关记忆的记忆；暗线则是讲述对英格兰历史的复制和重构，在怀特岛上建立一个主题公园，是对英国的国家记忆。两者的共性在于：“过去永远不是简单的过去，而是能够让当下心安理得地存在的依据”（5）；记忆是一种持续的自欺欺人，外表和内在之间总会受到一些宣传、贩卖或者营销因素的干预和影响。因此，小说中不仅涉及玛莎回忆自己一段记忆的记忆，还有关于英格兰在怀特岛上主题公园的自我塑形。从主题公园“英格兰，英格兰”的题目及其重复的关系，就可以推测后一个是前一个的重复或者模拟。巴恩斯曾说过这部小说是“关于英格兰、真实性、探索真相、发明传统以及我们如何忘记历史的”（Observer，2009：27）。

2.1　玛莎的自我塑形与自我建构

玛莎的第一段记忆是厨房地板垫子上的英格兰行政区拼图版，并具有这个国家的框架。她通常沿着海岸线开始拼图，但最后总是少一块，顿时觉得世界不完美，“一股悲伤、挫败和失望的情绪就会笼罩着她”（4），直到父亲出现拿出那块拼图，“斯塔福德郡已经找到，她的拼图，她的英格兰，还有她的内心有变得完整了”。在玛莎心里，“拼图是构建国家的一个简单的隐喻”（Pateman，2002：76）。可以看出，玛莎对拼图所构建的虚拟身份有认同感，而且这种认同感影响自我的完整构建。玛莎玩弄拼图也是对她性格的培养和建构自我的过程，在她看来，性格培养“一定是你具有的某样东西，或者一旦有什么事情发生在你身上会改变的东西”（15）。母亲告诉她，父亲离开家是因为他在口袋里找不到他放的诺丁汉图块，为了不想让她失望，他就去找那一块了，只不过花的时间比他想象得要长得多，但她相信他找到那块拼图后会回来的。因此，她觉得是她的拼图把父亲弄丢了，从而自责又难过，认为一切都是自己的过错，是自己造成父亲的消失和母亲的痛苦，并告诫自己以后千万不能再粗心和愚蠢了。几年后，她慢慢意识到父亲和那块拼图都不会回来了，无论是对于拼图还是英格兰，玛莎的心也不再完整了：“无法填补她内心那个准确的、唯一的、锯齿般的缺口”（29）。

正在培养个性的阶段，玛莎的自我建构受到侵蚀，在母亲的影响下认为男人要么很坏要么很弱，而女人一定要坚强，要照顾好自己。为了坚强，她每天扔一块拼图，一个学期下来，整个拼图就被扔进垃圾桶了。这似乎也暗示了她与父亲的决裂。“她并不清楚自己是要记住过去还是要忘记过去。像这样她绝不会培养成自己的性格”（20），她对自己的自我身份和国家身份感到不安和不确定。父亲的背叛让她慢慢长大，她的性格逐步确立，变得更加聪明，认为妈妈说的规律是对的，“他们犯的是他们的错误，现在你犯的是你的错误”（26）。因此，“二十五岁以后，你不能再对父母有任何责怪”成了玛莎的人生信条。当再次见到父亲时，她向他要诺丁汉郡的图块，但他不记得了。为此她永远记恨他。因此，父亲的背叛和诺丁汉郡的缺失是玛莎内心永远的痛，她的内心不再完整。

后来，玛莎应聘到杰克·皮特曼（Sir Jack Pitman）公司并参与“英格兰，英格兰”主题公园的建设，成为主题公园的首席执行长官。情人保罗认为杰克老板是她父亲的替代品，而怀特岛的英格兰复制品也替代了童年时的英格兰版图的拼图。在处理英格兰国王的问题上，她和保罗就发动政变一事发生争执。保罗认为玛莎既背叛了杰克老板，是弑父的行为，又背叛了他。玛莎则进行自我反思：在工作中面对一个问题或决定的时候，她思维清晰，逻辑严谨……到了晚上，这些品质就消失了。为什么要对保罗这么苛刻？只是因为对自己失望吗？母亲的教导和过去的经历，让玛莎认为不能责怪任何人，不能责怪怀特岛的项目以及英国历史。一切只能怪运气。她清楚自己想要什么："真实、简单、爱情、善良、友情、乐趣，还有美好的性爱也许要排在第一位。"（161）后来，保罗取代了玛莎的位置，玛莎被杰克老板驱逐出怀特岛，并将她列为岛上不受欢迎的人。去和马克斯博士告别时，马克斯博士相信她能在"已被弃置的救赎体系的残迹中"（284）自我塑形。

小说最后，玛莎经历了数十年的漂泊后再次回到怀特岛的安吉利亚村，她的生活孤独而无聊，"像一只候鸟般飞回安吉利亚的，而不是作为一个狂热分子的回归"（207）。她变得平静，并融入村子的生活，个性上抛弃了母亲之前讲的生活规律，"终于适应了这里的安静的……重复生活，适应了村民们的小心谨慎和毫无隐私，乐于相助，精神乱伦，适应了这里的漫漫长夜"（307），"不再为私人问题感到烦恼"（308），不再去争辩生活的意义。她的人生"幼时聪敏，成年心灰意冷，最后竟落得一个老处女的下场"（309）。米拉克（James J. Miracky）认为，《英格兰，英格兰》结尾充满了悲伤，玛莎沉浸在虚幻之中，幻想重构纯真，充满着孤独和忧郁。

2.2 英格兰的自我塑形及其身份重塑

主题公园"英格兰，英格兰"试图模拟、重构英国的历史，再现英国的历史和文化，重塑英国的身份。英格兰的历史和文化特征被浓缩到怀特岛上的一个主题公园里：大本钟、白金汉宫、亚瑟王和罗宾汉等神话中的人物，还有由演员扮演的传奇人物，如约翰逊博士。所有这些人和物都是复制历史和真实世界的人和物，并履行他们既定的、可预测的、被弱化了的职责。在小说中，"英国人擅长传统，他们还擅长发明传统"（30）。怀特岛取得了很大成功，"一种光明、现代的爱国情感迅速发展起来。这种爱国情感不是建立在征服故事和深情朗诵的基础之上"（243），这种构建的国家身份与真实的英格兰国家身份不同，具有热烈的爱国情感，而且这种情感产生了"一个骄傲的新的岛国"（243）。这种乌托邦式的岛国最终取代了英格兰大陆或老英格兰，并传播了对原始土地的负面看法。在那里，

“人们背负着昨天、前天、前天……”（244）。被剥夺了所有历史特征和大部分人口的英格兰，被重新定义为“被自己的历史疲劳的民族”（235）。通过对历史的重演，英格兰重构了历史，因为“记忆就是身份”（300）。在岛国，“英格兰，英格兰”成了“英格兰”的国家身份，“岛国本身也在竭力忘记除此之外的任何历史”。在一次采访中，巴恩斯评论说：“《英格兰，英格兰》更多是关于一个国家的虚假事实的创造，这些粗糙的图像代表真实的东西。写完这本书后，我偶然读到了勒南[①]的一句精彩语录：‘错误理解历史是一个国家的组成部分。’这句话本可以作为这本书的题词。错误的历史也是创建一个国家的一部分。你构建那些解放的神话、对抗压迫者的神话、勇敢的神话。它们通常都有一定比例的真实性，所以很容易形成神话，但成为一个国家以及变成一个国家也取决于这些神话的延续。”（Guignery，2006：59）

在巴恩斯看来，怀特岛国的身份源于错误的历史记忆，记忆本身就可以成为一种身份。这种身份与神话的构建和延续相关。岛国和英格兰展现的都是英国历史和文化中光彩的特征，主要的历史人物和情节都被简化和浓缩，进行“现代神话的重新定位”（148），如卖橘子的成为查尔斯二世的情妇、新教妓女。为了隐瞒英国国王查理二世情妇（114）内尔·格温通奸、恋童癖和“三人同床”的历史，玛莎建议改为：“让她年长些……没有儿童，没有其他情人，也没有社会或宗教的背景。然后，她可以是一位来自中产阶级的女孩，最后跟国王联姻”（115），“她的精华就像她的果汁，被浓缩了，她仍然是她曾经的版本，或者至少是游客的版本……”（223）。这些修改可以适应现代游客的认知需求，从而激发了人们的爱国激情。因此，巴恩斯的历史书写“通过我们自己的流行形象和历史拟像来寻求历史”（Jameson，1972：135），具有认知科学上所说的具身认知性。

① 欧内斯特·勒南（Ernest Renan, 1823—1892）。

3 玛莎的依恋之爱与悲怆之情

依恋（attachment）是心理过程发展到一定阶段的产物，一种感情上的联结和纽带。它是一种社会行为，维系社会层级中的相应位置（Winn，2001：1034），是人与人之间的亲密关系主要源泉之一。[①]霍根（Hogan，2011：112）认为童年时期是父母与孩子之间建立依恋关系的关键时期，一个人的依恋模式在这一时期确立，而且与朋友或配偶之间在某个时期也会形成依恋关系。因此，家庭成员之间（特别是父母与孩子之间），朋友、恋人以及某物之间在人生的某个时期会出现依恋或依恋之爱。依恋、依恋危机、依恋疏离、依恋缺失会激发情感系统，产生相应的情感反应。从情感理论而言，依恋是一种亲密的关系，会产生愉悦的情感效应，而依恋危机、依恋疏离或依恋缺失是相对于"失去"而言，因此会带来焦虑、创伤，产生悲伤的情感效应。[②]布雷德福（Bradford，2011：94）指出："巴恩斯将萎缩的怀旧情绪带到了生活中。"这种怀旧情绪本质上可看作一种依恋的情感。这种依恋的情感或者怀旧的情绪有一种令人喜爱的伤感。即使是那些本应以可悲、荒谬而突出的人物，也往往被赋予了一种悲剧的气氛。《英格兰，英格兰》虽然是一部关于政治的小说，但其中也充满着保罗和玛莎的浪漫之爱和玛莎对父母、拼图以及"英格兰，英格兰"的依恋之爱。

小说的叙述始于玛莎对童年的回忆，那时正是玛莎个性培养的关键期，也是依恋形成的关键期。有一天父亲突然离开了家，妈妈告诉玛莎他出去给她找诺丁汉拼图块了，可能时间会久点，但早晚会回来的。幼小的心灵难以承受失去父亲的伤害，而且还把父亲离家归结于自己的错，"一切都是她的错……是她造成了父亲的消失和她妈妈的痛苦"（17）。父亲对家庭的背叛给玛莎幼小的心灵造成了深深的伤害，尤其杰西卡·詹姆斯对她有意的恶作剧，让她受到惩

① 其他两个源泉是寻求系统（seeking system）和性爱系统（sexual system）（Fisher，2004：77-98）。

② 有关依恋与悲伤情感效应的研究，请参见谢弗等（Shaver and Tancredy，2001：63-88）。

罚，人们认为她玩世不恭，并把这一性格问题归结于她的家庭——“玛莎的家庭跟其他的家庭不一样”（15）。当她妈妈被人接走时，“总让玛莎想到她的妈妈也会消失”，所以她心里非常害怕，一是因为可能她从此就会成为孤儿，二是他妈妈经常被男人抛弃。她父亲的离开以及“这些来来往往的男人”（23）在她懵懂的心里埋下这样的想法：这些男人都会伤害她妈妈。因此，出于对妈妈的依恋和关心，她总是装病把妈妈拖在家里。

妈妈的生活哲理对玛莎的个性培养起到了关键的作用，男人在她心中不是很好就是很弱，这种刻板印象和认知石化让她不再相信男人，也为她在小说结尾的孤独一生埋下伏笔。正是父亲和父母关系对她的影响，让她觉得男人靠不住，一切都只有靠自己，“女人一定要坚强，要照顾好自己”（19），并形成她的一条人生信条：“二十五岁以后，你不能再对父母有任何责怪”，“受伤是童年的一部分。不允许对他们再有任何责怪。不允许”（26）。无论是她以后在怀特岛上的工作，还是和保罗的浪漫爱情，都体现出关键期形成的依恋风格对她的影响。

拼图是玛莎记忆的起点，对父亲的依恋主要是对拼图的依恋。父亲带走了诺丁汉郡，使英格兰版图不再完整，从而造成依恋的缺失。与此同时，拼图的缺失也喻指了玛莎父亲的缺失，她要找回来的是拼图。她在厨房走廊发现的一片橡树叶，她认为，只要她把这张叶子作为想起父亲的信物，那么他也会保存好那块缺失的诺丁汉图块。虽然她清楚诺丁汉郡图块和父亲不再回来，但她仍抱有希望，希望她和妈妈的泪水“可以把她的爸爸带回来”（19）。父爱的缺失让玛莎学会了坚强，她试图通过扔掉拼图块来培养个性，但扔完后还是不清楚“她是要记住过去还是要忘记过去”。（20）当她父亲主动找她后，才知道他当初抛妻弃女的原由是因为爱上了另一个女人。她一直期盼的诺丁汉郡图块也没有找回，因为她父亲忘记了。按照她的人生信条，她过二十五了，不能再对父母有任何责怪，然而她违背了这条信条，“她会因为这件事一直记恨他”（29）。父爱的缺失犹如拼图的不完整，从而玛莎的心也不完整，尽管她父亲回来，可缺失的仍无法弥补，如同第一次拼图时由于缺少一块拼图块。此时，一股悲伤、挫败和失望的情绪笼罩着她。在怀特岛上时，情人保罗甚至认为杰克老板是她父亲的替代品。

玛莎在怀特岛的主题公园“英格兰，英格兰”做首席执行长官，和保罗发生了一场轰轰烈烈的爱情，并和保罗一起试图排挤杰克老板，但讽刺的是保罗坐上了她的位置，而她却被无情地赶走，并被列为“岛上不受欢迎的人”（283）。玛莎离开时，“她拉开厚重的大门，勉勉强强关上，但是没有上锁，以免还有别人会来。因为这就是你的大棚，还有鲜花和故事”（287）。这为玛莎以后的回归埋下伏笔。“你”既可以指别人，还可以指“玛莎”。当玛莎结束数十年漂泊回到安吉利亚[①]时，海关官员声称“迷途知返是一件好事”（299）。她发现“旧英格兰失去了它的历史地位，它也就完全失去了自我意识”（300）。初回到一个“夜不闭户，路不拾遗”的小村子时，“玛莎有些伤感”（306），这与她之前的生活形成了鲜明的对比，对以前生活的依恋让现在的她产生心理落差，从而感到忧伤。因此，有人说她“是在怀念远方明亮的灯火了吧？”（303）。“远方明亮的灯火”可能暗指明亮的大城市。最后，她“终于适应了这里的安静”（307），这说明玛莎的经过一段时间，适应了这里生活。她觉得自己就像一只候鸟飞回安吉利亚，“她没有性生活；她在变老，她知道自己的寂寞”（307），回到“孤独”的老处女们的生活。

“山村狂欢节揭幕”庆典“可能表现出一种鄙夷的悲怆”（Bradford，2011：96）。然而，安吉利亚虽然落后，但小村子的生活宁静，没有纷争，夜不闭户，这恰好是现代社会的“乌托邦式”的生活。村子的生活“既不是田园牧歌，也不是反乌托邦”（306）。在玛莎看来，真正意义上的怀旧是“怀念自己可能永远不会知道的事”（310）。就玛莎的内心活动而言，她不像纯真的孩子们那样在真实和虚假中转变，而只看到虚假纯真与快乐，透露出一种因依恋情感而产生的世俗沧桑的悲怆。

① 安吉利亚是旧英格兰改名后的称呼。

4 结　语

情感应置于历史语境中加以考察，《英格兰，英格兰》中的“真实”身份与“虚构”身份体现了社会历史背景对小说人物塑形的影响，为情感认知的研究提供了语境输入。就情感系统而言，《英格兰，英格兰》中的玛莎经历了童年时对父亲的依恋疏离、成年时怀特岛上的爱情与权力之争的依恋危机，以及老年的依恋缺失。小说中的怀特岛又何尚不是对昔日“日不落帝国”英格兰的依恋，所体现的“英国性”也是依恋情感的体现。这种依恋情感最终都在似真非真、似幻非幻的历史重复中消耗。无论是玛莎自身的身份构建还是怀特岛对“英格兰”历史的重现，都体现了历史是具身认知的，历史总是处在真相与虚无之间。历史已逝，怀特岛对历史的重演在一定程度上体现了对历史的依恋缺失，而这种缺失又随着处于依恋危机、依恋疏离和依恋缺失的玛莎，油然产生一种悲怆的情感。

参考文献

[1] BIANCA LEGGETT. The Age of Suspicion and Replenishment: Alternatives to Metanarrative in the Work of Julian Barnes// Guignery, Vanessa. Worlds within Words: Twenty-first Century Visions on the Work of Julian Barnes. Sibiu: Lucian Blaga University Press, 2009: 26-38.

[2] BRADFORD RICHARD. Julian Barnes's England, England and Englishness// Groes Sebastian & Peter Childs. Julian Barnes: Contemporary Critical Perspectives. London: Continuum International Publishing Group, 2011.

[3] FISHER HELEN. Why We Love: The Nature and Chemistry of Romantic Love. New York: Henry Holt, 2004.

[4] GREENBLATT STEPHEN. Renaissance Self-Fashioning: From More to Shakespeare. Chicago & London: University Of Chicago

Press, 1980.

[5] GROES SEBASTIAN. Peter Childs. Julian Barnes: Contemporary Critical Perspectives. London & New York: Continuum International Publishing Group, 2011.

[6] GUIGNERY VANESSA. The Fiction of Julian Barnes. Hampshire: Palgrave Macmillan, 2006.

[7] GUPPY SHUSHA. The Art of Fiction: CLXV, Julian Barnes. Paris Review, 2000/2001(157):55-84.

[8] HEAD DOMINIC. Julian Barnes and a Case of English Identity// Rod Mengham and Philip Tew. British Fiction Today. London: Continuum, 2006: 15-27.

[9] HOGAN PATRICK COLM. Affect Studies. (2016-08-31) [2022-02-22]. https://doi.org/10.1093/acrefore/9780190201098.013.105.

[10] HOGAN PATRICK COLM. What Literature Teaches Us about Emotion. Cambridge: Cambridge University Press, 2011.

[11] JAMESON FREDERIC. The Prison-House of Language: A Critical Account of Structuralism and Russian Formalism. Princeton. NJ: Princeton University Press, 1972.

[12] NÜNNING VERA. The Invention of Cultural Traditions: The Construction and Deconstruction of Englishness and Authenticity in Julian Barnes' England, England. Anglia, 2001(1): 58-76.

[13] Observer. He's Turned Towards Python. (But not the dead Flaubert's Parrot sketch...): Interview with Julian Barnes// Vanessa Guignery & Ryan Roberts. Conversations with Julian Barnes. Jackson: University Press of Mississippi, 2009.

[14] ONG DESMOND, ZAKI JAMIL, NOAH GOODMAN. Understanding Affective Cognition: Frontiers in ModelingVReasoning about Others' Emotions. Proceedings of the Annual Meeting of the Cognitive Science Society, 2017 (36):84-85.

[15] RICHARDSON ALAN. The Neural Sublime: Cognitive Theories

and Romantic Texts[M]. Maryland: The Johns Hopkins University Press, 2010.
[16] ROMERO BETSABÉ NAVARRO. Playing with Collective Memories: Julian Barnes's England, England and New Labour's Rebranding of Britain. Valladolid, 2011(32): 241-261.
[17] SHAVER PHILLIP, CAROLINE TANCREDY. Emotion, Attachment, and Bereavement: A Conceptual Commentary// M. S. Stroebe, R. O. Hansson, W. Stroebe & H. Schut. Handbook of Bereavement Research: Consequences, Coping, and Care. Washington, DC: American Psychological Association, 2001: 63-88.
[18] R STAATS SARA, MARJORIE A STASSEN. Hope: An Affective Cognition. Social Indicators Research, 1985(3):235-242.
[19] STOTT CORNELIA. The Sound of Truth: Constructed and Reconstructed Lives in English Novels Since Julian Barnes's Flaubert's Parrot. Tectum Verlag, 2011.
[20] WINN PHILIP. Dictionary of Biological Psychology. London and New York: Routledge, 2001.
[21] 李颖，李会芳. 论朱利安·巴恩斯的法国情结与英格兰性反思. 湖南科技大学学报（社会科学版），2020(4): 45-51.
[22] 罗媛. 历史反思与身份追寻——论《英格兰，英格兰》的主题意蕴. 当代外国文学，2010(1): 105-114.
[23] 王一平.《英格兰，英格兰》的另类主题——论怀特岛“英格兰”的民族国家建构. 外国文学评论，2014（2）: 78-89.
[24] 王一平. 朱利安·巴恩斯小说的当代“英国性”建构与书写模式. 国外文学，2015(1): 74-80, 158.
[25] 朱利安·巴恩斯. 英格兰，英格兰. 马红旗，译. 南京：译林出版社，2015.

认知诗学“关键词”

情感历史主义

李丹云

【摘要】情感历史主义是外国文学研究中，继“认知转向”“情感转向”之后重新强调历史维度的文学批评范式。它摒弃了历史主义决定论和文本中心论，同时又吸收借鉴了历史主义和新历史主义的历史视角和思维，特别是在认知历史主义理论基础之上，回到人的主体性，专注情感的生物性、文学性、文化性、历史性的继承发展关系。本文简要厘清了情感历史主义的理论关联和基础，提出情感历史主义的主要特征在于关注情感的历史、情感的文化建构性以及关注特殊情感社区中情感群体，在情感脚本和规则的制约下，如何在情感事件中表征情感。情感历史主义的研究范式大致可以分为情感科学和情感后结构主义两类，各有所长，各有侧重，相互借鉴和支撑是新的趋势。

【关键词】情感历史主义；情感科学；情感后结构主义；特征；范式

情感历史主义认为情感随历史、文化背景不同而变化，既要强调历史的连续性、承接性，也要关注历史的批判性和文化诗学内涵。目前学界还未正式确立“情感历史主义”的学理内涵和重要地位。因此，我们有必要厘清其内涵及主要特征，与历史主义、新历史主义、认知历史主义的理论关联，然后转向情感历史主义的主要研究范式，进行引介和评述，以期为认知诗学和文学认知研究提供新的视角、理论、方法和术语借鉴。

作者简介：李丹云，女，四川外国语大学博士研究生，海南医学院副教授，研究方向为认知诗学、医学英语教学。

1 “认知转向”“情感转向”“情感历史主义”

20 世纪以来，外国文学研究在认知科学的兴起和发展助力下，也经历了“认知转向”(cognitiveturn)，且呈现出理论视域拓展（借鉴认知语言学、认知科学领域的理论）、研究方法更新（实验室神经科学研究、文本细读、访谈）、研究路径延伸三个突出特点（熊沐清，2019)。其中，最为突出的特征是，研究路径在原有经典文学研究领域之上增加了“认知”的维度，比如诗学延申为“认知诗学”，叙事学延伸为“认知叙事学”，类似的还衍生出认知后殖民研究、认知生态批评、文学达尔文主义、文学中的认知障碍研究、神经美学等路径。到大约 20 世纪 90 年代中期开始，西方人文社会科学领域开始出现“情感转向”(affective turn)（熊沐清，2019：302)。在这样的双重转向背景之下，学界对认知和情感之间的关系和区别有所论争，具体表现在“情感科学”是否应从属于认知科学，还是应当成为一门独立的学科。熊沐清教授认为文学情感的研究对象，即情感、感觉、情绪、态度等的性质和理论基础都以认知科学为基础，因而可以将“情感转向”视为广义的认知文学研究的一个十分重要的方面(2019)。无论是真实世界中人们体验的情感，还是文学虚构世界中人物的情感，抑或是读者或观众的接受情感，按照霍根(Patrick Colm Hogan)的理解，都可以统称为“文学情感”(literary feeling)(Hogan，2011：54)。“文学情感”研究呈现出情感叙事学、情感生态批评、情感地理学批评三大范式(2019)。然而，本质上而言，无论是哪种批评范式，都无法脱离情感历史主义的视角和维度。

“情感历史主义”(affective historicism)最先由霍根在其文学情感研究专著《文学与情感》(Literature and Emotion，2018)中提出，该研究范式认为情感在不同时期、不同文化中是不一致的，随历史变化而变化(62)。他重点关注的是作者的历史性，认为特定作品的时空背景、社会文化背景是由作者设定的，而不是由读者或者观众设定的；其次，正如汉斯·罗伯特·姚斯（ Hans Robert Jauss ）所说的那样，一部新作品可能会和当代读者的期望视野相去甚远。一部作品的复杂性和细微差别可能需要几十年甚至几百年的时间才能为读者所理解。因此，读者的历史性可能导致最初受众的理解和反应是有限的，甚至往往被认为是错误的。这意味着作者可能以某种微妙的方式，利用当时历史和文化定义的原则和做法，可能会以一种对于当代读者不那么明显的方式来表现文化和历史主题的隐含变化。

2 历史主义、新历史主义、认知历史主义

情感历史主义自然以历史性为理论基石，更侧重文学批评中的认知和情感的历史关联。历史主义是研究文化史、文学史、思想史等历史的哲学方法。近代以来，历史主义代表人物包括维柯、卢梭、伯克以及黑格尔，到现代历史哲学家柯亨、克罗齐、狄尔泰、斯宾格勒等，虽然各自理论基础和视域不同，但都强调历史的总体性发展观，后来这种观点受到批评，政治思想家卡尔·波普尔（Karl Raimund Popper）就是反对的典型代表之一，他认为“历史命运之说纯属迷信，科学的或任何别的合理方法都不可能预测人类历史的进程”（《历史主义的贫困》，伦敦，1957，第 1 页）。在波普尔看来，历史主义要求权力集中，是一种历史的整体论、乌托邦主义和历史的决定论。当然，历史主义更是遭到俄国形式主义、结构主义、新批评和解构主义的反对和清算。限于篇幅，仅略作铺垫，此不赘述。

新历史主义诞生于 20 世纪 80 年代英美文化和文学界，是一种不同于旧历史主义和形式批评的“新”的文学批评方法，一种对历史文本加以释义的、政治解读的“文化诗学”（朱立元，2014）。它与历史主义的区别主要在于历史主义选择了历史的客观决定论，而新历史主义则清算了文本中心论和历史决定论，认为文本具有历史性，历史也具备文本性，使得“历史与叙述”“政治解读与文化诗学”成为文学批评的热门话题（2014）。其代表人物包括格林布拉特、海登·怀特、多利莫尔、蒙托斯、维勒等人。新历史主义并非全“新”，只是在 20 世纪西方文论注重“共时”“文本自足性”研究的主流中，融入了历时的、动态的、情境的视角，重新注重文学与权力话语、文本与历史、

艺术与人生的关系。新历史主义与文化唯物主义学者在作品中积极地寻找一种固有的、不可同化的他性，一种距离感和差异性，强调我们不要把看上去似是而非的、关于自我的现代假设强加给遥远的历史文化。他们认为不存在超越历史的或普遍的人的本质，人的主体性是由文化代码构建的，这些文化代码定位和限制了我们所有人。

认知历史主义指运用认知科学理论历史地看待文学和文化，是一种认知文学批评方法，强调主体认知的历史性、社会性、文化性和具身性对文学批评的影响，主张从共时与历时的层面进行认知文学批评（蒋勇军，2019：159）。在西方人文社会学科“认知转向”的基础上，认知历史主义文学研究强调认知理论、历史与文学体裁、文学文化接受、身份认同、文学史与文化审美之间相互作用的密切关系。它不仅关注文学的历史，还涉及文化的历史和生物进化史，文学认知历史主义应承认人类身体和心智的历史发展性。因为在理查森看来（Richardson），历史“不仅包括社会、文化和政治各方面，还涵盖生物（包括进化和基因）以及地球物理学”（Richardson，2010：xi）。因此，认知历史主义关注的范围相对于前文所述的历史主义和新历史主义，视域更宽广，同时针对性更强。更宽广是因为它加入了认知的维度，没有人的活动参与的文学和历史是无法想象的，也是不可能的，而人的活动主要受其认知活动的控制和影响；另一方面，称其更具针对性，是因为认知历史主义摒弃了历史决定论和文本中心论，回到人的主体性，关注人的生物进化、认知加工和发展与文学生产和接受、文化社会的历史承接性和发展性。

本文对于认知与情感的关系已有所谈及，整体上来说，情感是认知不可分割的一部分。狄克逊（Dixon）认为情感是一种现代观念，一种文化建构。感觉（feeling）是大脑中发生的某些事情这个概念是在19世纪早期发明的（2003）。语言学家安娜·维尔兹比卡（Anna Wierzbicka）认为，只有一个词可以直接从一种语言翻译成另一种语言，那就是“感觉”（feel）（Wierzbicka，2013）。但是我们所能感受到的远不止人们通常认为的情感：既有身体上的疼痛、饥饿、温暖或寒冷，以及触摸某物的感觉，当然也有悲伤、委屈、孤独、焦虑这些非常微妙的心理感受。仅在英语中，就有不同的术语在历史不同时期被用来描述某些类型的感情。我们有“性情”（temperaments）（指人们的情感使其行为的方式）、“激情”（passions）（指身体首先感受到的影响灵魂的情感）、感情（sentiments）（当你看到美丽的事物或某人的不道德行为时的感觉）。随着认知心理科学和情感科学的发展，取而代之的是一个笼统的术语，它描述了大脑处理的一种特定的感觉——情感（emotion）。“情感”是一个新的边界不清的盒子，要想定义什么是情感是困难的，因为情感是一个文化建构的现代概念，不同文化历史时期的人对情感的认知不一样。同时，情感又是普遍的，否则就无法达到某些基本的认同和理解。情感既是天性使然，又是后天培养的结果。因此，回归人的情感历史主义探究符合文学认知研究新的理论趋势和潮流。

3 情感历史主义的主要特征

情感历史主义的内涵就其本质而言，可以分为三大特征：第一，往往要追溯情感发展的历史；第二，与文化建构主义（cultural constructivism）紧密相关，又有所侧重；第三，情感历史主义尤其关注特定历史时期情感事件中的情感社区（emotional communities）、情感异类（affect aliens）、情感脚本（emotion scripts）。

3.1 情感的历史

关于情感的历史，这方面的著述已有不少，大致可以分为四类，一类是从整体上定义什么是情感，什么是情感的历史（Oatley，2004；Boddic，2018；Firth，2021）；另一类是具体历史时期的特定情感与其他因素的关联，比如“帕尔格雷夫情感史研究”系列著述（Palgrave Studies in the History of Emotions）就探讨了不同历史时期的情感与战争、情感与疼痛、情感与语言、身份、情感与教育、情感与灾难和死亡等因素的相互关系。第三类主要探讨的是情感研究与其他科学学科的关联，例如情感与医学和历史的关系（Alberti，2010）、情感与心理学发展史的依托关系等（Oatley，2018）。当然，还有一些散见的某些具体情感的研究，比如，阿尔贝蒂（Fay Bound Alberti）认为孤独感意味着现代情感的诞生（2019），芭芭拉·罗森韦恩（Barbara H. Rosenwein）就提出了有“邪恶的”（vice）愤怒和“美德的”（virtue）愤怒之分。这些著述有的丰富全面，有的立意新颖，为我们从整体上把握情感和情感历史的发展提供了洞见和启发。

3.2 文化建构主义

就文学研究实践而言，情感历史主义首先是揭示情感的历史，部分源于文学作品，部分应用于文学作品。霍根认为情感的历史包含了一系列不同的历史和心理学假设，因对文化建构主义（cultural constructivism）的依附程度不同而异。文化建构主义认为，情感不是生物学预先赋予的，而是由文化建构的（Plamper）。表面上初看，情感的历史似乎是以文化建构主义为前提的。这在某种程度上是正确的，但这种建构程度有很大不同。康斯坦（Konstan）评论说“情感的历史是一个场所，在那里，建构主义（constructivist）和普遍主义（universalist）的情感理论可能富有成效地交相辉映”（206）。对于情感的文化建构主义，学者们见仁见智，有的持否定态度，认为情感事件（emotion events）的轮廓在不同文化和历史时期几乎没有任何连续性。文艺复兴时期的忧郁（melancholy）与当前的抑郁（depression）之间几乎没有联系，即使文艺复兴时期的愤怒或快乐和现在同名的情绪之间的联系也很微弱。而更温和的观点则认为“情感语言”（emotion language）或者叫情感文化（emotion culture）在创造或转变情感体验方面发挥了作用，而不仅仅是表征而已（Soriano &Ogarkova，242）。人们并不是在“艾滋病”一词被用来命名一种疾病之后才开始死于艾滋病的，特定现象的文化观念与现象发展方式之间往往存在某种联系。对艾滋病的诊断会在病人身上产生生理反应，而这些生理反应会影响病程的预后，这一点在情感反应方面更加明显，艾滋病的例子本身很大程度上就涉及情感问题。

我们需要简要阐述一下社会建构的概念，因为在讨论情感是如何建构之前，应对文化建构情感和意义有一个更好的认识。首先，社会建构经常被模糊地用于指共同信念或意识形态和社会塑造的事实（socially-shaped facts）。例如，假设有人认为女性多愁善感（emotional）和男性冷静克制（stoical）是社会建构的，这可能意味着女性更情绪化，而男性更坚忍是一种训练的结果，而非天生倾向；也可能意味着根本就没有这种差异，只不过是一种社会意识形态错误引导人们去认为女性更感性、男性更坚忍罢了。即使在事实中，建构也常常被含糊地用来表示由社会化产生的环境倾向。法恩（Fine）认为“男人的同理心并不比女人差，如果就事论事只就同理心而言的话”（2010：21）。其次，“社会化”的提法无法区分可改变的偏好或习惯性的、根深蒂固的程度，即浅社会化和深社会化的区分。从文化建构角度看，成长关键期经历的是深度社会化，其情感可能存在显著的文化或历史差异，至少在特定情感类别的社会分布类型上如此。例如，父母教养方式的改变很可能会影响到孩子的依恋方式（attachment styles），即人际关系反应方式。教养方式在文化或历史上的差异可能会改变特定社会中安全依恋和不安全依恋的比例。例如，当代美国社会已经将约会行为规范化，甚至在青少年早期，有限的性接触（如接吻）是被允许的，甚至是鼓励的，但有规定允许的性接触类型以及特定的时空限制（比如道晚安时的亲吻是被允许的）；这在中国的育儿主流实践中，青少年早期无论何种程度的亲吻相信也是很难受到父母的允许或鼓励吧。当然，这并不是说其他类型的性接触就不存在，但社会结构制定了相关规范和实践，其他形式的性接触可以根据这些规范和实践来判断，并据此发展。多元爱恋（polyamory）或许就和美国社会文化中劝阻人不要太依恋某一个人，也不要在年纪太小的时候就“稳定关系”一样。这种养育方式虽然不会改变与性欲或爱情有关的基本情感系统和过程，但它会改变一个人对欲望和依恋的间接激发的暴露，并改变人的性情。浅社会化则是情感倾向的发展，在能使人的情感反应产生偏见的情感记忆或认知过程的基础上形成，这种发展是高度多变的，这种变化是一种特殊经历，是传记式的和表征性的。美国人对“9・11”事件有情感上的记忆，虽然并不是所有人的反应都如出一辙，但它们往往有一些粗略的模式。这种情感记忆可能非常重要和持久，但一般不会像关键时期经历所形成的情感结构那样不可逆转。如果我们不考虑创伤的极端案例，基于“9·11”的情感记忆的仇外心理（xenophobia）应该不会像形成于儿童早期社会化过程中的仇外心理那样根深蒂固（Hogan，2018）。

3.3 情感社区、情感异类、情感脚本

情感历史主义关注特定社会、历史、文化语境中，处于边缘的、不为人注意的特定人群的情感研究。芭芭拉·罗森韦恩（Barbara Rosenwein，2006）的“情感社区”是我们理解情感价值的一个很有价值的概念。普兰普尔（Plamper）认为，情感社区是一群在表达情感方面有相同的准则的、重视（或不重视）同样的感觉的人（2015：68）。关键在于这不仅仅是表达问题，更是一个评价问题。情感后结构主义者艾哈迈德（Sara Ahmed，2010）的“情感异类”是指情感反应与社会的情感规范不一致的人，这个概念可能在政治分析和批判中很有用武之地。此外，文学批评家们已开始关注情感规则（norms）与脚本之间的复杂关系。“脚本”通常指的是话语权力和文化规范，遵循脚本就可以达到规定的（prescribed）情感状态（Tomkins 1987；McNamer，2007）。脚本是定义特定事件展开的标准方式的认知结构，情感脚本组织我们对某些情感事件的前因后果的模拟，会产生人身份和社会身份，它还有行为评估功能，例如，对于任何特定的情绪，或与情绪密切相关的成分（如诱发条件），可能有不同的脚本，这可能涉及不同的评估或产生不同的情绪诱发轨迹。以弗雷德里克·贝恩（Frederika Bain，2015）对不同剧本中有关杀人或夺人性命的分析为例，贝恩研究了早期现代对处决（execution）和谋杀（murder）的描述。处决是被社会接受的，谋杀则被社会否认，这两种形式都与情感密不可分。贝恩说：“一般意义上的情感缺失，及程式化的（stylized）情感表明了处决的恰当性，由此说明颁布处决命令的统治者的合法性。相反，那些命令、见证和经历谋杀的人

往往表达出强烈或不认可的情感。”（221）贝恩的观点明显适用于政治戏剧，但对《罗密欧与朱丽叶》的情感阐释也并非毫无启发。世人皆知提伯尔特对罗密欧非理性的愤怒是导致他杀死茂丘西奥而酿成谋杀的部分原因。然而，从贝恩提供的历史和情感背景去理解，则使得整个情节更加复杂。富有同情心的茂丘西奥也是愤怒的，他也有杀人倾向，因此他有部分罪责。用亚里士多德的术语来说，他没有用理智克制愤怒构成了悲剧性缺陷，这也解释了他的痛苦，因为有罪而被称为悲剧人物，尽管对他的惩罚超出了他应承担的罪责。实际上，罗密欧是有过之而无不及，他杀死了在朱丽叶墓旁阻拦他的帕里斯伯爵，直接构成了谋杀罪。但是，为什么读者对他的谋杀觉得情有可原，是因为社会同情罗密欧的立场，认为他的愤怒强度要大得多，因此更难调节，因而可以表示理解和接受吗？三人中只有班伏里奥诉诸法律和克制情绪，他敦促“茂丘西奥和提伯尔特撤退到一个僻静的地方，或冷静地处理你们的不满”（Ⅲ. i. 48-49）。班伏里奥提供的两种建议只是要求延迟、中断情感反应回路（circuit of emotional response），并未将情感与理性对立起来，他实际上要求两人模拟公众冲突的后果，模拟的后果是可怕的，因为艾斯卡勒斯亲王已下令对扰乱和平的人判处死刑（ii .92 93）。第二种选择则更为包容，也是更为高级的情感调制，涉及更广泛记忆和模拟，即对不满的理智思考，也就是人们常说的“三思而后行”。这些细节揭示了为什么历史上某些情感事件仍然会引起今天观众的情感反应，它们证明了更广泛的人性原则。

然而，情感历史主义并不太关注这些潜在的共性上，而可能会强调如何调制情绪，消除理性与激情之间的历史对立。霍根（2018）认为情感是激励性的，强调过程性、动态变化性，而不是对情感的理性或非理性的定性说，因为理性是通过信息处理来运作，而信息的处理是一个随着信息量的流入而逐步变化的过程。文学历史主义者特别关注关于文学对细节描述的理论或哲学。帕斯特·盖尔（Gail Kern Paster，2004）认为理解文艺复兴时期的情感表达和当时的医学理论关系是很重要的，比如“四体液说”（theory of the four humors)。帕斯特对早期现代身体的研究突出了情感和情感生态的物质性或心理生理学基础，强调内在自我和外部世界之间的交换，认为性别和阶级结构早在医学论述和早期现代戏剧中留下了情感的烙印。回到《罗密欧与朱丽叶》的分析，提伯尔特经常表现出他不受控制的脾气（Ⅲ.i.158），桀骜不驯的性格是因为他缺乏控制，这可以理解为一个不愿遵从君主意愿的臣民总是想破坏和平一样，或者也可以把提伯尔特的情绪反应理解为仇外（out-group disgust）、个人羞耻和因羞耻而愤怒的复杂情感。情感历史主义认为，这些分析对情感价值观的政治经济思考有所启发，认为克制个人情感的方式可能是屈服于权力当局意识形态的结果。无论如何，体液说、脾性说等分析让我们越来越关注情感的具身性。毕竟，情感表达会经过过滤和调制，身体的即时和累积反应或许更为直观和真实，关键要在于我们如何发现情感和身体的复杂关系。

反过来，我们的情感理论和情感脚本知识可能会影响我们对原因和结果的模拟。它们可能会影响在情感反应过程中被激活的记忆，我们感知到的，我们得出的推断，我们思考的反应等等。在某种层面上，非物质的自我完全依赖于物质的大脑——因此恳求大脑去思考，没有思考的大脑，自我是无助的。但与此同时，非物质的自我又有足够的自主思考能力来得知大脑有没有为自我提供足够的信息。我们想说明的是，随着我们对情感和情感的历史知识了解得越多，我们的情感反应和阐释就更为复杂多样。在每一个历史时期和每一个群体中都存在一定程度的理论多样性，在一定程度上，关于情感和其他话题的观点也是多重和矛盾的。没有简单的、统一的世界观来标记一个时期的所有作品，也不存在单一的福柯式知识论。因此，独立的理论不需要在给定的文本实例或跨案例中始终保持一致。正如米克和沙利文（Richard Meek & Erin Sullivan，2015）所言，文艺复兴时期也存在着类似的唯物主义和二元论情结。例如，忧郁的概念是复杂和不一致的，其实，多重性并不完全与唯物主义与二元论或唯心主义相对立。正如德鲁·丹尼尔（Daniel Drew，2013）所借用的莎士比亚《皆大欢喜》中的一个例子，剧中人物哲人杰奎斯（Jaques）说不同的职业有不同种类的忧郁，个体也有自己个体的忧郁（Ⅳ. i. 13-22）。可见，英国文艺复兴时期的文学想象中存在着多种忧郁，而今天的我们则可能不太会接受这种诗意的“忧郁”概念，而更容易理解医学领域内作为疾病术语的“抑郁”一词，即使是像愤怒或恐惧这样进化而来的古老情感也不是简单通用的。任何特定的情感事件都涉及来自不同情感系统的特定神经元群的激活，个人的、历史的情感记忆的选择性激活，以及对原因和结果的独特模拟结果所构成的。

情感历史主义观还强调文学体裁与情感的历史是紧密相连的。尽管广泛的情感导向型体裁在不同文化和历史时期都相当稳定，但某些具体作品出现在特定的文化背景或特定历史发展中，也往往与情感密不可分。斯泰梅斯特（David Stymeist，2015）对早期现代“焦虑小说”的研究是情感体裁分析的好例子；哥特小说与恐惧情感的关联；战争文学艺术承载着强烈、复杂的历史情感；英法百年战争在其抒情形式和跨海峡文学交流中被很好地记录下来；17 世纪的英国内战在一幅大地风景画中为我们呈现。对近代早期的边疆殖民暴力的理解常常被田园主义的文学情感记录所歪曲。第一次世界大战与英语抒情诗的亲和力，反恐战争与数字档案的紧密联系。在美国“9・11”恐怖袭击的背景下，战争题材小说与勇敢、创伤情感研究日益突显等等，不一而足。这些都为当代文学研究中的情感历史主义研究范式提供了可以调用的广阔资源，文学中的情感历史主义是一个潜在的丰富的研究领域。

4　情感历史主义的主要研究范式

霍根（2018）认为根据指导具体情感理论形成的一般解释前提和社会目标，情感历史主义可以归纳为两大取向：情感后结构主义（affective poststructuralism）和情感科学（affective science）。前者主要理论来源于后结构主义，包括福柯和德里达的解构主义话语分析，常与精神分析传统的元素相结合。福柯的话语分析批判性地考察了学科在其理论化、制度结构和实践中的组织方式。比如谁授权说或写，权威度如何，说者和作者应该做何表述和假设，可能会造成什么结果，这些结果如何通过制度执行。又比如，在精神病学中，精神病学家、临床心理学家，执业护士的权威是什么；什么样的诊断和治疗是可以接受的；哪些法律和其他机制可以控制相关人员的行为（例如，他们获得药品的途径）。此外，情感后结构主义部分源于文化研究，已超越传统马克思主义对经济的关注，更加关注政治分析和社会激进主义（social activism），福柯话语分析者倾向于对他们所研究的学科真理性主张持怀疑态度。

4.1　情感科学

广义上的情感科学研究来源于认知科学，是由一系列经验主义方法和不同理论共同的解释类型来确定的科学研究。情感科学家很可能利用神经学数据、语言测试、对人类和非人类动物的行为和因果关系进行研究。有人质疑情感科学家是在投机取巧地利用个人实验，玩弄数据。但是，还是要看到至少在遵循情感科学规范时，情感科学家们会试图协调大量来自不同渠道的数据，尽可能地做出合理、恰当的解释。贡萨加（Gonzaga）和同事们提出了不同的观点，他们参考了情感科学的方法，包括对主观经验、交流展示、关系结果和生理标记的研究，来测试不同功能的假说（2006：163）。鲁思·莱斯（Ruth Leys）认为情感后结构主义就是质疑某些政治争论和理性如何运作的解释。具体地说，"声称我们人类是充满了潜意识情感强度和共鸣的物质生物，这决定性地影响或制约着我们的政治和其他信念，以至于我们忽视了这些情感强度和共鸣，这将是危险的"（2011：436）。

然而，情感科学领域的研究者对学科偏见的批评似乎并不那么强烈，这有利有弊。一方面，福柯式的怀疑主义是对受情感科学影响的文学理论家和批评家的一种有益的反作用力。另一方面，这也可能导致研究者对科学探究的价值过于无动于衷，并过度倾向于历史决定论，以致他们无法承认或接受普遍的模式，而这些模式对科学探究是至关重要的。解构主义从德里达对意义和知觉的阐释开始，认为没有完整的语义或知觉存在。在以逻各斯为中心的思维方式中，我们相信（或默认）这种存在建立了认知、语言和经验的组织和规范原则，而解构主义则揭示了逻各斯中心主义及其存在形而上学的矛盾。德里达认为，意义或经验总是会被取代的，任何给定术语的意义都不是某种直接充分的，而是与其他术语的区别，以及在该事物无休止的一系列延迟（deferral）中不断变化。意义不是稳定的中心，而是不稳定的传播。例如，情感后结构主义者经常以明确或含蓄的解构方式来构建他们的分析。情感后结构主义者格雷格和赛格沃斯（Melissa Gregg &Gregory Seigworth，2010）暗示了对逻各中心主义的解构，没有纯粹或原始的情感状态，如何开始？即使术语“原始”一词，也与特定的哲学传统有所关联。关键他们是要表明，总是存在着一种传播当中的情感游戏，没有中心，因此没有最终稳定的情感系统。然而，解构主义分析声称揭示了某一假设确切的术语，实际上也是以假定的派生术语为先决条件的，本身就是矛盾的假设。尽管如此，在语义上进行二元颠覆，即差异和延迟决定意义仍然是许多当代文学理论的中心，其中也是很多情感后结构主义作品的研究导向。

4.2 情感后结构主义

至于精神分析学，霍根认为情感后结构主义借鉴的是精神分析的传统，而非精神分析，因为情感理论家经常将心理描述和解释基于拉康甚至更激进的反心理分析的作家，如德勒兹和加达里（Félix Guattari）的主流心理分析框架。这些原则与精神分析学中假定的原则是一致的，包括因果过程、重复模式、论证模式，甚至是简短的社会话语中的惯用偏好。例如，就因果原则而言，情感后结构主义作者可能会假设思想和行动是无意识的。换言之，他们倾向于假定一个人没有意识到自己的冲动，因为意识到它们是会感受到痛苦的。相比之下，情感科学则认为大多数无意识的东西要么是由于心理结构问题无法进入意识，要么是由于信息处理受限而被误解。至于论证模式，精神分析传统倾向于依赖临床证据或单一案例，有时甚至是轶事式的，而精神分析则是依靠受控的、实验研究或广泛的统计研究。

但是，我们需要确定的是，情感科学和情感后结构主义的区分不是一个绝对二分法，两个维度的学科交融和借鉴也成为新的趋势。许多理论家将情感科学和情感后结构主义两个研究方向的原则和目的结合起来。例如，唐纳德·威尔斯（Donald Wehrs）将安东尼奥·达马西奥（Antonio Damasio）的神经科学与朱丽娅·克里斯蒂娃（Julia Kristeva）的后结构精神分析结合在一起；安·卡普兰（E. Ann Kaplan）可以轻易被归为情感科学家，但她也与情感后结构主义联系在一起。情感后结构主义者也经常引用情感科学中的实验或理论，但是并不是说个别理论家整合了情感研究的各个分支，就产生了独立的综合理论，学科借鉴是选择性的，而非系统性的。确切地说，情感后结构主义和情感科学方法是观点、术语、模型、实践、话语的综合体，只是这个综合体倾向于分成两组，理论家们都可以借鉴两者中的某些元素，只是从理论发展史来看，这些目标的倾向存在连续性。许多文学批评家和理论家就利用认知科学和情感科学来进行政治分析和批判，比如后殖民时期和少数族裔文学作品就借鉴了认知和情感科学的研究成果，有助于政治批判分析。

情感后结构主义和情感科学的批判性分析涉及三个大的领域：社会组织、语言和心理，这就相应地促进了情感研究和社会学、语言学和心理学，尤其是与发展心理学的跨学科融合。社会组织制度的后结构主义分析仍然受福柯影响；情感科学分析更有可能利用泰弗尔（Henri Tajfel）等人发展的群体社会心理学（social psychology of groups）。情感后结构主义的语言层面涉及德里达的解构主义；情感科学的语言政治分析可借鉴莱考夫（George Lakoff）认知语言学。此外，情感后结构主义者通常借鉴广泛的精神分析原则或对精神分析传统的回应来探究政治倾向的心理根源，尤其是对德勒兹和加达里的借鉴；而情感科学家则可能会分析人类认知的启发和偏见，或者吸收社会神经科学的成果。他们在兴趣上有所趋同，大都或多或少可以归为两者中的某一类。例如，格雷格和赛格沃斯的《情感理论读本》（*Affect Theory Reader*，2010）就属于情感后结构主义的研究范畴，因为该书未收录达马西奥、勒杜克斯（Joseph LeDoux）、潘克塞普（Jaak Panksepp）、奥特利（Keith Oatley）、弗里达（Nico Frijda）、霍夫曼（Martin Hoffman）及其他当代情感科学领域的重要人物的研究成果。情感后结构主义的关键人物包括德勒兹和加达里，他们在情感科学研究中几乎是不为人知的。无论是他们，还是劳伦斯·格罗斯伯格（Lawrence Grossberg）或马苏米这样有影响力的情感后结构主义者，都没有出现在《情感与情感科学牛津指南》（*The Oxford Companion to Emotion and theAffective Sciences*，2009）一书中，即使像福柯这样具有广泛影响力的人物，在《情感理论读本》中举足轻重，但在《牛津指南》中也地位有限。

5 情感历史主义的理论价值与意义

从古至今，哲学家们一直渴望将历史与虚构分开。尽管柏拉图已经将诗人从他理想的共和国中驱逐出去，但他在描述哲学的终极真理时仍然不得不使用神话。因此，这样的学科界限从一开始就被证明是脆弱的。对亚里士多德来说，历史与诗歌的区别不是在于目的的严肃性，而是在于每一种论述所特有的概率和可能性的不平衡问题。因此，虽然俄狄浦斯认为他不可能杀死他的父亲并娶他的母亲，但索福克勒斯的戏剧《俄狄浦斯》的叙事力量表明，他为避免这一结果而采取的每一步都使这种可能性更大。“事实上，诗歌比历史更具哲理性，因为它有更大的自由来表现哲学所期望的完整理解。”这是汉密尔顿在撰写“历史主义”这个术语时的基调。他认为，在诗歌中，概率是一切；另一方面，历史不得不关注更多可能发生的事情（Hamilton，2003）。惠勒（Demian Wheeler）认为，在本体论和宇宙论的层面上，历史主义可以归类为过程哲学（process philosophy）的一种，强调世界的相互联系和“流动和关系的本质”（Wheeler，2020：9）。杜威（John Dewey）提出了事件本体论，声称“每一个存在都是一个事件”（Dewey，1925：61）。詹姆斯（William James）在其《激进实验主义论文集与多元宇宙》（*Essays in Radical Empiricism, and A Pluralistic Universe*,

1971）中，唤起了一个正在形成的世界，一个在运动、在变化、在时间中的世界。他认为“生命的本质就是它不断变化的特性”（1971）。可以说，情感历史主义从整体上主张文学情感历史的事件性、偶然性、过程性、流动性、关系性和变化性。

情感作为一门学科的历史可能会认为文学是可疑的、不可靠的，然而，文学文本恰恰给历史提供了一些细微的线索和依据。索里亚诺和欧加科沃（Soriano &Ogarkova）认为，情感的概念表征潜力可能超出表象的语言范畴；在语言群体中，语言差异倾向于以偏爱的、默认的方式来对情感现实进行分类和处理（2015：242）。如果既不能假定连续性，也不能假定差异性，这就引发了一个问题：在一个情感事件中，历史或文化上究竟发生了什么变化，以及变化的程度是什么？文学作品可能不是对前现代个体实际情感体验的准确记录，但正如霍利·克罗克（Holly Crocker）认为文学文本是一种呈现和触发情感的媒介，因为情感在故事中传播，而这些故事又通过阅读行为依附于身体（2017：91）。因此，他说文学对我们批判性地理解“中世纪的人们如何介入他们巩固情感的身份认同方式”至关重要（92）。萨拉·麦克纳默（Sarah McNamer）在对中古英语宗教文化的基础研究中，肯定了文本在前现代情感研究中的中心地位，因为文学是“情感的主要档案”。文学还是情感干预的档案，需要最大程度的感知（sentience）和关注语言的运作方式（2007：242）。麦克纳默认为，文本实际上可以产生复杂的情感效果，并把它们运用到身体政治（body politics）中。在麦克纳默的描述中，中世纪的祈祷文本是情感表演的脚本，它们就像忠实读者阅读的私密脚本，表现适当的精神感受（246）。

6 结 语

文学研究中情感历史主义沿袭人文社会学科的“认知转向”和“情感转向”，强调生物进化、社会历史文化因素潜移默化的影响。情感历史主义是历时的、动态的研究范式，我们无法否认特定历史时期、特定社会文化背景中特殊情感事件在历史长河中所承担的看似微妙，但实则耐人寻味的角色和价值，尤其关注特定情感社区中所谓的“情感异类”群体，因为情感确实具有很大的可塑性。其次，情感历史主义研究范式可以扩大对情感科学的借鉴范围，霍根在论及情感历史主义时，关注的是处于特定历史和文化联系中与作者身份有关的文学情感问题，缺少对文学作品读者的历史性关注，这是该范式可以继续丰实且大有可为之处。在认知科学、心理学、神经科学的飞跃发展助力之下，针对读者的眼动实验、反应时等认知心理科学实验能为文学的阐释和解读提供多元依据。因此，文学情感历史主义可以先从情感事件和情感调制入手，确定哪些是社会历史文化的变量，增加定量分析，通过借鉴情感科学，尤其认知情感科学的研究方法，提高研究的客观性，将情感后结构主义的批判活力与情感科学的实证分析有效结合，是情感历史主义研究范式中一种非常现实且富有潜力的跨学科整合。

参考文献

[1] S AHMED. The Promise of Happiness. Durham: Duke University Press, 2010.

[2] F BAIN. The Affective Scripts of Early Modern Execution and Murder//R Meek, E Sullivan (eds). The Renaissance of Emotion: Understanding Affect in Shakespeare and His Contemporaries. Manchester: Manchester University Press, 2015: 221-240.

[3] H A CROCKER. Medieval Affects Now. Exemplaria, 2017, 29 (1): 82-98.

[4] J DEWEY. Experience and Nature. Chicago: Open Court, 1925: 61.

[5] T DIXON. From Passions to Emotions: The Creation of a Secular Psychological Category. Cambridge, UK: Cambridge University Press, 2003.

[6] D DREW. The Melancholy Assemblage: Affect and Epistemology

in the English Renaissance. New York: Fordham University Press, 2013.

[7] C FINE. Delusions of Gender: The Real Science Behind Sex Differences. London: Icon, 2010.

[8] G GONZAGA, R TURNER, D KELTNER, B CAMPOS, M ALTEMUS. Romantic Love and Sexual Desire in Close Relationships. Emotion, 2006: 163-179.

[9] M GREGG G J SEIGWORTH. The Affect Theory Reader. Durham and London: Duke University Press, 2010.

[10] P HAMILTON Historicism (2nd edition). London and New York: Routledge, 2003.

[11] P C HOGAN. Affective Narratology: The Emotional Structure of Stories. Lincoln and London: University of Nebraska Press, 2011.

[12] P C HOGAN. Literature and Emotion. Oxon: Routledge, 2018.

[13] W JAMES. Essays in Radical Empiricism, and A Pluralistic Universe. New York: E. P. Dutton, 1971: 145.

[14] H R JAUSS. Toward an Aesthetic of Reception. Trans. T. Bahti. Minneapolis: University of Minnesota Press, 1982.

[15] D KONSTAN. History of Emotion// R. Meek & E. Sullivan (eds). The Renaissance of Emotion: Understanding Affect in Shakespeare and His Contemporaries. Manchester: Manchester University Press, 2015: 206-207.

[16] R LEYS. The Turn to Affect: A Critique. Critical Inquiry, 2011 (37): 434-472.

[17] S MCNAMER. Feeling//P. Strohm. Middle English: Oxford Twenty-First Century Approaches to Literature. Oxford: Oxford University Press, 2007:241-257.

[18] R MEEK, E SULLIVAN, eds. The Renaissance of Emotion:

Understanding Affect in Shakespeare and His Contemporaries. Manchester: Manchester University Press, 2015.
[19] G PASTER. Humoring the Body: Emotions and the Shakespearean Stage [M]. Chicago: University of Chicago Press, 2004.
[20] J PLAMPER. The History of Emotions: An Introduction. Trans. Keith Tribe. Oxford: Oxford University Press, 2015.
[21] B ROSENWEIN. Emotional Communities in the Early Middle Ages . Ithaca: Cornell University Press, 2006.
[22] D SANDER, K R SCHERER. The Oxford Companion to Emotion and the Affective Sciences [M]. Oxford: Oxford University Press, 2009.
[23] C SORIANO A OGARKOVA. Linguistics and Emotion// R. Meek & E. Sullivan (eds). The Renaissance of Emotion: Understanding Affect in Shakespeare and His Contemporaries. Manchester: Manchester University Press, 2015:240-242.
[24] D STYMEIST. Anxiety Fiction: Domestic Poisoning in Early Modern News, Arden of Faversham, and Hamlet. Explorations in Renaissance Culture, 2015(41): 30-55.
[25] S TOMKINS. Script Theory// E. Joel Arnoff, A.I. Rabin, & Robert A. Zucker (eds). The Emergence of Personality. New York: Springer, 1987: 147-216.
[26] A WIERZBICKA. Imprisoned in English: The Hazards of English as a Default Language. Oxford, UK: Oxford University Press, 2013: 75.
[27] 蒋勇军. 认知历史主义视阈下庞德的英美批评. 西华大学学报（哲学社会科学版），2019: 38(2): 6-12 + 24.
[28] 熊沐清. 外国文学研究认知转向评述. 英美文学研究论丛，2019: 295-310.

研究新论

叙事学研究的多元创新与进展
——《叙事学与意识形态》评述

杜 坤

【摘要】 20 世纪 90 年代以来西方叙事理论出现了跨学科的研究派别，后殖民主义叙事学就是其中的一个。2018 年出版的《叙事学与意识形态：后殖民主义叙事学中磋商语境、形式和理论的协调》将经典叙事学的形式分析与后殖民主义文化历史阐释紧密结合，对叙事形式与意识形态之间的辩证关系做了进一步的阐释。书中的每位作者在学科领域内用不同的方法探讨后殖民主义叙事学关注的一些问题，并提出了一些新的概念和方法，拓展和深化了后殖民主义叙事学研究。

【关键词】叙事学；后殖民主义叙事学；意识形态；语境；形式

0 引 言

经典叙事学自 20 世纪 60 年代兴起，以热奈特、查特曼等人为代表，对叙事作品的人物、时间、空间、事件结构、聚焦等的构成成分、运作规律和话语结构展开研究，然而“自从查特曼为文本类型辩护以来，叙事的概念有了很大的扩展。从某种意义上说，它已经变得更加抽象——现在人们更多地把它理解为一种散漫的模式（a

基金项目：本文系国家社会科学基金重大项目“认知诗学研究与理论版图重构”（20&ZD291）的阶段性研究成果。

作者简介：杜坤，女，四川外国语大学博士研究生，讲师，主要从事英美文学和认知诗学研究。

discursive mode），甚至是一种认知形式。这样构想出来的叙事不是超越，而是从语境中出现：它处于交流的社会环境中，处于可识别行为的环境中，处于生物学上人类具身环境中”（Dwivedi，Nielse & Walsh，2018：5）[①]。可以说，叙事学研究将注意力转向了结构特征与读者阐释相互作用的规律，转向了对具体叙事作品之意义的探讨，注重跨学科研究，关注作者、文本、读者与社会历史语境的交互作用（申丹，2003），走入后经典叙事学研究，女性主义叙事学（Feminist Narratology）、认知叙事学（Cognitive Narratology）、修辞叙事学（Rhetorical Narratology）、后殖民主义叙事学（Postcolonial Narratives）等补充经典叙事学范畴，呈现出跨学科、跨文类等特点，从不同的角度为丰富经典叙事学研究做出贡献。

2018年，俄亥俄州立大学出版社出版了一部文集《叙事学与意识形态：后殖民主义叙事学中语境、形式和理论的协调》（*Narratology and Ideology: Negotiating Context, Form, and Theory in Postcolonial Narratives*）。三位编者 Divya Dwivedi、Henrik Skov Nielsen 和 Richard Walsh 分别来自印度理工学院（Indian Institute of Technology Delhi）、丹麦奥尔胡斯大学（Aarhus University）、英国约克大学（University of York）。他们认为“叙事学与后殖民文学批评的相关性以及对叙事学的后殖民主义批判的可能性，在文学研究与后殖民主义理论关系的背景下产生。叙事理论的发展为文化、政治和意识形态霸权机制的关键参与提供了杠杆，特别是后殖民主义的权力关系通过叙事小说的资源进行协调”（22）。因而，选取的文章都是从叙事角度出发，把理论思想的充分性放到意识形态情境阅读中接受考察，讨论后殖民小说中的叙事学问题，因此文集以殖民主义叙事命名，或者说是更广泛的“语境叙事学”（contextualist narratology）（1）。可以说，本书集中了当前后殖民主义叙事学研究的最新成果，将叙事形式分析与文化阐释紧密结合，进一步推进对叙事形式与意识形态之间辩证关系的认识，使得后殖民叙事学研究

① 文中所有只标有页码的引文均出自该文集。

继续沿着多元创新的态势发展。

1 文集内容概述

本书正文除“导言”外，其余13个章节分为5个部分。导言部分针对“叙事理论中的形式主义和意识形态”“后殖民主义文学批评和叙事”和“后殖民文本的叙事学问题”展开论述。

第一部分“叙事问题”（Narrative in Question）的3篇文章主要探讨文学作品中对国家、身份、历史的意识形态和政治斗争的叙事形式和技巧。帕特里克·霍根（Patrick Colm Hogan）结合情感记忆理论（the theory of emotional memory）和创伤研究，分析在遭受国家危机的受创伤社会背景下的克什米尔叙事。他发现文学作品和民族思想中普遍存在着民族主义情节化（the emplotment of nationalism）（37），因而可以说叙事结构影响着意识形态。马丁（Martin Loschnigg）的文章借用弗鲁德尼克（Monika Fludernik）的认知叙事学理论，以3名加拿大南亚裔作家作品为文本：瓦桑吉（M. G. Vassanji）的 *A Place Within*（2008）、翁达杰（Michael Ondaatje）的 *Running in the Family*（1981）和密斯特里（Rohinton Mistry）的 *From Firozsha Baag*（1987），分析了移民和返乡的意识形态含义以及作品的叙事策略。移民视角由存在的经验框架和反映框架组成，这些框架使国家成为一个不完整的、不断想象的结构。许多复杂的叙事技巧，如元叙事和传统叙事中故事内叙述，结合在一起创造了一种后殖民叙事身份，从而背离了西方自传文学霸权。乌达亚·库马尔（Udaya Kumar）关注的是印度西南部喀拉拉邦当代小说中的客体呈现以及其与叙事意义复杂协调等问题。他以N. S. Madhavan的马拉雅拉姆语（Malayalam）小说 *Lanthanbatheriyile Luthiniyakal*（*Litanies of the Dutch Battery*，2010）为研究对象，关注叙事对象的地位，探讨了其与经典叙事学的一些基本区别，指出小说从人物的内在性中打破了叙事和公众记忆，提出叙事允许一种“愉快的记忆”（delectation of memory)(86),而其他话语却没有。作者 Madhavan 实现了这一点,他没有通过传统的聚焦方法,而是通过其他形式和流派的叙事诱导,如连祷(litany)、诗歌(欧洲和南亚)和对话。

第二部分"叙事区域(类、元、内)"[Zones of Narrative(Para-,Meta-,Intra-)]的 3 篇文章详细论述了类文本、元叙事层、层次及其在叙事中越界等所产生的一些叙事学问题。普林斯(Gerald Prince)以塞本尼(Ousmane Sembene)的 *Les Bouts de bois de Dieu*(*Banty mam Yall*)为研究对象,发现具有调解、粉饰和解释功能的元叙事符号(metanarrative signs)在意识形态上控制着意义与交流。他探讨了元叙事符号与多语言的殖民和后殖民情境书写之间的密切关系,在这种关系中,语言在单一交流中相互作用的同时,也沿着经济政治和文化轴发生相互作用,叙述者也都会与经济政治和文化轴相连。科普兰(Sarah Copland)的文章展示了修辞叙事学在把握特定叙事文本—类文本关系中的权力结构的效力。以 Mulk Raj Anand 的 *Untouchable* 和 E. M. Forster 为其写的前言为研究对象,探索前言中修辞策略所展现的特定的、局部的语境,而不只是假设作者与代书前言作者(allographic preface writer)的动态关系或被殖民者与殖民者之间普遍的、全球性的动态关系存在,解读真实读者和作者的读者(authorial audience)之间动态关系,即殖民者的序言和被殖民者的文本在进行简单化和程序性的误读时而被忽视的动态关系。阿尔伯(Jan Alber)的文章着眼于拉什迪(Salman Rushdie)的小说 *Midnight's Children*(1981)中叙事策略的具体意识形态功能。作者把自己的分析与其他后殖民主义批评家的阅读进行比较,展示对小说的叙事学分析可能会产生什么样的阅读效果,并试图确定叙事技巧的意识形态分支,通过分析这些叙事策略一方面认同小说主人公西奈的观点,而另一方面则揭露西奈是一个理想主义的梦想家,他没有意识到自己的想象和实际行为之间的差异,行为始终与他自己的道德标准相抵触。

第三部分的 3 篇文章探讨的是叙述声音和叙述者(voice and the narrator)的问题。金里奇(Marion Gymnich)以一部描述博帕尔毒气悲剧的小说——辛哈(Indra Sinha)的 *Animal's People* 为研究对象，探讨了权力的协调，特别是代表沉默的受害者和被赦免的压迫者的权力。小说中，叙述在个人声音和公共声音之间的转换，对博帕尔灾难的描述是强调在虚构和非虚构文本中对受害者的描述，导致一般化和忽视承认个性和多样性的需要。(153) 此外，无论是在新闻媒体还是小说文本中，当涉及道德问题对痛苦的表征和感知时，叙述者作为公共声音的具体建构，可能会唤起实际读者某种不安。奥尔森 (Greta Olson) 通过对可靠和不可靠叙述的研究揭示了可靠模型的意识形态基础。在这个模型中，不可靠是一个缺点。在哈米德(Mohsin Hamid) 的 *The Reluctant Fundamentalist* (2007) 中，一个美国的穆斯林移民使用了不可靠的叙述以及对第二人称的模糊使用，用以与恐怖主义意识形态对话和对抗。这些特征表明叙事学模型，即可靠性模型，需要被历史化。通过观察殖民语境中出现的不可靠性归因，揭示不可靠叙事模式所特有的人性假设，论证了叙述者的不可靠性如何作为意识形态批判的策略。费伦 (James Phelan) 的文章详细分析了拉希里 (Jhumpa Lahiri) 的 *The Third and Final Continent* 中可靠叙述和人物之间对话的处理。通过对以往评论的分析考察，他首先提出两个问题，分析后认为后殖民理论提供的关键概念和政治关注阐明了拉希里的主题目的，且修辞学理论更详细地描述了作者实现这些目的的方式，甚至增加了对故事的情感和伦理层面的理解。当回到修辞层面上，这不仅是对可靠叙述、人物对话以及他们之间协同作用的理解，也是对叙事交流本身的理解。反过来，这些叙述技巧也补充了后殖民主义的主题，因为它们都具有了陈述、解释和评估的功能。

第四部分“策略、叙事与后殖民”(Strategies, Narrative and Postcolonial)中的 2 篇论文比较和衡量了叙事学和后殖民批评对文学作品策略的价值。弗鲁德尼克的文章首先回顾传统层面上叙事学是如何处理意识形态的。然后对文本的解释建立在对阅读过程的概念化上，或者建立在一个动态模型上，试图将辛菲尔德 (Alan Sinfield)的见解与叙事学相结合。选取 Nayantara Sahgal 的 *A Time to be Happy*（1957）和 Mohsin Hamid 的 *How to Get dirty Rich in Rising Asia*（2013）这 2 部小说为研究对象。尽管它们都以反讽为基本策略，却展示了两种截然不同的意识形态处理方式，这种差异可以通过观察阅读过程发现以及考察意识形态是如何及时传达中获取。巴塔查里亚（Baidik Bhattacharya）的文章细致地分析了印度独立时期孟加拉语讽刺作家 Paraśurām 的作品集 *Galpakalpa*（1952）的叙述策略。在这些讽刺中，他们对非殖民化和后殖民历史有着不同理解的方式，在想象中分离后殖民地和国家的可能出现，即使是短暂的，对这个短暂时刻的关注也为那些反对后殖民主义的人提供了理论指导。文章以对死亡的修辞为出发点，探讨了后殖民地与民族主义侵占之间的归化关系，反思后殖民历史中非殖民化的影响，作者认为这种叙事关系是通过编史的元虚构和预期叙事技巧具体建立起来的。

第五部分，"叙事、理论、意识形态"（Narrative，Theory，Ideology）对叙事学与意识形态的关系进行了更为广泛的理论反思。巴尔（Mieke Bal）首先对"透视"（perspective）和"凝视"（gaze）提出了批评，认为它们常常与聚焦混淆，重新解释了聚焦及其与视觉分析相结合的潜力，并通过对拉希里的小说 *The Namesake* 和印度艺术家马拉尼（Nalini Malani）的视觉艺术作品的分析进行了说明。巴尔认为斯皮瓦克反聚焦的提议有助于强调聚焦对后殖民主义叙事学的特殊意义。然而，巴尔指出后殖民主义叙事学实际上应该让位给"迁徙美学"（migratory aesthetics）（235），甚至让位于"批判叙事学"（critical narratology）（247）。最后，迪维亚（Divya Dwivedi）揭示了阅读的意识形态，从而开启了对阅读这个容易被忽视概念的质疑。为此，她提出了"收件人功能"（addressee function）的概念，收件人功能是意识形态的，因为它控制着意义的扩散。对比萨扬（O. V. Vijayan）的小说 *The Legends of Khasak* 的叙事声音细读，揭示了这种意识形态对叙事意义控制的抵制，这种控制是以一种特殊的聚焦形式出现的，称之为分散聚焦（dispersive focalization）（252）。作者将修辞叙事学和自然叙事学与后殖民主义文学理论进行比较，揭示这些构想获得的具体操作方法以及各自的意识形态价值。这种比较与其说是一种理论方法优于另外两种，不如说是收件人功能在两种方法中的思想运作。

2 文集的特点和意义

整体而言，本文集具有创新性、专业性、多元丰富性等特点。

首先，文集的创新性体现研究领域内的创新性。叙事学理论家弗鲁德尼克在《走向“自然”叙事学》(*Towards a 'Natural' Narratology*, 2005）一书中专辟一节讨论三个方面的意识形态框架（女性文学、后殖民研究、权力话语）与叙事学的关注结合。他指出叙事学分析与包括族裔文学在内的后殖民文学在方法上可以互相借鉴，互为补充。因为后殖民文学和少数族裔文学的最重要一个叙事学研究领域是对叙述者的语言和所代表的对话的语言、方言或习语的选择。（Fludernik，2005：274）第二个研究领域是形式创新，比如第二人称小说就有着明确的意识形态问题。所以说，后殖民主义的理论和批评不能排除对文本进行叙事学研究的必要，民族和叙事问题、人物的典型性问题、语言形式问题等都是叙事学领域内加以探讨的方面。同时，经典叙事学遭到后结构主义和历史主义的夹攻，研究势头逐渐回落（在美国尤为明显）。顺应读者反应批评、文化研究等新兴学派，关注读者和语境的后经典叙事学也就应运而生（申丹，2003)，因而将叙事学带到了后殖民主义批评中，推进了当前关于语境叙事学的必要性和难点的讨论。

该书编者认为后殖民主义叙事学将后殖民主义与文本形式和文本权力的叙事学和意识形态分析领域联系起来，并提供方法来解决语境主义叙事学的问题。采用经典叙事学的模式和概念来分析后殖民文学作品，注重作品与叙事规约之间的差异性，深入探究叙事形式差异与文化历史之间的互文关系，使得后殖民文学的研究立足于文学范畴的叙事性，注重读者和社会历史语境，有意识地吸取有益的理论概念、批评视角和分析模式，以求扩展各自的研究范畴，克服自身的局限性，这种将形式研究与文化政治批评相结合的路径对于后殖民文学研究具有启发和推进作用；同时，对后殖民文本的叙事学介入也检验了叙事学抽象的局限性以及特定的局限性，引发了对叙事学中各种概念和流派的语境主义范围的思考（24）。因而，编者期许也许可以将批判叙事学分析从后殖民研究扩展到全球化研究、移民研究等，例如，非文学的、非虚构的作品，以及非正式的口头叙述，包括那些在南亚和其他地方殖民统治之前产生的作品。（29）这些都将是未来可以开拓的更为崭新的研究领域。

其次，各章作者都是该领域的专业研究者，其中许多人更是该领域的知名学者，如费伦、霍根、弗鲁德尼克等。他们多年从事叙事学研究，有比较丰富、影响广泛的相关著述。在这些文章中提出了一些新的阐释框架、分析方法或新概念，对理论深化发展具有重要意义，例如第一章的“破碎的故事”（Fractured Tales）、“殖民创伤”（Colonial Traumas）、“损毁的故事”（Disfigured Stories）（同37），第二章的“叙事返程”（Narrativizing Return Journeys）（55），第四章的“元叙事符号”（Metanarrative Signs）（93）等，特别是第八章提出了“走向批判的文化叙事”（Towards a Critical, Culturalist Narratology）的设想，已经非常明确地且大大超越了经典叙事学的形式研究范畴。这些新概念被用于文学分析则更为新颖，既反映了该领域的新成果，又提供了新的启发和借鉴，使后殖民叙事学研究的产生新的可能性。

最后，该书研究对象集中、视野多元、理论与方法丰富，分析的文学作品大都来自南亚，包括斯里兰卡、巴基斯坦和印度，以及加拿大、美国和英国的南亚裔作家的作品。这种集中为的是针对一个历史背景对多个叙事理论和叙事概念进行持续考察，而不是随意地在不同地区的文本上套用文学经典理论问题。南亚的殖民主义问题是后殖民理论研究中一个重要的甚至占主导地位的部分，这一点在叙述学家对后殖民主义的援引中尤为突出。文学的主题和意识形态分析离不开叙事的惯例和技巧，离不开体裁和历时性，离不开语义学、互文性、叙事诗学之间的复杂互动，离不开对读者解读的指导作用。（24）该书的文章聚焦于南亚，不仅以例证的方式证明后殖民主义批评可能会从叙事学观点中获益，同时也从叙事学的理论话语中挖掘出潜在的意识形态内涵。文章通过探讨内容和形式的关系，运用叙事学的概念和叙事分析的丰富理论方法，针对修辞、韵律、叙事特点、技巧和手段等问题，以一种或多种方式阅读有关南亚的文学叙事，以了解这些文本如何阐明意识形态并在意识形态层面进行干预。虽然一些文章的分析结合了文学史和特定体裁的历史进行细读，将形式维度置于内容之上以寻找与美学相关的概念，讨论反殖民抵抗、移民等后殖民时期的常见主题，但是同时也涉及一些并非后殖民主义独有的研究问题，例如关注创伤和叙述、个人和公众记忆的关系、对公共历史来源的文学研究，以及将叙事与新帝国主义资本主义和全球化的政治相结合。可以说，这些文章作者的选题范围很大程度上取决于后殖民叙事学本身的理论核心框架，既关注意识形态与叙事理论互动的原则问题，又以后殖民文学的理论问题检验这一原则问题的语境主义为前提。由此产生的文章对后殖民小说及其批判理论语境进行的叙事学论述，反映了后殖民意识形态主题对叙事理论本身的探究。

3 结 语

作为后经典叙事学领域中的一种批评方法，“后殖民叙事学”虽然目前尚未形成具有体系的“学派”（王丽亚，2014），但是该书编者认为在后殖民语境中揭示叙事结构、叙事学概念和框架的解释性和理论的重要性也是十分必要和重要的。尤其是通过对南亚文学研究的展望，丰富了参考框架，可以有效地扩展到其他新兴领域，打破狭隘的学科认知，把叙事形式分析与后殖民社会、历史和文化紧密结合起来，为当代后殖民叙事学批评理论的发展做出贡献。

参考文献

[1] DIVYA DWIVEDI, HENRIK SKOV NIELSE, RICHARD WALSH. Narratology and Ideology: Negotiating Context, Form, and Theory in Postcolonial Narratives. Columbus: The Ohio State University Press, 2018.

[2] MONIKA FLUDERNIK. Towards a 'Natural' Narratology. New York: Routledge, 2005.

[3] 申丹. 叙事学. 外国文学，2003（3）：60-65.

[4] 王丽亚. 后殖民叙事学：从叙事学角度观察后殖民小说研究. 外国文学，2014（4）：96-105.